DANCING WITH MR. D

Lisa Kleinholz

AVON BOOKS
An Imprint of HarperCollins*Publishers*

This is a work of fiction. Names, characters, places, and incidents are products of the author's imagination or are used fictitiously and are not to be construed as real. Any resemblance to actual events, locales, organizations, or persons, living or dead, is entirely coincidental.

"Violet" by Hole copyright © 1997 Mother May I Music. All Rights Reserved.

Edward Abbey, *Desert Solitaire*. New York: Touchstone, Simon and Schuster, 1968.

Edward O. Wilson, "Is Humanity Suicidal?" *In Search of Nature*. Washington, D.C./Covelo, Calif.: Island Press/Shearwater, 1996.

AVON BOOKS
An Imprint of HarperCollins*Publishers*
10 East 53rd Street
New York, New York 10022-5299

Copyright © 2000 by Lisa Kleinholz
ISBN: 0-06-101412-5
www.avonbooks.com

All rights reserved. No part of this book may be used or reproduced in any manner whatsoever without written permission, except in the case of brief quotations embodied in critical articles and reviews. For information address Avon Books, an Imprint of HarperCollins Publishers.

First Avon Books paperback printing: December 2000

Avon Trademark Reg. U.S. Pat. Off. and in Other Countries, Marca Registrada, Hecho en U.S.A.
HarperCollins® is a trademark of HarperCollins Publishers Inc.

Printed in the U.S.A.

10 9 8 7 6 5 4 3 2 1

If you purchased this book without a cover, you should be aware that this book is stolen property. It was reported as "unsold and destroyed" to the publisher, and neither the author nor the publisher has received any payment for this "stripped book."

"Lisa Kleinholz blend... ...s of small-town life and p... ...ps, and the rock music s... ...ase and grace. As a writer, I admire her talent. As a reader, I am smitten with her characters."
Kate Flora, author of *Death in Paradise*

"Lisa Kleinholz is to mysteries what Eric Clapton is to the guitar. Her fast-paced plots are leavened by the heartrending complications of relationships that always ring true."
April Henry, author of *Heart-Shaped Box*

Praise for Lisa Kleinholz's previous book
EXILES ON MAIN STREET

"A debut of great promise and verve, with an unforgettable heroine to carry its provocative story."
Laura Lippman, author of *The Sugar House*

"*Exiles on Main Street*, with one of the best openers, is just the beginning of what should be a long-running series."
Ft. Lauderdale Sun-Sentinel

"Crackling suspense, an affecting cast of complex characters and a fascinating window on Cambodian culture combine in a stunning debut mystery novel."
Amherst Bulletin (MA)

"Kleinholz's debut is replete with compelling personalities, particularly the rock 'n' roll refugees."
Publishers Weekly

Also by Lisa Kleinholz

EXILES ON MAIN STREET

ATTENTION: ORGANIZATIONS AND CORPORATIONS
Most Avon Books paperbacks are available at special quantity discounts for bulk purchases for sales promotions, premiums, or fund-raising. For information, please call or write:

Special Markets Department, HarperCollins Publishers, Inc., 10 East 53rd Street, New York, N.Y. 10022–5299.
Telephone: (212) 207–7528. Fax: (212) 207–7222.

*For my mother, my sister, and my daughters—
divas all*

ACKNOWLEDGMENTS

I owe a debt of gratitude to many people who contributed to this book.

For help with writing: Carolyn Marino and Jeffery McGraw, my editors; Mary Alice Kier and Anna Cottle, my mentors and agents; Bruce Carson, who solved a key problem; Jeannine Atkins, Rebecca Fisher, Dina Friedman, and Paul Kaplan, who brainstormed, kibbitzed, and encouraged; and Courtney Love and Hole, whose music provided inspiration.

For help with research: Mishiara Baker, who did the legwork; Edward H. Cotton, who taught us that even trees need love; Jim Armenti, Yehuda Jordan Kaplan, and Mark Alan Miller, who explained the technical and psychological aspects of the recording process; Nicole and Noah Ross, who coached me on dialogue and dinosaurs; Jan Steenblik and Jim Warner, who consulted on weapons; Stephanie Kaplan, Randy Koch, Vince O'Connor, and Blair and Dianne Whitham, who provided background on environmental and building regulations; and Dr. Stanton Kessler and Dr. Loren Mednick, who generously answered some last-minute questions on autopsies. All mistakes are mine alone.

I've exaggerated and simplified, especially concerning land-use and wetlands law. As far as I know, the spotted blue newt is a creature that resides only in my imagination. The decline of amphibians is real. Scientists, as usual, do not agree on the cause.

It may nevertheless be the case that these small beings are singing not only to claim their stake in the pond, not only to attract a mate, but also out of spontaneous love and joy. . . . Has joy any survival value in the operations of evolution? I suspect that it does; I suspect that the morose and fearful are doomed to quick extinction. Where there is no joy there can be no courage; and without courage all other virtues are useless.

EDWARD ABBEY

Prophets never enjoyed a Darwinian edge.

EDWARD O. WILSON

Chapter 1

Some blame global warming, others blame El Niño. But I blame all my troubles on rock 'n' roll. Because when the rhythm starts to sizzle, I'll be with all the other divas vogueing down the frying pan handle right into the fire.

I'll admit I felt a twinge of panic at the idea of welcoming my husband's ex-lover for an extended visit. That the fling between Vivi Cairo and Billy Harp had been over years before didn't ease my anxiety. Neither did the fact that Vivi, at forty-six, was fourteen years my senior. She had enough attitude to upstage the entire Lilith Fair tour with barely a tilt of the chin. At least, that's what I heard through the grapevine.

You don't maintain a twenty-eight-year career near the top of the charts without titanic talent, drop-dead looks, and the drive of a squadron of fighter jets. Not to mention an ego the size of Vesuvius and a temperament just as explosive.

I had crafted a counter-strategy. I'd play the role of perfect wife—at least for the three weeks she intended to stay. That meant getting home on time, which wasn't always easy. I'd whip up gourmet meals every evening. I figured she couldn't cook. What diva could? I'd chosen my wardrobe weeks ago: Hollywood with a dash of innocence that I didn't think she could match. After all, in

Annie Lennox's words, divas were "born in Original Sin."

I'd be nurturing and Madonna-like as I put the kids to bed. Then I'd sit in with Vivi and Billy to keep an eye on them while they discussed their upcoming album. This collaboration, growing out of her success with tunes Billy had written for Vivi the year before, would give my bass-playing husband the comeback vehicle he craved.

Billy was a refugee from rock 'n' roll, but lately he'd been yearning to take another ride on the glory train. Much as I resisted, I'd begun to realize Billy needed to follow his dreams, even though we still hadn't recovered from the nightmare finish that ended his first dance with fame—that most dangerous diva of all. No drugs, Billy had promised, and no tours. And I'd relented. As a former theater brat—my dad, Bobby Szabo, had been a Broadway song-and-dance man—I was a believer in second and third acts.

So, I convinced myself I had Vivi's visit under control. Then fate, namely Whit Smythe, my boss, intervened.

At five P.M. on the dot I turned off my Discman. I'd been listening to *Live Through This*, Courtney Love's CD released just after Kurt's death. Before that it had been Alanis Morissette.

I'd been listening to divas, old and new, for the past two weeks, soaking up the persona the way you'd prepare to go into snake country—by injecting diluted venom to build up an immunity, so a bite from the real thing wouldn't kill you.

Vivi and her boho entourage were scheduled to land at eight-thirty. Billy intended to meet them at the airport, an hour's drive south. I'd planned a late dinner for the whole crew. And it was going to be *fabulous*.

I'd just shut down my computer when Whit caught me. Owner, publisher, and editor-in-chief of the *Greymont Evening Eagle*, Whittimore Covington Smythe III is a thin, serious New Englander. Since he's not the demonstrative type, I've learned to read his code of subtle expressions and gestures. A slight lift of the eyebrow. A tap of a thumb on a desk.

Today, although his face betrayed nothing, the fact that he'd come looking for me instead of picking up the phone spoke volumes.

"Zoë, what's on your agenda tonight?" he asked.

"Company. Why?"

"I've got a problem. The Environmental Commission is voting on the Plaza project, and Barbara can't be there."

"Is she all right?"

"Fred went into the hospital an hour ago."

"Oh. I'm sorry."

Whit handed me a sheaf of notes. "You're going to have to take this and run. I don't think Barbara's going to be back for a while. We agreed you're the best person for the job."

The shadows under Whit's eyes deepened. Barbara Warwick was an old-timer. She had started writing for the paper during Whit's grandfather's reign. Her husband, Fred, suffered from chronic heart trouble. Judging from Whit's expression, Fred was seriously ill.

A tiny drum in my ear went thump a-thump bump. I wondered if I could manage somehow to dash home for an hour to get the buffet ready before Vivi's arrival. At the same time, I felt concern for Whit, who looked upset.

"Tell Barbara I hope Fred feels better soon."

Whit nodded brusquely and plowed on. "I called Craig Detweiller. He says he's sending in bulldozers the minute the decision comes down. Tim Boudreau decided to withdraw his opposition last night. He and Craig worked out some kind of a deal."

Tim was a high school biology teacher who headed the local Sierra Club chapter and served on the Environmental Commission. Craig, a developer, was a big man in town.

"Who else is fighting this thing?"

"Cassandra Dunne." Whit barely concealed his distaste. "She called a few minutes ago in a rage. Threatened to chain herself to a tree. As far as I know, she's the last holdout."

The project, proposed for a site at the north end of town, was embroiled in controversy. Though I hadn't paid close attention, I'd been aware of the ongoing dispute since Billy and I had moved here a year and a half earlier.

Imagine the animosity between the antagonists in, say, *Star Wars*, transplanted to a New England college town, and you might get an inkling of the ferocity of the emotions involved. With the exit of Tim Boudreau, the struggle promised a face-off between the two major players: Craig, who headed the Plaza consortium, and Cassandra, a.k.a. the "Green Queen." People in town really hated her.

Darth Vader versus Princess Leia. Only central casting had got things backwards. I'd seen Detweiller a couple of times, and he seemed like a nice enough guy—a youngish forty-two, relaxed, smooth. Cassandra, on the other hand, was a well-known crank, and she'd definitely moved past the ingenue stage. Imagine a ranting, menopausal Princess Leia, single and childless. No Luke Skywalker or Han Solo waited in the wings to come to her rescue. She'd have to wage this battle alone.

The drumbeat fragmented into a complex pattern of cross-rhythms and syncopations. Forget rock 'n' roll. I began to think opera: Brunhilde versus a well-mannered Siegfried, who might fight dirty for his right to party.

No. No more late deadlines, I'd promised myself. At least not till Vivi Cairo left. It was obvious I couldn't get out of this, but I might be able to get help.

"I have a slew of guests coming from California," I stammered. "Is there someone I could share the byline with, at least for tonight? Billy's counting on me doing this dinner." In spite of my attempt to hide my emotion, I was dismayed to hear the pleading in my voice. I was desperate.

Whit's mouth twitched at one corner. "Can't Billy take them to Chinese? The meeting's bound to be over by nine, nine-thirty."

I reflected. Billy, Vivi, and the others couldn't possibly get back to the house before ten. I swallowed. There were my kids. My two little Wookies.

Whit reached for my phone.

"What are you doing?"

"Dialing Cassandra. She's planning some crazy action. She was raving. Everyone else is on assignment, Zoë. Tomorrow I can take Mark off sports. But tonight he's covering a big game."

Mark Polanski was my archrival on the paper. As Whit well knew, the mere mention of his name was enough to make me leap unto the breach. I could also read between the lines. As a rule the quieter Whit's demeanor, the more acute his irritation. At this point his voice was barely a whisper.

"I'll take care of it," I said.

He handed me the phone and walked off without another word.

"Ms. Dunne? This is Zoë Szabo from the *Eagle*. The Plaza site? Fifteen minutes? I'll be there."

The music I'd listened to earlier flooded my ears, the sound of Courtney screaming in "Violet:"

*"Go on, take everything, take everything. I want you to.
Go on, take everything, take everything. I dare you to."*

The rhythm wasn't complex anymore, just that old rock 'n' roll taking everything. Later, I'd remember, I asked for it.

Chapter 2

The sky sparkled a sapphire blue as I walked a brisk half mile to the Plaza site. A few fleecy clouds lent a picture-postcard sweetness to the panorama of fancifully painted Victorian houses leading toward the busy intersection of Stanhope and Webster. A left at the light took you to the sprawling State University, while a right led to Greymont High.

Today's paper had run a story about the record-breaking heat this fall. Although it was the middle of October and the trees had begun to turn color, the mercury still reached into the seventies. Tomorrow it was supposed to approach eighty, which was absolutely unheard of.

Even though I'd grown up in Manhattan, I'd spent the past decade in LA, so I enjoyed the unseasonable weather. After the previous winter—my first in icy Greymont—I dreaded the onslaught of darkness and snow. Summers in New England were short. As the leaves turned gold, I grew homesick for California; I yearned for the beach, the rough surf, and green foliage all winter long.

Finally, I arrived at the weedy park where I was to meet Cassandra Dunne. At its center stood one of the main objects of contention: a magnificent two hundred-year-old maple. Its grand spread of greenery was shot with bright orange and red. Because of this tree the lot had remained undeveloped despite constant pressure to build.

I spotted Cassandra seated cross-legged under the maple. A lean, faded woman without a trace of makeup, she had loosely clasped graying hair with copious strands flying free. Despite the warmth, she wore a moth-eaten Mexican sweater over baggy jeans.

"Hi," I said. "I'm Zoë."

Most people's faces are asymmetrical to some degree, but Cassandra's was downright lopsided. Her right eye, a sandy hazel, was set about a quarter inch higher than her left, which was a watery blue. Her crooked mouth went up at one end and down at the other. With her tilting body, the overall impression was one of imbalance.

She gaped a little rudely at my outfit—a tight lavender skirt and skimpy top—then at my ultra-short, bleached platinum hair. Lastly she shot a scornful look at my heels, high enough to rival K2. My excuse is that the added height lends authority to my meager five feet, four inches, but obviously she didn't think so. Her expression was the familiar "What planet were you hatched on?" that I often receive in Greymont. But it was edged with annoyance, as if she found me too frivolous to cover a serious issue like hers.

"I recognize you," she said, "from your picture with that article you wrote last year for *Rolling Stone*."

"It's always nice to meet a fan," I kidded. The story had been on the murder of a Cambodian refugee here in Greymont.

"Oh, I didn't say that."

Ignoring the slight, I offered her my hand.

She studied my long nails painted chartreuse and sealed with a coat of glitter. For my four-year-old daughter Smokie's amusement, I'd glued silver stars to the tip of each nail. In contrast, Cassandra's hands were rough, nails bitten, knuckles thick, skin cross-hatched with little lines. I felt slightly sorry for her; she had no one to dress up for.

"More objectionable was that piece about the bear," she said with condescension, perhaps sensing my pity. "You got it all wrong."

What the hell had I written about the bear?

"For future reference," she added, "large predators invade human territory only when there's a scarcity of prey. Bears in town indicate habitat loss."

"I stand corrected." I smiled again, as if to say, Let's keep this friendly. "How would you like to answer a few questions about the Plaza project?"

She stared with those funny eyes. "I'm surprised Whit's letting you do this. He hates me. I know too much about his personal life. By the way, I'm annoyed with you."

"Are we still on the bears?"

"You didn't bring a photographer!"

I held up the range finder that the paper consigned me and snapped her photo.

"No. No, you need a telephoto lens. For when I get up there."

"You're going to climb the tree?"

"Unless you intend to stop me."

I pasted on a smile and took a deep breath. As the mother of two little kids, I was used to having my patience tested, but she was beginning to get on my nerves. I stole a glance at my watch. My mind ticked off the seconds like a taxi meter. Just do the interview, I told myself. Don't confront.

"Craig Detweiller responds only to hardball tactics. When he sees the photo, he'll know I mean business."

I switched on my micro-recorder. "Why don't you start at the beginning."

She eyed the machine skeptically. "Craig and his cronies. You've been here long enough to know Stuart Livingston and Mavis French?"

I nodded. Stuart, whom I'd interviewed once, was the town manager. Mavis, a shop owner, headed the Environmental Commission.

Cassandra went on. "Those three and your boss are colluding to cram this mall down the throats of the taxpayers."

I began to understand why everyone at the paper made snide remarks about the woman. "Where does Whit fit in?"

"Do some research. You'll see. I'm not going to connect the dots."

Okay. Next question. "Your plan is to sit in the tree, until when?"

"Until we get an injunction. We're filing as soon as the courthouse opens tomorrow."

"Who is 'we'?"

"What do you mean?"

"Who's joining you in this action?" I wanted to wrap up and go home.

"Shira Weiss, the attorney representing our group, the Living Earth Coalition, and . . . a few others. I admit Craig has seduced a number of people. The Sierra Club, for one. That's his greatest talent, by the way, seduction.

They'll realize soon enough that his promises are hollow. Of course, by then, it will be too late."

"I take it you're referring to Tim Boudreau."

Her pale cheeks grew ruddy. "Among others."

"You assume the commission is going to vote for the variance?"

"Don't be naive. With Stuart Livingston's hand-picked chair? And Craig's golf buddy on the board?"

Cassandra was right. A picture would tell the story. No need for me to drag this out. Best would be one of her in the tree with Detweiller's bulldozer threatening. I made a mental note to stop by the site around sunrise and to bring a photographer.

Final question. "What's your basis for filing?"

"That meadow over there is the only habitat in the region of the spotted blue newt, which is on the EPA threatened list. I have a biologist's report."

"May I see it?"

"You'll get a copy at tonight's hearing."

"What's the biologist's name? Do you have a phone number?"

"Not so fast. I know how you media people work—playing us off against each other. No, I'm holding these cards close to my chest."

For a moment I considered whether to leave it there. I get testy when people start badmouthing the media. Amazing how they're usually the same ones who are trying to get you to publicize their cause. Figuring she would say no, I threw out, "Why don't you show me this newt's habitat."

A magical thing occurred. The combative pose suddenly melted. Cassandra shot me a loopy grin, and the churlish expression vanished. "Really want to see?"

"Sure." Inwardly, I winced. What I really wanted was to go home.

"You'll have trouble in those shoes, but I'll walk slowly."

In mountain boots, she strode swiftly ahead and then waited for me to catch up, as I teetered gingerly in my high heels to keep from sinking into the soft earth.

Near the center of the area, she knelt. The subtle reverence pervading her struck me suddenly as poignant. She was so, so . . . weird. But a childlike wonder began to seep through that defensive exterior.

"Place your hands on the soil. Feel how spongy it is. In the spring, this is swamp."

I crouched and touched the earth. She was right.

She crawled along. I tiptoed after her.

"I don't know if we'll see any newts now. They dig themselves into the mud and hibernate through the winter." She waved an arm. "About four acres can be classified as seasonal wetlands. Detweiller, Smythe, French, Livingston—the real estate mafia—they'll tell you they're going to restore wet areas elsewhere to replace what they're filling in here. But it's death for the newt."

"Can't the animals be moved?"

"Nope. Like salmon, they remember where they've been bred. They migrate throughout the area in summer and fall, then come back in the spring to breed in pools created by runoff and snowmelt. The biologist can answer your questions better than I can. She'll be at the meeting. I talked her into doing this as part of her master's thesis. Women are generally better at ecology than men and more willing to pitch in for free. As creatures who give birth, we tend to be more connected to nature. You're smiling. Why?"

"That doesn't jibe with the letter you wrote to the paper this fall."

"Which one?"

"You said being a parent was the supreme act of selfishness."

"Well, that's true. I have figures about how much energy each child in the West consumes. I guess you found that offensive because you have two kids. Four and six. Right?"

I stared at her for a second.

"Oh, I've researched you. It's listed in the town census."

I'd used these listings myself as a reporter, but I found it disconcerting to have the tables turned on me.

"Chaining yourself to a tree," I summarized, letting it go. "Isn't that an extreme thing to do for a creature that's about three inches long and slimy?"

She chuckled. "Slimy? Not really. And I'm climbing, not chaining. Finally, why do you assume that you and your kids—who I'm sure are very sweet—have more right to this space, this earthly paradise, than the spotted newt? Or, for that matter, the red ant, the earthworm, the eastern bluebird, the green spider? I'll tell you why. You're humanocentric."

I laughed. "That's good. Humanocentric. Can I find it in Webster's?"

"I'm talking about saving the planet, and you're worried about spelling! The newt is EPA-listed, and humans think they're cute. That's why I'm framing my opposition around them. But a spider, an ant, a vole, has just as much right to this earth as Mavis French and Craig Detweiller. More. All the creatures want is to live. Mavis and Craig have shelter and food. That should be enough, but no! Why do we need a three-story retail plaza with a parking garage? Cars, pollution, global warming? So Mavis can get rich. And Craig can get richer! Force-fed consumption. That's what it boils down to."

"What if you're denied an injunction?"

"As long as the site is threatened I'll stay in the tree. Let Craig demonstrate his lack of respect for life by cutting me down. Even human courts agree that's murder. He won't dare."

Vertical creases scarred the space between her faded eyebrows. I could hear the quiver in her throat as she exhaled.

"How about food?"

"I have provisions. And"—her voice swooped up half an octave—"a neat sling chair."

That answered my question about how she was going to stay through the night without falling.

"May I see?"

She unpacked the bag and pulled out a blue fabric contraption. She demonstrated how it could be hooked to branches. I examined it and decided she'd be pretty uncomfortable.

"Toilet facilities?"

"Ever heard of a chamber pot?"

"Are you sure you can climb up there all by yourself?"

"I took an intensive tree-climbing course in the Pacific Northwest last summer. A hundred-foot maple is nothing."

I took my cell phone from my purse and called Kate Braithwaite, the staff photographer, who agreed to come down with a telephoto lens.

Despite my grudging sympathy, I considered the whole thing a joke. Years in Hollywood have made a cynic of me. No one wants to put a message across to the media that doesn't have some payoff. So far as I have personally experienced, the payoff is most often financial, although some people are such narcissists that the publicity itself is enough.

"You're sure you're not doing this just to get your picture in the paper?"

Cassandra lifted her face sharply.

"A funny question," she spat at me. "Did you enjoy the publicity when your husband overdosed and nearly died?"

A shiver passed through me despite the unseasonably warm sun on my back. How did she know? Billy's overdose—which had come close to destroying our marriage—had happened over three years earlier, long before we'd moved to Greymont. Aside from a few lines in a minor fan magazine, there hadn't been any publicity. She'd said she'd researched me, and now I began to realize that she'd gone to a good deal of trouble. Did she make it her business to dig up dirt on everyone in town?

"That story was not widely reported."

"A bad reputation sticks like a shadow. I've learned the hard way. You will too."

With that, Cassandra slung a rope ladder over the lowest branch and shimmied up the trunk with efficient, angry, jerking motions.

She hooked her rope higher and continued up through the branches, bounding and dangling through the thicket of leaves tinged with scarlet.

A couple of kids ran from their parents, who were returning from shopping to cars parked at the edge of the lot. They crouched near the foot of the maple and gazed up into its limbs at the woman returning to the treetops like an elongated orangutan.

At last from a perch about eighty feet up, Cassandra

waved at the children. She let out a weird, self-conscious laugh that echoed through the October air. All she lacked was a pointed hat and a broom. The children must have thought so too, because they shrieked and scampered back to their parents.

A few minutes later, Kate appeared. A twenty-five-year-old equestrian champion, Kate Braithwaite was a tall, athletic type with classic American features and a long swinging braid down her back. Though our styles were different, we were the only two women under fifty at the paper and we'd quickly become friends. Most of the time, we had female fun together—shopping, talking about men, comparing favorite movie stars and musicians, consulting each other about recipes and household furnishings, and just plain joking around.

But recently our friendship had deepened. In June she'd gone through a painful breakup with her old high school beau. We'd spent the summer comparing notes on difficult times. That's when I confided in her about my troubles with Billy. She told me about her younger brother, who'd died two years earlier, after a long bout with leukemia. Her parents hadn't recovered. They relied on her for emotional support, which was draining. Her older brother, Ron, though he lived in town, wasn't much help.

Kate was one of those people—I considered it a Yankee trait—who masked her feelings. Usually she managed to maintain a relentlessly cheerful front. Today, however, she was uncharacteristically dour. Especially when she caught sight of Cassandra. Dutifully Kate took a couple of photos, rolling her eyes at me between shots.

"Not your favorite person?" I teased.

Dancing with Mr. D

"Please! She's got my vote for Crazy Lady of the Year. Ever notice they're all transplants?"

Like most inhabitants with roots deep in Greymont's history, Kate had the utmost disdain for the current population of professors, yuppie exiles from the rat race, and self-styled activists who were either holdovers from the sixties or new age imitators, pushing their agendas on the much put-upon natives.

When she lapsed into her anti-transplant mode, I always felt uncomfortable. Billy and I, after all, were among the newest arrivals. My style was decidedly un-Greymont, despite my recent attempts to tone down my fashion statements from in-your-face punk glam to modified glam with post-punk accents. Kate decried all newcomers for raising taxes to pay for fancy additions to the schools. When she broached that topic, I was guilty as charged. I wanted good schools for my kids.

Although I hadn't paid close attention to the debate over the Plaza project, I felt ambivalent about it. Billy and I had been lured by the unspoiled countryside: the farms with horses and dairy cows, and the many conservation areas with hiking trails, streams, and wildlife.

I adored the charm of the central business section with its brick storefronts and Victorian houses transformed into colorful shops. I wasn't sure I wanted a mall stuck in the midst of it, despite the fact that I'd probably be the first to check out Starbucks or the Gap. And the extra parking it promised would make my hectic life easier.

"So," I asked as we left the site, "what's Cassandra after? She says she's trying to save a rare newt."

"She wants her fifteen minutes on the front page of a

national paper or an interview with Mike Wallace bad-mouthing people like my dad."

"What does she have against your dad?"

"Oh, it's a long story. She ruined his chance to sell his land. I'll never forgive her."

"When was this?"

"It doesn't matter. But I just hate giving her this publicity," Kate added as we strolled along the bright streets toward the *Eagle* offices. "Everyone's going to say, 'Oh those big bad people killing defenseless little amphibians.' But she's the evil one. She's driven more people into bankruptcy than the IRS, the State Tax Assessor, and the Commonwealth Creditors Association put together."

"I detect a note of bitterness."

"Yes."

"Anything you want to talk about?"

"No."

We walked in silence, the customary stream of small talk stifled. I thought about Kate's father selling his land. He owned one of the prettiest farms in the area. I loved taking my kids Smokie and Keith there to pick strawberries and blueberries, to see the newborn calves, to gather pumpkins. It would be a shame to lose that beautiful tract to a subdivision.

"Kate," I said quietly, "is your father having problems again?"

She turned on me. "Must you be so nosy?"

I bit my tongue. We passed the ice cream parlor and a bookstore.

"Kate," I ventured as gently as I could, "I didn't mean to pry. I'm offering to lend a friendly ear, but only if you want one."

"I'm sorry. It's one of those days."

I grinned. "Forgiven."

She smiled, making amends, but her dark brown eyes, usually so guileless, were clouded.

Chapter 3

If things hadn't been so hectic, I probably would have given more thought to Cassandra perched precariously in the top of the tree. At the very least I would have driven by on my way home to make sure she was okay. But our house was in the opposite direction, and today was Billy's turn with the car.

Billy and I were still straining under the mountain of debt caused by his drug crisis and a contractual dispute with his old band, Alamo, now defunct. Even though the royalties from Vivi's album sales had boosted our income, my job at the paper didn't pay well. Billy's labors—filling in occasionally in local bands and teaching an adolescent Cobain wannabe or two—were sporadic. My hours, which constantly shifted, had caused enough conflict that we'd decided to use the extra money to hire a regular baby-sitter rather than buy a second car. So today I had to get where I was going on foot.

By the time I arrived home Billy had left for the airport. "When did he leave?" I asked Dania, our sitter, a second-year art student at the State University.

"Oh, about a half hour ago. He was worried about traffic over the bridge."

That was uncharacteristic of Billy, who almost invariably ran late.

"What enormous pumpkins!"

"Aren't they cool? We had a bumper crop this year, so I brought these for the kids."

"Love your hair, by the way."

Dania's long hair had gone overnight from Day-Glo orange to neon green. Until recently I'd added streaks of bright color to my own close-cropped 'do. But now, being a New England mom and a professional newswoman, I'd settled for bleaching it platinum, retaining a few dark roots as homage to my punk past.

Luckily, I'd put together most of the buffet the night before. Dania, the kids, and I set everything on the dining table in no time. The perishables—upscale cold cuts and cheeses—stayed in the refrigerator. Dania, who'd planned to watch the kids during the party anyway, had instructions on the final preparations in case I didn't make it home ahead of the crowd.

After kissing Smokie and Keith, I jogged the mile or so to the nineteenth-century brick Town Hall. This time I was smart enough to wear sneakers and pack my heels in my roomy turquoise shoulder bag with Madonna's face silk-screened on the front.

The energy I'd expended to be punctual turned out to have been a waste. Folks milled about the gold and green Town room, chatting and maneuvering, the commission members among them.

While I waited for the meeting to start, I cornered Kate's dad, Erwin Braithwaite, a farmer with a bushy beard, flannel shirt, and suspenders. Despite his troubles with Cassandra, he sat on the board deciding her petition—an obvious conflict of interest.

Ron Braithwaite, a contractor and Kate's older brother, was in deep conversation with his dad when I interrupted. I nodded hello to Ron. A surly, muscular man in workclothes, Ron glowered at me a moment, then murmured a few words to his father and hurried out of the room.

"Have you considered abstaining?" I asked Erwin.

"Zoë, if everyone who had a gripe against the woman abstained, there'd be no one left to vote."

I smiled tolerantly. "Now say something nice for the record."

Erwin pulled at his beard. "Let me put it this way. If Cassandra Dunne were run over by a truck in the middle of town, there'd be partying in Greymont for weeks. Most everyone here would agree with me, although they might not have the guts to say it."

"I'll do you a favor, Erwin, since your daughter's a friend. I won't quote you."

I did, however, begin to canvass the room to see if his assertion held up. But as I roamed, I found my thoughts zooming back to Vivi. What would she wear? How would my outfit compare? What on earth would I say to her? *How was Billy in bed, way back when he was barely out of his teens?* What would she answer?

When the meeting finally came to order, over an hour was spent in a review of minutes and old business. Not until nine-thirty, as I was debating whether to cut out before the vote, did the chair, Mavis French, call on Shira Weiss, Cassandra's attorney.

After forty excruciating minutes of verbal wrangling and posturing by various commissioners, the vote was finally taken. Shira, whose law degree was from Harvard, and who'd spent two years in a top New York firm before coming home to work for "the cause," did her best for her client. She was diplomatic and well-spoken, as was Rachel Lopez, the biology grad student, who made an enthusiastic presentation, complete with colorful graphs and charts.

But as expected, the Plaza won, four to three, despite considerable discussion—some blatantly scornful—of the plight of the newt. Tim Boudreau, the local Sierra Club head, went out of his way to say that the newt was threatened, not endangered, and could be found in other parts of the state, which seemed to sway a couple of the commissioners to the side of the project.

Shira requested a delay in construction to give her time to file an appeal. I watched Tim carefully, thinking he might back the motion. But he went with the prevailing sentiment in the room, and the delay was defeated, again by his single vote.

Whoa, I thought, that was a switch for him. I noted that he looked anxious and unhappy as he voted.

It was ten-thirty before things wrapped up.

"Excuse me," I said, approaching the crowd of people around Craig Detweiler, the developer. "Mr. Detweiler, I'm a reporter from the *Eagle*. Do you feel vindicated?"

Detweiler looked in my direction. He was a medium-sized man, supremely relaxed, healthy, with a teddy-bearish cast to his face.

He grinned triumphantly, shaking my hand. "Yes."

"I hear you're planning to send in the bulldozers."

"Absolutely. Tonight."

"Why the rush?"

Though he was still smiling, I detected steel in his voice. "This is Greymont. I have to strike while the iron is hot. You know"—he looked around at his cronies, who were laughing—"someone might find a hundred-year-old ordinance and shut me down again. I assure you, the tractors are rolling." He checked his watch. "The minute the ruling came down, I called my contractor."

"What if there's an appeal? The biologist's report—"

High on his success, he turned to his admirers. "Listen, if that biologist comes looking for the newt," he bragged more to his audience than to me, "she's going to have to go through the mud molecule by molecule. The ground is being turned over tonight—thoroughly."

"And the maple?"

"Tomorrow morning. At the crack of dawn, the chain saw will be buzzing."

He waded into the crowd. "Mr. Detweiller," I shouted, "what about Cassandra Dunne?"

"We'll talk tomorrow!"

I sought out Shira. "Craig says he's sent in the bulldozers. He's going to make molecules out of the newts."

Shira, weary though still feisty, replied, "We're filing in state appeals court first thing tomorrow. I've also petitioned the EPA."

"Were you surprised by Tim Boudreau's vote?"

Her black eyes flashed. "He warned me, but I didn't think he'd go through with it."

"What's going to happen tomorrow with Cassandra in the tree? Craig says he's going to cut it down at dawn."

"What?"

"She climbed the tree as a protest. Didn't you know?"

Shira looked angry. "No. We're supposed to be in court in Boston. That woman is driving me mad! Ah, that's off the record. I'm sorry, Zoë, I'll give you an interview tomorrow."

"I need something before deadline—early morning."

"We're disappointed, but determined to press our suit.

Excuse me. The biologist just walked out the door. I have to catch her."

She ran off. I packed up my notes, deciding the controversy could wait. Billy, Vivi, and the band needed me more.

When I turned the corner onto Amethyst Lane, I heard the dull thump thump of a bass. I quickened my steps. As I approached the privet hedge delineating the front yard of our small Cape at number nineteen, the spectrum of sound broadened. A jazzy piano and rhythm guitar dueled over who could drive the power chords the hardest. Lights burned brightly in every window both at our house and at number twenty-one, the grand yellow Victorian next door, which belonged to our neighbor Morgan Swan. The elderly professor doted on Billy and had generously offered to put up Vivi and her crew for the night. Then they would move to the Vermont studio where they were recording.

By the time I entered the mudroom, the piano had clearly won and was winding out in a wild Jerry Lee Lewis rush of percussive crashes. The frenzy of two-fisted pounding pulsed through the progression like a train hurtling across an empty prairie at ever-increasing speed.

I kicked off my sneakers and slid on my heels, grimacing as my feet cried out in protest against my sassy shoes. I tugged my lavender skirt and arranged my sleeveless top—in a color called Whisper. I checked my makeup in the hall mirror, adding a bit of dark lipstick—a shade some marketing type had dubbed Temptress. I examined my short-cropped hair, brushing it with my fingers to give it a little "poof." With the tip of my pinkie, I smoothed the glittery mauve shadow from where it had caked in the creases over my eyelids. Licking my lips to make them shine, I gave myself a "good luck" salute before sucking in my breath and going to meet the competition.

From the living room the music thundered. The bass egged on the piano with big imaginative leaps, pushing the tempo. Billy's velvety tenor sang lyrics I couldn't quite discern. I recognized the tune as one he'd been working on over the past month. A lead guitar picked out the melody and then threaded a counterpoint as Billy sang louder. A familiar, gravelly but oh-so-sweet soprano joined in with a yearning harmony. Lately Billy, after doing a lot of listening to Sinéad O'Connor, had been raiding his Irish roots. His melodies had taken on a haunting, modal quality.

Through the archway I saw Billy standing behind the pianist. Across the room were two guitar players. One was a young guy with a huge belly. He leaned on the blue notes, fingers moving on strings with finicky precision. Then he screwed up his puffy cheeks, sprinkled with acne, in an aching expression. His head shook back and forth, as if saying, *No, no, no,* and his double chin jiggled. His hands artfully cascaded down the frets to a low note that buzzed and reverberated and fed back in a way that made you feel that the world could end and you wouldn't care, if only the music played on.

The other guitarist—not nearly as good but more pleasant to look at—was an aging hippie. I recognized him as the legendary Spots known by that name alone. He was the owner and chief engineer of Wonderland Sounds, one of the top studios in the country.

Spots wore a flowered smock and baggy chinos. A bandana kept his voluminous gray hair from falling into his face. Sporting love beads with a peace symbol, the guy was a one-man Grateful Dead road show.

Dancing with Mr. D

He may have looked like a grandfather, but he moved like a hipster. Swinging his butt and kicking out one leg, he played a vintage Gibson Les Paul, circa 1959. The electric guitar must have been worth its weight in gold.

Behind him was a short, pensive black man with cornrows, who had to be Charles Duck, the drummer. In a suit that could have been worn by a Wall Street executive, but sans necktie, Duck knocked the drums almost as an afterthought while he flirted with a red-haired backup singer in gypsy garb. Despite the laid-back demeanor, he was always right on time, as skillful as they come.

But the person who drew my attention was the pianist, playing as if there were no tomorrow. Although I'd seen many photos of Vivi Cairo over the years, I'd never actually met her. I recognized the straight, nearly black hair, glossy and expertly cut. From her back I could see only that she was much thinner than I expected, with a Scarlett O'Hara waist, delicate shoulders, and slim but feminine hips.

Instead of the garish Versace-type garb I'd seen her wearing in publicity shots, her clothing was plain: a snug pair of dark blue jeans, a silver Navaho belt with small medallions embedded with turquoise, and a black form-fitting T with cap sleeves, which revealed tanned arms with sculpted muscles.

As she turned, I caught a glimpse of her face. Her features were at once exotic and familiar: high, pronounced cheekbones; generous lips; a crisp, pretty nose; arching eyebrows; and large, luminous deep blue eyes, almost Asian in shape. Her skin was incandescent despite her age. I couldn't discern even a hint of a wrinkle.

Vivi suddenly stood, banging on the keys, pace ever quickening. "Hit it, Billy!"

He took a short solo. She wove the piano chords in an

intricate pattern, staying well out of the way, but matching him move for move. He pulled it way back and then turned to the young guitarist. They played one more chorus and abruptly stopped with a smash-fest of chords that rivaled a freeway pile-up. Billy grinned at Vivi and the two of them laughed raucously.

"Shit," she said.

"I was wondering if you were ever going to get back to that A chord."

"Hell, Billy, it's a little low for my voice. Just trying to give you a nudge in the right direction. Can we try it again in C sharp?"

Everybody laughed.

The drummer heckled from the sidelines. "Cerita requests B flat, so she can make the high note."

"Cerita will damn well sing it where I want. 'Cause I'm the fucking star." This was delivered so cheerfully that it didn't sound insulting. Vivi smiled at the gypsy woman.

"Told you she'd bitch," Cerita said with a chuckle.

"That ain't bitchin', child," Duck said. "That's sweet talk. She got to work up to bitch."

Vivi ignored him. "I mean it, guys. Let's try another key. A's so fucking dull."

Billy ran through a quick progression in C sharp. He broke off, basking in the smile she shed on him.

Okay. She was gorgeous, model-thin, glamorous but understated, a fabulous musician with a voice that bordered on miraculous. Billy couldn't take his eyes off her. He wore a silly half grin, very sexy, his eyes heavy-lidded. He leaned against the back of our blue velvet settee, which faced the old-fashioned stone hearth.

In fact, there wasn't a person in the room whose eyes weren't riveted on Vivi: The young guy with the acne practicing the suspension and the II chord. Spots, plucking his Les Paul. Duck and the sultry red-haired gypsy, Cerita. Our sixty-something neighbor Morgan, stretched out in our worn flowered recliner, mouth open in admiration. Even the kids nestled in the oversized chair with Dania. Smokie, my wild four-year-old girl, dark brown eyes as big as saucers, stared at Vivi Cairo as if she had stepped off the silver screen into our tiny living room.

Even I couldn't take my eyes off her. She was so focused and magnetic. Charisma. She had it in spades.

When she turned in my direction, seeming to sense my presence, everyone else did too. It was like having a spotlight fixed on me. At that moment I would have done anything she asked; just to please her would have given me such joy. That was the power of the spell she cast. I had met superstars before, but no one of this caliber.

"Zoë!" She wrapped her arms around my shoulders and kissed my cheeks. "Billy, you didn't mention how beautiful she is! Your kids are adorable."

Smokie perked up. Keith laughed and hid his face behind his knees.

"And thank you for the delicious spread. We were starved after the flight. Billy wanted to go bar hopping, but I just wanted to lay back and kick out."

She laughed as if some marvelous idea had struck her. "It's beautiful here. You're so lucky. What a charming town. I didn't think there were any places like this left in the world. Untouched by time. And, Morgan!" She tripped over to my elderly next-door neighbor with his sagging jowls and thinning hair and hugged him as if he were Warren Beatty. "What a treasure. And so sweet to put us up tonight."

Morgan blushed, enjoying the blessing of this effervescent goddess.

I'm not usually shy, but in the presence of this woman I suddenly felt self-conscious. "I appreciate your coming here, so Billy doesn't have to be away from home."

Her smile displayed perfect teeth. "He has a family. I don't. Besides, I've always wanted to record at Wonderland Sounds. Spots has such an incredible reputation. I'm stoked."

The young guitarist, whose name was John Cano, mumbled something about being wiped out. He returned his guitar to its case. "You have anything to drink, man?"

"There's beer in the refrigerator," Billy said.

John disappeared into the kitchen.

I introduced myself to Spots and asked about his guitar. His pink bow lips formed a natural smile. "This is one of the first Les Pauls made. When Clapton recorded with her at my studio, he signed her for me. This baby's my favorite ax, though she do weigh a ton!" He tucked his treasure into its case.

"How was your day?" Billy asked, coming over and resting a hand lightly on my shoulder.

"Hi," I said, giving him my sexiest smile. "Oh. You wouldn't believe. I had to interview this crazy environmental radical intent on stopping a building in the middle of Greymont."

Billy turned to Spots. "Zoë's converted."

"Yeah," said Spots.

"She used to write about music. Now she's doing small-town news."

Spots looked at me, his eyes doing the guy thing. A few years ago, I would have been annoyed, but with Vivi around, I felt flattered.

"Hey," Billy said, holding up one hand. "My wife."

"Only while you're looking," Spots said. "Hey, Zo. How you doing?"

"So tell us about the crazy environmentalist," Billy said, teasing me along. Like he was showing me off.

"Her name—get this—is Cassandra. She's ranting about doom. Right now she's sitting in the top of a maple to prevent the contractor from cutting it down in the morning."

"Cassandra," Spots remarked. "That's not a name you hear every day."

"In Greymont you hear it bandied about a lot, often accompanied by colorful adjectives. She's a controversial figure." I gave him a thumbnail sketch of her latest crusade.

"If you're looking for nuts," Billy joked, "Greymont's full of 'em."

"Hey, Bill," Spots shot back, "guess you fit right in."

Billy laughed. "You might want to stay awhile."

"Naw, I got it good where I am. We're all nuts there."

John wandered back into the room, obviously unhappy about the selection in the refrigerator. "Oh, man. Any hard stuff?"

"Nope," Billy answered easily. "This is a drug-free zone."

"I have some single malt at my place," Morgan said.

"Man, you are just what the doctor ordered. Hey, Viv, I'm beat. I'm going to pack it in."

Morgan rose from the recliner with difficulty. "I'll join you. Anyone else?"

Spots slapped Morgan on the back. "Single malt sounds good to me. Your place drug-free too?"

"Not so far as Scotch is concerned," Morgan said affably, as he herded Duck and Cerita toward the door, with Spots close on their heels.

I noted that the magic words to make folks vanish were "drug-free zone." I glanced anxiously toward Billy, hoping he wouldn't be tempted. No, that was dumb. Of course he'd be tempted. I prayed silently for him to have the strength to resist.

"Don't let them walk all over you, Morgan," Vivi rasped. "Boys, behave yourselves."

John shot her a sarcastic glance. "Let me get a sandwich. I'll be right over." He stuffed about a half pound of ham between the two fragments of roll he'd torn apart with his hands, dropped various veggies and cheese slices into the center, and looked at me. "Got mustard?"

"Sure." I started toward the kitchen.

"Don't wait on him. He can get it himself," Vivi said. "Fat Boy," she shouted playfully.

John returned. "Who you calling fat, woman?"

Vivi laughed. "You! Get your own mustard."

"Lucky you pay well, woman."

"Here," said Billy. "I'll get it."

"Dania," I said quietly to our baby-sitter, who had watched with hardly a blink since the moment I'd arrived. "Maybe it's time to put the kids to bed. Then you can go home."

"Oh, sure. Sorry." She gathered them up. Smokie was half asleep. Keith rubbed his eyes. I kissed them and whispered that I'd be up soon.

I sat down, wishing I could have a little taste of that single malt Morgan had offered. I studied Vivi, taking in her magic. She reminded me of an exotic black cat, part Siamese, maybe part Abyssinian.

She gazed at me with an expectant, questioning smile. "So," she said finally. Her voice was low, guttural, the rasp accentuated by her near whisper. "Do I meet the test?"

"I admit I was curious."

Her lips parted. "It was a long time ago. A different lifetime almost."

"Do I?"

"Absolutely. The day he met you, Billy called me and said he'd found 'the one.'"

"I didn't realize you were that close."

"Yes, we were close."

"I thought you'd broken up long before we met."

"Oh, we did. But you know how things are."

I nodded, although I didn't.

"He's a great guy. Take good care of him."

I nodded again, the edge of a knife beginning to cut at a raw place inside. I tried smiling. It didn't quite work.

Vivi rose from the piano bench, turning slightly, contemplating the keys, and then played carelessly four or five notes of an old McCartney song. "Pretty tune," she whispered to herself. "Hey, Billy!" She ambled toward the kitchen. "Find that mustard yet?"

"John just left by the back," Billy said. I heard him uncapping a beer. He allowed himself one a night. It was his reward for getting through another day without resorting to anything more potent. Sometimes I wished he didn't have to work so hard to keep from slipping.

"I'm going to say good night," Vivi said, resting an arm on his shoulder. She was taller than me by several inches, but much more delicate.

Billy glanced toward me and winked. "Hey. My wife's watching."

She laughed softly and patted him on the stomach. She let her body swing in a casual half turn, dipping with a kind of funky wriggle. "I'll be good. 'Night, Zoë. What time are we driving to Vermont?"

"One or so. Why don't you come over for breakfast."

"Righto! I'll see myself out."

She let her shoulders sway with that funky rhythm and danced out the door.

Billy shook his head. "Want a beer?"

"Is there any wine?"

"Chardonnay."

He uncorked the bottle and poured me a glass. Before handing it to me, he leaned down and nuzzled my ear. Dimming the lights, we took our drinks into the living room. It was quiet. The children were in bed; Dania had gone.

Billy sat down on the oversized chair. I perched on the arm. He slid a hand under my skirt.

I sipped the wine, which was just the right blend of tart and smoke, and studied the room. The rose walls suddenly struck me as dingy.

"Leave you speechless?" Billy asked.

"You could say that."

"Jealous?"

"Me? Never."

"If you're jealous, honey, I've got the cure."

"Oh yeah?"

"Yeah . . . Man, I hate pantyhose. The guy who invented them must have been a Republican. Why don't you take these off?"

"I will on one condition."

"What?"

"Tell me the whole story."

"Sure you want to hear it?"

"Just don't lie."

He sighed. "I'll give you the short version."

"Deal."

"Boy arrives in LA. On his first audition, he lands a gig playing bass with the opening act for Vivi Cairo, who has two songs on the charts and is a humongous star. This was over twenty years ago. You were like eight."

"Twelve."

"Nope, I was twenty. You were eight. So you can't remember how big a star she was. Major. Major. I could barely cut it. I don't know what they were thinking when they hired me. Guess I had the look they wanted."

"You're very pretty, I know."

"I was way out of my league. Freaking before every concert. Terrified I was going to screw up. She had a band behind her of guys—like they were real pigs. They had women in the hallway, the closet. They had a contest— who could screw the most sets of twins. It got so you couldn't go to the bathroom without—"

"Okay, you don't have to get graphic."

"I was a shy kid. She was nice to me."

"And you were nice to her."

"It was a gift, what she gave me. I figured if I was good enough to sleep with Vivi Cairo, I could cut it on stage."

"Funny how guys work these things out in their heads."

"Remember that big record producer, Sammy Samuels? Vivi and he had a thing going for a long time. When he split for that TV star, Vivi started hitting the drugs hard. I felt, you know, she'd helped me, boosted my ego. I took up with her again for a while. Just before I met you. It helped. She pulled herself together.

"I hadn't given her much thought in recent years. But then when I slammed against the wall"—this was Billy's way of referring to the crisis—"she heard about it through mutual friends. On her next upswing, she called to see what she could do. Bought two of my songs. And look what happened. We've got a hit. Contract for a whole album with the company footing the bill for a month in the studio, which is almost unheard of these days."

His soothing voice drifted into silence.

"You never told me."

"I told you we'd been lovers."

"Not in this detail."

"Zoë, I love you. But there are parts of my life that just don't belong to you. I'm telling you now."

"She sounds like a great lady."

"She is."

"It would be easier if she were a bitch on wheels."

He grinned before reaching up and switching off the light. And then he kissed me. Billy was a playful, teasing lover. He took his time. The night was pitch black with no moon. Through the windows, the leafy branches were opaque against the more translucent sky.

Later, much later, from the depths of our caresses, I thought I heard something out there in the dark. A sharp cry in the far distance. I paused and listened. After a long silence, a cat yowled. The sound was as faint as the wind, as far away as the stars.

Chapter 4

I've suffered from a distrust in the benevolence of the universe since I was seventeen, when I lost my mother to a swift and virulent liver cancer. Whenever things start to go well, I wonder what evil might be lurking around the bend, poised to unveil itself with a gloating smirk. Once the worst happens, I have so far managed to dig up the courage to resist. Though the villain may be defeated, the evil at the core seems to live on, concealed, licking at its wounds, biding its time, gathering the strength to strike again.

This morning I was off my guard. Since things seemed to be going pretty badly already, I didn't expect them to get too much worse. For one, after making love, Billy disappeared into his basement hideaway to work out some new chords for the tune he'd played with Vivi and to find a better key for her voice. The remarks I'd interpreted as musicians' jests, he took seriously. He wanted very much to please her. When I awoke the next morning, his side of the bed was still empty. I'd risen well before dawn in order to witness Cassandra's confrontation with the chain saws.

After dressing, I noticed the light in Keith's room. I found him already awake, complaining of a sore throat. I checked his tonsils while he went "ahh."

"I can't see any red." I took his temperature. "Normal."

Keith had inherited my Scottish mother's coloring. His strawberry blond hair was damp against his forehead. His gray eyes regarded me forlornly. He groaned. "It's really raw, Mom."

I wiped his wide brow with my palm. "I'm sorry, honey."

Keith had inherited my mother's artistic sensitivity as well. Already we could see he was unlikely to follow in the footsteps of the legendary rocker we'd named him after. Tall for his six years and bright, but introspective, Keith Richard Harp—the kids took Billy's last name—would probably grow up to be a scientist. He could identify about thirty kinds of dinosaurs, recite the periods in which they lived and the dates they went extinct. His idea of a great time was sitting on the floor of his room reading.

This was exactly why Billy and I were concerned. He didn't connect with other kids, although he communicated well enough with adults. Morgan felt he was gifted and had begun tutoring him in math and teaching him to play chess. Awesome, yes, but also sad. Despite a superhuman effort from his teacher, Keith was having trouble adjusting to first grade. Some afternoons he'd confide to me in tears that the kids made fun of him. A big athletic kid named Ellis had been bullying him. I'd hesitated about complaining. The kid was Mavis French's son; it was touchy.

"Did anything happen with your friends yesterday?" I asked casually. This was the third time in the last few weeks that he'd attempted to beg off going to school.

Keith shrugged. "At lunch Tommy said I couldn't sit with him."

"But Tommy's your best friend."

Dancing with Mr. D

Keith muttered something so softly I couldn't hear.

"What sweetheart?"

"He's not really my friend anymore. He likes Ellis better. He was saving the seat for him."

Ellis again, I thought with frustration.

"Aw." I patted his shoulder. Keith wrapped his arms around me and buried his face in my neck. "Maybe we can think of something to do."

He lay back on his pillow and sulked.

"Why don't we invite Tommy over one afternoon next week?"

He shrugged.

"A play date might remind him what fun you two have together."

"I don't think it would work."

"We could try."

He moved his tongue against his cheek. "Guess what?"

"What?"

"My tooth is loose."

"Let's see. Wow! It's really wiggly."

He grinned. "Lots of kids get a dollar when they lose a tooth."

"My dad used to give me a pearl."

"A real pearl?"

"Yeah. He spoiled me. You know what, hon? I think we'll try to send you to school today."

He moaned dramatically. "I'm sick. I feel horrible."

"Have the nurse call me at work if she thinks you need to come home. I'll dig up your dad and tell him what's going on. You can sleep for an hour or so."

I gave Keith another hug and went off to find Billy. He wasn't in his basement studio. He wasn't in the kitchen. Maybe he'd wandered over to Morgan's after I'd gone to bed. Billy usually got the kids up and ready for school, because I often had to be at the paper early for last-minute work on deadline.

The *Eagle* was one of the few remaining afternoon dailies in the country. Whit held space on the front page for late-breaking stories. The last edit was transmitted at ten, and the paper hit the stands by two.

On early days, I'd come home and spend the afternoon with the kids. Several evenings a week, I covered committee meetings or arts events. That was both the blessing and the curse of working for a small-town paper. The constantly shifting schedule and assignments kept the job interesting, but were tough on family life.

When I covered a political controversy or a crime, my hours stretched way out of proportion to my pay. Billy had been more than generous about being flexible. But whenever Whit asked me to cover a last-minute story, we experienced considerable strife over who would watch the kids. Since we'd hired Dania, the conflict over schedules had nearly vanished, and I suffered much less guilt. With Vivi and the band here, though, Billy's days and evenings were going to be full. If Keith or Smokie got sick, I didn't know what I was going to do.

After a brief search, I found Billy on the far side of Morgan's wraparound verandah. The sky to the east was turning softly gray. Vivi snuggled in a quilt, knees tucked under her, on the porch swing. Billy lay on the floor, his stocking feet propped on the wooden swing. Vivi's hand rested lightly on one of his blue-jeaned shins.

Billy whistled as I approached, as if there were nothing out of the ordinary about him lying there with Vivi caressing his feet at five A.M.

"Off to work?" he asked.

I nodded hi to Vivi. "Keith is complaining of a sore

throat. I think he's just trying to get out of going to school."

Billy nudged the swing gently with his foot. "I can take him to the doctor. We're not going to the studio till this afternoon. Anything you want to do in town, Viv?"

"I'd like to see where you work, Zoë."

"They'd get a kick out of a visit," I said. "Mind having your picture on the front page?"

"Free publicity? Let's do it, Billy." She made it sound like a lark.

"We'll stop by after I take Keith to the doc."

"Speaking of which, it'd be great if I could use the car."

"Sure. I, uh, Viv rented an extra one, so I can commute to the studio and back."

"Thank you," I said.

"Don't mention it," Vivi said.

"You didn't get any sleep last night," I said to Billy, then kicked myself. I did not want to wear my heart on my sleeve, but it had sneaked up while I wasn't looking. I guess I was distracted by the things Vivi was doing to Billy's toes.

"We had a lot to talk about."

"Did you work out the key change?"

"Yeah, we're going to do it my way," said Vivi. As pleasantly as a soft breeze on a summer night. Only it was October, even if it didn't feel that way.

Billy pushed the swing harder, and she giggled. "Like shit," he said.

"We'll take a vote."

"You're paying them. Of course they'll vote your way."

Her throaty laugh resembled a purr. "Duck won't. Ever honest, ever true. Unlike some folks."

"I'll let you two fight this out in private." I was determined not to play the part of jealous wife. "Don't forget to check on Keith and drive Smokie to school."

"Vivi will remind him, dear. Don't worry." Flaunting it. As if to say, when I finish playing, you can have him back—whatever's left.

"Never worry," I responded. "That's my motto."

I arrived at the Plaza site just as the first rose tints heralded the pending day. I parked across the street. To my relief the grand old maple was still standing. I strained to catch a glimpse of Cassandra in the topmost branches, but the broad canopy of leaves, black against the pearly dawn, blocked my view.

A hastily erected fence of orange plastic stretched around the site. The adjoining area that had been overgrown with weeds and wild grasses was enclosed within the partition. An enormous back hoe and bulldozer stood guard at the center of the area. Yesterday Cassandra and I had trooped through tall grasses, knelt and touched the spongy earth into which the newts had dug for the winter, awaiting the death and resurrection of the warming sun.

Now bare soil, reddish and raw, covered the space that only twelve hours earlier had been a verdant meadow. The whole area, save for a wide circle around the maple, had been bulldozed clear. Craig Detweiller's crew had made sure the newts wouldn't be allowed to stop this project.

As I approached with a growing sense of unreality, yesterday's testy interview began to take on depth. Disgust rolled through me like surf breaking across a long flat beach. I remembered my own silent scoffing at Cassandra's language, at what I'd considered her overwrought accusations. The real estate mafia, she'd called them. Well, from now on, I would treat her with more respect.

I gazed high into the branches of the tree, searching for the sling chair.

"Cassandra?"

There was no answer. I squinted, trying to discern in the increasing light some sign of the woman. I checked my watch. Kate should be here any minute. We'd agreed to meet at five-thirty. She was a few minutes late. The dawn grew brighter. A light breeze rippled through the leaves. At last I caught sight of something dangling way up high. Yes. Now I saw it clearly—the dark blue fabric of that crazy contraption Cassandra had shown me yesterday. I moved to get a better angle, and the sling chair came into full view. The straps flapped loosely and the expanse of fabric twirled and twisted. The breeze blew a little more strongly. The seat seemed strangely empty as it turned slowly, knotted, and unwound.

I wondered if she'd shimmied down the tree to try to stop the bulldozer. Perhaps the police had already come and arrested her. It struck me as odd that no one was here at all. I was annoyed that Kate still hadn't shown up. She was usually punctual. Expecting her to be here, I hadn't brought a camera, and I absolutely had to have a photo of the destroyed meadow for today's paper.

Whit would be at the office. He'd surely know of an arrest. I took my cell phone from my bag, but decided at the last minute to explore more thoroughly. I headed toward the orange bulldozer at the center of the property.

Halfway through the ring of tall grass that still surrounded the old maple, on my way toward the excavated area, I noticed a depression where the stalks seemed to be bent. I drew closer. Two or three heavy limbs of the maple, bursting with scarlet leaves, had fallen to the ground.

I was almost upon the broken branches when I noticed what appeared to be a crumpled mass of clothing among the flame-colored leaves. I stepped quickly forward, ignoring the fact that my heels were beginning to sink into the soft mud.

As I drew even closer, I saw a tangle of denim, patches of cream and gray and muted brown. Something told me to stop before it was too late, but I ignored this inner voice and spurted ahead. Because I had to look. And then I had to look away.

Cassandra Dunne lay sprawled under a heavy branch. The two different-colored eyes, pupils black and dense, stared as if startled. Her nose and cheeks were bashed. Out of her mouth drooled a lake of blood. I didn't get sick, though, until I noticed the crack in her skull and the gray ooze that clotted her matted hair.

My hands went clammy. I felt the sweat at my forehead. A huge shiver rattled through me. The horizon, pink with the first rays of sun, tilted nauseatingly, like a ship hit by a rogue wave. My legs crumpled, and I knelt, retching a vile fluid from my empty stomach.

Chapter 5

After calling 911, I tapped Whit's speed dial code into my cell phone and pressed send. My emotions raced wildly, from horror to sadness to fear. My stomach still felt unsettled. I looked out my car window for signs of the police, worrying suddenly that someone sinister might be lurking behind one of the buildings. My hands trembled. I tried to steady them as I held the tiny flip phone, listening to the electronic chirp.

"Whit!" I exclaimed with relief as soon as he picked up, "You'll never guess. Cassandra Dunne—she's dead!"

"Slow down. Where are you?"

"I'm at the Plaza site. Whit, I found her. It was horrible."

"You called the police?"

"Yes."

"Have they arrived?"

"Not yet." I could hear my heart pumping away.

Whit was quiet for a moment. He was unflappable in the face of catastrophe, a habit formed while working the crime beat back in Boston when he was young. "Start at the beginning," he said. "Try to calm down."

"She fell. At least I think she did. Her skull was—" I stopped myself, because the dizziness began to attack. An uncomfortable sensation under my tongue made me swallow. I tried desperately to control it.

"Describe exactly what you saw."

I took a couple of slow breaths. Then I told him about arriving at the site shortly after dawn, looking everywhere for Cassandra, discovering the bulldozed field, and then finding the body.

When I finished, Whit asked, "No wounds that might have been inflicted by a weapon?"

The pounding of my heart slowed as the possibility that it might have been something other than an accident became clearer. "Not that I could tell. She was covered by a limb."

"Did it appear as if she'd fallen in the last hour? Or had she been there—say, all night?"

"I have no idea," I said, the confusion rising. "Why?"

The resonant blare of the fire station horn pierced the early-morning silence. Cassandra's lopsided face floated through my mind. A flash of the ooze seeping from her skull. I fought off the nausea.

"While you wait for the police," he said, "why don't you read me what you have on last night's meeting. I'll write the story, so we can make today's paper."

I told him everything. When I finished, Whit said, "Sit tight. I'll send Mark down with a camera."

"But Kate—" I didn't want Mark Polanski horning in on my story. And then I caught myself short, suffering a pang of conscience as I remembered the interview the previous afternoon. Cassandra's childlike delight with the newt. Her hand, rough, touching the earth. A human being had died, and I was reacting like a hardened reporter, trying to beat everyone else to the scoop. Forget your feelings, a voice inside me cautioned. Get the story. The sad truth is that in the news business, nice girls not only don't finish first, they are rarely given a second chance to get in the running.

"If Kate's not there now," Whit was saying, "she's not coming."

In vain I scanned the panorama of the surrounding village for Kate's pickup truck. Instead, I saw the police chief's car turn the corner, lights flashing. An ambulance followed.

"Police are here."

"Pin them down on as many facts as you can. They won't want to give you a time of death, but it doesn't hurt to ask. Be sure to check in before deadline."

"Will do." I let out a groan. A shiny red Miata, its convertible top down, ran the light at the intersection. The car turned down the street toward me and screeched to a halt across from my ten-year-old Civic.

A jock sporting a grin as big as the Grand Canyon and an ego to match, hung over the side and waved. "Hey, Szabo! *Qué pasó?*"

"Don't bother calling Mark," I muttered to Whit. "He's here." The competitive spirit surged, clearing away my ambivalence like a cold slap of water. I was ready for combat.

Not one to waste words, Whit grunted and hung up.

I watched the oversized boy hang a U-turn with tires squealing. He parked and bounded out of his car, all six feet, two inches of him. He wore his basic uniform: jeans, baseball jersey, hightops. No baseball cap—too funky for Mark. He went for the clean-cut, boy-next-door look complete with short hair the color of wet sand and large features that reflected his Polish heritage. His build was athletic with shoulders that pumped iron and a neck that could stop a train. At twenty-seven he was five years my junior, a fact he never let me forget.

I'd had my moments of exasperation when I vowed he should be chained to his sports desk and let out only to cover the games. But Whit took a more benign attitude toward his go-get-'em style and his tendency to lead with his left. Not that I didn't get into tight spots myself . . . or use prose that veered dangerously into Zone Purple, as we called it down at the paper. But I prided myself on having a little more humility than my rival. A former star pitcher on the State University ball team, he had the high self-opinion that came from always having been picked first when sides were being chosen.

Mark smirked as I teetered over in my heels to meet him. I was still green from my encounter with the body.

"Hey, Szabo. Lose your breakfast?"

"Did a little bird tell you about the fresh corpse," I answered testily, "or was it the scent of blood that attracted you?"

"I have a scanner. What's your excuse?" He gave me the once-over. "Cinch you weren't out for your morning run."

Mark had a point. I'd dressed to impress Billy, not for maneuvering over rough terrain. My narrow skirt with a kick pleat, in a pale wheat color, may have been foxy, but it was not a practical choice for today. To add insult to injury, my black top with clutch collar and bare shoulders provoked a wolf whistle from the uniformed cop accompanying the police chief, who headed in our direction.

"Hey, Mark," I said loudly enough to be overheard as

we converged on the cluster of police and paramedics, "Told you not to wear those tight pants."

The cop laughed, and we exchanged greetings. It was a small town. We'd tangled at crime scenes before.

Chief Sodermeier, a fuzzy old guy two years short of retirement, didn't crack a smile. "Zoë. Where is she?"

An uneasy quiet blanketed our group. The sky was yellow. A haze had settled on the valley. The air was muggy despite the early hour. The mercury would certainly top yesterday's, which had climbed into the high seventies. It was the warmest October on record. Like a surrealistic painting, the town had been dabbed with autumn color, but was still awash in summer heat. *Global warming? So Mavis can get rich. And Craig can get richer!* Cassandra's voice echoed. The funny eyes jerked open wide. I felt warmer than I should have, even in this unnatural weather. My stomach went queasy.

I thrust the vision from my mind and focused on the present. The police followed me through the break in the construction fence, toward the spot among the grasses with the telltale burst of red leaves.

One of the paramedics, a woman with lean, tough features, bent over the body and began a preliminary examination. I looked away, afraid I might be sick again, embarrassed and filled with the ominous horror that came from approaching a human corpse.

"Zoë," said the chief. "Do you want to tell me what happened?"

"She climbed the maple yesterday afternoon. I came to report on her threat to confront the tree cutters. But when I arrived, there was nobody here." I pointed to the blue fabric contraption still dangling high in the upper branches. "She wasn't there. Then . . . then I saw."

Chief Sodermeier glanced toward Mark.

"I got here when you did," Mark said, no longer so jaunty. Still he searched the area with his eyes. We all did.

"Is she . . ." I hesitated.

The paramedic said curtly. "No question. She's dead."

"Any idea how long she's been like this?" Sodermeier asked her.

The attendant frowned toward me and Mark, and glanced at the uniformed cop.

"Chief," the officer suggested, spelling it out for him, "should we make the usual calls?"

"What?" Sodermeier stared in bewilderment. After a long moment, he got it. "Yes. Get Brannigan. And seal off the site."

A holdover from simpler times, Sodermeier met situations like this with the dazed confusion of a parent faced with an offspring caught shoplifting.

Detective Kevin Brannigan headed the Western District homicide squad. The police station in Greymont had minimal facilities. The crime lab people, medical examiner, and detectives were based in Sheffington across the river, about twenty minutes away. It wasn't out of the ordinary for them to be called in to confirm an accidental death. But I guessed the paramedic had found something suspicious. I wished I had her cool in the presence of the corpse. Unlike Sodermeier, she seemed totally unfazed.

"Chief," I asked gently, "is there any chance of foul play?"

His white eyebrows went up vaguely. "Oh, it will be a couple of days before we can answer that."

"Come on," Mark butted in. "We're on deadline." A Nikon hung from his neck. He snapped photos, liberally moving around the accident scene despite warnings from the cop.

The paramedic eyed him, then glanced at me. Something was wrong. Two minutes of conversation with her, I was certain, would have elicited insights, but with Mark hovering that was impossible.

Sodermeier tried to be helpful. "It looks pretty cut and dried, Zoë. I can't imagine anyone climbing up there and pushing her."

"Can you estimate the time of death?" I asked the paramedic.

Sodermeier responded. "Now you know we can't answer that. Why don't you run along and let us do our work. Call this afternoon. I'll fill you in as much as I can."

I studied the paramedic, who knew more than the rest of us, just from having touched the body.

"Is she still warm?" I asked.

The paramedic stared at me as if I'd said something outrageous.

"Can I safely say she died after midnight?"

"Zoë," said Sodermeier.

"If I could get some answers by ten—" I pleaded. Begging is my first tool of the trade, because it's effective. No telling what people will say if you only ask with an undercurrent of urgency. Reporting the news is not for people with a strong sense of pride or delicacy. We are the original junkyard dogs.

"I know, I know." The chief sighed. "You're on deadline."

Meanwhile, Mark sauntered over to snoop around the bulldozer, ostensibly to get a picture. The uniformed cop, plainly pissed, ran after him.

It was obvious I wasn't going to get more now. So, as they started unrolling the yellow police-line tape, I left

Mark to await the homicide squad, whose standard script I knew by heart, and trotted off to plow more fertile ground.

"Craig Detweiller, please?" I was in my Honda with the cell phone. The woman on the other end sounded half asleep.

"It's early," she objected. "Who is this?"

"Zoë Szabo with the *Greymont Evening Eagle*. It's urgent."

"Zoë!" Detweiller's husky voice boomed. In contrast to the woman, he sounded as if he'd been up for hours. "What can I do for you?"

"There's been an accident. I'd like a comment."

Wariness crept into his tone. "Where? What is this about?"

"Cassandra Dunne. She's dead."

"You can't be serious. When?"

"Sometime last night. She fell out of the tree."

"Tree? What tree?"

"The maple she climbed at the Plaza site. Don't tell me you didn't know. The police are here now. She's dead."

Silence, then: "Forgive me. This is a shock. What do you want?"

"A comment. I'm on deadline."

"Give me a moment."

"Did you know she'd climbed the tree?"

"I'd heard rumors that she might do something like this, but I thought she'd back down. Actually, because of those rumors I asked the crew to go in early—to get the jump on any protesters."

"They've been here all right."

"Did they cut down the maple?"

"No, but the ground's been turned over."

"Yes. That was done last night."

"Her death solves one problem," I said. "You don't have to worry about her appeal."

His tone, which had been almost panicky, grew milder. "Zoë," he said, softly chiding, "that's unfair . . . but I know you have a job to do. As for a comment: Got a pen?"

"Of course."

"All right, say this: I'm deeply saddened. Even though I disagreed with Ms. Dunne's assertions about the environmental impact of the Plaza construction, I found her a worthy adversary and I shared many of her ideals."

Sure, I thought, but I wrote it down.

"What time did the construction crew go in?" I asked. If I could pin that down and match it to time of death—

"I'll have to check."

"Isn't it odd to send people to work in the dark?"

"Zoë, I need to talk to my crew boss and find out the facts. Call me in a couple of hours."

"But you just—"

"Two hours. I'll get back to you."

"One more thing—the biologist's report."

"What about it?"

"You told me last night that she was going to have to go through the mud molecule by molecule to find any trace of the newt."

After the briefest hesitation, he emitted an easy laugh. "I gave in to feelings of frustration. I apologize."

"Okay," I said, not believing my ears. He'd confirmed the threat I'd heard him make the night before. That meant I could use it, no problem. Even Whit would have to agree.

"Is that enough?" he asked.

"For now. Thank you." I snapped the phone shut. My spirit soared like an eagle on an updraft. Predator that I was, I thought I had him clasped in my talons.

Chapter 6

Two hours later, nearing eight-thirty, I stood behind Whit's chair, staring with dismay at the headline on his monitor: PLAZA PROTESTER DIES IN PLUNGE.

Whit had written the story from what I'd dictated that morning. The facts in his bare style seemed to hide much more than they revealed. He'd made Cassandra sound suicidal, while I had wanted to show how she was mocked in town, how desperate she'd appeared when I'd talked to her, how much hostility she'd garnered, and how many threats she'd provoked.

Plus, I wanted to investigate the collusion of the real estate interests with the town boards. I wanted to explore the problem of volunteer government—totally unpaid, with very little expertise except what was fed them by the people who had the most at stake. Their decisions—especially in regard to irreplaceable species and habitats—could have far-reaching consequences. The story had great potential, I thought. I could use Cassandra's death, including the murky circumstances, as my takeoff point.

Unfortunately, Whit wouldn't entertain the notion.

"Absolutely out of the question," he said, with a force that surprised me.

"Why?"

"Zoë. Have you read Hal Gaffney's column's lately? He's been ranting about rabid Chicken Littles."

"So this will add balance." Gaffney, I thought with annoyance. He was always on the wrong side.

"Correction. *He's* providing balance. Everybody and his sister is writing about the environment. I've got Sylvia Toravian on planting native shrubs so the birds will be happy. Ann Chatsford opposing building anything larger than a toolshed. Barbara has her series on the monarch butterfly sanctuary. And—"

"Okay." I sighed. "But no one has studied the interaction between the town boards and the real estate interests."

Whit's voice tightened to a dry whisper. "Town Meeting is notoriously anti–real estate and anti-business. This is an unfortunate death, pure and simple."

Town Meeting is a form of government peculiar to small-town New England, where ordinary citizens gather, spring and fall, to vote on issues that elsewhere are handled by town councils. Like all forms of democracy, it was contentious, messy, and slow-moving. Hal Gaffney and his pro-business crowd argued it was outdated and unwieldy. Area activists were happier with the format; at the end of the day, they usually came out on top.

"Humor me," I pleaded, ignoring the warning signs. "Let me play you some tape—"

"Summarize," he said between clenched teeth. "I don't have all day."

Whit hated tape more than anything. If you couldn't nail your quotes with a couple of quick strokes of the pen, he was ready to ship you off to the networks—which he placed only slightly above the ninth circle of hell.

I read him Erwin Braithwaite's remark about partying

in Greymont if an accident should befall Cassandra. And Craig's mutterings about the molecules. I wanted to contrast this with all his pontificating about "shared ideals."

Whit frowned. "I'm not in the business of printing that sort of thing. It borders on libel."

"These are verifiable quotes. I have them on tape."

Whit's facial muscles tensed. "Those are careless statements made out of frustration built up after years of delay."

"Frustration leads to anger. Even rage."

"As far as the police are concerned," he reminded me, "this was an accident."

"You were the one who brought up the possibility of foul play—this morning on the phone."

"What did Chief Sodermeier say?"

"Nothing. They're waiting for the autopsy."

"We can wait too. We're not going off on a tangent that we'll later have to retract. A newspaper is not a gossip sheet. Others may have forgotten, but I know the difference."

"How about the bulldozed wetland?" I pressed. Here was an angle that might keep the story alive. "They did that to preempt an appeal. Craig admitted as much this morning!"

"You're putting words in his mouth," Whit said quietly. His cheek stiffened.

I bit my tongue.

Whit swiveled around in his chair to gaze out the bay windows overlooking Main Street and, beyond that, the broad Common. The swath of grass was still green, despite the yellowing leaves of the beeches and oaks.

He took a moment to consult with his ancestors, who seemed to be part of the very air. His roots went back farther than the oldest buildings in sight: Town Hall with its slate roof and clock tower, the whitewashed Lord William Inn, and the ivy-covered spires of Greymont College in the far distance.

"We're too close to press time to change the story," he said at last. "We'll print it as is."

"It's your newspaper." I packed up my notes, not hiding my disappointment.

"If you want," he added by way of concession, "write a follow up for tomorrow. Just keep it balanced."

I brightened, jumping on it. "I'd like to do an in-depth with Detweiler."

"All right. But we're not spear carriers for the ecofeminists or anybody else."

"Yes, boss."

His eyes met mine. They were a washed-out blue. "Tread lightly," he admonished.

"Oh, I will," I assured him. "A sidebar on the newt might be enlightening. Not a manifesto—just science. I can call some college professors . . . they're always good for a little obfuscation."

"Go ahead, but find spokesmen on all sides, and Zoë—"

"Yes?"

Whit's eyes met mine again. "If you get into local personalities, do your homework. Don't embarrass people needlessly. Remember, these are our neighbors. We have to live with them."

"Sure. I don't need a partner to work on this. I can probably wrap the whole thing up in a day or two."

I wasn't sure he'd heard me.

"Whit?"

"Hmm."

Dancing with Mr. D

"We don't need Mark on the story, do we?"

He seemed to reawaken to my presence. "Mark? If you want help, go ahead and ask him."

"I can manage alone."

On my way back to my cubicle downstairs, I stopped by Sharon's desk to get my messages.

"Billy called," she said. "The doctor said Keith's fine. He'll stop by later."

I dialed Billy, but got the machine. Why wasn't he answering? For a moment, a pale green cloud drifted into my conscious mind, but I repressed it. If I was in a state like this now, where would I be by the time Billy finished the album?

Focus, I told myself. I had a story to write, a death that seemed somewhat suspicious. I didn't want Mark to get the upper hand just because I was too involved in my personal life to pursue the story with my customary zeal. I remembered the lesson I'd learned from my actor father. No matter what, even if your world is falling apart, the show must go on.

I glanced at my notes and punched in the number of Detective Brannigan. A short conversation with his assistant disclosed that he was still at the Plaza site. She reiterated that the death was being categorized as an accident pending the autopsy, which they'd scheduled for tomorrow.

It was approaching deadline and the energy level in the newsroom was high. I loved the buzz of activity, the pressure, the game of "gotcha" reporting. Busily writing or calling, everyone seemed to be aided by a ghostly force of old-time newsmen and women hovering near. I could almost hear the clickety-clack of manual typewriters, echoing from the distant past.

I spent the next few hours on the phone. First, I called the fire station to talk to the paramedic I'd seen at the crime scene. She was on another run—a stroke in North Greymont. Then I tried the cop I liked to banter with, but he was out in his patrol car.

I went through the street directory, which lists phone numbers by address, and called residences around the Plaza site. Several people said they'd heard shouting around twelve-thirty, but students were always walking home drunk around that time. Last night seemed no different.

One man did mention that he was awakened around two in the morning by a loud rumbling noise. He looked out the window, saw nothing, and went back to bed. The noise had stopped shortly afterward.

I spoke to a loquacious doctor I often used as a source. He gave me a few pointers on how forensics people determine time of death. From my description, he guessed Cassandra had died within two or three hours of when I'd stumbled on the body—anywhere between two and four in the morning. He confirmed that a fall from that height could have killed her.

I phoned the town manager, Stuart Livingston, who murmured words of sympathy and regret. Then I reached some of the environmental commissioners, who made various statements of shock and, of course, sadness—none remotely convincing. Even the people who'd voted in Cassandra's favor hated her. One man told me he'd been on the verge of resigning, but with the news of her fall, he'd reconsider.

"That's a pretty strong statement," I said, a little shocked at his willingness to speak ill of one so recently dead.

"You couldn't get a variance to rebuild your porch steps without her jumping up to protect some vernal pool—half the time in a place that would stay dry in a flood. She'd come back time after time on the same project.

"Anyone who's served on a town board," he added irritably, "has been subject to the barrage of paper she's filed on every proposal brought before it, including punctuation changes in bylaws. She was a one-person procedural nightmare. Go ahead and quote me."

The only board members I couldn't reach were Mavis French and Tim Boudreau. I'd called Boudreau earlier and got no answer. High school teachers are incredibly difficult to reach because they're always in front of a class. I called again. Aha. On a break, he came to the phone.

"I assume you've heard about the accident?"

"No. What happened?"

"Cassandra Dunne. She's dead."

"Oh my God," he whispered. "It can't be. When?"

"Sometime during the night." Vague enough. Brannigan would be proud.

"Oh my God, did she fall?"

"Yes. I'd like a statement for the paper."

"From me?"

"Yes."

I waited while he summoned some thoughts. He sounded stunned. I liked that. I typed the word. *A stunned response from Environmental Commission member Tim Boudreau, who said—*

"Well, it's . . . it's dreadful. We collaborated often in the past, but recently we'd had our differences. No don't say that. Sounds terrible. I have to think." He sounded flustered.

"Could we meet? I need background," I pressed. "How about right after school? Three. Three-thirty?"

He said he'd get back to me, which meant if I pestered

enough he might talk. "Listen," I persisted, "I'll be at your classroom when school lets out." I assumed he had a regular room. "Okay?"

He muttered something noncommittal and I said goodbye cheerily, as if we were the best of friends and the date was carved in stone. If people think you believe they've agreed to talk, nine times out of ten they will. It just takes a certain amount of chutzpah to put it across.

As I hung up, Mark wandered in, looking miffed. Guess he didn't get too far with the police. I gave him a little wave hello.

"Hey, Szabo. *Qué pasó?*" There he went again, mauling my Hungarian last name by trying to say it with a phony Mexican accent.

"What's the matter? Couldn't get a date with that cute cop?"

He made a face. "Don't start."

"So how's my friend Brannigan?"

"He sends his regards."

"Get a photo?"

"Page one center. Missed your byline."

"It's right next to your picture."

"No. That reads, 'W.C. Smythe III, with reporting by . . . '"

I shrugged. "What's Brannigan's take?"

He was at his desk, two down from mine, in the large high-ceilinged room of the old Victorian building that had housed the *Eagle* offices for over a century. People buzzed back and forth.

"I'll make you a bet," I said.

Mark punched numbers into his phone. "I'll wait," he said into the mouthpiece. "What?" he asked me, receiver at his neck.

"It was no accident."

"You've got a lively imagination, Szabo."

"How come the chief was so tight about the time of death? They're worried about alibis. I can read them like cards."

"Tarot?" Before I could reply, he turned away. "Hey," he murmured into the mouthpiece, "want to meet for coffee?"

Now, either he was asking for a date—not likely with a breaking story on deck—or he was trying to sweet talk the paramedic I hadn't been able to reach earlier. Hmm.

I flipped through my notebook, pretending to be in deep concentration while I spied on him. Paramedic, I decided when he put down the receiver, with an expression like he'd swallowed a canary. A few minutes later, there was nothing left but the grin.

So, what next?

I looked at the big clock on the wall. It reminded me of the one in the stuffy Manhattan private school I'd attended as a kid. The huge face was framed in antique wood, the numerals were Roman, and the minute hand quivered with every tick. Nearly noon.

Start at the top, I decided. Call the big honcho before he left for a power lunch and see where that led. I dialed his office. A secretary with a refined British accent answered. Detweiler must have given her my name, because as soon as I identified myself she put me right through.

"Yes, Ms. Szabo?" he said pleasantly.

"I'd like an interview." I prepared myself to use whatever argument might be necessary to talk him into it.

He hesitated. "What's your schedule like?"

"Wide open."
"How about now?"
"Great," I said, masking my surprise. "I'll be right over."
It shouldn't have been so easy.

Chapter 7

I took the elevator to the third floor of the magnificent nineteenth-century bank building that Craig Detweiler had bought and renovated. It still housed a bank, but a large new addition provided a row of retail shops on Stanhope. The offices of his company, Delstar, took up the entire penthouse floor. They were beautiful. The ceilings were high, the windows large, the decor subdued except for the wall hangings and paintings.

The receptionist's name was Alida Kai. I noted it carefully. People close to the source can sometimes provide better information than the source himself. She sat at a huge natural cherry desk backed by high arched windows that looked down on Stanhope's restaurant row. On the desk was an impressive telephone system with something like forty different lines. Interesting, for an office with few employees. Other than Ms. Kai, the place seemed empty.

Craig Detweiler came out to meet me. Like many powerful men, he exuded confidence. But unlike most, he didn't seem to be driven. Everything about the man—even his well-cut olive jacket, tan slacks, gray shirt, and ivory tie—appeared to be casual and friendly.

His nose was small for his wide face. His eyes were

engaging, his jaw broad, his hair blow-dried and well cut.

"Hi, Zoë," he said, reaching out to shake hands. "Sorry I was rushed last night."

"I appreciate your meeting me on such short notice."

His gaze met mine, sizing me up. But I had to give him credit. Unlike most Greymonters, he didn't stare at my clothes or spiky punk hairstyle. In fact, his glance didn't wander from my eyes.

"It's the least I can do, considering the circumstances. Alida," he said to his secretary, "Hold my calls."

He escorted me down a wide corridor to his office. Decorated in the same style as the reception area, the suite was enormous, with windows on two sides and a skylit dome at the center. His elliptical cherry desk had no visible drawers and was completely bare. No papers. No clutter. Not even a phone. The only sign of work was a seventeen-inch flat-screen computer monitor on a shelf, where I finally spotted a small black cordless cradled in a futuristic holder.

On the walls hung original artwork eclectic enough that it had to be self-chosen. A Jasper Johns oil dominated the wall behind the desk. I saw in a glance that Craig Detweiller was a man of wealth and taste.

He led me to a group of sofas and stuffed chairs in muted shades of teal.

"Tea or coffee?" he asked, as I took a seat by a floor-to-ceiling window that overlooked the trees surrounding the stone library next door. The hazy sky seemed to fill the room. The atmosphere was warm and damp. New Englanders, even wealthy ones, are notoriously thrifty when it comes to climate control. In October, no matter how warm, air conditioning is out of the question.

"Nothing, thank you."

"Are you sure? I'm going to have tea."

Dancing with Mr. D

He rang his receptionist, who brought in a tea tray and left. There were two mugs and a pot large enough for several servings. The colors matched those of the carpet. He picked up a small plastic container in the shape of a bear and drizzled honey into his mug. His grin indicated he thought the honey bear was a cute touch. A whimsical fellow—that was the message.

"Sure I can't tempt you?"

"I just had lunch," I lied. Truthfully, I would have liked coffee, but I made it a rule not to eat or drink while conducting an interview. Too distracting.

"You were up early. Poor Cassandra." He sounded genuinely distressed. "Bad news to wake up to."

"Sorry."

"Don't apologize. I admire competence. I reward it in my own people. I'm sure Whit does the same."

"How many employees *do* you have?" I segued, looking around. "The place is as quiet as a—" I stopped short, feeling a chill.

His gaze grew somber. "Yes," he said, "I feel it too. She was quite a presence. It won't be the same town without her."

He didn't answer my question about employees, but I didn't push it. I could find out later.

"Before we get started," he said, leaning forward like an eager pupil, "I have to tell you I was a big fan of your father."

"Really?"

"My family used to summer in Cape Cod. Your father played the Music Tent. We went season after season. He always brought the house down. What a showman!"

I didn't bother to hide my pleasure. Few people in Greymont had heard of my father, and those summers in Cape Cod, with my mother painting dunes and wildlife, my dad performing nightly, had been some of the happiest of my life.

He raised a hand before I could speak, "I remember you too. In *The Sound of Music*. I hate to think how many years ago. You must have been, oh, four or five. We thought you were very cute, especially my mother."

"Like a trained poodle." I laughed, appreciating the memory.

"Not at all. I remember when your ringlets got caught on a doorknob."

"The wig came off, and I went running back for it? The stage manager almost died!"

"Did he? The audience just loved it."

"Unbelievable that you remember."

"As I said, we looked forward to those theater nights. Jennifer and I went back this July on our honeymoon. We're hoping to make it a habit."

"You're a newlywed?" I'd checked an old story in the *Eagle*, which mentioned a divorce. Jennifer, I thought, must be wife number two.

He beamed. "Don't I look it? Met a gorgeous girl far too young for me. I finally convinced her to marry me last summer."

"Congratulations."

"I'm an old buddy of your boss, you know."

Behind the casual charm, I detected a purpose. Establishing connections, with my dad, me, now Whit.

"He didn't mention that."

"He wouldn't."

"Why not?"

"I'm sure he wouldn't want to influence your reporting."

"It's difficult in a small town to avoid conflicts of interest." Ah. Here we were, right where I wanted to be. "Speaking of which, it's interesting how many Environmental Commission members had wrangled with Cassandra in the past."

He nodded and took a sip of tea. "Yes, it's hard to avoid, especially with real estate. Practically everybody willing to volunteer for town boards is a property owner and has something at stake."

Craig rested his hands on his knees, still leaning forward, for all intents and purposes, completely nondefensive.

"Cassandra made an accusation about that before she died," I said, giving him time because I wanted to watch his reaction. He set his face in a casual smile, preparing to hear some negative comment.

"Yes?"

"She said that the Environmental Commission was hand-picked by you."

He didn't cover with the smooth, artificial laugh I'd anticipated. "Well, I'd say the closeness of last night's vote is a better indicator than any denial I can make. But if you want one—"

"Why would she say something like that?"

Now he laughed. "Zoë. You talked to her. Can you tell me why she'd say half the things she said?"

"Actually, she seemed quite coherent."

"I'm not going to argue the point. And as I said, I'm truly saddened by her death. It's a tragic accident."

"I wonder how it happened."

His hazel eyes met mine. He let them go cold, impartial. The rest of his face was earnest. "I do feel responsible. After all, it was my order that sent the contractor and crew there last night. I've allowed myself to let my impatience overtake my common sense. I should have told them to wait until morning."

The hum of an engine outside broke my concentration. I remembered the loopy laugh, the lopsided gaze. I saw the funny eyes staring.

"But that would have given them time to go to court and get an injunction."

He didn't seem to take offense. "No court in the state would grant one, not after the prolonged hearing process we've been through."

"Why, then, did you insist on having people work in the dark?"

"You have to understand. I knew she was planning something. The sooner we bulldozed, the better. In Greymont, there are all kinds of nuts eager to climb on the bandwagon. I wanted to preempt a demonstration if I could."

"Who is the contractor?"

"Ron Braithwaite."

Kate's big brother. My throat tightened.

"We took plenty of outside bids," Craig added, noting my discomfort. "Ron came in very low. We knew he could do the job. Your colleague, Barbara Warwick, reported that last spring. A couple of people objected—in Greymont, someone always does—but we won approval in Town Meeting." He leaned toward me again. "The process has gone on far too long.

"You know," he continued, looking weary, "I wish Cassandra had been willing to talk to me about this. I called her several times. Even went to see her. She slammed the door in my face."

"When was that?" I asked.

His jacket fell open, revealing faint stains of sweat.

"A few days ago."

"Why?"

He leaned forward again, palms on knees, legs apart,

face somber. His tie, pale against his darker shirt, was loosened.

"I found a guy, believe it or not, who said we might be able to move the tree without killing it."

"A two-hundred-year-old tree. You were going to transplant it?"

"Disney did it in Florida."

"I assume his budget was bigger than the Plaza consortium's."

"They brought in jungle-clearing equipment. I read about it and thought it might be a bone I could throw." He took a quick breath as he shifted again, a man whose medium size and height seemed somewhat inflated by his ego. "Zoë," he said, putting his fist gently on the glass coffee table between us, his gaze calculatedly level with mine, "I consider myself an environmentalist." Like he was telling me a secret, a confession he was embarrassed to voice. "We investigated the claims about the salamander—"

"Spotted blue newt."

"Yes, newt." He flashed a quiet grin, like it was just between him and me. "I was willing to compromise, but she held out for everything."

"What are you going to do now? Are you going to move the tree?"

He shook his head. "I could have sold the idea to the consortium, especially as I was willing to pay the lion's share. Now that she's dead, I think everyone is just going to want to get this thing over with as quickly as possible and move forward."

"You've said you consider yourself an environmentalist."

"Yes."

"Can you give me an example or two?"

"Sure." He leaned back now, one hand on his thigh, the other lifting in an open gesture, as if he could point to something on the wall that would prove it—perhaps in one of the showy abstract paintings. "The Clarendon preserve. Up in North Greymont, on Framingham Road. We donated most of that land last year. And on the south side of town, the Gemini conservation area. I bought that property fifteen years ago—first land I purchased. I considered building. It would have made a lovely development. Big lots. Nice pond there, and a stream. Good frontage. I could have kept within all the regulations. About ten years ago, I decided to donate it instead. Look back over the records of the Green Trust. You'll see Delstar, my company, is the largest donor."

"If you're such a generous guy," I said, meeting the open, baby-face look, "why was Cassandra fighting you?"

I could tell he was itching for a duel, trying his best to resist, trying to keep it low-key and casual.

"You're hurting my feelings, Zoë. I am a generous guy." He threw open his hands like a musketeer trying to show he was unarmed, while keeping a stiletto hidden in his boot and maybe a bodkin or two up his sleeve.

"You didn't answer the question."

"If you read the biologist's report, you're going to see a lot of inconclusive statements. Talk to Tim Boudreau. He says the tree is diseased, that it's going to die in a few years anyway, and that the newt is not in any danger of extinction.

"Cassandra wanted to stop that project at all costs. It wasn't about the tree or the newt. I'm sorry to say, I think she had problems. I'm not being facetious. Some people have to find a way to make themselves feel important. This was her way, and it got out of hand."

"So you're saying she asked for it."

"Don't put words in my mouth." He held up a finger as if I'd been naughty. "Now, I've probably gone and said a whole lot more than I should have."

I put my pen and pad in my bag. "It sounds as if you knew Cassandra fairly well."

"I try to know as much as I can about my opponents."

He stood, signaling the end of our interview.

"Thanks for your time," I said.

The easy smile returned. "Don't mention it. Call if you have questions. I'll be more than happy to answer."

He walked me out to the lobby. When the elevator arrived, he offered me his hand. "I can't tell you how much I've enjoyed meeting you and having the opportunity to express my appreciation of your father."

As the elevator took me to ground level, I thought, Craig went to see Cassandra. I would have loved to have been a fly on the wall. What had they said to each other? Who might know? A friend, I thought, someone she might have confided in, or a neighbor.

The revolving door of the Delstar building opened onto a new row of storefronts. Most prominent was Mavis French's store, the Byzantine Fling, which sold imports from cooperatives of native people worldwide. Walking by on my way from the meeting with Detweiller, I peered through the window. It was filled with Day of the Dead mementos from Mexico, tin trays from Thailand, and batiks from Bali.

It had already been a very long day. It was after one, and my stomach, finally recovered from my morning queasiness, had begun to ache with a quiet hunger. I wanted to go to the office, maybe grab a snack, type up my notes of the interview with Craig, and ponder the possibilities. But I saw Mavis French inside. She headed the Environmental Commission. I couldn't pass up the chance to talk to her in person.

Remembering my talk with Keith this morning, I hesitated. Ellis, the boy who was bent on excluding Keith, was Mavis's son. I'd already felt a twinge of anxiety about the possibility of having to discuss the problem with her. Did I really want to press her for a reaction to Cassandra's death?

Finally, I put aside my doubts and went in. The tin bells on the door jangled, announcing my entrance. Mavis was a formidable-looking African-American woman of thirty-five. She wore a chic linen dress in shell pink and pearl earrings that set off her rich chocolate skin. A close-cut natural hairstyle emphasized her long neck. She stood at a back counter going over a new shipment with an employee who seemed duly cowed.

"Yes?" she inquired when I approached. Her tall frame and flawless posture radiated a potent blend of attitude and savoir faire.

"Zoë Szabo. From the *Eagle*." I flashed a smile. "Your son and mine are in the same first-grade class. We met at the open house at school a few weeks ago."

She took me in as if I were an exotic botanical specimen. Her glance started with my short, spiky, bleached hair, then wandered over my outfit, which was definitely too trashy for her taste. It settled on the row of studs along my right earlobe, and the skeleton—silver and Mexican—which dangled from the left. I always wore it in October, in honor of Halloween. Maybe the earring won her over. I caught a glimmer of good humor in her expression.

"Yes. I remember."

"I enjoyed hearing Mr. Keene explain hands-on math. He seems to be a good teacher."

She responded skeptically. "Ellis's brother had him two years ago. I prefer a traditional approach. He has trouble keeping the class in order."

"Yes, Mr. Keene could do better with discipline," I answered. Even though she'd given me an opening, I decided that this wasn't the time to voice my concerns about Ellis. "The reason I'm here is that I'm reporting the Plaza story. I wonder if you've heard about the accident?"

Mavis's expression soured. "Oh, yes. Miss Dunne."

"Would you care to comment?"

"Comment?"

"What were your feelings on hearing of her death? I'm asking all the board members."

"Mmm," she murmured as if she didn't quite believe me. She took a few moments to think, and I waited. Then in a voice low but composed, she said, "My heart went out to her, as a fellow human being."

"How well did you know her?"

"Not well."

"Were you aware that she planned to protest the ruling?"

"No."

A little frustrated at the one-word answers, I asked, "Do you think it's proper that Delstar bulldozed before she had a chance to appeal?"

"Yes."

"Could you explain why?"

She seemed annoyed at my question. "The waiting period had run out," she said with crisp enunciation. "Her attorney submitted a last-minute motion. We heard it even though we were under no obligation to do so. Therefore, yes, I feel it was proper. And, remember, she'd been through a full state review on a separate complaint about the same project."

"But to bulldoze at night—"

"That may have been inappropriate. But I can't speak for the board."

Okay, inappropriate, that I could use.

"Do you think she might have been startled by the noise of the machinery?"

I should have guessed from her gaze that I was getting a warning sign. "What happened and how," she finally said, very slowly, "is beyond my province."

"When did you find out she'd climbed the tree?"

She hesitated.

"Did you know yesterday?" I pressed.

"I heard this morning. On the news."

I wondered if this were true. Her demeanor was stiff and uncomfortable. "How well do you know Craig Detweiler?"

"What do you mean?"

"How close are you?"

Her eyes grew stony. "We've worked together. He's my landlord."

"You've worked together? On what?"

"That's irrelevant."

Like a hound on the scent, I felt my ears perk up and my nose twitch. "He had a sizable financial stake in the case before the commission. Did you consider recusing yourself?"

"If you mean to imply—"

"You're active in the Chamber of Commerce, which helped fund the consortium. Your landlord is the prime promoter and investor. You see no conflict of interest?"

She drew herself up, seeming to add an inch or two to her stature.

"I have an interest," she said in a resonant alto, "in the welfare of this town and of the poor in the developing world. If that is in conflict with a tree and a newt, I make no apology. I put people first."

"But not people like Cassandra Dunne?"

Her glare could have sunk the *Titanic*.

"If you'll excuse me," she said icily. "I have a business to run."

As I left I recognized that in my eagerness to penetrate her defenses, I'd alienated her more than I'd intended. But, I still wondered, how well did she know Craig? Did she have something at stake in the Plaza decision—beyond the obvious? I knew she was slated to have one of the largest spaces for an expanded store. But that wasn't a good enough reason for her unease. Maybe it was just annoyance at being grilled by a pushy white girl. But maybe there was something else, some secret she didn't want me to discover.

Then, with an awful flip of my stomach, I realized that I had just about ruined any hope of enlisting Mavis's help in bridging the rift between Ellis and Keith. Whit's words of this morning echoed faintly. *These are our neighbors.* What had I done? For a quote I might not even use.

I returned to the office battling self-critical feelings. I had no qualms about most of my questions, but I had jumped on her "putting people first" statement. It wasn't one of my more tactful moments. I'd been smoother with Craig. But then he didn't have a kid who was telling my son's friends not to play with him.

I'd switched from writing about rock to news because I wanted to explore the real world rather than tout the artificial glamour of celebrity. I'd wanted to be like Lois Lane, going after the bad guys with daring. To my dismay, I'd begun to learn that reporters had to delve into the personal lives of everyday people. Sometimes in a way that bordered on the offensive. You couldn't always tell whether you were on the trail of a breakthrough or just intruding on someone's privacy. Still, I wondered what kind of business dealings Craig had with Mavis. Why had she been so quick to evade my question?

Reporting this story might be trickier than I'd thought. Whit wasn't sold. And the key players had clout—not only with the paper but with the whole town.

Yet I couldn't let go. In the story I'd reported last year on the murder of the Cambodian, I'd learned that those who died violently had trouble resting. They badgered the living. The memory of Cassandra had begun to eat at me.

Chapter 8

It was nearly two when I returned to the office. Billy had assured me he and the band were leaving early in the afternoon for Vermont. I felt a little deflated, thinking that I might have missed him. But as I drove past the *Eagle* building, a Victorian painted in shades of green from pale sea mist to dusky moss, I saw a throng crowding the sidewalk. On the steps leading up to the entry stood Vivi Cairo in all her splendor. Wearing a skimpy raspberry top and black karate pants, she gossiped animatedly as she signed autographs—a goddess basking in the adoration of her fans.

My sigh of resignation was tempered by the expectation of spending a few minutes with Billy before he took off for Vermont. I pulled my Honda into the back lot, feeling more upbeat. To my annoyance a green Taurus occupied my favorite space. I vaguely recognized it as one of the cars Vivi had rented.

After fifteen minutes looking for another place to park, I gave up. I drove past the Community Center on the other end of the parking area and crossed Revere Street. I pulled behind the post office and found a spot marked: "Postal Customers Only. Violators Will Be Towed." I left my battered old Civic there, complaining under my breath at the inconvenience.

As I passed the Indian restaurant, the scent of curry enticed me. Maybe I'd get some takeout for lunch. A fantasy of Billy and me talking over a quick meal fluttered pleasantly on the aroma of spice in the air. I'd had nothing but coffee all day.

Then I thought of Vivi's model-slim figure and Billy on the porch caressing her feet. No. Better skip lunch. When I reached the *Eagle* building, the crowd had grown. Billy, in full rock-star garb, hung close by Vivi's side. Lean in black jeans and loose purple designer shirt, he projected the magnetism that had first drawn me to him. Two gold chains graced his neck. The blue veins at his temples contrasted with his deep tan, tempering the prettiness of his fine-hewn Irish features. Deeper in the crowd were Duck and Cerita, having a heart-to-heart with a couple of young hip-hop wannabes, whose eyes were shining with pure adoration.

Despite the fact that most of these folks saw Billy on Greymont's streets almost daily, they invariably asked for his autograph after having collected Vivi's.

"Hey, gorgeous! Zo, I'm talking to you!"

I whipped around to see Spots, the recording wizard and hippie emeritus. What can you say about a guy who wears tie-dyed painter's pants held up by stars-and-stripes suspenders, over a Ben & Jerry's T-shirt?

"Hi, Spots!"

Even though he was looking in my direction, his eyes seemed to be focused on that distant galaxy known as the sixties.

"How long do we wait on this dog and pony show?" Spots whined.

With him was John, the fat lead guitarist, who followed him around like a St. Bernard puppy. John, with his ample belly, teenager's acne, and dirty clothes that looked like he was waiting to send them home to Mom for a washing, was no exile from the Haight.

He looked like a very large fourteen-year-old kid who'd spent all last night behind the barn smoking his first stinky cigars. Under the blemishes, he was ghostly pale. And his T-shirt was wet with sweat. He'd probably stayed up too late and imbibed way too much. Spots wasn't an ideal role model.

My maternal side felt concerned. "How's it going, John?"

"I'm bombed," he said, ill-at-ease.

"Already?"

He shook his double chin and snorted a laugh.

Having heard his audacious riffs last night, I knew he could play rings around anyone in the band, even Billy. But he didn't have that laid-back veneer that musicians, no matter how uptight, tended to develop with age.

"What say we sneak in the back?" I suggested. "I'll take you on the ten-cent tour while Vivi communes with the masses."

They followed me around to the *Eagle*'s rear entrance. I showed them the offices and introduced a few reporters who hadn't joined the throngs of fans. Afterward, I bought a couple of sodas from the machine and sat down with Spots at the large table in the glassed-in porch off the kitchen, while John found a bathroom.

"I had quite a wild day today," I told Spots, after we'd chatted for a few minutes about his plans for recording, and I'd fended off a couple of fairly crude advances. He was old, but he assured me he hadn't slowed down. As a ploy to distract him I found a copy of today's *Eagle*, pushing it across the table to him. "That woman I mentioned last night," I said.

Hardly listening, Spots idly glanced down at the paper,

his eyes skimming a couple of below-the-fold articles. Then he turned it over and noticed the headline.

His mildly bedazzled expression suddenly vanished. He squinted at the picture that Kate had taken yesterday of Cassandra high in the tree. And the other taken by Mark of the paramedics and police surrounding the body by that time draped discreetly.

I watched his face morph through a series of emotions as he absorbed the news.

"You knew her?"

He lifted his chin, gazed at the ceiling. His eyes watered. He let out a heavy breath.

"How did you know her?"

Spots finally heard me. "Back in my youth." His thick lips, bow-shaped and pink, stretched into a quizzical smile.

"When you were kids?"

"No."

I made a wild guess. "Were you lovers?"

Spots looked into that faraway galaxy of his. I was about to repeat the question when he spoke. "We had a thing going there for a while."

Astonishment only hints at what I was feeling. It was like the earth wobbled on its axis before it got a grip and started moving again—and I wasn't sure if it was still spinning in the same direction. For a moment, I couldn't speak.

"When?"

A dim smile. "Years ago."

"How did it end?"

He tapped the paper. "You wrote this story?"

I nodded.

"Honey, if this is for your paper—"

"I'd love to know about her background before she

moved to Greymont." No way I was going to let go of this.

"I only knew her briefly."

"How long? A month?"

"Little more than that."

Behind the deliberate vagueness, I noted a clarity deep in his eyes. "Six months?" I pressed. "A year?"

He shrugged. "Can't really remember."

John came back and sat across from Spots. He took a sip from his soda and gazed out the porch windows at the back lot.

"When was this?" I asked. "The sixties?"

"No, no. In Vermont. Up at the commune."

"You lived together?"

"It wasn't serious. You know how things were in those days."

"Not really."

"Very free. Partying. Lots of great tail."

John guffawed, as he did at any mention of sex. His sense of humor seemed to have stuck somewhere around seventh grade.

"No strings attached." Spots's grin turned to a leer. "Hell, times might have changed, but I don't. Want to tango?"

I tilted my chin and shot him a "now don't be a naughty boy" glance. It was one of the many tricks in my "dealing with obnoxious come-ons and rude stories" grab bag from rock interviewing days. Talk about sexual harassment! I could have sued the entire roster of male recording artists residing within commuting distance of LA. One of the reasons I quit writing about the music scene was that I got tired of having to deal with this crap. But the upside was that behavior like Spots's seemed fairly tame.

"I'm married, so I'll have to pass," I said lightly, trying

to let him down gently. It wouldn't do to wound the male ego, especially as I figured he was hiding something that could help with my story.

"You know what they say about old dogs, darlin'."

"We'll have to catch each other in the next incarnation." I leaned closer and whispered, "Tell me about Cassandra."

"Not much to tell."

There was more to this story. I could tell by looking in his eyes. He wasn't trying to come on to me, just wanted to divert my attention. "What was she like?"

His laugh was evasive. "I've taken a lot of drugs. My memory isn't what it should be."

"You remember her name. Was she pretty?"

"She was okay." He glanced at the photo of Cassandra taken the day before. "The years didn't treat her too kindly."

I noticed that John was following the conversation with more than idle curiosity. He leaned over and scanned the headline. PLAZA PROTESTER DIES IN PLUNGE. His acne went white.

"John, what's the matter?" I asked.

"What in the hell's keeping Vivi?" Spots interrupted. He suddenly rose. "I wanted to do a sound check today. That damn woman. I bet she's still out there yakking with the public."

Okay, I thought, maybe Spots knew something he didn't want John to hear. Or maybe he was afraid John would say something he didn't want me to know. It was definitely worth a follow-up.

Vivi Cairo had just entered the lobby. The reporters and staff gathered around her. Billy stood at her side. Sharon, the receptionist, hung on Vivi's every word. And Vivi didn't simply effuse, she gushed. Even Whit, who had descended halfway down the stairs, seemed to be mesmerized, caught in the spell of her star power.

"Zoë!" Vivi cried out. A sweep of her hand indicated the varnished fir wainscoting. "This is where you work? It's so quaint. Like the inside of an exquisite antique."

"Let me introduce you to my boss," I said, steering her in Whit's direction.

He descended the rest of the way, a whimsical grin gracing his usually serious mouth. "Pleased to meet you, Miss Cairo."

Vivi's laughter rang out like a Lorelei's song. "Please, it's Vivi."

Whit was usually so reserved, I shrank inwardly when Vivi threw her arms about him and kissed his cheeks. But Whit, fussing a bit, took her hand.

"You sang one of my favorite songs," he said, a blush creeping from his neck to his ears as I watched in shock. " 'Heaven Sent.' "

Vivi brightened, if that was possible. Her wattage could have lit Times Square for a week. She closed her eyes, swinging to an inner beat. She began to sing in a whisper at first, and then in that wine-dark soprano with overtones of patchouli, licorice, and smoke.

The room hushed. Vivi sang through a verse. Then Billy, in his clear tenor, laid down a harmony, not taking the limelight, just enhancing her glow. When they were done, everyone burst into applause.

Mark, at the top of the stairs, held up a camera. "Hey, Viv!" he shouted.

She glanced in his direction, sultry as soon as she noticed the Nikon, showing her better profile.

"Zoë," Mark said. "Step over." He motioned me to get out of the picture. He snapped as soon as I moved.

Then Vivi called, "Now take one of the two of us together. We're like sisters." She reached out with those model-thin arms and pulled me close. Mark dutifully clicked away. He got a shot of Whit between Vivi and Billy. Then one of Whit, still blushing, alone with the diva.

"Mark," Whit said when the photos were taken. "Write a short piece. What she's doing in Greymont, the new album."

"Let's take a walk, Mark," she suggested. "You can shoot some candid photos of me in this lovely town. I'm inspired. New verses have started to flow into my mind." She wrapped her arm in Mark's.

I murmured to him. "Want me to cover that game for you tonight?"

He shot me a snide, close-mouthed smile.

Vivi beamed at me. "Want to tag along, little sister?"

"I have a story to write," I said. "But thanks." Inwardly, I blessed her for baby-sitting my rival so I could make calls undisturbed.

"Oh, before you go—" I grabbed Billy. "We need to talk about Keith."

He gazed after Vivi, clinging to Mark's arm, with the rest of the band close on her heels. When they finally exited, stage right, it was as if the air had escaped from the room with a *whoosh*.

"Okay, party's over," Whit announced. "Back to work." He disappeared up to his lair. The others returned to their desks.

"There's nothing to tell, Zoë," Billy said when we reached the kitchen. There was a studied laziness about him, a softness. His dark eyes, full of poetry and molten lava, bored into mine. A question in there, an impatience. "The kid's fine."

"No sore throat?"

"He just didn't want to go to school. I was the same way. Every six-year-old pulls that stuff at one time or another."

"He loves studying. He's been unhappy. In the last couple of weeks, the kids have been teasing him. I think it's serious."

"Keith will toughen up. You duke it out once or twice. Kids start to respect you."

"*Duke* it out?"

I could just imagine the expression on Mavis French's face if our sons got into a fistfight. And I'd seen Ellis. He was scrappy and strong. He'd be sure to beat Keith to a pulp.

"I grew up in a tough neighborhood," Billy persisted. "I learned to fight before I could walk."

"Spare me."

"We can't protect him forever. Some lessons a kid has to learn on his own."

I'd learned street lessons too, most of them hard. "We ought to support him. Help him make friends."

"I don't want him to be a mama's boy."

"What old-fashioned bull!"

"What do you want me to do? Threaten to pound the kids if they're not nice to my boy?"

"I'm not going to dignify that with an answer."

We glared at each other.

Billy sighed. "I'll talk to his teacher."

"When?"

"When I finish the album."

"Billy, that'll be months!"

"Three weeks—at the outside."

"It'll be too late."

"Let go, Mama Bear. Have faith in your son. He'll learn how to stick up for himself."

I dug my teeth into my lip.

Billy caressed the nape of my neck. "Give him the month. If he doesn't work it out, I'll take it up with his teacher. Okay?"

A lump entered my throat.

"It's a guy thing."

"Guy thing—that's baloney."

The shock of seeing Cassandra's limp body had begun to overtake the numbness. Strains of Bob Marley's "No Woman, No Cry" echoed on sympathetic strings deep in my heart. And then I thought maybe Billy didn't know.

"You heard that Cassandra died this morning?"

He was taken aback. "Hey—no. Aw, honey." He touched my arm.

"I found the body."

"Aw, shit." He pulled me close, holding me. His body was so warm, so gentle. I felt reassured.

"What happened?" he murmured, touching my chin and looking me deep in the eyes.

"She fell out of the tree."

"Gee, I'm sorry." A shadow passed over his face. "This means more work for you, doesn't it?"

It felt good that he cared. I nodded.

The shadow darkened. His expression became less sympathetic. "You know, I'm going to be at the studio day and night. I'm not going to be able to help with the kids."

So much for empathy. All he cared about was the album. I pulled away.

"Don't be like that."

"Billy—"

"No. This is my chance. And it's not just for me. It's for both of us. Forget the ego thing for a moment, think of the money."

"I know."

"It's bad timing. But I've made a commitment."

I nodded, feeling teary, glad Vivi wasn't around to interrupt.

Billy sighed, sounding peeved. "I'm not going to be able to drop everything and run down here to get you out of any scrapes."

"With all that street-fighting experience, maybe you ought to give it a try."

"Seriously. Be careful."

"When will you be home?"

Guilt tinged his grin. "We're going to set up the sound. Spots wants to try several different types of miking. Sometimes we work better late at night. You know how it is."

"Right."

"Zoë, you're getting that tone—"

"What tone?"

Like two chary gunslingers in a tape loop of the *OK Corral*, we faced off.

"Why can't you trust me?"

"It's not you I don't trust."

"Could have fooled me." As bitter as the last dregs of yesterday's coffee.

I wanted to hold him. Wanted to love him. Wanted to melt into his arms. But we stood there shooting verbal bullets. Then desire and panic overtook me. I reached out. He clasped my hand.

We were transported to the beach at Malibu. Purple sunrise over the mountains, the sea black behind us. The bad times hadn't happened. The world was still new.

Outside an autumn breeze rustled the yellowing branches. A leaf drifted to earth. Through the windows of the glassed-in porch, I could see the dirt lot filled with cars, most of them cheap foreign models, many years old. Whit's blue Volvo was one of the few that had been recently washed. Greymont was not a showy town. Beyond the lot were the backs of the restaurants and shops on Stanhope and Main.

It was New England, not California, I reminded myself. A few weeks before Halloween, not the midst of a glorious spring. The bad things had happened.

Billy left soon after in the new metallic green Taurus Vivi had rented him. Vivi, Duck, and Cerita followed in a silver Carrera. Spots and John led in a van painted for Vivi—a surprise from her record company. The name of the album—EVE'S AMBITION—was emblazoned in purple and gold over a jungle mural on one side, a shimmering Vivi as Eve on the other.

Chapter 9

On my way back inside, I ran into Kate at last. She was halfway out the door, camera bag in tow. Around her neck, as always, dangled a chain with a gold heart and tiny diamond. A few strands of hair wandered uncharacteristically from her thick chestnut braid. Her skin, despite a tan, seemed sallow.

"Where were you this morning?"

"Oh, Zoë." She looked frazzled. "I overslept."

"You're probably better off. You heard—we found the body." I shivered.

"It must have been unpleasant."

"Yeah, it was."

"I'm sorry I let you down."

I shrugged. "Mark enjoyed prancing around with the Nikon. You made his day."

She smiled tensely. "I'm on my way to a shoot."

"Is everything okay?"

"Oh, sure. Just tired. You know, my mom. She wanted me to spend the night."

I nodded, sympathizing. Her mother had a tendency to place hysterical late-night calls.

"Let's have dinner," I suggested. "Billy won't be home until late. I could use some company."

"Not today."

"Tomorrow?"

"Maybe." She squeezed past me, not meeting my eyes.

"We'll talk. I've got lots to tell," I added, raising my voice as she walked swiftly down the street. She tossed her bag in her old pickup and drove off. Yesterday, I'd attributed her distance to a brief bout of moodiness. Now I wondered if it was something more serious.

"Oh, Zoë," called Sharon as I passed her desk, "it was so exciting to meet Vivi Cairo!" She beamed. A total fan. "What's she like in private? Is she always that friendly?"

"She's a peach."

Sharon gave me a knowing glance. "Yeah—I wouldn't want my husband spending too much time *recording* with her."

I laughed lightly.

"Still," she effused, "I can't believe somebody I know is doing an album with Vivi Cairo. Is Billy going on tour? Oh my God—what I've heard about musicians and tours—trashing hotel rooms and groupies—oops, sorry."

"Thanks, Sharon. The next time I need reassurance, I'll call you for a quick consult."

She really was embarrassed. "I put my foot in my mouth, didn't I?"

"Don't worry about it. I've heard worse. Anyway, we've agreed, a tour is not on the horizon. Shoot! It's after four."

"What's the matter?"

"I just blew off an interview."

"Tim Boudreau?"

"Yeah."

"He called. He had to cancel. He wants to meet you tomorrow."

"Saved! Thank you." I glanced at the slip of paper with Boudreau's home number and a tentative meet at a coffee shop in the morning. I went back to my desk and checked in with Dania, telling her I'd try to be home by six. That ought to give me time to collect enough information so that I could write the story tonight after the kids went to bed.

It would border on a fifteen-hour day, but I just couldn't let go. If I didn't file a story by tomorrow morning's deadline, Mark would surge ahead of me. He had something percolating on the police side. Probably from that paramedic.

Still, I didn't have anything else to do with my evening. Billy wouldn't be home till two or three in the morning. I felt a pang of loneliness. Feeling the need for someone to whom I could pour out my heart, I thought of Cletha. I hadn't spoken to her in ages. Cletha Fair had been close to my parents. In her mid-sixties, she was nearly a substitute mother. Billy and I had moved to Greymont at her suggestion, and it had been her recommendation that had secured me an interview at the *Eagle*.

I'd never forget Whit's look of disbelief when he'd glanced over my résumé or his disdain when he'd asked what made me think writing reviews of rock concerts qualified me for straight reporting.

"Well," I'd stammered, smiling as winningly as I could. "I can put words together. And I'm willing to start at the bottom. Obits. Birth announcements. Garden club news. I'll do just about anything."

"These clips," he said, frowning.

"I know," I said, "They're a bit—"

"Yes," he agreed. "A bit—"

"I realize that when you report a robbery you don't describe the victim's voice as a 'whiskey-drenched drawl.'"

"Yes," he agreed, deadpan. "I would hope that you'd

retire 'drenched' for anything other than to describe a flood or a storm."

It had been either my abject willingness to start from scratch or Cletha's urgings that had won me the job, maybe a combination of both.

Despite the falling out we'd had last year, I had a soft spot in my heart for her. I decided to risk a call.

"Cletha!" I said cheerfully. "Zoë."

"Hi."

"Long time no see. How are you?"

"We're doing well. And you?"

"So-so. Billy's recording an album. And the whole crazy crew has descended."

"They're recording in Greymont?"

"No. Vermont. At Wonderland Sounds. Ever hear of it? The studio's got a pretty good rep. Vivi Cairo's here."

"Who?"

That's what I liked about Cletha: she didn't keep up with the names. Too busy saving the world. "I'd love to get together sometime. Maybe you can come and have dinner. You and Prith."

"We'd like that. He's doing much better. He's enrolled in an ESL program at the community college."

"That's wonderful. Let's set a date as soon as I finish this story. You've heard, haven't you, about Cassandra Dunne?" A leading community organizer, she knew all the activists, regardless of cause.

"So that's what this call is about."

"No, not at all. Did you know her?"

She responded warily. "I did."

"What can you tell me?"

"On the record?"

"That's not necessary. You've been quoted a lot. I'm

looking for someone who knew her well, a close friend or family."

"Have you talked to Ann Chatsford?"

"No. What's her connection?"

"Cassandra was her tenant. She must be terribly upset. I should call. Ann is ninety-two years old. Cassandra did her shopping, cooking, and odd jobs around the house. Off the record, Cassandra was a difficult person. She alienated everyone, even her allies. Or especially her allies. She was impossible to work with. I tried once or twice and swore I never would again."

"When was this?"

"Ten years ago or more. But don't quote me. It's old gossip, not worth going into. Talk to Ann. She's probably the only person in town with a good word to say."

This was exactly what I had been hoping for: a friend of Cassandra's and a neighbor. I didn't even bother to call. I just looked up the address and drove over.

I found Ann Chatsford in the garden behind her whitewashed brick Colonial on Coolidge Avenue. She was digging up dahlias to winter over in her root cellar. A bundle of energy, though frail, Ann had tight white curls with pink scalp showing through, liver spots, and a nose that dominated her thin face. She wore a pair of pastel plaid pedal pushers and a white cotton blouse with a Peter Pan collar that could have been displayed in a museum of vintage clothing.

"I'm writing a story on the death of Cassandra Dunne," I explained after introducing myself. "Cletha Fair suggested I talk to you."

Ann eyed me inquisitively. After a moment, she leaned

toward me and whispered. "You solved that murder last year, didn't you?"

"Well, I helped."

"Don't be modest. If you don't blow your own horn, who will? Some people say your dress is too flashy, but I like your spunk. I never go out without lipstick." She wore a smear of bright red on her wrinkled lips. "What's that color called?"

"Heart to Heart."

"I like it."

I laughed, feeling an affinity for her. "Glad you approve."

"I suppose you want to see Cassandra's apartment?"

"That would be terrific. The police didn't seal it off?"

"Hmph! They didn't do a blessed thing. Could you get those tools for me, dear? I hope you're not going to be like them! Accident. She was murdered, I tell you."

"What makes you think so?"

"Cassandra lived in that apartment for fifteen years. She was an expert woodsman—person I suppose you'd say these days. Someone who could survive in the wilderness for a month with nothing but a knife and a compass. It's absurd to think she'd fall."

Some people talk too much, others too little. Ann was one of the former. She kept up a constant monologue. I followed her to the cellar, where she put away her gardening equipment, then to her kitchen, where she got her keys, then to the carriage house and up the exterior stairway that led to a studio apartment. Despite her age, I had to hustle to keep up with her.

"The police barely inspected," she told me with a spark of anger as she unlocked the door. "I asked them to take fingerprints, but they treated me as if I were senile.

"She built the bed and the table herself," Ann said, her eyes reddening as she looked around. "She was very handy. She did all my repairs. All my shopping. Before she went yesterday, she made sure I had plenty in stock. It was as if she knew something might happen."

There was a sadness about the apartment. A loneliness. The large room was monastic, tidy, and spare. It held a narrow bed, a bookshelf, and a kitchenette in desperate need of an upgrade. The stove looked like something my grandmother in Stalinist Hungary might have used. There were no knickknacks, no posters, not even a clock or a calendar.

On the desk, I noticed a day book. Being careful to touch only a corner, I flipped through the pages. There were descriptions of weather, walks, and observations of nature written out in a cramped hand, always in the same blue-black ink. Most entries were only a line or two. The last was dated the previous Friday. It read:

Finches and crows. 62 degrees at sunrise.

A strange epitaph, I thought. Its impersonal quality was mirrored by the spareness of the small apartment. The only objects that were imbued with feeling were the pieces of furniture that she had crafted herself.

Ann kept up her patter, telling me Cassandra had moved in right after the Gemini Hill Farm fight. They'd met in a demonstration against the subdivision.

"We chained ourselves to a huge old beech." Ann boasted, describing the battle in detail. At first Cassandra and she had stood alone, but eventually others joined them. "Those were grand times," she concluded. "There were no compromises and no backroom deals."

Ann would have gone on all evening. Somewhere in the midst of her ramblings, I murmured about having to get home to my kids, and we drew the conversation to a close. On the way out, I followed her downstairs to the drive where I'd parked my car.

"Oh," I said before leaving. "I meant to ask. Did Cassandra have visitors last week?"

"Her lawyer came by a few times. And Tim Boudreau."

"No one else?"

Ann frowned, eager to help. "I did hear a car Saturday night—very late. When I asked who'd come, she said no one. But I'd looked out, and there was a car. You know how black they can look. I remember thinking, 'Why aren't the headlights on?' Cassandra swore no one came. But the next day she decided to climb the maple. I was afraid for her."

"Why?"

"Ordinarily, I wouldn't have objected. I'm a believer in direct action. Other people called her a zealot, but I'm old enough to remember when Greymont was mostly farmland and woods. None of these awful malls and flimsy houses slapped together and stuck just anywhere."

"Do you think it might have been Craig Detweiller?"

Ann turned her face to the sky. Her dominating nose seemed even larger in profile. Above us stretched the branches of a huge old sycamore. At last, she said, "Maybe. But I assumed it was Tim. They had an awful fight a few months ago. He came by a few times in the past month, trying to patch things up. But it always ended in an argument."

"About what?"

"The Plaza site."

"I thought he decided to change his vote the day of the meeting."

"Yes. But he'd been thinking about it for quite some time."

After a couple of tries, I managed to start my Honda. I'd had this trouble intermittently in the past winter, but now it seemed to be happening no matter what the weather. The engine finally turned over and purred reassuringly.

I waved good-bye to Ann and drove through the streets lined with stately old homes and grand trees. Despite the heavy atmosphere, the slanted afternoon light took on traditional hues of autumn. Sunset burnished the fading greens and pale golds of the thick foliage.

I put a tape on—*Blondie's Greatest Hits*, continuing my diva training. But Debbie Harry was just too much fun. I sang along with the boisterous chords and trashy humor of "Hanging on the Telephone" and forgot the horrors and sad feelings, focusing instead on the music.

About a mile from home, I reluctantly hung a right following the narrow road over the train tracks, toward the strip mall on Route 88 on the east side of town. I had one person I had to try to catch before I could call it a day. I didn't want to talk to him, since he was Kate's brother. But I knew I couldn't put it off.

Lit with dim fluorescent lights, RB General Contracting appeared to be a business run on a shoestring, but then most contractors in Greymont ran their offices out of their homes. Either Ron was doing relatively well or he liked to show off. From the look of the place, it was hard to tell which. On the walls were framed photographs of undistinguished new homes. A trail of white dust covered the linoleum tile.

A woman in her late twenties sat at a desk near the phone. In a playpen in the middle of the room sat a chubby-cheeked child, holding a ring of plastic keys in primary colors.

"Hi," she said as I approached. "Can I help you?"

She wore a floral print dress straight out of Kmart. Her pale brown hair was styled in a pageboy.

"I'm looking for Ron Braithwaite."

"He'll be back in a few minutes. I'm his wife, Sandra. Are you thinking of building? You might want to look through our idea book."

I shook her hand. I'd tried to reach Ron a few times today, and he always seemed to be out when I called. I decided not to tell her I was a reporter. Didn't want her to slip into the back and give him advance warning that I was here. "I'll take a peek at that idea book."

Relief flooded her face.

"Do you live here in town?"

"Yes."

"Own or rent?"

"Own. I'm thinking about getting something bigger." I didn't add that I also thought about winning the lottery and buying a Jaguar. "How old is your baby?"

Her smile relaxed. "Nine months. Aren't you, sweetie?"

The baby smiled at the sound of his mother's voice. He pulled himself up to a stand, reached up and teetered a moment, then plopped down in a sit. "Mmmumum."

"They're so sweet when they're babies. I wish they never had to grow up."

"I know what you mean. Mine are six and four."

"Really? I have a six-year-old, too!" We chatted about our children for a few minutes, until finally Ron Braithwaite arrived.

About thirty, tall, with the build of a wrestler, Ron wore a black T-shirt with sleeves cut out. His face was long, forehead pronounced, hair thinning. The biceps in his deeply tanned arms bulged. His blue jeans were streaked with grease and mud. His boots were thick with dirt.

"Oh, Ron, honey," Sandra said.

Ron Braithwaite took me in and scowled. Although we'd never formally met, gauging by his expression, he recognized me.

"You're a hard man to track down," I said lightly.

Physically there was a strong family resemblance between him and Kate—a square jaw, athletic build, and long legs. But in style they were light years apart. Kate was a horsey Ralph Lauren type; Ron reeked of stock cars and plumbing supply stores. Kate was cheerful and compliant, almost to a fault when it came to her mother. From what Kate had told me, her brother was tightly strung and caused his parents all sorts of heartache.

"What do you want?" he asked.

"Craig Detweiller mentioned—"

His expression flashed extreme irritation. His biceps flinched and his hands, marked with ropy muscles, tautened.

Sandra let out a nervous laugh and swooped up the baby. "Hungry?" she cooed. "Excuse me. I'm going to feed him."

Ron ignored her, staring fixedly at me.

"I'm doing a story for the paper on Cassandra's death. Craig said he sent you to the site after the hearing."

Ron said nothing.

"I wanted to know if you had any interaction with Cassandra. You must have seen her up there in the tree."

"No."

"You didn't notice her?"

"No."

"She was found dead this morning."

"Yeah, I know that."

"I thought you might have talked to her when you arrived at the site last night."

"No." His stare made me uncomfortable.

"When did you find out about her death?"

The sound of his breath was hard and masculine. I could smell his odor, a mixture of sweat and soap. "Where do you get off asking these questions?"

"Just doing my job."

"For the record, huh?"

"Yes."

"Public has a right to know, huh?"

"Sounds like Kate's schooled you well." I grinned appeasingly.

He smiled, but not particularly nicely.

I switched to a more businesslike approach. "Well, for the record, what was your response when you heard of her death?"

"It happened about two years too late." He laughed at my ill-concealed surprise at his response. "I hated her fucking guts."

Okay, I thought, I can play hardball. "What time did you go to the site?"

"Eleven."

"That's when you bulldozed the grounds?"

"That's what Craig told us to do. I left my foreman to finish the job."

"You were scheduled to work this morning. But neither you nor the crew showed up. Why not?"

"Craig called. He said we'd better hold off."

"When was that?"

His head bent forward. His eyes lowered down at his black leather motorcycle boots. I guessed that his feet were a size fourteen. Considering his height and he-man build, they didn't seem out of proportion.

Dancing with Mr. D

"Five. Something like that."

"How did you find out Cassandra was dead?"

"Craig told me."

"When?"

"When he called."

"Did you see anyone else near the site last night?"

A smile of aggression, not a smidgen of humor or friendliness in it. "Somebody might have walked by. We were doing a job. Machinery makes a lot of noise. Like I said, I wasn't there long."

"Could I have the name of your foreman? I'd like to give him a call."

His stare grew less pleasant. Perspiration beaded on his brow. "Time's moving along. I suggest you do the same."

Chapter 10

"Mommy! Mommy!" Smokie ran toward me, her dark hair cut in short bangs, her tiny nose and bright mischievous mouth smeared with cheese sauce from her macaroni. Still a little shaky from my conversation with Ron, I dropped to one knee and took her small body in my arms. At four, she still hadn't lost that trusting innocence of early childhood. I drank it in appreciatively, wishing I could remake the world for her into the benevolent place she believed it to be.

"Hi, snugg'ms," I said, kissing her nose.

"What does snugg'ms mean?"

"It's a term of endearment."

"What's a deer mint?"

I smiled. "Something you tell someone you love."

Dania hovered, ready to leave. After I paid her, we consulted the calendar and arranged a schedule for the following week that I hoped would do.

"Hey, Keith," I said, giving him a hug after Dania left. He sat sullenly at the table, reading a book while supposedly eating. His macaroni was untouched. "How was school?"

Keith read his book, saying nothing. "Did you hear me?" I asked.

He looked up, reluctantly. "What?"

"School?"

He pursed his lips and then said matter-of-factly, "I hate it."

"What happened?"

"Ellis called me a donkey."

"Oh, hon. Do you want me to call your teacher?"

He mumbled something. I repeated my offer. "No," he muttered.

"If he's calling you names—"

"I called him a name."

"What?"

"A stupidosaurus. I said I was a lexovisaurus and I was going to stomp him."

I'd hoped this disagreement would simmer on the back burner for a while, but it seemed to be escalating. I wondered how long it would take for Mavis French to get over our little confrontation today. Neighbors. I sighed.

"We should talk about name-calling," I ventured. "People who call names are usually pretty insecure. Sometimes the best thing to do is just ignore them. They're trying to make themselves feel big at our expense."

Keith focused on the book, ignoring me.

"Keith? Did you hear me?"

"I don't want to talk about it."

I was so tired, I hugged him and let it go for the time being. Despite Keith's moodiness, the next hour or two passed in a pleasant low-key fashion. The three of us played Sorry! Smokie won. Keith did his homework with me in about two minutes, then he closeted himself in his room with his dinosaur collection.

I gave Smokie a bath. We sailed her boats in the tub,

letting them capsize for fun. After the shock of discovering a corpse, taking care of my children helped me pull back a little from my growing obsession with Cassandra. A person had died, but the pulse of life continued.

Finally, around eight, after tucking Smokie into bed, I sat at the kitchen table, booted up my laptop, and wrote my article, placing a few more calls to round out my story.

Using old clips I'd dug up from the newspaper's morgue, I traced the history of Cassandra's battle to save land from developers. I marked a few milestones: her arrival in town just before the battle over the Gemini Hill Farm; her brief leadership of the Sierra Club chapter; her decision to found the Living Earth Coalition shortly afterward; her opposition to the Braithwaite subdivision proposal; and her recent fight over the Plaza site.

I focused on Cassandra, her cause, and tried to present what I imagined she believed her mission to be: to preserve the earth in its present beauty. I quoted Ann Chatsford on Cassandra's deep belief in environmental preservation. I cited the biologist's report on the newt and some of the other documentation from the Environmental Commission decision. I kept the tone as neutral as I could, knowing Whit didn't want to sensationalize the fight, but I did try to present her side. Summing up someone's death, you are taking account of her life. I wanted people to pause for a moment and think, not about the dissension she'd caused, but the reason she believed it was necessary to do so.

Then, needing a scientist's quote on the newt, I called Morgan, who was a physics professor, in addition to being a music fan with broad and eclectic tastes. He liked everything from early music to grunge. (I swear, the professor and I had engaged in a heated discussion on the Seattle sound only a few weeks before.)

Although he was pushing seventy, he still taught a few courses at Greymont College. He gave me the name of a local zoologist. I told him about finding the body and complained about Billy having to be out most of the night.

"I'll keep you company," he suggested. "We can have a game of chess."

"I don't know if I can concentrate that hard."

"I'll go easy on you."

I should have called the zoologist, plugged in the quote, and gone to bed, but the horror of having found a body still hadn't worn off. The intensity of the day's interviews with Craig, Mavis, Ann, and Ron had my mind buzzing. I was afraid I'd have nightmares. The house felt empty without Billy.

"Come in," I greeted Morgan, about fifteen minutes later. With his thinning gray hair, droopy eyes, and sagging cheeks, he reminded me of the creatures in Smokie's beloved Mercer Mayer stories. "Make yourself comfortable. I'm just finishing up my piece."

"I'm not interrupting?"

"No, but I still have to call your friend."

Morgan poured himself a glass of white wine and set up the chess board while I phoned the zoologist, who agreed that the newt was not endangered—at least not technically speaking.

"Just between you and me," he added, "all creatures are losing more and more habitat. And habitat loss leads to species extinction—sometimes quite suddenly."

"Why didn't you speak up at the Plaza hearing?"

He sighed. "I'm no expert on that particular piece of land, so I couldn't speak with authority. But the loss of each acre of wilderness, even small patches, brings us closer to the brink."

"The brink of what?"

"We are now in the midst of the greatest mass extinction since the end of the Mesozoic era, which wiped out the dinosaurs. The former was caused by an asteroid, we believe. But the current extinction is caused by man.

"In addition to the large mammals, we are losing untold numbers of smaller species: insects, mites, worms, corals, tiny crustaceans that make up the plankton of the seas. Many of them support the system of life in ways we still don't understand.

"We don't know when it will be too late. When the delicate web of life will lose so many strands that it won't be able to support our own species."

"What are we supposed to do? Stop building entirely?"

"You're right, it's a complicated question from both a technological and a political vantage point. Scientists disagree. It's not an easy position to sell."

I was surprised at his assessment. I'd considered Cassandra a wild-eyed extremist. Now this staid college professor was sounding the same alarm.

"Did you know Cassandra Dunne personally?"

"No."

"What did you think of her crusade?"

"I try to avoid local politics. I will say that self-styled environmental activists can do more harm than good. They prophesy doom and destruction. When they're proven wrong, it's a setback for more reasoned argument."

"Well, thank you," I said. I stuck the "web of life" statement into the newt sidebar and wondered what Whit's reaction would be. Then I rummaged through the refrigerator, found some fruit and sliced turkey, and arranged it on a plate to share with Morgan. I poured myself a glass of Chardonnay, diluted it with seltzer and ice so it wouldn't knock me out after my long day, and went into the living room to play chess.

As I pushed out my first pawn, I said, "Your friend turned out to be as much of a doomsayer as Cassandra."

"Really?"

"It makes you wonder what the world's going to be like for Smokie and Keith when they're adults, not to mention their kids."

Morgan was silent. "Remember, academics need to get research funded. The more we convince people of the importance of what we do, the more money comes our way."

"You're saying he's biased."

"We all are, dear." After three moves, Morgan took one of my knights. So much for his going easy on me.

We played for a while. I suspected that he could have won in the next two moves, but he delayed the assault, preferring to test my IQ in a series of skirmishes, which almost always led to the loss of one of my pieces. I frowned, looking over the board. Finally, I brought out my queen.

"Dangerous move." Morgan eyed me in a grandfatherly manner, then he sighed. "I enjoyed the excitement last night," he added.

"Vivi's a hoot, isn't she?"

"Dazzling."

"Yeah, she's dazzled my husband right out of my house."

Morgan studied me over his bifocals. "Tell me if I'm overstepping my bounds, but if I were you I'd let Billy be."

I took a sip of my watery wine and fought the urge to argue.

"He's worked very hard to be a good father and husband," Morgan added gently. "We've talked. He was worried about Vivi coming. Worried about how you might react."

"He didn't tell me that."

"A man has his pride. Give him some space."

"I am. I didn't argue when he said he didn't know when he'd be coming in tonight—if at all."

"He's an artist. He needs to be free to do his work. Music is a collaborative venture."

"Well," I said, trying to steer to safer ground, "you were very generous to put them up last night. They must have kept you awake into the wee hours."

"Oh yes. I didn't sleep well."

"What were they doing, playing music?"

"Billy came over early in the morning to play something for Vivi."

"I know."

Again Morgan glanced over his bifocals. "Mmph. Are you sure you want to move your queen there?"

"Huh? Oh. Can I take it back?"

He nodded. I moved the queen somewhere else. From his frown, I guessed it wasn't much of an improvement.

"That young guitarist—"

"John?"

"Yes. He and Spots were out till all hours."

"Really?"

"Yes. I refused to let them smoke marijuana in the house. They left pretty quickly. They didn't get in until shortly before four."

Now he had my attention. "How do you know?"

"I sleep lightly. I went downstairs because I heard noise. They were just returning—and it looked as if they'd done more than smoke a marijuana cigarette."

"They were really stoned?" I asked, the fear rising. I looked at my watch, wondering what Billy was doing right now.

Morgan said nothing. After another few minutes, he took my queen.

I groaned. "What's your reaction to the death of Cassandra Dunne?"

"Honestly?"

"Of course."

"We're well rid of her."

"Morgan!" He sounded almost as bad as Ron Braithwaite.

He put up both hands. "She was a madwoman."

"Sometimes people appear crazy, but only because they have a good reason. Your friend," I added, by way of illustration, "said that the last ten percent of habitat loss is what kills most of the species. Maybe it wasn't so absurd for her to fight for a few acres of wetland in town."

He shook his sagging face. "I served on a committee with her once. I swore I never would again."

"That's what Cletha said. What did she do?"

"Some people argue to make their case. They may not be very bright and their arguments may be totally irrelevant, but they're sincere. Not Cassandra. She threw tantrums that were simply unforgivable. If she had used that argument about habitat loss, some of us might have listened."

I considered this while I studied the board. The wine, even watered down, had gone to my head. It was after eleven. Even though I hated the thought of going to sleep, I was having trouble fighting off drowsiness. From the clips of Cassandra's battles, I remembered that arguments about habitat were always brought up. At times they were countered intelligently; most often they were dismissed out of hand.

"Didn't she help keep Greymont as beautiful and untouched as it is? There are so many conservation areas and hiking trails."

Morgan sighed. "Other people work for the same things in much less divisive ways."

We played a while longer. Morgan, I thought, must have had a bit too much wine, because I saw a great move and managed to swipe his queen. I felt triumphant.

"Did she have any particular enemies?"

Morgan studied me. "She and Craig Detweiller were almost always at odds. Of course, he's emerged as one of the more enlightened developers in town. I like the man."

"He's so slimy."

"Anybody working with a charitable organization knows Craig will help out. He always makes a sizable donation. He was instrumental in setting up the Green Trust, which funds most of the purchases of conservation land in town. You could make a case that Craig is one of the unsung heroes of the environmental cause. I can see by your expression that you don't agree."

"What did his father do?"

"Nothing particularly distinguished. Some sort of sales."

"Where did he get his money?"

The wrinkles on Morgan's face rearranged themselves into an expression of uncertainty. "I suppose he got lucky in real estate."

"What do you know about Ann Chatsford?"

Morgan smiled. "You're grilling me tonight."

"You're my Greymont griot. You've been here forever and you know everyone."

"Well, dear, it's a bigger town than you think. And there are a lot of transients, college people moving in and out."

"And Ann?"

"You want my honest opinion?"

"Sure."

He shook his head dismissively. "The woman can't stop talking."

"You're an old chauvinist," I teased.

"My wife accused me of it once or twice." Despite the joking tone, his eyes misted. He still mourned her, even though she'd died many years before.

"Tim Boudreau?"

"Don't know the fellow. Uh oh. You shouldn't have made that move. Check."

I glanced down at the board. After a few moments of pondering, I pushed my remaining bishop in front of my king.

Morgan clucked and moved a pawn. "Checkmate."

I cried out in dismay, but I can't say I didn't expect it. "I wasn't much of a challenge, was I?" I said ruefully, as we put away the game.

"You should play more often. Keith will give you a good game."

I walked him to the side door. "Thanks for the company."

"Anytime, dear. Anytime." He patted my arm. "Now

don't worry about Billy. He'll be just fine. And if you need help with the children, don't hesitate to ask."

"Good night," I called after him. I watched to make sure he made it across the yard to his house. When the lights on his porch went out, I closed the door.

Billy stumbled into bed sometime around three in the morning. I opened one eye, looked at the clock, and rolled over. When I woke up at six-thirty, he was fast asleep. I tried to ask when he had to be at the studio, but I couldn't understand the answer he mumbled.

In the bathroom, I snooped a bit, examining Billy's shirt in the wicker laundry bin, going so far as to sniff it. Nothing out of the ordinary. No telltale smudges or dusting of powder, white or otherwise. The only scent was that of Billy's skin and tobacco. I cast my mind back on the band and didn't remember seeing any of them smoke.

I reflected on my chess game with Morgan. I'd been so distracted by my story on Cassandra that I hadn't paid attention to the trap he'd set for my king. Was I ignoring something by focusing only on the obvious? Had something other than her environmental zeal contributed to her death?

I added up all I'd learned in the previous day. Craig and she were enemies. Craig claimed to have visited her a few days before her death to try to talk her into a compromise. According to Ann, right after that visit, Cassandra had decided to make her last stand by climbing the maple. The Braithwaites hated her. And she had numerous other enemies, including, possibly, her ex-ally Tim Boudreau, who'd cast the deciding vote against her motion.

Had she made some kind of a threat against him, a threat that he later feared she might carry out?

And then there was Spots. Was it a coincidence that he'd arrived just before her death? An ex-lover, who seemed visibly upset when he read of her plunge. An ex-lover, who had been wandering through the streets of Greymont in the wee hours of the morning, at approximately the time she'd died.

Chapter 11

The weather had turned. The air, in the mid-fifties, felt like October at last. I dressed quickly, choosing a pale lichen suit with a sleeveless plum top and open-toed heels in a matching wine suede. Though the flippy skirt was short and the hues were a tad vibrant, this was one of my more conservative outfits—the better to reassure Whit that I was not going to go off the deep end and become an environmental extremist. And it was adaptable. If the weather turned warm I could leave the jacket in the car. This morning it was cool enough that I was happy to have it.

I took an appraising glance in the mirror, put on some deliciously dark lipstick, called Deep Desire. Then, after examining my row of earrings and studs, pulled in my tummy and regarded my profile. I put on a dusting of glittery pink eye shadow, some purple liner and mascara. When dressing in such a subdued manner—I mean, gosh, I was wearing a suit!—I liked to go a little wild with my makeup.

I went in and kissed Billy good morning. He opened his eyes and groaned. "What time is it?"

"Seven."

"Ungphm." At least that's what I thought he said. He rolled over.

"Morning, darling," I breathed close to his ear.

He groaned again. His shoulders were bare. They were comfortable, lean shoulders, attached to long, elegant arms. Billy's chest was mostly smooth, but he had a fine line of dark hair leading from a diamond between his ribs to his belly button. I touched one of his nipples.

"Come on, babe," he murmured half asleep, catching my hand.

"I didn't see you at all last night."

He sighed, opening his eyes, smiling tolerantly but obviously wishing to go back to sleep. "Sorry."

"Coming home earlier tonight?"

His face clouded. "Zoë. I hate to say this—"

"Then don't say it."

"Don't be that way—"

"Billy."

"You know it takes almost two hours to drive here from Wonderland Sounds?"

He took my hands in his. I pressed my lips together, trying to hide my feelings. His finger traced a design on my breast. Neither of us spoke for a few minutes.

"You're dressed up all pretty."

I laughed. "So are you."

He shook his head, smiling. "After the album's done, we'll take a weekend somewhere. Just you and me. We can leave the kids at my mom's. Hey, she adores them."

"I'd love to take a weekend."

"Good. So would I."

"It's nice to be close, to sit here and talk, even if it is only for a few minutes."

Billy's lashes were thick. His chin was covered with a soft, sexy stubble. He graced me with a long gaze from those large, dark, smoldering eyes of his. I was putty in his hands.

"Babe," he said gently, "I want to get the album done as quickly as possible. That means working intensely. I don't like it any better than you, but the best thing for me to do is to spend as much time there as possible."

"It's only been one day."

"Yeah, but I've got a two-hour drive. I can't commute every day."

"Where are you going to sleep?"

"Spots has lots of room. Don't give me that look."

"You're not taking up with Vivi again, are you?"

He fixed his gaze on me. "No." He paused. "I need you to believe that."

I looked in his eyes and nodded, banishing my feelings of insecurity. What could I say? I hoped he was telling the truth.

"When do you think you can get home?" I asked in as light a tone as I could manage.

"I'll try to do two nights there, one here."

I nodded, swallowing back the lump in my throat. "I'm being silly."

"I told you this was going to mean some sacrifices. But it's worth it. This is such an incredibly lucky break."

"Yeah. For both of us. And the kids, too."

"Glad you understand."

"I do, Billy." My expression didn't match my words. During the ensuing silence, we exchanged a series of somber looks.

"I love you," he whispered, touching my cheek. "Only you. I know I haven't always been a saint . . . But sometimes the only thing that's kept me going is knowing that you were out there. Even when we—those months we weren't together."

This was as close as he ever came to mentioning the crisis. Though neither of us spoke the word, the memory of all that had happened filled the room like thick smoke.

The "crisis" is my way of referring to the chain of events that nearly ended our marriage. After years of glitter and paste, writing celebrity interviews, and traipsing after Billy and his band, Alamo, I'd begun to yearn for something real, something true.

Meanwhile, the stress of trying to revive sagging album sales, touring, wild spending, and escalating doses of cocaine began to land Billy in one hospital after another. The debt grew like weeds in an untended garden.

The climax came shortly after Smokie had been born. She was at my breast at three in the morning as I attempted to tap out a piece on late deadline when the call came from Kyoto, Japan. Billy had OD'd after a concert. I dutifully filed my piece, then maxed out the last credit card, packed up Smokie and three-year-old Keith, and flew to his side. Billy survived; our relationship didn't.

Once he was out of danger, I told him I'd had enough. I fled to my dad's duplex on Central Park in New York. Billy checked into rehab.

Six months later, he showed up on the doorstep, fully recovered, clean, swearing he'd had it with the band, drugs, touring, and the LA rock 'n' roll rat race. It took a year to sell off everything, get out of the bad contracts he'd signed, and start hacking away at the jungle of debt. I'd been offered a staff job at *Rolling Stone*, but Billy wanted to move to the country. Against my better judgment I succumbed to his charm. We moved to Greymont, away from temptation.

Just before we left, my dad died. Those two years were such a nightmare that I try to suppress them. Sure, I miss LA—the surf, the sun, the pretty people, and the buzz of importance—but I'm free from the ache and the tears.

On warm nights when the kids are asleep, Billy and I stand on the back porch and gaze at the stars. I feel like Dorothy. I've just clicked my heels. We're not in Oz anymore. But is the storm really over? Is this really home?

As Billy and I regarded each other this morning, the past wound itself into our unspoken thoughts. It threaded its way around my heart and choked off my more tender feelings. As always, his gaze melted my resistance, but still, he could read me well enough to catch the concern in my eyes.

He smoothed my hair, then drew his hand gently across my lower lip, smiling. "I love you," he whispered once more.

I allowed my expression to soften moderately. "I love you too."

His chocolate eyes seemed to burn, melting my heart with their poetry and volcanic fire. "Thank you for making this easy."

I didn't say, You're welcome because, frankly, I didn't feel it. I kept thinking, this too shall pass and maybe it will all turn out fine. Then I went to wake up the kids.

"Give him space," Morgan had said. Well, I didn't have much choice. He would have taken it whether I offered or not.

I helped Smokie dress and didn't even argue with her when she insisted on wearing mismatched socks: one orange with blue fish, the other black with snowflakes. I popped Eggo waffles in the toaster, arranged them on plates, cut them into bite-sized pieces, and poured maple syrup. I was so upset I could barely get down two sips of coffee. Keith didn't want to ride the bus because he said the kids were too noisy. Since I had to take Smokie to preschool anyway, I didn't object. The drive to her school, up to the northern section of town, past dairy farms and fields—a patchwork of black, tan, and green—was gorgeous at this time of year. The hills beyond the farmland were filled with the colors of autumn, and the sky was majestic. Not one cloud marred its sparkling, rich, cornflower blue.

After dropping off the kids, I went to Flora's, an espresso bar halfway between the *Eagle* building and the high school, where I'd arranged to meet Tim Boudreau. I arrived before him, ordered a cappuccino—skim—and an almond biscotti, and sat down at a table outside. A mild breeze rustled gently through the fading leaves of the crabapples and hawthorns lining the path down the pedestrian alley toward Stanhope. The air was fragrant with roasting coffee, sweet pastries, and the freshness that marks summer's end.

From where I sat I could see the back of the post office, where I'd parked, and the Unitarian church, where teens and peddlers gathered on sunny afternoons in autumn and spring. The walkway led past a Szechwan restaurant toward Stanhope, creating an L of shops off the street. To the left were plantings, benches, chess boards, and a path to the Community Center.

At eight-fifteen, Tim Boudreau rode up on a beat-up blue racing bike. He locked his vehicle to a rack near the planters, removed his helmet, drew a manila envelope out of dirty green panniers, took a clip off his pants cuff, and walked toward me at a quick pace.

Tim was a pleasant fellow in his mid-thirties, with a reddish mustache, hair pulled back in an unobtrusive ponytail, and pale freckled skin. His style was of the "live simply so that others can simply live" school: jeans, faded Henley shirt, Birkenstocks.

"Sorry I'm late," he said. "My first class is at nine, so

we'll have time to talk." He shook my hand in an earnest manner as he spoke. I judged him to be a contra-dancer. His movements were graceful, limbs long, and he was heavy into eye contact. His thin lips broke easily into a smile.

"I'll buy you coffee," I said.

"Oh, no need." He disappeared inside and brought back a steamed soy drink, the mere thought of which made my nose wrinkle.

He tossed the envelope. "I found a bio we printed when Cassandra ran for Select Board."

"Thanks. This is great." I glanced over the bio. Born and schooled in Wisconsin. Became an activist with the anti-nuke movement. Opposed Seabrook. Member of Town Meeting for the past ten years.

We engaged in some small talk about the weather, biking, and the difficulty of finding parking in town.

"I never have trouble," he said with a grin and wave at his bike.

"You ride in all weather?"

"Oh, yeah."

"That's admirable."

"I try to do my share. Besides, it keeps me healthy."

"I suppose you don't have kids to carry around."

"No." He smiled gently. "I have friends who have kids. You're right. That is a tough one. Too bad the buses don't run more often."

"Tell me about Cassandra."

"Where should I start?"

"When did you meet?"

"Back about ten years ago, when I was in grad school at the university. I did my master's thesis on rare beetles in a field near the Gemini preserve. Cassandra used it to persuade the owner to donate his entire tract to the Green Trust. We didn't even have to go to court."

I pulled out my pad. Next to my notes on Cassandra, I wrote *Green Trust*. This was the second or third time the name had come up.

"That's pretty persuasive," I said.

Tim's eyelids closed. He glanced down at his hands. They were the color of buttermilk, with fine reddish hair on the knuckles. He nodded. "Yes, she talked a number of people into donating land. I think that's why some of us made allowances for her." He paused, a shadow of unease crossing his lips. "She initiated the drive to set up the trust and talked people into giving money and land to get it going."

"I thought Craig Detweiller did that." At least that's what Morgan had said.

Tim gave me an odd look that I couldn't quite read, then said, "Yeah. He was involved too."

"What can you tell me about her group, the Living Earth Coalition?"

Tim grinned and shrugged. "It was made up of anyone who happened to show at a demonstration that day."

"So it wasn't a real organization."

"She tried, but she wasn't easy to get along with. I guess you could call me a member. I tried to promote it by holding regular meetings and organizing outings, but it fizzled."

"Is that why you quit?"

"Partly. We also had ideological differences."

I met his gaze. "How so?"

"There are two factions of the environmental movement in town. I used to be in what people call the radical fringe. You know, we should get rid of all manufacturing, we should live in caves, walk or bike everywhere, and read by candlelight at night. But I've found that position isn't very convincing," he added without irony.

"I've learned to compromise, to find allies, and forge coalitions. Cassandra didn't like that. She accused me of joining the establishment to make it easier to get along at the high school." He laughed shyly. "She called me a liberal, which in her book was right up there with fascist."

"So it was purely political, your falling out."

Tim glanced toward Revere. A steady stream of cars moved down the street past the post office. He nodded. "Well, I wouldn't say 'purely.' She had a difficult personality."

"Can you give me an example?"

"If Cassandra didn't get her way, she fought dirty."

"How?"

"She made threats."

"For example?"

He blushed slightly. "She made it her business to find out people's secrets. She'd threaten to expose them if they didn't go along with her."

"Did she carry out the threats?"

"I don't know. But she did gossip."

I decided to press a little harder. "Who had a grudge against her?"

He smiled at me for a moment, seeming to deliberate over whether to answer. Finally, he said, "You must know about Craig Detweiller. They were archenemies. They battled over every sale, every deal Craig made since Cassandra arrived."

"That's kind of funny considering they worked together to create the Green Trust," I said, musing aloud.

"Well." Tim laughed. " 'Worked together' isn't an accurate description of what happened."

"I gather this was before your time?"

"Oh, yeah, but people talk."

"What happened?"

"From what I hear Cassandra twisted his arm."

"How?"

"There were the Gemini demonstrations—"

"And?"

He glanced away skittishly, then met my gaze. His soft green eyes were gentle. "This is gossip, so don't quote me, but people say she knew some kind of secret."

"Really? A secret about Craig?"

He nodded.

"Any idea what it was?"

He shrugged. "Maybe about his romantic life. Don't say I said so, but he's had his share of affairs. Maybe she threatened to tell his wife. Of course now that's ancient history. They're divorced. And the Braithwaites were pretty mad at her. There was a time when Erwin threatened to break her neck."

"When was that?"

"A few years ago, when Drew, their son, was diagnosed with leukemia. Erwin tried to sell his land to a man who wanted to build condos. Cassandra tied the sale up in appeals. Erwin nearly declared bankruptcy. The medical bills were enormous. A lot of people never forgave Cassandra for that."

"Were you one of them?"

Tim made eye contact. "I thought it was cruel, but I'm relieved the land wasn't developed. Craig Detweiller did a nice thing."

"Really. What?"

"Well, the story goes that he secretly bought some rights to the land and is holding it in trust for the family."

"And that's not widely known?"

"It's held by a company no one ever heard of. Cassandra told me Craig was behind it."

"How would she know?"

"Oh, she had her ways." He averted his eyes. Maybe it was the freckles or the spot of red where he'd cut his cheek shaving, but he struck me as honest. He wiped a trace of soy milk from his mustache.

Tim named a few other developers, a couple of whom had gone bankrupt after Cassandra ruined their deals. In fact, just about the entire Chamber of Commerce at one time or another had crossed swords with her.

"Do you know if Cassandra actually exposed anyone's secrets?"

"Oh, yes. If you talked to her for any length of time, she'd tell you smut about almost anyone whose name happened to come up. She knew who was having an affair, whose marriage was about to break up, who had a gambling problem, who had a hand in the till."

"What did she have on you?"

He smiled tolerantly. "My life is an open book."

"Not one little skeleton in the closet?" I myself had a number of skeletons I wouldn't want blasted on the front page of the paper.

"Nothing anyone could use to blackmail me."

"So you weren't afraid to vote against Cassandra at the hearing?"

"No. But even if I had been, I would have done what I believed to be right."

I wondered if maybe Craig had something on Tim that had convinced him to switch his vote. "I was surprised to see you argue against the newt."

"Well, I'm not on the radical fringe anymore," he said.

"Don't you believe in protecting the newt?"

"As I explained at the hearing, I have a master's in biology. Although locally they are disappearing, there are plenty of newts all over the Northeast. That's the difference between the moderate and the radical side. Moderates believe there's room for compromise."

"'Act locally,'" I quoted, teasing.

He smiled thinly. "Now you sound like Cassandra."

"But didn't you only decide to change your vote within the last few days?"

He paused, touched his fingers to the nearly empty glass that had held his soy milk. Then he looked at me a little coyly. "Yeah."

"Why? I'm just curious."

"I guess I decided it was time."

I waited. He said nothing. Finally, I said, "Time for what?"

"To make a clean break. See, I felt sorry for her. She'd lost so many allies."

"Forgive my asking, but were you romantically involved?"

He smiled tolerantly again. "No."

I changed the subject. "Maybe you can help with a few details about the Green Trust. Who runs it? How's it set up?"

"A board of trustees."

"Who appoints the trustees?"

"The initial benefactors vote."

"Can you name the benefactors for me?"

"That's a secret."

"You just said the records are public."

"Yes, but with a trust there are ways to protect the identity of individuals."

"Do you know who the benefactors are?" Like it was going to be a secret just between him and me.

Tim blushed. "No, I don't."

"How about the trustees?"

Tim drew in a breath. "Well, I suppose you'll find out. I was one."

"Really? When was that?"

"Oh, for about a year. I stepped down a few weeks ago."

"Why?"

Eye contact. "Personal reasons."

"Who else is on the board?"

He named a few people. One was an ecology professor at the university. Another was a friend of Cletha's who served on the Sierra Club. A third was my boss, Whit Smythe.

"Who took your place when you stepped down?"

"No one yet, but they were thinking of asking Mavis French."

Things were getting cozier and cozier. "Oh. Why?"

"They like to have someone who's also on the Environmental Commission."

A cold knot formed in my stomach. "What was Cassandra's relationship to the trust?"

Tim smiled. "Combative."

"But she helped found it."

"According to her," Tim said softly, "they'd betrayed her."

"What do you think?"

He averted his eyes, touched his buttermilk-colored hands to his soy drink. "Honestly?"

"Of course."

"She'd had some kind of breakdown before moving here. I think she was skirting closer and closer to the edge."

"In other words," I said, "you think she was crazy."

Tim looked me straight in the eyes and said, "I wouldn't rule out suicide."

"You think she killed herself."

He did something odd with his lips, as if a piece of food were stuck between his teeth. He glanced toward the post office, then toward the concrete planters, then he met my eyes and said. "I think . . . I think she was ready to give up."

"Give up what?"

"I don't know. This is just intuition on my part, but she had some kind of thing about Craig. Ever since he remarried, she acted wilder and wilder. Don't put it in the paper that I said this."

"All right."

"I think she was hung up on Craig."

Chapter 12

Back at the office, I typed in the last-minute changes on my story summing up Cassandra's environmental stance and the various reactions within the town. About half an hour before deadline, I decided to call Detective Brannigan to see if there was any change in the official position that her death had been accidental. The autopsy had been scheduled for today. I wondered whether it had been done.

I was able to reach him, but he refused to comment. "We'll have a preliminary report this afternoon."

"I'm on deadline. The paper won't be on the stands until two. I'd hate to print that it was an accident and have the radio scoop me before we hit the stands."

He sighed. "Sorry."

"What is your theory?"

"Conjecture is your domain, Ms. Szabo, not mine."

"That was an ugly bash she had on the head. I've tried every which way to imagine how it could have happened in a fall. I keep drawing a blank."

"You disappoint me. Usually you exhibit quite a flair for creativity. Oh, do me a favor."

"Name it."

"Print an item saying we'd like to talk to anyone in the vicinity between midnight and five yesterday morning.

Dancing with Mr. D

We have an 800 number. Anonymity is guaranteed."

"Midnight and five—so that's the time of death?"

He grumbled something that I took to mean yes.

"If you're looking for witnesses, you must suspect it wasn't an accident."

Brannigan responded with a snort.

"Somebody climbed up that tree and pushed her?

Brannigan said nothing.

"What if I write, 'Police are not ruling out foul play'?"

He grunted a begrudging okay.

"Thank you."

"Express your gratitude by not sending up smoke signals before we make our statement."

"You'll keep me posted?"

"I trust you'll make sure that I do."

I called Whit and told him about the police request, adding that my story was slugged and in the system.

"Oh, and I did a sidebar on the newt."

"Fine," he said, distracted.

"I found an adorable picture. I like the little guy. He's five inches long, orange with blue spots on his back. And the cutest bug eyes."

Whit actually laughed. "I'm looking at your story right now. It's an inch too long. Ah. I'll cut this. We're okay." He hung up.

I ran to Kate, who was in the photo room with the newt picture.

"Hi," I said. "How about dinner tonight? My place? We can rent a video and commiserate with each other?"

Kate, her hair clean, carefully braided, looked fresher, happier today. "Sorry," she said. "How about tomorrow?"

"Hot date?" I asked, keeping it short because we were about twenty minutes to deadline.

"I wish! No. It's my mom. She's having a terrible time, Zoë. I'll tell you about it tomorrow."

"Great, we'll talk later."

She flashed me her normal cheerful smile, but her eyes still looked troubled.

While I was on the third floor I stopped in at the old-fashioned morgue. Bigger newspapers with larger budgets have computerized their back files, but not the *Eagle*. We had clippings files that someone had tediously indexed, and we had just linked into a database that coughed up newspaper files from all over the country, if you just looked for the right thing. I was no whiz. Mark, who loved electronics of all sorts, was the resident expert.

I copied the old *Eagle* clips on Cassandra. There were several dozen, going back fifteen years to the first mention of the Gemini development, which she'd successfully defeated with a large group of activists.

I found a photo of her with Ann Chatsford and several others chained to their beech tree. Fifteen years hadn't changed Ann much, but then she'd already been old at seventy-seven. Cassandra, though, had been much more attractive that I'd expected. Vigorous, lean, and outdoorsy, she cut a pretty impressive figure. And she came across as surprisingly articulate, not loopy or overwrought as she had in more recent interviews.

I stuffed all these in my Madonna bag, entered the task of reading through them on my mental to-do list, and went downstairs.

Mark was hunched over his keyboard, working intently despite the fact that we'd passed deadline. I went to the kitchen on the pretext of getting coffee. On my way back I peeked at his monitor, where I saw a column of numbers.

This summer, he'd scooped me on an exposé I'd spent

a month preparing about kickbacks on maintenance contracts in Sheffington. He'd gotten hold of my notes, done some hacking, and come up with the smoking gun I hadn't managed to unearth. I still hadn't forgiven him.

I sat down and called the foreman on the Plaza project. What a jerk Ron Braithwaite was, I thought, refusing to give me the guy's name. He could have saved me the trouble of having to look it up. The foreman turned out to be as easy as Ron had been hard.

"Yeah," he said. "She was in the tree. I told the police yesterday. She was hollering, throwing stuff."

That was a colorful detail. Too bad I'd missed deadline.

"When did you leave the site?"

"Around eleven thirty or so."

"And Ron left earlier?"

"Yeah. He had a family problem. His mother, or something." I wondered if maybe Ron had returned. I'd try to find a tactful way to ask Kate or her dad, Erwin.

"What happened with Cassandra?"

"Nothing. I ignored her. The bulldozer drowned her out. Detweiller asked us to cut the tree down, too, but we told him that was crazy. Even without the broad up there. We could have killed ourselves. He wanted us to bring in spotlights. There was some bad blood between those two, I tell you."

"Forgive me for asking, but she was alive when you left?"

"Alive and screaming."

"Did you see anyone else around?"

"Police asked that too. Nope. They wanted to know where I was the rest of the night. Just for the record, I was in bed with my wife. She'll vouch for me." He laughed. "Glad I wasn't in bed with somebody else. I'd be in big trouble."

"Thanks for being so helpful. When are you slated to go back to work?"

"I wouldn't hold my breath waiting. The police put everything on hold until they get all their questions answered. And we've got Town Meeting coming up next week. They'll probably find a reason to delay. They always do. That's why we were so eager to get started. Detweiler was shitting bricks. I've never seen him so mad."

"When was that?"

"After he talked to the police."

"When?"

"Yesterday morning. We had a meeting at his place. Ron, me, Craig—around nine o'clock. He wanted us to go cut down the tree, but we told him the police were swarming all over the place. He didn't believe us. He had a loud conversation with Chief Sodermeier. If it was up to the chief, he would have let us go ahead, but the state homicide guy just laughed. Two weeks, they said, at the very minimum."

I thanked him and hung up. While I was pondering my next move, Mark, straddling his chair, elbows on the backrest, scooted over and began pawing through my photocopies.

"What's all this?"

"None of your business."

"'Cassandra Dunne,'" he read from one of the clips, "'a former leader of the Clamshell Alliance—'"

"Where'd you get that?"

"You had it right here."

"I missed that one."

"See? Already I'm helping, Szabo."

I hurriedly gathered the papers and packed them into my bag.

"Your kind of help, Mark, I can live without."

"I transmitted a piece on your friend Vivi and the band. I got a great picture of her by the steps of Town Hall with that old hippie and the pimply guitar player. She was perched on their shoulders. Whit's titled it DIVA DAZZLES DOWNTOWN. Page one. Above the fold."

I was annoyed. My follow-up on Cassandra belonged there, with the picture of the newt, not Vivi. Upstaged on both fronts, I was finding it harder and harder to keep a stiff upper lip.

"How nice."

He ignored my acid tone. "She's crazy about frogs. Says they're disappearing."

I unlocked my lower drawer and withdrew my notes. I thought it was time to investigate the Green Trust and Detweiller's real estate deals.

"She's interested in the lizards."

"What lizards?"

"The ones Cassandra wanted to save. Guess they're goners now that she's dead."

"Newts," I corrected him with a saccharine smile. "Speaking of Cassandra, what did the cute paramedic say?"

"Spying?" He grinned with surprise, then shrugged. "I wasted twenty minutes and two cups of coffee. She's not exactly my idea of cute. But I've got something else, right up your alley."

"What?"

"Vivi. She has this foundation. They have a thing about amphibians. She wants to do something about Cassandra. I mean, she was serious." He raised his eyebrows.

I didn't know whether that was good news or bad. On the one hand, it was an excuse to go to Vermont. On the other, I didn't like her nosing in on my beat. I had a hard enough time outmaneuvering Mark. I wondered if he was going to try to use this angle to horn in on my turf. "Is that what you're working on?"

"Huh?"

"You had numbers on your screen earlier."

"Statistics."

"What kind?"

"Hello? Football? The university has the first decent team in a decade. Take a look."

I examined his screen. A table listed the statistics on top college players, passing and yardage and the like, which he'd downloaded from the Internet.

I returned to my desk to pack up my notes. I'd decided to drive to Sheffington to check the Hall of Records for dirt on Craig Detweiller, his company, and, while I was at it, the Green Trust.

As I was on my way out, Mark said. "Now what is it you don't want me to know?"

I laughed lightly. "Suspicious, aren't you?"

"Something with numbers." He regarded me closely. "Anytime you need help with the computer, just ask."

"You're so generous."

"I am. Give me a chance."

"Right. Like last summer when you scooped me on my own story."

He couldn't suppress a smirk of conceit. "Yeah. I guess that was kind of rotten. Remember, we did share the byline."

"On my investigation, after you butted in—unrequested."

"Hey, sorry." His arms spread in a gesture of conciliation. "I owe you. Listen, to make up for it, why don't I help you with research." Bright-eyed and innocent.

"What do you want me to look up? Phone records? Financials?"

"That's good. Real good. You stole one story. You think I'm going to give you a chance to do it again? You're about as sorry as a fox in the chicken coop."

"Aw, Szabo. You're breaking my heart."

"You don't have a heart, Polanski. You have a scoreboard."

Chapter 13

An hour later I was in the Registry of Deeds. I spent the rest of the morning combing through files. The records were only computerized back to 1988. Everything else was recorded by hand on cards dating back to colonial times.

I scrolled through Detweiller's records on the computer, whistling when I looked up the paperwork on his house. He'd spent $4.2 million the previous year to build a state-of-the-art mansion in South Greymont on a thirty-acre spread. In Southern California that might have been considered middle class, but it was beaucoup bucks for Greymont, where even the wealthy were frugal and building costs were relatively low. Ludwig of Bavaria could have built a fantasy castle in the Heritage Valley for less.

Other entries included a small house in the town center, which he'd inherited from his mother and sold. He'd also owned some apartment buildings and a condo complex, which had been transferred to Delstar a decade earlier.

Then I checked Delstar. Ah. Here was the action. Entries scrolled down the screen. The old card files contained even more. I copied down all Detweiller's and

Dancing with Mr. D

Delstar's citations and had copies made. I did the same with the Green Trust.

In the swamp of information, one thing popped out. The Gemini Hill Farm. In 1979, it had been purchased by a company called Saragossa. In 1980, an agreement to develop was signed by Saragossa and Delstar. Later that year, Saragossa applied for a variance from the town of Greymont. The Environmental Commission refused the petition. In 1982, Delstar bought the property. Two years later, Delstar donated the entire 140-acre holding to the Green Trust. That was the first land acquired by the Green Trust.

I ran the Braithwaite name through the catalogues. Kate's father Erwin's land had been in the family since 1875. A few months before her younger brother Drew's death from leukemia, a right-of-way was acquired by a company called SilverSeed. The amount of money paid was modest: $20,000.

Someone like Mark with his computer hacking skills could probably dig up all kinds of dirt on Detweiller and Delstar, I thought with a twinge of temptation. If only the guy could be trusted. *No.* If I asked Mark for help, he'd steal the whole pie.

Also under Braithwaite was Ron's house, a three-bedroom in East Greymont. A check on his construction company revealed the purchase of a thirty-acre plot two years ago. Despite an ambitious subdivision plan, he'd built on only three lots. Only two had been sold. I wondered what his credit report looked like.

I left the registry feeling impressed by my new ability to shift from would-be gonzo journalist to stealthy investigative reporter exploring the nefarious nether world of electronic data. I'd had no idea how much I could learn about my neighbors—just from their real estate transactions. What other kinds of information were hiding in public records, accessible to those of us who tattled for a living?

I stopped for lunch at a small sandwich shop in Sheffington, which was known less for the cuisine (pre-gentrification American) than the clientele. Police and court officers hung out here on their lunch breaks from the county courthouse, a Gothic sandstone tower in the middle of town.

I ordered chicken noodle soup and a Diet Coke. I had eaten only a few spoonfuls of soup, which wasn't very good, and was nursing my soda when Detective Brannigan walked in. He was a short, wiry man with the face of a street tough and an air of impatience. His clothes looked as if he'd acquired them by rummaging through the giveaway barrel at the Salvation Army.

He was at the counter ordering a sandwich and a cup of coffee.

"Hello, Detective," I said.

"Ms. Szabo. I had a hunch I might run into you today." He collected his change, depositing it in the pocket of his ill-fitting jacket. "I'll be in the back booth," he told the waitress.

He brought his coffee over and sat down across from me.

"I feel honored," I said, meaning it. "I was about to pounce."

"Saved you the trouble." His sandwich arrived. Bacon and egg on rye. "Been living on doughnuts and coffee since yesterday morning."

"The autopsy report," I said. "You have the results."

He ate for a few moments. "Yup."

"And?"

He looked me in the eye. "I'm on my way over to Greymont. We'll have a press conference with the police chief this afternoon."

"You want to give me a hint or should we play twenty questions?"

"No question about it. Somebody killed her."

He seemed to enjoy my startled reaction. I hadn't expected him to tell me.

"On purpose?"

He nodded, eating his sandwich. I studied him. His nose had been broken once in his youth. His chin could only be described as pugnacious. Despite his flinty features, humor glinted in his eyes. He liked his work. He didn't expect much of the world, and he seemed to be willing to accept it on whatever terms were dealt. He thrived on late nights, early mornings, and bad coffee. Cruelty, brutality, and gore didn't faze him.

"How?"

He wiped his mouth, then took a tissue from his pocket and blew his nose. Returned the tissue to his pocket.

"Well, Ms. Szabo, as much as I'd like to accommodate you, I can't."

"Why not?"

"Because this one was a surprise." He seemed to derive sadistic enjoyment out of dangling this information in front of me. "And if I tell you, you tell the public, and we're no longer in control of the investigation."

"Curare and a blowgun," I suggested.

"I like that. But, no."

"A swift blow to the temple with a blunt object."

He lifted his sandwich and took another bite.

"Gunshot," I suggested.

"One," he said with a knowing look. "I don't want you to make random guesses—especially not in print. Two. Watch yourself. Off the record, we were close to saying it was accidental, when my ME noticed something and we ran some tests."

"Poison."

"Szabo. Do yourself a favor. Refrain from speculation. Refrain from amateur detective work. You're a nice-looking woman. You got two lovely kids. You don't want to tangle with this one."

I studied his poker face, and a light clicked on in my head. If something so minor that it might have been overlooked by the medical examiner indicated murder, it certainly couldn't have been a gunshot wound. Not the ugly bash on the head either. I'd lay odds that had happened as she hit the ground. Poison, I thought, or maybe the murderer had pushed her. A shove might be hard to detect.

"Detective," I said, "was the murder weapon a fist? A karate chop, maybe, to the back of the neck?"

"You don't give up, do you?"

Something in the way his eyes creased told me I was on the right track. That and the fact that he hadn't denied it. Of course, I thought after a second, it could have been some kind of injection of a poison or drug that was hard to detect. Either way, the murderer would have to have climbed the tree.

"Who are your suspects?"

"You're kidding."

"An arrest imminent?"

"No."

"Any leads?"

Dancing with Mr. D

"A few. This entire conversation is off the record—you want something to print, come to the news conference at three."

The press conference was held in Town Hall in a small room overlooking Main Street. Only four media people attended: a team from the local all-news radio station, a reporter from the *Sheffington Sun*, and me. Even Mark didn't appear. I found out later that he had an exclusive interview with the coach of the university basketball team, who'd just been hired away by the NBA.

Detective Brannigan and Chief Sodermeier presided. Brannigan made a short statement. The homicide squad was investigating. They believed Ms. Dunne had been murdered. They placed the time of death between midnight and five in the morning. They were withholding all other details.

Frustrated, I walked back to the office and wrote a tiny item for the paper. Then I went up to see Whit. I found his office door was ajar, which meant it was okay to come in. I gave a little tap and entered. He was on the phone, deep in conversation. He held up his hand. I stepped outside to wait until he was finished. As I did, I heard him saying:

"Tonight? No I can't get away that early. How about ten? My place. Yes. Me too. Yes. Bye."

I shook my head, trying to get rid of the cobwebs. Whit was a notorious loner. The paper was his personal life. Maybe he was arranging a delivery. But at night? With words like "My place" and "Me too"?

"Zoë," he said, "come on in."

I walked into his office. He wore a yellow oxford shirt, a light blue jacket, and a tie the same hue as his jacket. His hair, which he wore very short, seemed recently cut. I caught a slight whiff of aftershave. Confirmed, I thought, enjoying the secret.

"It's official," I said, "Brannigan just announced Cassandra was murdered."

Whit frowned. "Have they charged anyone?"

"They're still working on a list of suspects."

"Well, I have something else for you to do in the meantime." He held a folder bursting with papers, some still in brown mailing envelopes. "Here are the warrants and position papers for Town Meeting. Barbara's out for the rest of the year."

Town Meeting, which took place in autumn and spring, was a New England tradition, a gathering of several hundred citizens to decide on the budget and other questions of importance. Normally I would have considered it a plum assignment, but not while I was in the midst of pursuing a murder story.

"How's Fred?" I asked.

"He's not entirely out of the woods, but he made it through the first forty-eight hours." He sighed. "I know it's last-minute, but I'd like you to update the summary of what's on the agenda. Can you get it to me by deadline tomorrow?"

I took the sheaf of papers, which weighed several pounds.

He relaxed in his leather chair—the same chair depicted in the oil painting on the far wall facing his desk—a portrait of his great-great-grandfather and namesake who'd founded the paper.

"The Dunne story can rest until the police come up with a suspect."

"I've been checking the files on Cassandra. There are some things that strike me as curious."

"Such as?"

"The Green Trust. Craig Detweiller," I ventured gingerly, worried about Whit's response. "Craig says he's an old friend of yours."

"He is."

"I know you're on the board of the Green Trust, but—"

His eyes met mine momentarily. The blue of his jacket brought out their color. He clasped his hands together and leaned forward.

"Zoë, you're new to Greymont. On the one hand, it's good to have a fresh approach, a new set of eyes, so to speak. On the other hand, it's not worth rehashing these old battles unless you come up with something along the lines of MAN BITES DOG."

"How about MAN BITES NEWT?"

His lips pursed. "I don't think so."

"I have a strong gut feeling," I pleaded.

"You think there's a connection with the Green Trust?"

"Maybe."

For a few seconds, he scribbled on his memo pad, blue circles. He filled them in with dark slashes of his Pelikan fountain pen. "We've devoted far too much ink to the trust and all the various factions, pro and con," he said at last.

"Whit—"

"Drop it."

"I'll still track the murder investigation," I insisted.

He conceded with a nod. "But make Town Meeting your first priority. The police will let us know when they have a suspect."

A glance told me that arguing would be futile. Not that I intended to follow orders. When I found something newsworthy, I'd come to him. Until then I'd keep my digging to myself.

"What's the latest in jock soaps?" I asked Mark when I returned to my desk with a soda, ready to pack up for the day. It was four-thirty on a Friday. I was contemplating a trip to Vermont tomorrow afternoon, and if I were going to be away then, I wanted to spend some time with the kids today.

"Oh, there's a little thing called the World Series," he said, not looking up from his computer.

"Don't tell me you've traded college football for a mere national story?"

"Actually, Szabo, I have. But not baseball. Coach just turned pro, gave me the exclusive. Good-bye Greymont, hello *Sports Illustrated*!"

"Why stop there?" I said. "ESPN is probably panting for you."

My phone rang. It was Dania. Keith wanted to talk to me.

"Mom?"

"Hi hon," I said. "I'm just on my way home."

"Mom?"

"What do you want, sweetie?"

"Can you homeschool me?"

I sighed. "We'll talk about it when I get home."

"I want to talk about it now."

"Did you have a bad day?"

"Jackson is getting homeschooled."

"But, honey, his mom doesn't have a job."

He mumbled something.

"What?"

"Ellis called me a donkey again . . . and stupid!"

Dancing with Mr. D

Anger flared through me. Monday, I decided, I was calling Mr. Keene. If that didn't work, I'd call Mavis. "Listen. I have two little things to do here, then I'll be home. We can have a long talk. Okay?"

He grumbled, but agreed to wait till I got home. Then we'd go over our options.

After I returned the receiver to its cradle, I stared at the phone sadly, wondering what I could do. I realized that despite my effort to be upbeat, he could sense I didn't have a clue as to how to smooth his way with his classmates.

"Keith?" Mark said.

I looked up with surprise. I nodded.

"What's the story?"

I hated to let a superjock like Mark know how my little boy was being tormented by his classmates. But the subject was bothering me, and my two mainstays for this type of conversation, Billy and Kate, were incommunicado.

"He's not getting along with the kids at school," I admitted.

"What's the dynamic?"

I restrained my initial knee-jerk impulse to utter a putdown. "They're making fun of him. Calling him names. They probably think he talks funny because he uses big words. It's painful to have to stand by. I wish I knew what to do."

Mark rolled his chair closer. "How about Billy?"

"What about him?"

"What's his take?"

"He wants Keith to punch his way out. I mean, it's absurd. Keith is a sweet, sensitive, intelligent six-year-old."

"If you don't mind my butting in—"

"Actually, Mark, I do."

He shrugged, rolling back toward his desk. I brooded for a couple of minutes about Keith, about Billy. Finally, curiosity got the better of me.

"Okay," I said, "I give up. What would you do?"

Mark glanced toward me, as if unsure whether to release the pearl of wisdom lurking in the depths of his brilliant mind. Finally, he said, "Get him involved in a sport."

I laughed snidely. "That's your solution to everything."

"Hey, it's worth a try."

"He hates sports."

"Maybe that's a cover because he feels he's not very good. Town has a great soccer program. I know all the coaches—parents, volunteers. Want me to see if I can find him a team?"

"Sure," I said sarcastically. "Do I look like a soccer mom?"

Mark didn't smile. "Why not?"

"I can't see Keith charging around a field, kicking a ball."

"Nothing healthier than fresh air. Get out in the autumn, all the leaves falling. Lots of running. It's fun." Mark looked around to see if anyone was listening. The newsroom on a Friday afternoon was quiet. He met my gaze with a frank expression. "If you use your body, you feel better about yourself. You begin to project confidence. He doesn't have to be the best on the team."

"What if he's the worst?"

"Nah. I won't let that happen."

"You're going to wave a wand and say this kid will be a competent player?"

"I can do the next best thing."

Dancing with Mr. D

"What?"

"I'll come by a couple afternoons. Teach him some skills."

"You'd do that?"

"Sure."

"Why?"

"Keith's a good kid." His wide-eyed stare protested innocence.

"Thanks," I said quickly. "I'll pass."

He shrugged. This time, though, he didn't turn away. He waited while I wrestled with the idea. Growing solemn, studying me.

"You'd honestly be willing to do that?" I finally asked.

"It'd be fun. I don't have any nephews." Again with the innocent look.

"It's sweet of you to offer, but—"

"Hey, what are you doing tonight?"

I opened my mouth, prepared to say I was busy. But my Friday evening was a big zero. Billy wasn't coming home. Kate had begged off my dinner invitation. More problems with her mom.

"You have a game to cover."

"That's tomorrow afternoon. Listen, why don't I pick up a pizza. I'll drop by my place for a soccer ball, be over"— he checked his watch, a huge Casio lap timer— "in a half an hour? I'll kick the ball around with him, drop a few hints about joining a team. At six all these kids do is chase the ball. He doesn't have to be Pele."

I tossed my stuff into my bag. "All right," I said lightly. If he got any ideas about peeking at my notes or any other accoutrements, I could handle it. I hadn't spent ten years interviewing rude boys with guitars without learning a few dodges.

"Going home?"

"Yes."

"I'll walk you to your car."

"Don't bother. I'm parked at the post office." It was a hike.

I threw my bag over my shoulder, slipped on my high heels, and scampered out ahead of him. He followed me down the back steps.

"Jump in," he said, pointing to his Miata parked next to Whit's Volvo. The freshly polished red sports car gleamed in the angled sunlight of late afternoon. "I'll drop you."

Hey, I couldn't resist. It was such a cute car. Unlike mine, the inside was spotless. No plastic juice cups on the floor.

"Thanks for the ride," I said when we reached the small lot in back of the brick post office.

Mark sat there, gloating and gunning his engine, while I climbed into the beat-up Civic, covered with a layer of dust, into which some jokester had scratched, "Wash me."

As it turned out, it was lucky he was there. The Honda had decided to play possum. No matter what I did the engine wouldn't turn over. I swore under my breath, pumping the pedal and grinding the starter.

After a few minutes, Mark emerged from his car and opened my door. His arm motioned me aside with a flourish. "Make way for an expert."

With the greatest reluctance, I handed him the keys. Despite his boasting, even Mark couldn't get her to start. Finally, we maneuvered the car into a position to roll down toward the street. Mark pushed while I sat behind the wheel. I popped the clutch, and the engine finally kicked in with a reassuring rumble.

Mark poked his head in my window, "See you as soon

as I pick up the pizza. Better get that starter fixed. I know someone who specializes in Japanese imports."

"I have a mechanic."

He flashed his ivories. "Maybe it's time for a switch."

"I'm happy with the guy I've got now."

Chapter 14

As promised, Mark arrived with the soccer ball and pizza. "Hey, Szabo. *Qué pasó?*" He handed me the pizza box and started tossing the ball into the air.

"Keith," I called. "Guess who's here?" I found a platter for the pizza and turned the oven on low. "He's in his room with his dinosaurs."

"Hi, Mark!" Smokie said, grinning with all the four-year-old charm she could muster. She held her favorite stuffed rabbit by one ear.

"Hi, Smokes." He shot her a jaunty look, tossed the ball into the air, and caught it spinning on a finger, moving back and forth as it began to wobble almost immediately.

"Whoops!" He caught the ball as it fell.

Smokie's dark brown eyes widened. "Can I try?"

"Gee," I said, "you could moonlight as the entertainment at birthday parties."

Mark knelt down, tried to get Smokie to hold her knuckle stiffly, then attempted to spin the ball on her tiny hand. It was a fiasco.

"You do it," she insisted, poking his shoulder.

"Okay. Watch carefully."

After a few minutes, lured by Smokie's peals of laughter, Keith appeared in the doorway. Keith knew Mark, but they weren't exactly buddies.

"Hey, Keith." Mark tossed the ball again, spun it on his finger. "Oops!"

Keith's lips parted in an expression of restrained inquisitiveness. "How do you do that?"

"Want to go outside and kick this thing around? I'll show you some tricks."

Smokie grabbed at the ball. "I do! I do!"

"Maybe next time," Mark said gently. "Today your mom asked me to show Keith a few soccer moves." He glanced sidelong toward Keith. "What do you say?"

Keith raised his shoulders in a European shrug that I swear he inherited from my father. "Well," he muttered, as if he were doing me a big favor. "If Mom says I *have* to."

Mark winked. "Let's give it a shot."

While they played outside, I kept Smokie busy with her stuffed rabbits. Wild for my attention, she made me sit on the sofa while she ministered to a family of ten—in all sizes and colors—with her doctor kit. She gleefully inoculated them, while I played the role of worried mama begging her to cure my sick babies.

Nearly an hour later Mark and Keith burst back into the house. "How about that pizza," Mark said.

"Yeah, Mom, how about that pizza!" Keith echoed, gazing admiringly at Mark. I don't know what Mark had done, but he'd worked magic with my little boy. I hadn't seen him so excited in weeks.

I tossed a salad and served pizza slices. Mark goofed around with Smokie, who was a little suspicious of him. Smart girl, I thought. He'd been over before, always on business. This was the first time he was just hanging out. While not bubbling with enthusiasm over soccer, Keith had been intrigued by Mark's fancy footwork. At dinner Mark balanced the salt shaker on a grain of salt, demonstrated some sleight-of-hand with a paper napkin, a spoon, and two glasses; and watched with interest as Keith bit his slice of pizza into the shape of a lexovisaurus. Smokie munched hers into a rabbit. Not to be outdone, Mark nibbled his into the shape of a soccer ball, and then, of course, gobbled it up.

Later, Keith demonstrated a simple drill. He derived great pleasure from the fact that Smokie, usually more adept, found the maneuver beyond her. Patiently and proudly, he slowed it down and taught her.

As Mark prepared to leave, he handed Keith a flier about Pee Wee soccer. "Want to try it?"

Keith read and reread the flier. "Go once," I urged. "If you don't like it, you don't have to go back."

Keith shrugged. "Okay."

Mark tousled Keith's hair. "You'll be glad you did. I'll pick you up in the morning."

"You don't have to do that," I demurred. "I can get him there."

"Hey, I want to show Keith around. Let everyone know he's a special pal of mine." Mark flashed me the "I'm not such a bad guy" wink. "Right, buddy?" He punched Keith lightly on the arm.

Keith punched him back. "Right."

Mark feigned injury. Keith giggled.

"That's right. That's right. Gimme five."

Slap. Slap.

Keith said, "Gimme ten." He hit Mark's proffered hands really hard.

"Aw, you can do better than that," Mark protested.

Keith repeated the motion, smacking his hands down on Mark's.

"Hey, ouch! With the handshake, dude. Right." Mark grabbed his sweatshirt. "Catch you tomorrow."

"Catch you tomorrow, dude!" Keith shouted.

Dancing with Mr. D

We watched the red Miata rumble in the driveway a moment before zooming out, running through the gears like a race car. I sighed. Eight o'clock on a Friday. The weekend stretched out before me.

The rest of the evening passed quietly. I tucked Smokie in, then read to Keith. For the first time since school had started, he actually seemed eager for the next day to come.

"Looking forward to joining the team?" I asked. Suddenly, the reticence that had tarnished the last few weeks returned. His gray eyes went dark. Trouble stiffened his soft mouth.

"Yeah." The word was uttered without conviction. "Mom?"

"What, hon?"

"What if the other kids don't like me? What if they don't want me to be on the team?"

My heart went out to him, hoping he wouldn't be hurt. "Why don't we wait and see what happens. We'll cross that bridge when we come to it."

"Or we'll just jump in and swim."

"Yeah." I brushed his blond hair from his forehead. Just like me: Jump first, think later. He drifted off to sleep, a happier kid than I'd seen in a long time.

Later in the living room, sitting with my laptop and the Town Meeting agenda, I began to feel lonely for Billy. Why hadn't he called? I wouldn't miss Keith's debut for the world. But in the afternoon, if I could find someone to watch the kids, I might take a ride to Wonderland Sounds and see what my wayward husband was up to—and maybe corner Spots and find out more about Cassandra.

I called Dania, but reached her answering machine. Silly me. Nine o'clock on a Friday evening. Of course she was out. After leaving a message, I considered calling Wonderland Sounds. But I decided against it. Why give them a warning?

And, I remembered, I had to be careful not to let my plan slip out to Mark at tomorrow's game. So far I was the only one who knew about the Spots-Cassandra connection, and I wanted to keep it that way. I wasn't sure what excuse I would use when I arrived unannounced, but I told myself I'd think of something. Like Keith, I'd just jump in and swim.

Then, unable to procrastinate any longer, I opened the Town Meeting packets, read Barbara Warwick's draft of the warrant summary, skimmed the update Whit had handed me that afternoon, and revised Barbara's story.

The task took about an hour. I read my piece over, then scanned the new agenda for controversies that might seem ripe for the plucking. A motion entered within hours of Cassandra's death struck me immediately. It had been offered by Ann Chatsford and my pal Cletha. In light of Cassandra's martyrdom, they proposed that the entire area be set aside as a park in her honor. Smiling in anticipation of Craig Detweiller's dismay at the proposal, I toyed with the idea of calling him tonight.

Gee, maybe I could interview Vivi about her amphibian group. That was just the excuse I needed to hang around Wonderland Sounds. I could snoop on Billy and Vivi, *and* subtly interrogate Spots about Cassandra. Meanwhile, here in Greymont, I might use Vivi to push people's buttons. Imagine Craig's reaction if mega-star Vivi Cairo, and maybe even some of her Hollywood buddies, got involved in the drive for the park. The thought of him squirming warmed my heart.

I should have had enough experience with celebrities

Dancing with Mr. D

to realize that even a mere mention to Vivi might unlock a Pandora's box. But the prospect of stirring up trouble clouded my judgment.

I plugged in my modem, transmitted the story, and went to the kitchen. The kettle boiled. I poured the scalding water over a peppermint tea bag in my favorite mug. A hunger pang struck when I saw the leftover pizza. To save myself from temptation, I dumped it into the trash, then examined my figure in the hall mirror. Wanting to be the fairest one, seized suddenly by doubts.

Saturday morning went better than I dared hope. Wearing baggy shorts and a loose university T-shirt despite the chill in the air, Mark drove Keith over in the Miata. Smokie and I followed in my Honda. The soccer fields covered a huge open area next to one of the elementary schools.

Mark, who occasionally wrote up the kiddie games, was still remembered from his days pitching for the university baseball team. He sashayed around, introducing Keith as his special buddy.

A word here and there had prepared the coaches to put Keith in a group that wasn't too competitive. Mark had even found a child-sized pair of shin guards. And the mild-mannered coach of his team had a brand-new bright turquoise team T-shirt. That had to be a good omen—my favorite color.

While Mark helped Keith get acquainted with his new teammates, I wandered about hand-in-hand with Smokie, wondering at the bounty before me. I had never realized the limitless opportunity to schmooze presented by kids' sports. All the movers and shakers of Greymont were there.

I saw Craig Detweiler with a young woman who had

to be his new wife. Her hair was pulled into a bouncy black ponytail. He wasn't kidding when he'd told me she was far too young for him. I would have suspected she was his daughter except for the way they couldn't keep their hands off each other. Would you believe it, he'd married a cheerleader. He appeared to have a son on the Orange team. A boy kept running over to him, talking, then running back in to play.

Across the expanse of green, I spotted Mavis French in a suede car coat, watching her son Ellis dribble the ball down the field. I toyed with the idea of going over to say hi, but I chickened out. Maybe next weekend, I thought. After I'd talked to the teacher.

But then I saw that the coach of Ellis's team—the Greens—was none other than Ron Braithwaite. He busted ass like a drill sergeant. At one point he had his entire crew of six-year-olds on the ground doing push-ups. Kate stood nearby with Ron's wife.

"Hi, Kate!"

"Hello, Zoë," Kate said, more cheerfully than I'd expected. "You know my sister-in-law, Sandy."

Smokie saw one of her preschool friends, and ran off to play. I waved to her parents. "We met yesterday. Hi, Sandy."

"What are you doing here?" Kate asked.

"Mark just talked Keith into taking up soccer."

"Mark's here?"

"Why don't you go over and say hi?" I teased. She had such an obvious crush.

Kate held a copy of today's *Eagle*. "Ooh, can I take a look?" I asked.

"Sure."

"Hmph. At least I made page one," I grumbled. The

short item announcing that Cassandra's death had officially been pronounced murder was below the fold, but it had a decent-sized headline. "Yesterday, Vivi Cairo and her band made the top spot. My story was relegated to the back pages. And I had the cutest picture of a newt."

"Page three," Kate said, "is not the back of the paper. You should see where he put my story on the new equestrian team."

"At least it wasn't buried in auto and real estate ads. Whit has a thing about the environment," I complained, without paying too much attention to the fact that my audience wasn't exactly sympathetic. "He cut my most important quote." The one on the web of life. "Kate," I added, "you could be such a doll."

"Uh oh. What do you want now?"

"You couldn't sit for me later this afternoon?"

Her smile evaporated. "I promised my mom—"

"I want to drive up to Wonderland Sounds to drop in on Billy. My sitter is tied up all weekend."

"Maybe tomorrow."

"I'd like to go today, but if I have to put it off till tomorrow, I'll call you. Oh, please, don't tell Mark."

"Why not?"

"You know the way he steals stories."

"It's about Billy," she said, "not a story."

"Right. Still, I'd rather he didn't know." I turned to Sandy, who stood there eavesdropping shyly. "Is your son on the team?"

She smiled eagerly. "Yes. Ronnie Jr. He's over there."

I glanced over at the field. The boy she indicated was far in back of the cluster of children who surrounded the ball. He was a spindly kid with an unstylish crewcut and a hesitant way of running, as if he had hiccups.

Ellis rushed down the field to growing excitement of the parents and made a beautiful goal. Mavis waved her arms. "Go, Ellis!" she shouted.

Ron, face reddening, instead of cheering for his star forward, yelled at his son for lagging behind. A tiny spark of pity for little Ronnie flared inside me. He was so outmatched by the other children, yet he seemed to be trying so hard.

Just then, in his baggy soccer shorts, Mark jogged over. "Hey," he shouted, "Keith's doing great. You should go watch. Hi, Kate."

A ray of sun lit her eyes. Her strong mouth stretched into a wide smile.

"Get a load of those knees," I kidded.

Mark shot me a cheesy grin. "Don't stop there." He patted his stomach. "Check out these abs."

"Conceited," teased Kate. Her laugh was throaty.

I leaned forward and murmured, "He wants you to punch him in the gut so he can demonstrate how tough he is."

"Sure," he said easily, spreading his arms. "Go ahead."

"While you two are conversing," I said, ducking away, "I see someone I have to talk to."

I managed to tear Smokie away from her friend, and the two of us walked around toward Mavis French.

"Hi," I said.

She nodded politely, but her eyes dubiously scanned my outfit: orchid leggings and a chenille sweater in a color called Blush.

"If I was a little overeager the other day, I apologize." I flashed my most winning smile.

"Mmm hmm."

"That's your son, Ellis."

"Yes." She paused. "The black child."

I stumbled on, ignoring the acid-drenched tone. "With our sons in the same class, I wanted to . . . smooth over any hard feelings."

"Oh?"

"You've heard, I assume, that Cassandra's death has been reclassified as murder?"

She stared unnervingly. "Ms. Szabo, I have said everything I have to say on the subject. Please don't disturb me again."

I stammered, but nothing would undo my question or her suspicions. Sheepishly, I slipped away, kicking myself. The best thing, I decided, was to let Keith solve his own problems. Everything I did only made matters worse.

I meandered across the fields toward Keith's game. After watching for a while, I took Smokie and set out to find Craig.

"Zoë," he greeted me. "Have you met my wife, Jennifer?"

Jennifer appeared to size me up as a rival. The two of us would definitely have joined different cliques in high school. Jennifer was the type who went out with jocks and gave blowjobs to preserve her virginity. I was of the arty rebel persuasion, with in-your-face clothes, tattoos in naughty places, and a reputation that caused boys' mothers to cringe.

"Jenny," Craig said, "this is Zoë, the reporter I told you about."

We shook hands. "I hate to corner you on your day off, Craig, but did you know that the police have concluded that Cassandra was murdered?"

"Murdered?" Jenny's face sobered. "How? Do they know who?"

"No."

Craig drew a carefree arm around Jenny and pulled her boyishly to him. "Zoë," he said, his eyes colder than his smile. "I make it a rule never to discuss unpleasant things when I'm relaxing. Call me on Monday."

I was about to press on, when I became aware of Ron Braithwaite on a field not far from us. The game was over, and he was with his son Ronnie. Sandy with her baby in the stroller watched from the edge of the field.

Ronnie, face red, sweating profusely, raced to one end of the field, kicking a soccer ball zigzag around a line of cones. Back and forth he went, again and again. His father barked orders. If he stopped, Ron insisted he go back and start over. Ronnie, Jr., no older than Keith, though much smaller and thinner, ran as if his life depended on it, but his legs were short and he was weak. Finally, halfway down the field, he stumbled and fell.

"Get the hell up and do it again!"

The boy lay still on the ground.

"Get up, I tell you!"

I wandered closer, Smokie on my hip, weighing me down.

"Ron—" Sandy said meekly. Ron glared at her. She went silent.

The boy, face teary and frightened, scrambled to his feet. He kicked the soccer ball, moving it around one of the cones, panting, totally winded, almost drunk with exhaustion.

"Hey, Ron," I called, "go easy. He's just a kid."

Ron, his back toward me, froze. Slowly he turned around. "Excuse me?"

"Maybe it's time to call it a day," I said, hanging back uncomfortably.

We stood for a moment, a few yards apart. Ron met my

gaze with a fierce glower. "When I want your opinion, I'll ask for it."

I held Smokie close. If there hadn't been so many people around, I would have backed off. The guy was scary.

"Ron," Craig called affably from behind.

The man shifted his glare to Craig, who jogged forward. Ronnie Jr. scampered off to his mother.

I watched Craig jolly Ron out of his rancorous mood. Within a few moments, Ron had even tilted his head in a half grin, though his eyes burned with menace, especially when he glanced my way.

Sensing that the kid would be all right, I wandered back, putting Smokie down to run ahead. She threaded through the dwindling crowds to find Mark and Keith. It was nearly noon. Time to go home.

"When are you going to take your car to the shop?" Mark asked, after we'd walked to the Honda. He waited until I'd managed to get her started.

"First thing next week," I promised.

"Remember—if you need me to run down any statistics? I saw you talking to Craig Detweiller. The two of you looked pretty intense."

"I'm on top of it," I said, not without edge. Then I thought twice. "Thank you for helping Keith."

He shrugged. "Hey, it was fun. Wasn't it, kid?"

Keith grinned. "Slap me five, dude!"

Morgan didn't appear until six, but he quickly agreed to baby-sit in exchange for a home-cooked meal. I explained that I had a last-minute story assignment. All right, I lied, but I didn't want to have an argument about giving Billy space.

I took the back way to the Interstate, then crossed the

Vermont border. As I climbed into the mountains, the lavender and pink colors of dusk illuminated the darkening vistas. Remembering my argument with Morgan over grunge sound, I put Nirvana's *Nevermind* on the tape deck and listened to Cobain pumping the power chords. I remembered Vivi, Spots, and John, playing on the night of their arrival. John, though young, was a better guitarist. Too bad the talent didn't come in a prettier package.

Then I thought about Billy. Talent and looks. I could understand how attractive he must have been to Vivi so long ago, when, face it, she could have had anyone.

I pressed the gas pedal harder. The Honda, with its four-cylinder engine, had trouble making the inclines. As soon as the grade began to steepen, I'd lose power. The automobile zipped down the declines. I played a game of keeping up with a fast moving car with a double row of red taillights. During a long ascent, I'd almost lose sight of the distinctive lights, then I'd go downhill at breakneck speed to catch up.

A half hour passed this way. Intermittently glancing in my rearview mirror, I became aware of a large vehicle with high mounted headlights—probably a small truck or an SUV—seeming to play the same game with me. Falling back, then catching up.

I switched albums, this time U-2, and drifted off into fantasy land, imagining that Billy's project with Vivi would turn out a hit and generate money like the old glory days in LA. Then I could afford, say, a new Saab. Hey, why not go whole hog, and conjure up a Mercedes-Benz?

Suddenly, headlights loomed close to my rear. Some drivers had no patience. I was in the left lane, gaining on a truck, which had come between me and my friend with the double row of taillights. I pressed the pedal to the metal and approached eighty. My Civic began to tremble. I gunned the engine and pushed ahead of the truck. As soon as I could, I pulled to the right lane so the aggressive headlights behind me could pass, but they had disappeared.

A little while later, I exited at the ramp toward Sparrowville. A small village in the Wolfshead ski area, Sparrowville was known for the group of hippies who'd settled in a network of old houses. When the commune had disintegrated in the late seventies, the remaining members had divided up the property. One of these was an enormous barn, which Spots had refashioned into a recording studio.

He'd made several classic albums here around the time when I started writing for *Rolling Stone*. Since then his reputation had grown. Big groups made the trip to Sparrowville like pilgrims to Mecca. You hadn't arrived unless you'd recorded at least once at Wonderland Sounds.

The meandering two-lane road climbed higher into the mountains. A steady flow of traffic streamed in both directions. I drove the five miles through back country on badly groomed dirt roads, taking first a right fork, then a left, until at last my headlights illuminated an enormous psychedelic sign.

In brilliant colors a blond Alice had been painted on a huge mural in the guise of a Hindu goddess. Her multiple arms fanned out, hands blending with waves and fish, lightning bolts and raindrops, clouds and sunshine, rainbows and stars, and rabbits. Hordes of rabbits. They jumped through the spaces between Alice's arms like horses over hurdles. They danced boogaloos and bagatelles, minuets and macarenas, tangos and twists, in twos and threes surrounding the many-armed girl.

Above the mandala huge letters proclaimed: WELCOME TO THE RABBIT HOLE.

Around the greeting in a feathery glow-in-the-dark script were the words: <> Silver Wind Farm <> Wonderland Sounds <> Ye Who Enter Here, Abandon All Hype <>

Part of me was charmed. The other part, the skeptic, worried about the druggy subtext. Too many talented people had bought into that dream and checked out at the psycho ward or the morgue.

I proceeded down the mile-long driveway. Electric lights beckoned from behind a thick grove of evergreens. Around a bend loomed a huge barn, painted in bright colors. Strings of tiny blue lights dimly outlined the roof. The name of the studio was stenciled on the side in ornate barely decipherable psychedelic script that could have graced a Grateful Dead poster, circa 1968.

My beams shifted as the road turned. I drove along an alley of trees. My headlights caught patches of color among the dense evergreens, marking a purple farmhouse and a series of outbuildings. It was like a summer camp in the off-season.

A sign with a curled arrow twisted in an ironic knot indicated a driveway to the right, which I followed. Painted faces of animals, like Iroquois masks, loomed from the trunks of trees.

On a wide stretch of grass about a dozen cars, vans, and pickups were parked. I pulled up alongside a van with a woman resembling Vivi painted on its side. Her arms branched like a tree of life, inhabited by frogs, lizards, turtles, salamanders, and snakes. The words EVE'S AMBITION swayed like a banner.

A rumbling resonated in the distance. Thunder? Or had someone followed me? I listened to the dark sounds of night. An owl hooted. Boughs rustled in the mild breeze. High above, in the black dome of the sky, a silver arc delineated the fragile edge of the moon, light and shadow inverted. Banishing my fears, I walked toward the farmhouse.

Chapter 15

"Hey, Zo! Come on in. We're just sitting down to dinner." Spots wore a Hawaiian shirt with red macaws over a long-sleeved Henley. His chunky arms enveloped me in a bear hug.

"My neighbor offered to sit," I said, gently disengaging. "So I thought I'd visit. What a cool place."

"Your timing's great. The gang's in the kitchen."

I followed him down the hall. Faded oriental carpets covered the polished oak floors. Platinum records, posters of bands, framed photos, and other rock memorabilia cluttered the walls, which were painted in intense colors. The hallway was crimson; the spacious parlor through glass French doors, deep plum.

"Hi," sang Cerita as we entered the huge modern kitchen. She stirred a pot of chili on the large stainless steel stove, which matched a Sub-Zero refrigerator built into the far wall.

At a table long enough to feed an army sat Duck and John, charts spread out around them.

"Sit down," Duck growled in his deep bass. His face was broad, cheeks pronounced, eyes bloodshot but friendly. Despite the cornrows, he looked more like an executive than a drummer, in his subdued shirt and flannel slacks. "Billy's in conference with her majesty. They should be down any minute."

Dancing with Mr. D

"Bill!" Spots shouted into the hallway. "Pull up your pants—the ol' lady's here!"

Cerita, in a skimpy black lace blouse and full red skirt, greeted me with a hug. "Don't pay any attention to him. How ya doin', Zoë?"

"Terrific. How's the recording?"

"Only two days, and we're already a week behind," Spots complained, coming to taste the chili. "Mmm! Needs more of the hot stuff."

"No more for you. We got to put you on ice," Cerita shot back, removing his hand from her derriere. "Doctor's orders."

John smirked. His bright yellow-green T-shirt bore the slogan VIVI CAIRO—FRESH FRUIT—THE TOUR. In front of him stood a two-liter bottle of tequila. He filled a shot glass, drank, then grabbed a lime, and sucked on it.

"Take it easy, kid," said Duck.

"I play better stoned."

"To your ears, maybe."

"John, let me get you something to eat." Cerita placed a bowl of chili in front of him.

"Did you make all this?" I asked, looking around in awe at the platters heaped with food.

"Oh no. Spots has a cook. I just spiced up the chili. Grab yourself a drink. They're in the fridge. Stay for dinner. You see there's plenty."

"Thanks." I found a soda and popped the tab. "Someone at the paper mentioned that Vivi's involved with an amphibian foundation. I thought I might do an article."

"Remind her to sing you the froggy song," Duck said. "She added a verse about the newts in memory of that woman who died in your town the night we arrived."

"That was creepy." Cerita shivered.

John glanced at me. Uneasily, I thought, wondering how I might corner him alone.

Just then, with a burst of chatter, Vivi and Billy made an entrance. Billy's hand grazed the back of Vivi's gray blouse, which she wore over a long black skirt. The simple clothes seemed to amplify her radiance. Her exotic features and luminous eyes overflowed with energy. Everybody turned as she came in, like flowers toward the sun.

"Got a gal here," Spots kidded, "says she lost a dog answers to the name of Billy Harp."

"Hi." I grinned.

"Arf," Billy barked. He gave me a light kiss. "Happened to be in the neighborhood, huh?"

I tilted my chin a little coyly. Okay, so I hadn't put anything over on him. Still, here I was.

"Zoë!" Vivi trotted over and kissed the air by my cheek. "Welcome. What did you do with the kids?"

"They're with a sitter." I gave her a squeeze and met Billy's gaze again.

"Busy day?" he asked.

I nodded.

"Me too." He touched Cerita's arm. "This chick's a sweetheart. Working overtime."

"Want good cooking, you know where to come."

"Hungry?" Billy asked me.

"No. I, uh, actually came to"—it was obvious I was here to scope out the scene—"see how everything . . . was going. But I got this great idea. Vivi, how about a feature on you and the amphibian cause? We could do a couple of interviews while you're here, if Spots doesn't mind. Maybe work something up to appear when the album does."

The air filled with a juicy, gossipy pause.

"That's good, Zoë," Vivi said. "You have to hear 'Froggy Night'! Billy's been helping me with it." Her smile turned liquid when it touched on him.

Spots chuckled. "Bill's all heart."

"Yeah," said Cerita. "And you're all—" She didn't have to finish. The others concurred, laughing. The conversation continued, but it seemed to fade into the background.

"Too bad you didn't call." Billy touched my arm. "I could have told you this was a bad time. We'll be working late."

"I didn't hear from you, so—"

"Well," said Vivi with a meaningful smile. "I'll let you two talk in private."

The others gave us space, getting dinner, sitting down, eating. Billy and I moved to a corner by the windows. Outside the night was dark except for the sliver of moon, which had risen higher and peeped through the black branches.

"How's Keith?" he asked.

"Mark took him to soccer this morning. He seemed to like it."

"Mark. What's his angle?"

"He overheard a call I had with Keith and suggested sports, so we're trying it."

Billy frowned. At first I thought he was concerned about Keith, but then I realized his gaze had drifted toward the window.

"Problems with the album?"

His voice dropped so Vivi wouldn't overhear. "The execs nixed one of her favorite songs. She took it hard. Duck's great. Such a pro. Let me get some chow, and we'll talk. Have something."

"Billy's behaving," Spots confided as we approached the table. "Right, Viv?"

"Absolutely."

Billy ignored the ribbing. "Spots has a great setup. All the comforts of home."

"Then some," Spots said. "Maid service. Breakfast in bed."

Duck said, "Have to try that tomorrow."

"It's true," Vivi piped up. "They brought coffee."

"Vivi, that was lunch," said Cerita.

The conversation went in a million directions. Cerita had a sharp tongue, which she didn't hesitate to use. Spots was ready with risqué comments. Duck easily gave in to a growling chuckle and kept the peace by doing the dozens on anyone whose remarks threatened to get out of hand. He often came to John's defense. Although the young guitarist's virtuoso playing made him one of them, his comments were so sophomoric, the others tended to put him down a bit cruelly.

I kept my sympathy in check. John was more like the rude boys I'd run with in my youth than I cared to admit. Billy had been different. Although the bedroom eyes and dark good looks had attracted me at the beginning, Billy's gentleness, his intelligence, his depth, and his refusal to play the dumb put-down game were the qualities that really got me. I studied him now, in love with him still. He tossed out a barb or two just to let the guys know not to mess with him, but it was obvious he found it distasteful.

Despite the banter, all through dinner the undercurrent of tension was palpable. Money, reputations, futures were riding on this venture. As the others joked, Billy fell silent, picking at a piece of cornbread, touching nothing else on his plate. If he was so anxious that he couldn't eat, the pressure must be weighing heavily. I felt for him, for all of them.

Vivi showed the stress by playing prima donna. Nothing was good enough. She'd asked for yogurt, they'd bought the wrong kind, not the organic brand she'd requested. Mineral water. They'd bought French; not the obscure one from the Italian Alps she'd asked them to special order. Her laughter verged on brittle, but still she sparkled. I wondered how she did it. When I get testy, it just sounds like complaining.

As I studied Billy, I realized that this would be his first work for a major label—for any label—since the OD in Kyoto. I saw the strain in the creases at his eyes when he glanced toward Vivi—how he longed to please her. And in the tightness of his chiseled lips when he smiled—how he yearned to feel the heat of the spotlight once again. I felt my own ambivalence. I loved him. I wanted him to be happy, but I couldn't forget the pain this trip had caused before.

The more anxious he became, the more laserlike his charm. In that way, Billy resembled Vivi. Even Cerita—I could see she was attracted. And Vivi—well, I suspected she'd never resigned herself to their separation, even if they had parted years ago. Still, Billy seemed blithely unaware of that. Or maybe he just hid it well.

A telepathic message passed between us. He pressed a finger against my wrist, tracing a line into my palm. He didn't say, *Jealous?* But his dark eyes implied it. He seemed to find it a turn-on. We exchanged glances. I wondered for a fleeting moment if Morgan could sleep at our house. If maybe I should spend the night here, with Billy.

"Cerita," Vivi was saying, her voice rising above the general buzz. Cerita had just unveiled a cream cheese flan. "What is this with the high-carb, high-fat munchies?"

"Vivi's idea of soul food," Duck kidded, "is listening to Aretha while eating celery."

Everybody laughed more than they would have if Vivi's behavior hadn't been so difficult.

I had to give her credit. She laughed with them. "God, I'm not that bad, am I?"

"Honey," Duck said, "you are worse."

"But we wouldn't have you any other way," Cerita added, giving her a reassuring hug.

"Okay, Cerita. You get that solo," Vivi said. Laughter followed and more ribbing.

Spots, despite his laid-back style, cleared his throat. "What say we do a run-through in a half an hour. Bass— Hey, Bill. *Bill?*"

Billy turned from me. "Basic."

"Basic but plush," Vivi said, giving him a little look.

Billy flashed an edgy smile. "*Plush?*"

"Hey, Vivi," Duck said to distract her, "you were going to sing 'Froggy Night' for Zoë."

Vivi took a swig of Evian. She screwed the top back on. "Yeah. Zoë, we'll talk later. Tonight I've got to work on sound." Her liquid smile fell on Billy. "And tempo."

"Viv," Spots interrupted, "you and Bill want to work out your differences before we start? Or should we just dig in and battle it out on tape? It's your money."

Vivi tore a section from an orange. "We'll work it out one way or another. Won't we, Billy?"

Billy glanced in my direction. Having grown up in the theater, I can take a cue. "Spots," I said, "how about a tour of the studio."

"Sure, Zo. Sure."

Vivi said, "Hey, if we wanted to kick you out, we'd say so."

"I wouldn't dream of disturbing your work." Thinking

that things were finally starting to follow the scenario I'd envisioned, I smiled. I felt calm. In control.

"Stay for the run-through later?" Billy asked me. His dark eyes said more.

"Maybe."

I excused myself, while Spots conferred with Duck. I walked down the hall, turned into an alcove that led toward the den. In the blue-tiled bathroom, with all new fixtures, I scrutinized my twin in the mirror and gave her a two-minute pep talk. For the first time in the last few days, I felt upbeat.

If Billy were a lawyer, I reasoned, would I feel hurt or worried about the hours he had to work while he was preparing a million-dollar case for trial? If he conferred with other lawyers on his team, even if some of them were gorgeous women? The situation was roughly comparable. Give the guy a break, I told my mirror image, beginning to feel more confident. Morgan's words came back to me. *He has his pride. Give him space.*

Good advice, I thought. Billy, though anxious, seemed copacetic. Vivi was already getting on his nerves. I would show him that I could back off, demonstrate that I trusted him with her, and at the same time talk to Spots in private. Two birds, I thought, one stone. And then, later—?

Maybe I should call Morgan now, about staying the night with the kids. I went to the den to look for a phone. Opening the door, I saw John, lurking in a corner near the old piano. Alone! Now was my chance to pounce. I couldn't believe my luck.

"John," I whispered, approaching him.

"Huh?" He glanced around nervously. Flushing, he stashed something into his pocket.

Good, I thought. He did know something about Cassandra. I'd sensed it all through dinner. "You have something to tell me, don't you?" I whispered.

He looked startled. But didn't deny it.

"About Cassandra," I prompted.

"I, uh, can't talk here."

"You saw her, didn't you?"

"Uh—I don't know anything." His eyes told a different story.

"You don't have to go to the police. I understand. I'm a reporter. I've never betrayed a source. You can be totally anonymous. That way, if you saw someone or something, your conscience can rest easy, but you don't have to be exposed."

He hesitated, tempted. "Don't tell Spots. We'll get busted if—"

"Our secret," I assured him. "What did you see?"

"Uh—" Footsteps sounded.

"Listen," I urged. "Meet me outside later?"

"When?" Reluctant. Unsure.

"Half an hour?"

He hesitated, wanting to unload. I could see it in the anxious way his fingers clenched. Finally, he nodded.

I breathed a sigh of relief. "Where?"

"Boathouse. Look for the dragon," he whispered.

Just then Spots entered the room. "John! Don't disappear. Keep your nose out of the powder. We want steady hands." Spots saw me. "Hey, Zo. Ready for the tour?"

"I'm dying to see this fabled studio." I bestowed my classiest smile, taking his arm and leaning close. "Word is Electric Lady is a mosh pit compared to Wonderland. I heard you built from scratch."

Weathered on the outside, high-tech with clean lines on the inside, the converted barn was cavernous. The two

Dancing with Mr. D

fully equipped studio suites were an acoustic engineer's post-millennial daydream, with huge live areas with high ceilings and hanging panels you could shift to adjust the acoustics, isolation booths, drum rooms, and more. Mikes, wires, and stands of all kinds were everywhere. The larger studio was big enough to fit two symphonic orchestras and the Mormon Tabernacle Choir.

The smaller studio where the Cairo crew was recording was decent-sized, but more intimate. Duck's drum set stood in the center. In a corner a nine-foot grand piano on wheels with a paisley quilt cover was dwarfed by the enormity of the room. I counted three keyboards, eight electric guitars, four basses, along with violins, dobros, kettle drums, other more exotic instruments, and a dozen stools and chairs for the musicians. The decor was functional, tending toward chrome, leather, and kilims in muted colors.

Inside the control booth, I felt as if I'd entered the cockpit of a spaceship in a high-budget science fiction flick. A twenty-foot console allowing mixing of 128 tracks, with knobs, dials, levers, meters, and multicolored lights dominated the long soundproof glass wall looking into the smaller studio. Other electronic equipment—MIDIs, synthesizers, reverb and delay units, computers, samplers—were stacked on racks against the walls.

"I'm never without this baby," Spots said, patting the Gibson Les Paul with the Clapton signature, which hung in a favored spot not far from the producer's chair.

He explained the recording process. Although the studio was fully digital, he also had analog equipment, because, he said, the warm sound of analog just couldn't be beat.

"State of the art," he kept repeating.

"This is fabulous. When did you build?"

"Oh, about fifteen, twenty years ago. Started small, during the commune days. When things started to pick up, I plowed the profits into equipment."

"You must have tales about all the great sidemen who've recorded here."

"That I do."

"Gee, I'd love to write a story."

"On me?" His bow lips etched a dubious smile.

"Sure."

"Nah. I don't want to be in the papers." He opened a drawer and slid out a sheet. "You want to know about me, read this."

It was a studio bio. Standard stuff. The veins on the back of his stubby hands stood out in bas-relief. I folded the sheet and put it in my pocket.

"Everybody likes free publicity. I'm going to do that piece on Vivi and the frogs. Why not you too?"

"I don't want to attract tourists. Leave me out."

"Afraid you might give too much away?"

"What's your angle, honey?"

"I'm trying to track down Cassandra's history. Pre-Greymont."

Spots fiddled with his dials, wires, and levers. It took a few moments before he spoke. "You came to the wrong place."

"Maybe the wrong time zone, but I'm in the right place. Why won't you help?"

His half smile was snide. "You psychic?"

"Maybe."

"She was just a chick with a taste for dicks." He said it with a snicker and watched for my reaction. I disappointed him. Dirty talk doesn't intimidate me. Rock 'n' roll is not a place for women who blush at the mention of anatomy, however gross.

"I was told she grew up in Rheinlander, Wisconsin, but they don't have any record of a Cassandra Dunne at the local schools."

"I can't help you there." Pale patches bloomed on his cheeks like time-lapse roses, white on a sea of pink.

"Did she change her name?"

"Haven't a clue."

"Other members of your old commune might remember."

"You'd have a hard time tracking them down."

"You could give me some names . . . phone numbers."

He squinted through his glasses. Behind the facade of cosmic whimsy alternating with sexual come-on, I detected agitation. My God, I thought. They'd seen the killer. That's why John was so nervous. Of course, with all the drugs they had in their systems, they were afraid to come forward. Maybe I could work something out. If I could just gain their trust, I could get the evidence without tipping off the police as to the source.

Spots flipped a switch. Music blared through six huge speakers. He flipped another. A medley of African drums burst forth. He dug a pouch out of a back pocket of his baggy chinos, sprinkled some dried leaves onto Zigzag paper, and rolled. He lit a match and sucked in the smoke, then offered it to me.

I shook my head.

He smoked his joint and peered through the glass into the dimly lit studio.

"Nobody has to know the information came from you."

"Yeah?" He inhaled again, then let go. His eyes grew wistful. Some moments passed.

"Did you meet her here?"

He nodded.

"When?"

"A long time ago."

"Twenty years?"

His fingers picked a piece of stem off his tongue. I waited, watching the memories travel slowly through his visage. After a minute or two he added, "We didn't use names. Not real ones. Most of us wanted to get off the grid."

"The grid?"

"Electric. Gas company. Telephone company. Drivers' license. Social Security numbers. Bank accounts. Credit cards. Big Brother. The grid."

I silently blessed the truth serum Spots had drawn into his lungs.

"Cassandra?"

"Disappeared down the Rabbit Hole. Like Alice."

"What was she running from?"

"Same old shit." He tapped ash into a tin jar on the console. "Now Cassandra was pure analog."

"I thought she was just a chick looking for dick."

"Oh yeah. A big green dick."

"*She* broke it off?"

The pale patches reappeared on his chubby cheeks. "I can mike you to sound like anyone you want. Aretha? Janis? Jewel? The artist formerly known as Vivi Cairo? Want to make a demo?"

"I'd like to know more about Cassandra."

"Thought you wanted to do a story on this studio. Maybe feature Vivi and Billy recording the album." His pink lips parted. "Blow by blow."

"Tell me who you saw. How she died. I guarantee anonymity."

"You are one curious pixie." Spots smiled cagily. He flipped a switch. Over the speakers I heard my own voice, whispering with heavy reverb the words I'd just said.

They echoed and interlaced, like waves breaking, ripping back into the tide, and rippling forward in a second rush toward shore.

Anonymity. Anonymity. Anonymity.

Spots laughed. "You like that?"

He flipped another switch, and I heard *blow by blow* repeated like an image in a hall of mirrors.

He mixed the two together. *Anonymity* bled into *blow by blow*. Then he added: *how she died, running from?, blow, anonymity, green* and *dick* then *chick*. Then *feature Vivi and Billy, running from?, blow by blow, big green dick, grid, grid, grid, grid . . .*

His smirk broadened. "Like I said, wanna make a demo? Who do you want to sound like? Chick? Or Dick?"

The white roses on his cheeks spread to his forehead, which had broken out in a fine mist of perspiration. Wildness bordering on panic swept through his doped-up eyes.

I drew my card from my pocket and wrote my beeper and cell phone numbers on the back. Under that I wrote: "Anytime." I underlined it.

He glanced at the card and said nothing. The crazy recordings echoed over and over, like vinyl with a scratch. We stared at each other, opponents in a weird chess match, eyeing each other from opposite sides of the funhouse mirror.

After slipping out of the room, I jogged to the car for my micro-tape recorder, just in case I could get John to talk. A few minutes later, at exactly nine-thirty as prearranged, I negotiated my way through the woods toward the lake.

I clutched a small flashlight, but didn't turn it on. The edge of the moon, sharp above the black mountains, shed barely any light. The intensity of the darkness frightened me. I sped up my pace, hoping I wouldn't run into anything I couldn't see.

Water lapped against the shore with a mild slapping sound. The shadows seemed enormous. Passing through a black patch, I felt a sudden panic as if I might not emerge into the light. As I drew closer to the lake, the rustlings grew eerier, the darkness blacker in the shadows, the stillness poised like a snake about to strike. Affected by the secondhand pot smoke, I guessed, my mind was playing tricks on me.

I found a boathouse. I turned on the flashlight and examined the walls. No dragon.

I heard the crashing of branches, someone running toward me.

"John?" Cerita's voice called out. She came running down the path.

"It's me," I called.

"Have you seen him?"

"No."

"Darn. Spots went to find him. Now they're both missing."

I asked about the dragon. She pointed to a dark rectangle about thirty yards away along the lakeshore. I hurried toward it.

I approached the boathouse, the painting on the side illuminated by my beam. I heard breathing. A soft panting.

"John?"

The only response was the black water lapping at the pier.

And then I saw it, a glimmer of lightness about twenty yards out into the water. I ran down the wooden treads of the pier. "John?"

I aimed my beam on the water. Bobbing in the darkness, my beam traced a pale green outline among the glinting waves.

Footsteps clattered. A light bounced from the water to the wood grain of the dock to the dark blue of Duck's shirt and into my eyes.

"Zoë—what's wrong?"

I pointed my light to the green bubble out in the water. Duck's flashlight followed the angle. Duck didn't pause. He kicked off his shoes and jumped. I followed suit. The shock of icy wetness woke me from my terror. I swam as fast as my limbs could pull me.

Duck shouted, "Damn. Damn!"

Together we struggled with John's huge body, dragging it back toward the pier.

By that time Billy, Vivi, Spots, and Cerita had gathered on the dock, holding lights, seeing what they could do to help. Spots jumped in to assist with the task of lifting John's unwieldy body out of the water. Billy knelt down to help. I hoisted myself on my elbows and scrambled out.

Everybody seemed paralyzed. Cerita was shrieking. Spots was cursing a blue streak. Vivi was repeating, "Oh my God. Oh my God."

"Help me turn him over," I said. I propped John's chin on his hands, straddled his back, and pushed down hard. Water gurgled out of his mouth.

I leaned back, hoping my muscles would remember the motions I'd learned so long ago. I prayed silently for the good air to rush in. Then I paused and repeated the motion.

"Call an ambulance," I shouted.

Cerita was sobbing. Duck, dripping, muttered curses. Spots kept trying to help me.

"I know what I'm doing," I said. "Someone call an ambulance."

Spots grabbed my arm. "Let me."

"I've got a rhythm going," I insisted.

He pulled me harder.

"Quit it," I snapped.

Billy pulled Spots back. "She knows what she's doing. She saved a kid a few years ago."

"Is he going to die?" Cerita asked.

"He's not going to die," I said. "Call an ambulance now!"

I kept pumping at his chest, waiting to hear a gurgle in his lungs pleading for air. After what seemed like a very long time, I still couldn't detect any indication of breathing. I hesitated.

Spots jumped forward. The light bobbed again. I saw John's eyes staring, filmy, cool, but I felt they were alive. Hope stirred within me.

We turned him over, and I bent down to rekindle life with mouth-to-mouth resuscitation. The cold lips were flaccid, their scent dank with pond scum and weeds and clay. It tasted like kissing death itself.

I kept at it. I didn't hear the others, their swearing, their cries, their murmurs of dismay, their hints at the possibility that he might not come around. I ignored their questions. I ignored their suggestions. I ignored their hands on my shoulders nudging me. I ignored the suggestions repeated louder, through a dull screen of concentration. I kept thinking perhaps, perhaps, perhaps, it was not too late. Perhaps, perhaps, the breath would come. Perhaps my lips would restore life. I kept going.

And then, after a period of time that I had no comprehension of, something inside me, some small voice, some whisper, echoed the words I'd tried so hard to block out. The wind came. It plastered the cold clothes to my skin. The wet lips I kept pressing, pushing air into, hoping to feel a response, grew increasingly colder and increasingly lifeless.

I stopped.

John lay dead on the dock. I sat numbly and gazed at his face as the others fixed a flashlight beam on him. Footsteps resounded on the boards from the boathouse.

It took three paramedics to carry him by stretcher up through the forest path to the ambulance. There, they tried to jump start his heart. But the body . . . cold . . . merged with darkness.

Chapter 16

Some chivalrous instinct, I suppose, persuaded the Vermont police to ask the men to stay and make formal statements, but allowed Vivi, Cerita, and me to wait until the next day.

The drive back to Greymont was tense. The mountains were dark against a dramatic night sky full of gathering storm clouds. The moon occasionally peeped out and edged the clouds with silver. Cerita slept. Vivi chatted on. About the album. All the hopes she had riding on it. About Billy. That he was being difficult, though, of course, he was a darling. About Spots. How he'd been pushing them all too hard. About John. What a great player he had been, and what a waste it was.

Finally, we arrived at the house. I woke Morgan gently. He always seemed so fragile when he slept, although his snore was mighty. His eyes at last blinked open. "Oh, Zoë." He looked about, orienting himself. "My, I must have drifted off." He sat in the old recliner, his favorite spot, Mac portable in his lap. He'd been doing some work—astrophysics calculations. He rubbed his face, stored his files, and switched off the computer.

"The children are fine," he said, still groggy as he put his things away: a thick book, a pen, an academic journal.

"Morgan," I whispered, "Vivi and Cerita are here."

"Oh. Fine, fine."

"I left them at your place. Is that okay?"

He noticed my expression. "My dear, what's wrong?"

I pressed my hand against my mouth, allowing the tears now that I felt safe. "John, the guitar player. Remember him?"

"Yes, of course. What—"

"He died tonight."

"My God! How?"

"He drowned. They think it was drug-related. He passed out and fell into the lake." I described the effort to revive him.

"Horrible," Morgan kept repeating as I spoke. When I finished, he added, "This album seems to have a curse. First Cassandra, now this."

"It does. And they won't stop. There's too much money sunk into it. They're going to keep going until they finish."

"Is Billy here?"

"He and the other guys are making statements for the police."

"I'd better go help the women get settled. Will you be all right?"

I assured him I would. After Morgan left, I checked on the kids, hugging them in their sleep. Then, to get the cold out of my bones, I ran the tub and bathed, but my mind kept racing so much that I couldn't sit still for long. I went to bed, but couldn't sleep.

Finally, I gave up and went downstairs. I'd been lying alone in the dark, unable to wrest myself from a rehash of the events of the night, the icy feel of the water, the taste of death on my lips. To stop the images from flying around in my head, I warmed milk with vanilla and honey. Then I sat at the computer and wrote a short piece on the accident for the paper.

I was in the midst of the sixth or seventh replay of the tragedy in my head: John's waterlogged body sprawled on the dock, the smell of his mouth, dank with pond water and the bitter flavor of tequila, the knowledge that I couldn't revive him. Suddenly something broke through. I looked around in the dark, startled to find myself in my own kitchen. And then I remembered that before I'd fallen into the reverie, I had been about to go through my files. The chain of events leading to the drowning began to loom in my mind again. I shook it off.

I needed to find a way to distract myself. My hands were on the file of clips I'd copied about Cassandra's crusade. Behind that was a folder containing the property transactions I'd collected at the Hall of Records. Pushing the memory of the pond from my thoughts, I delved into the material.

For the next half hour, I read scores of articles on battles over wetlands and proposed conservation areas. I pored through the myriad lists of properties and dates of purchase and sale. The details I wouldn't have had patience for at any other time gave me a focal point to fend off the unpleasant memories.

As I worked, I began to realize that without some kind of visual aid, I was never going to get a firm grasp on all these properties. In the folder was a lot map of Greymont. The best thing to do, I decided, was to map the property Cassandra had contested over the years. Then, make another showing exactly how each property had been disposed. Maybe I'd find some kind of pattern.

I had just begun working, when I heard a tiny rap. A dart of fear pulsed in the back of my throat. I held my breath.

I heard the rapping again. I was just about to try to turn off my lamp and hide, when I heard a voice cry, "Zoë?"

Scoffing at my own jumpiness, I turned on the porch light, and saw Vivi at the door, shivering. "Come in."

Her hair was mussed from tossing, unable to sleep. Her skin was pasty, eyes bruised with exhaustion. She wore black silk pajamas with a light sweater thrown over her shoulders. On her feet were embroidered Chinese slippers. "I can't sleep. I don't want to be alone."

"Would you like some warm milk?"

"Ugh. I couldn't stand milk." Shivering, she entered the kitchen and sat down at the table.

"Can I get you a warmer sweater?"

"Don't bother."

"How about a piece of toast?"

"God, no. If you have to eat, do it somewhere else. I couldn't stand to watch. I spent the last hour in the bathroom vomiting."

She met my stare. Neither of us spoke. It had been a very long night.

Eventually, I said, "The shock does wear off."

"Tell that to Cerita."

I went to the stove and put milk on to warm. I added a drop of vanilla and a teaspoon of honey.

"What a fucking nightmare." Vivi closed her eyes. "Has Billy called?"

"Not yet."

She slipped a silver flask from her pajama pocket and delicately unscrewed the top. She poured a capful and downed it. "Do you think they're still with the police?"

I checked the time. When I was younger being awake at four in the morning had been a symptom of adventure. It was the hour when you walked home in the rain, after the clubs let out, with a new special someone. Now, though, staring at a clock at 4 A.M. only meant trouble. Kids never had a fever of 105 when a doctor was within reach through a simple phone call. On the newspaper staff, it meant nothing short of a natural disaster: a fire, a tornado, a freak flood.

The milk began to steam. I took the pan off the stove and poured the hot liquid into my favorite handmade ceramic mug. The sweet scent filled my nostrils. "Sure you don't want some?"

She nearly turned green. "Want some of this?" Vivi said, her hand on her flask.

"No, thanks. I'll stick with the mild stuff." I took a careful sip from my mug. The honey felt soft going down.

For a moment, the weirdness of the situation struck me. It seemed positively unreal to be sitting here comforting my husband's ex-lover after the death of her band mate. She fidgeted with the cuff of her pajamas. Her dark hair, beautifully cut, fell in front of her eyes. Her edginess filled the cluttered kitchen.

The children's things were scattered across the floor. On the linoleum from two days ago lay a finger painting with sparkles sprinkled in swirling letters "S-M-O-K-E." Dania was better at creative projects than she was at picking up after them.

Vivi's slender fingers stroked the smooth wood of the oblong cherry table. Her hand brushed the stuffed rabbit near Smokie's booster seat. The fabric was a blue silk with pink velvet inside the ears and a fluffy pink tail.

Vivi pressed it to her chest, smiling like a kid, her charisma coming to the fore. "Sweet."

"Smokie's. She has a huge collection."

"Just rabbits?"

"Mostly."

"She'll drive them wild when she grows up. She's a charmer."

"Yeah." It reminded me of some of the conversations I had with Billy's sister. Children made safe subjects when you wanted to avoid certain topics.

"You know, I used to think I wanted kids. I envy you yours." Whoops. Not so safe as I thought. She read my mind. "Don't worry. I have no designs on your husband."

"The thought never occurred to me."

She grinned, propping the rabbit against a book on the table. "I am not the ogre you think I am."

Part of the star power was the intimacy implied in her gaze. She looked at me now as if we'd been friends forever. Despite my jealousy and resentment, I found myself feeling flattered.

"What a horrible night!" she said, veering toward less treacherous terrain. "I can't get John out of my head."

I studied the bubbles edging the milk in my cup. "Neither can I."

"He was an incredible musician. You know, I discovered him."

"Oh?"

"Yeah. A few years ago, some nothing garage band on an unknown indy label managed to get my address and sent me a demo. In my position, you learn never to open a package unless you know who it's from. I insisted my manager drive all the way from Laguna to my house in Topanga to pick it up. I wouldn't touch it. He groused, but, hey, that's why I pay him his fucking twenty percent.

"Two weeks later, I asked did you send back that package? He'd completely forgotten. I took it as a sign. My intuition had been telling me all week, *Open it and listen.* So I had him play it. The demo was dreadful. Typical mess. But the guitar player, John, was—just nuts. Really hot.

"I called him that day and asked him to audition. He was a baby. Seventeen. They all thought I was crazy, but I insisted on using him on my Fresh Fruit tour. Well, he was great. I can pick 'em, Zoë. I really can. He could have gone far."

Her dark eyes welled with tears. She plucked absently at the velvet ear of the toy rabbit. We were silent.

"What a waste," I said after a few minutes.

She bent forward. "Why John?"

I was wondering the same thing. What secret had he taken with him to the grave? I was afraid it might be something about Spots. Something terrible. I worried for Billy's safety.

Could John have passed out and fallen waiting for me? Had someone followed him down to the dock? Or lurked out in the woods, waiting? Had someone followed me to Vermont? Why John? Maybe I was crazy. Maybe it was the accident it appeared to be. The paramedics said summarily that he'd passed out and drowned. They didn't suspect foul play at all. Spots and Duck confirmed that he'd been drinking all day long and sneaking outside. Spots scornfully said musicians were fools. All of them were hooked on something—women, drugs, booze; sometimes just music alone was enough to screw them up.

"How were John's licks yesterday?" I asked. "Did he seem drunk or stoned?"

"I haven't the foggiest. The man played in the groove. None of my business how he managed to do it. Poor guy," she added, softening. "Only a kid."

"You know, the police say Cassandra's death was murder."

Her expression subtly changed from bewilderment to something darker—horror, apprehension? "Murder?"

The word lingered in the atmosphere.

I nodded.

"Oh," Vivi whispered. Her fingers trembled. She unscrewed the cap of the flask and poured herself another shot. For a few seconds she was too distracted to drink. Then, when she lifted it to her lips, her hands shook so that it spilled.

"Oh, God. Do you have a napkin?"

I studied Vivi. I wondered if she'd been dabbling. Cocaine. I knew all the telltale signs. Sometimes people drank to bring themselves down. I went to get a sponge.

"How was it done?" she asked.

"They're not saying."

"God." She shuddered. "Why would anyone?"

"She made a lot of enemies. This protest increased her unpopularity. They've been trying to build this mall for years."

"Your partner was telling me."

"Partner?"

"Yeah, Mark. He's a *babe*."

I winced. "He told me about your amphibian foundation."

Her eyes lit. "All over the world, you know, the frogs are dying out. Deformities. Tumors. Poisons in the water."

"A scientist I talked to says that we're in a wave of extinction. The last one killed off the dinosaurs. I looked in Keith's book—the frogs and newts survived that one. They might not be so lucky this time."

"Extinction," she repeated, slurring the word. "I—I want to give something back. Write that story you mentioned earlier. Go ahead—with my blessing." She sipped her vodka. "I'll help any way I can."

"Vivi, don't drink anymore. Have some tea."

"I'm beyond tea, Zoë, way beyond."

I heated the kettle. When it boiled, I poured a double dose of chamomile and added a spoonful of honey. I dropped in an ice cube so it would cool faster, the way I did for Smokie. I placed it before her, putting my hand on the flask, remembering the way Spots had taken the tequila from John and hidden it in the cabinet.

"Drink is just to stave off the craving. I need it to keep me from . . . the stronger shit." Her stare was shameless. I left the flask where it was.

"I have to get this album down before I fall to pieces."

I murmured sympathetic sounds.

"I cost them plenty a few years back. Screwed up big time."

"Maybe the best thing to do would be to put off recording for a few weeks."

"I can't."

"Why not?"

"Obviously you're too young to know about last chances. Billy's come up with some great songs. This is the best group of sidemen I've ever managed to get in one place—even without John. Spots is booked solid. It's now or never."

"So," I said, "I'll do that piece on your foundation." If Billy was going to spend the next few weeks recording, I wanted to have an excuse to drop in once in a while.

"Good." She smiled at me more genuinely.

I wanted to hate her, but I relented and smiled back. "Who knows? Maybe we can peddle it to a magazine."

Her eyes took me in. "I keep thinking about Cassandra," she confided. "I don't know much about her, but I feel close to her, as if she's talking to me. How horrible—

Dancing with Mr. D

to think she was murdered. Do you think they did it because she was going to stop the mall?"

"If so, it backfired. There's a motion in Town Meeting that's going to come to a vote next week. Some people want to make the area into a park instead."

"You don't say?"

"This terrific old lady—she's ninety-two. But what a live wire! Believe it or not, she's leading the charge." I was talking away, not noticing Vivi while I spoke. "Her name is Ann Chatsford, and she's 'Old Greymont' at its finest."

I glanced up. The plain fingers—no bright polish, just trim nails for her keyboard playing—fiddled with the silver top of the flask. But her hands didn't tremble. It was like watching a snake shed its skin and begin to rejuvenate.

"Zoë! I have just had an *inspiration*! When did you say that vote is?"

"A week or so."

"It's not much time, but, Zoë, I think we just might—"

"What?"

"Cassandra," she mused. "Here was a woman, completely unknown. She gave her life trying to save a poor defenseless creature from criminal greed."

"Vivi—"

"Criminal. What's the name of that wicked man who wants to build that monstrosity? A parking garage? A *Mall*? Cassandra. She couldn't even get her own hometown to pay attention to what they were doing to these small helpless amphibians. We can tie the album—*Eve's Ambition*—into Cassandra and her—what was it?"

"Newts."

"Zoë, I've got it!" Her eyes blazed like some crazy

Joan of Arc. "Zoë." She grabbed my hand. "You and I are going to do for Greymont what Sting did for the Amazon!"

"Sting? The Amazon?" What would Whit make of this? "Vivi—"

"Zoë, you're a genius!"

"Oh, it was your idea." I swallowed, trying to shift the blame.

"Don't be modest. You're the one who triggered it! We'll start out with a press conference. And a protest rally! I can get *People* in a New York minute. We'll do it right in front of that tree. They've been pestering me for an interview ever since my last overdose. Well, let them gawk. It's for a good cause."

"Vivi—"

"And Mark. What a honey!"

I couldn't help but make a face.

"He was spellbound when I described my Eve's Ambition tour. Did he tell you?"

"Yes. He did, but—"

"The two of you would make a great team. You can get a leave of absence, can't you? What's the name of your adorable boss? I'll call him in the morning. First thing."

"I can't get a leave of absence. I'm on a story."

"Don't you see this would be part of the story. The 'Murder of Cassandra Dunne.' No woman is an island. That will be my slogan. I've got to call my manager. What time is it in LA?"

"Too early to call. Remember, you need to put your energy into the album. The campaign can come later."

"Cassandra!" Her hands painted the word in a gesture. "Cassandra, wasn't she a prophetess?"

"She warned about the fall of Troy."

"My best lyrics are steeped in myth—just dripping with it."

"I'm sure they are."

"Remember my song about the swan? There was myth in that. And the one your boss liked."

"Yes, terrific lyrics—"

"Cassandra. I think I'll spell it with a K. Sounds more tragic, more Greek. Like Medusa, wasn't she?"

"No. Medusa was a monster. She had snakes for hair."

"Oh no. No. That's going too far."

"Yes, Vivi. Too far."

"Cassandra. We'll do all the Greek things. An Acropolis in the background. Maybe a Trojan horse and Greeks bearing gifts. And a tunic. Wouldn't I look good in a tunic?" She glanced in the mirror and flipped her hair. "Maybe I'll get a perm."

"Hey, I think it's time to go to sleep. We'll talk about it in the morning."

"But I'm not tired!"

"You're going to face the cameras. You need your beauty rest. I'll open up the couch, if you're afraid to go back to Morgan's."

She seemed to step back down to earth. The air in Greymont, maybe that's what did it, proximity to the Heritage River. Or the emissions from smokestacks in the Midwest. Seemed to turn even the most self-centered souls into Quixotes attempting to save the world and to joust at all those crazy windmills in their minds.

She reached for her flask.

"You can get to sleep without that now," I coaxed, the way I might try to talk Keith into letting go of his new dinosaur model.

"I'm not sure."

"You have a mission. You have to look your best."

"That's true."

I grabbed sheets from the hall closet, opened the sofa, made the bed, and gave her some towels. "Need music?"

"No, no. Music floods my mind with thoughts. I can't sleep if there's music playing."

I doused the lights and locked the doors. As I brought her a pillow, Vivi whispered, "John said he saw something. I suggested he talk to you. If I'd insisted, he'd still be alive. He was scared. Something about Cassandra's fall wasn't right. He kept reading that article from the paper over and over."

"Did you tell anyone?"

"No. Should I have?"

Saw something. That confirmed what I'd suspected. John had witnessed the murder. Had Spots witnessed it too? If so, how long would it be before someone caught up with him? Unless—no. I wouldn't allow myself to think it.

Chapter 17

On Sunday morning, Whit called to say he'd run the piece on John's drowning. When he heard that I'd tried to play hero and resuscitate John, Whit was concerned. "Do you want to take tomorrow off?"

"I'd rather work. It will take my mind off things, but thanks for offering."

That afternoon, Billy arrived alone. The Sparrowville police determined that John's death was accidental. His family had been notified. He had just turned twenty-one and, according to Billy, was one of the top guitarists in the business. Spots and Duck had stayed in Vermont to make final adjustments on miking the drums. The rest of them would start recording on Monday. Word was the A&R execs wanted Vivi's tracks done as quickly as possible because there were doubts about how well she would hold up.

Once Billy conferred with Vivi and Cerita, the decision was unanimous. Everyone felt it was best to soldier on. Spots said he could use practice tracks John had laid down. Vivi's keyboards could replace some guitar parts. Someone would dub leads in later. To salve their consciences, they decided to dedicate the album to John. Vivi and Cerita wanted to go back to Wonderland that night, so they could get an early start in the morning. Because there was only one car, Billy had to drive them.

"I'm going to miss you. The kids too." I said to Billy. It was two in the afternoon, and I was taking the sheets off the couch. Vivi had gone to Morgan's to shower and dress.

Billy kneeled on the floor, building a Lego-saurus zoo with Keith on one side and Smokie on the other.

"Daddy. I want you to see me play soccer," Keith said.

Smokie put her thumb in her mouth. "Me too."

Billy hugged her. Then, noticing the jealous look in Keith's large gray eyes, he reached out and pulled his son close. He cast his velvet eyes on me. "Why don't we take a walk?" He stood up. "Keith, go find your soccer ball."

Keith shouted, "Yay!" and ran to the closet.

Billy swooped Smokie up in his arms. In a black cotton jumper over red shirt and leggings, she squirmed gaily. He lifted her onto his shoulders.

Smokie grabbed a fistful of his hair. "Ouch!" he said.

"Mommy! I can touch the ceiling."

"Come on, Zoë." Billy held one of Smokie's feet with one hand and reached out to me with the other.

Billy treated us to a ride in his spanking-clean rented Taurus. After hearing so much about the Gemini conservation area, I suggested we go there. I was curious to see what everyone had been battling over. The sun peeped through the gathering clouds, casting a golden light on everything.

The preserve, abutting woods and hills, contained several trails and was located in the southern section of the town. A path led through wet areas into woods, then up a long, grassy hillside, still green, to an orchard planted on its crest. The gnarled apple trees were partly denuded, twisted, and gray. Pale yellow leaves clung to their branches.

Keith ran along, struggling to make his ball roll up the grassy path. Every so often, Billy would give it a sharp kick and Keith would go racing after it with Smokie close on his heels.

"Could you come down next weekend for his game?" I asked as the kids ran ahead. Keith had tired of kicking the ball. Billy carried it.

"We're badly behind schedule now. Everybody's so creeped out over John, I think we're just going to work straight through till it's over."

"The kids miss you."

A shadow of anxiety played on his cheek. "We'll get back to normal as soon as the album is done."

"You have a lot on your mind," I said, not so much to absolve him as to quiet the discomfort that had begun to thud in my chest.

"I do."

"How long do you think the taping will take?"

"About three weeks, depending on whether we can agree. After Spots does the rough mix, we'll meet with the A&R guys and battle over the sound. Chances are they'll at least call for a remix. Maybe another song."

"Oh, Billy."

"Careers are riding on this. Vivi needs a hit. So does her record company angel. He wants something that'll go to number one and stick for a while."

We walked in silence.

"I wrote a new tune. We're trying to convince Vivi to record it as a duet." He named a popular male singer half her age, whom he wanted to approach.

"What does she say?"

"Wants me to sing the part."

"She *is* trying to steal you away."

He laughed, his hand at the back of my neck. But there

was something in the way he shook his mane of dark hair and tilted his unshaven cheek that disturbed me. "Listen, Mama Bear. I'd never do anything to hurt you. Believe that."

I buried my face in the indigo warmth of his sweater. The rich scent of lamb's wool and woodsmoke reminded me of the fires we'd curled up in front of during the previous winter, watching the flames dance and sipping cocoa, toasting marshmallows, and talking late into the night while the children slept. Sometimes he took out his old guitar and sang me tunes he was writing.

At the top of Gemini Hill, Billy helped Keith and Smokie into the branches of an apple tree. The children surveyed the panorama of fields and hills studded with scarlet, burgundy, and lemon. Despite the partly gray sky, the sun broke through and illuminated the rich autumn colors. The mountains in the distance were a palette of evergreen, russet, and gold. The Heritage River meandered like a deep blue ribbon across the far meadows.

"How are you holding up?" Billy asked, as we strolled down the hill back toward the car. We'd been talking about John's death, how shaken up everybody was. The kids played, coming close, then venturing far, but always staying within sight. They scampered, playing with sticks, tossing leaves in the air, shouting.

"I'm a basket case," I said. It was nice just to be near him.

"Not easy being a hero."

"When you save someone, they're not supposed to die."

He kissed me gently. Keith and Smokie seemed suddenly to have caught the same wavelength. They stopped their games with sticks and leaves and started running down the green slope. Billy saw them coming. They ran toward him at full speed. Just in time, he dropped to one knee and they hurled themselves into his arms. He fell backwards. The three of them became a squirming, wriggling, joyful pile. My husband, my children, in a moment of light.

We took the back way home, following Whittier Street toward Greymont Center. Maples lined the way. The dark trunks of the stately trees reflected the burnished copper of the setting sun behind us. Rosy light poured from under the dark underbelly of clouds, streamed through the branches, and glinted in the rearview mirror. The dying leaves on the trees turned amazing hues in this bath of saturated pigment, as if they'd been painted by a cartoon artist. Reds were shot through with fuchsia. Oranges became so extreme they appeared to have pink coronas. Yellows went from an innocuous lemon to a sulfur so acidic it threatened to blind the eyes. Yet you couldn't stop looking, even though the feast of color was so intense that it hurt.

Against the trunk of one of the oldest trees, someone had fashioned a witch. In the glow of sunset it appeared lifelike: legs flung forward, arms askew, green face smashed into the trunk, astride a broomstick that had run smack into the tree. It was a joke. A lifelike joke. But what I saw was Cassandra.

That night Billy drove Vivi and Cerita back to Wonderland. On Monday the rains came. The sky blackened. The heavens opened. For four days it poured. When Billy left he warned me he wouldn't be back until they'd gotten a good chunk of recording behind them.

As far as Whit was concerned, the Cassandra story dropped out of sight. I had my afternoons off, but starting Tuesday, I would spend most weekday evenings at Town

Meeting. In the mornings, I wrote up my stories and made calls. With the relatively light load, I had time to research Cassandra's background, her connection with Spots, and her legendary battles to save Greymont's open spaces from the developer's ax.

I did call Brannigan and tell him about John's death. He was close-mouthed, sharing absolutely no information, making me reluctant to share mine.

"Do you think there could be any connection with the death of Cassandra?" I asked.

"Hmm? What makes you say that?"

"He was here the night of her death. Then, four nights later, he accidentally drowns in Vermont. It's a coincidence."

"I hope you're not withholding evidence."

"You know me better than that, Detective."

"I'll check into it." He hung up with a bang.

Monday afternoon I decided to take the kids shopping for Halloween costumes. It would get Keith's mind off his awful day and keep us from being cooped up in the house while it rained.

"Ellis told all the kids I had cooties, Mom," he said. "And no one would touch me."

"Oh, Keith. I'm so sorry."

"I said I would kick his butt with a soccer ball, and he said he was going to kick mine."

"Oh, honey!"

I tried calling Mr. Keene, the teacher, but he was gone for the day. I considered calling Mavis French. Better let the teacher handle it, I thought. After my faux pas at soccer on Saturday, I didn't trust my conflict resolution skills. I was still having flashbacks to the inky water, John's dank lips, and the sight of Cassandra's body, her

Dancing with Mr. D

eyes staring. I just wasn't enough in control to handle a tricky interpersonal situation. I left a message. Mr. Keene would call back.

Halloween shopping would give us all the escape that we needed. We went to Toys for Tots, on Stanhope, about a half mile from the Plaza site, which was still marked off by police tape. The grand maple tree stood, its leaves red and orange against the gray sky. The driving rain had transformed the bulldozed meadow into a sea of mud.

Smokie found a headband with two tall fluffy white ears lined with pink. She donned a white mask, dubbing it a "wabbit face." She grabbed a purple fairy wand with a pink glitter star. We found a skirt in a matching gauze, and her "Magic Wabbit Pwincess" costume was complete.

Keith was nowhere near so easy.

"I want to be a lexovisaurus," he said with a decisiveness that bode no good.

"What's that?"

He reminded me that it was a dinosaur, twenty feet long with green and purple skin, triangular plates like a stegosaurus's down its back, and a long purple tail with a spike. I wondered if this wasn't some creature he'd imagined, but he insisted it was real—though extinct, of course.

I consulted with the woman at the counter. After a search, she dug up a green felt mask that went over his head like a bag. It resembled a horse's head, with scales going down the back like a mane and red felt flames shooting from the mouth.

"No. That's a dragon," Keith said. "I want to be a lexovisaurus."

I exchanged glances with the saleswoman.

"This would make a wonderful lexovisaurus," she told Keith, her tone far too saccharine.

"It's not purple," Keith said.

"You could buy a nice shiny purple cape." She glanced at me. "From the fabric store?"

"No," said Keith. "It has to have a long tail with spikes. It has to be purple and green. It has to be fat and have no flames. That's what I want, Mom. Let's go to K.B.'s."

"Honey, I don't think they're going to have one. Nobody makes lexovisaurus costumes."

"They have to. Come on, Mom. They have to."

I gave in to his whim because he'd been having such a hard time lately and I enjoyed shopping with the kids. We put the dragon mask on hold in case we couldn't find anything better and piled into the Civic. Ever since I'd found the Cambodian woman dead in her car the previous Christmas, I'd only gone to Heritage Mall when I couldn't avoid it. Now, as I headed there, I told myself my fears were crazy. But a shiver ran through me.

In fact Halloween shopping wasn't giving me the escape that I'd hoped for. The visual cues—the witches, ghosts, goblins, ghouls, and cadavers that abounded in store decorations—were much too close to the real thing. They kept triggering memories. When we passed the movie theater, some joker was playing a horror tape of Dracula laughing. It ended with a blood-curdling shriek, and I jumped a foot in the air. Smokie and Keith thought that was pretty funny, how scared I was and how startled. I held their warm hands and tried to bury my fear.

We spent a couple of hours shopping, but, of course, found nothing to satisfy Keith. Smokie grew tired and whiny. Keith began to behave monstrously.

Finally, at the fabric store, despite Keith's howls of disapproval, I bought two yards of shiny green polyester and a length of metallic purple.

"That's wrong," Keith shouted. "I won't wear it! Put it back!"

"Please, honey. Just in case we can't find something better."

"NO." He was on the verge of a tantrum. "That means you're going to make me wear it and I DON'T WANT TO."

Embarrassed, I knelt down beside him. "Don't yell, please," I whispered.

He folded his arms in front of his chest with an emphatic frown.

"You know what that is?" I said, trying not to lose it—and failing. The stress had caught up with me and this was the last straw. I shook him hard. "That's the pout of a spoiled child."

"Mommy, Mommy," chimed Smokie. "I'm good. I'm good. Keith's bad."

Keith slapped her.

I grabbed his hand. "Do not hit your sister."

"She called me a name!"

"In school didn't you learn to use words, not your hands, when you're mad?"

"Dad says if somebody calls you a name, it's okay to hit."

"Bad Keith. Bad. Bad. Bad," chanted Smokie.

"Stop it!" I shouted at her.

"Hey," said a friendly female voice. "Could you use a hand?"

I looked up. It was Kate Braithwaite, the old, cheerful, and endlessly competent Kate. She was on assignment getting "cute" photos of kids painting Halloween windows.

"What's the problem?" she asked Keith.

He explained about the costume.

"Why don't we see what you have at home," she suggested. "Maybe we can whip something up."

Keith brooded. After a few moments, he said, "Okay. Let's see what we can whip up." He liked the words "whip up."

"Dinner?" I suggested. "I have the night off."

"You're on," Kate said. "I'll pick up a movie for when the kids go to bed. Tear jerker or romantic comedy?"

"*Jurassic Park!*" shouted Keith.

Kate tapped the tip of his nose. "You're going to be in bed, mister."

Kate arrived at seven. Dieting, I explained to her when I served sole baked in aluminum foil with red peppers and mushrooms. I hadn't realized how famished I was until I finished my first helping and went back for seconds.

After dinner, Kate listened to Keith describe what he wanted for his costume. Then she pawed through our closets. Finally, we found a pair of old silk pajamas of mine in shimmery peacock blue. We refit them for Keith, while Smokie danced around in her princess bunny costume.

Kate found a pillowcase and cut holes for eyes. She stuffed it with old stockings to form a snout. Keith spent an hour happily decorating the mask with fabric paints to make exactly the costume he wanted. With wire hangers and sheets, we fashioned humps that went down the back and the tail. As a result of Kate's ingenuity, we had a happy kid, and I'd recovered from my own bout of temper.

Once the kids were in bed, Kate and I settled down in front of the TV with an upbeat romantic comedy. Later, we sat in the living room, munching unbuttered popcorn, and talked. After some complaining about the recording schedule and having to survive without Billy, I told her about trying to resuscitate John and how I'd been having trouble shaking the memories.

"I know," she said, "I was with Drew . . . when he—" She pressed her hand against her perfect white teeth. She shook her head and her braid swung in an imperfect half circle. At first it appeared that she was smiling, but she was fighting back tears.

"I'm sorry." I touched her shoulder. We'd had this talk before.

She kept shaking her head, the braid continuing to swing. "I've had a tough week myself. My mom has been very depressed. She sits and stares, won't get out of bed. Last night, my dad called. Mom was in the cellar, saying she wouldn't come up until she found Drew. Like she thought he was a little lost kid."

"That's hard."

"We just passed the second anniversary of his death. Lots of sad memories."

I sighed. "Sorry. Boy, your whole family has been under a lot of stress."

"We have."

"Has it all fallen on you?"

She closed her eyes, resting her head on the back of the sofa. She wore a forest green turtleneck and Levi's. Our feet were propped on the coffee table. Her size nines—long and narrow, like her lanky legs—were clad in cotton socks the same color as her shirt. Mine, smaller but nowhere near as elegant, were bare. And my manicured toes were painted a glittery blue.

She opened her eyes and studied a spot on the wall. "Ron's been fairly helpful."

"The night Cassandra died," I said. "I heard he was at your mom's."

Her dark gaze met mine. "I don't know how we would have got Mom settled without him. It took most of the night."

The conversation took a few turns. She was training a horse for some people, and there were problems with the animal. She was trying to talk her dad into boarding horses, thinking about maybe quitting the paper to help start a business.

"Kate," I asked when I found a moment to slip it in, "there was a right-of-way bought from your dad by a company called SilverSeed."

"How did you know about that?"

"I've been looking into all the people Cassandra caused trouble for over the years. It came up." I didn't say Tim Boudreau told me.

She nodded. "It saved us. Drew was scheduled for a marrow transplant, but . . . there was no money. Craig said he knew some man who was considering buying property behind ours. The deal fell through, but Craig's friend bought the access just in case. Why do you want to know?"

"Just curious."

"I've always suspected Craig made a gift of the money." She bit her lip. "My father has a lot of pride. He'd sell the land, but wouldn't take outright charity."

"Your father didn't suspect?"

"Maybe he did, but he could maintain the pretense and save face." She smiled through her tears. "I wonder if there will ever be a time when it doesn't hurt."

"You'll always miss him."

I handed her a tissue. She wiped her eyes.

"A lot of good it did us to watch a comedy," she joked.

"This has been a tough couple of years for your family."

"God. You should see my mom. I don't know if she's going to get through this. She sits and stares and weeps. Dad. Well, you know men. They don't show it as much. He goes off and plows fields that he forgets to plant. He almost turned himself over on the tractor a few weeks ago, trying to hay the meadow. I'm so scared that something will happen to him or to Ron. I don't think Mom could take it."

"Ron can take care of himself."

"But, Zoë, he's so full of anger. And his finances. What a mess."

We were silent for a few moments. I heard the tick tock of the old clock on the mantelpiece, inherited from my parents.

"Kate," I said, "what do you think of Craig's new wife?"

"Jenny?" she said, brightening.

"Not that I'm trying to solicit gossip, mind you."

"We went to high school together."

"Ah, a treasure trove just waiting to be tapped. What was she like?"

Kate giggled. "We didn't exactly run with the same crowd."

"What clique was she in?"

"Drama."

My mouth fell open. "I would have laid bets on cheerleader."

"We didn't have cheerleaders."

"You don't have cheerleaders? What's wrong with you? Un-American?"

She laughed. "Greymont, being the most politically correct town in North America, ditched it back when I was in elementary school. Girls do track, field hockey, basketball, softball, swim."

"Was she in plays?"

"Yeah. She was pretty good. She played the lead in *Bye Bye Birdie*."

"Ooh, I have to reevaluate my entire take on her." We might have stuff in common after all. "So what's the scoop on Craig? Why'd she marry him?"

"From the look on your face I assume you don't find Craig attractive?"

"Do you?"

"Yeah. Kind of."

"That snake oil salesman?"

Her eyes brimmed with a secret she seemed to be dying to tell.

"Have you gone out with him?"

"No."

"You have a crush?"

"Okay. A tiny one."

"Now why do I think there's more to it than that?" I wheedled.

"Promise not to tell?"

"Hmm. Sounds juicy. Scout's honor."

She smiled shyly. "He made a pass once."

"What happened? When?"

"It was when my brother Drew was sick. He'd visited and offered me a ride. We stopped somewhere and parked. He asked about my family, how everyone was faring. He was very sympathetic. And, well, he put an arm around me—"

I waited. She looked at me funny. "That's it?"

"No."

"Oh, come on. Tell. I'll tell you one of my nasty secrets in exchange. I'm sure mine is naughtier."

She laughed throatily. She really blushed, which was unlike her. "Well, I found it flattering. You know, that he thought I was attractive."

"And—?"

"And . . . he touched me. And I touched him." She drifted off a little dreamily. Then she suddenly realized who she was talking to. "God, don't tell anybody!"

"I won't. Where did he touch you?"

"Just about everywhere." She blushed terribly. "We— It was very sexual. He was still married to his first wife. I felt guilty, but I liked it. I thought he'd call. But he never did."

"Did he ever make another pass?"

"He offered me a ride, but I didn't take it."

"Why not?"

Her strong jaw tilted. "Pride. And the boyfriend." Ex-boyfriend now.

What a creep, I thought. I didn't say it because Kate obviously felt otherwise.

"You're not in love with him?"

"God, no! You know my current crush."

Mark the shark. "Here's one for the treasure trove. Do you think it's possible Craig was involved with Cassandra?"

She laughed loudly. "Not likely."

"How about Tim Boudreau. Do you think there was any hanky-panky between him and Cassandra?"

"God, you're full of funny ideas tonight," she said, giggling.

"I admit, they're an unlikely couple."

"That's not the half of it. Of all people, I'd expect you would know."
"What?"
"Tim—he's gay."

Chapter 18

During the next few days the sky was dark, the rain unrelenting. It beat the foliage off the branches. Water rushed along the gutters and ditches. Red and yellow leaves swirled onto the wet pavements and were trampled underfoot. The children wore boots and yellow slickers. Keith begged for Mark to come by for another soccer lesson, but I told him it would have to wait until the weather cleared. I called Billy several times, but he was busy, distant. I told myself that this was normal, just a professional hard at work on a difficult project. I did manage to connect with Keith's teacher, Mr. Keene. He hadn't noticed any problem, but assured me he'd watch more carefully.

"Ellis is a great kid," he said. "Are you sure he's the one who's causing trouble?"

"He's the person Keith keeps mentioning. Ellis calls him names, won't let Keith sit with his friends at lunch, tells the boys Keith has cooties—"

"I'll talk to the boys."

"Thank you," I said, wondering if anything would be done.

In the meantime, most of my work energy was focused on Town Meeting, which started Tuesday evening. It would run for the next couple of weeks, nightly in the middle school auditorium. My evenings were spent taking notes on the proceedings. My early mornings were spent filing summaries of the previous night's actions and writing forecasts of what was to come.

The vote on the new proposal by Ann Chatsford and Cletha Fair to create a memorial park on the Plaza site instead of a mall was slated to be debated the following week. That promised to be a terrific fight. Until then the work was routine.

This left me with ample time to research some back channels. I spent the next few afternoons at home on the telephone. In my years on the rock scene, first as a camp follower, later as a writer, I'd made a good number of friends. As a result, my little black book brimmed with backstage sources. I called about fifty people, from aging groupies to well-known musicians to has-beens and perpetual wannabes.

I finally found what I was looking for early Wednesday afternoon. I reached my former editor at *Rolling Stone*. A brazen groupie in her teens and early twenties, Deirdre had slept with everyone from top artists to minor impresarios to roadies. About a decade ago, she'd gone back to school, earned a Ph.D., and started churning out scholarly books on what she jokingly referred to as tartology—women who slept their way to the top.

I asked her about Spots and Wonderland Sounds.

"Oh, Spots!" she cried. "Sure. What a horny guy. Yeah, I knew him way back when."

"At the commune?" I was home alone. The kids were still at school. Outside the rain flowed in sheets down the windowpanes. The leaves had faded into a smear of pale yellow and tan.

"Oh no, before that. In New York."

"What was he like?"

"We were crazy with youth," said Deirdre. "Spots had an excess of talent and women. I've always felt he was one of the few who escaped the worst temptations, although I've heard he made his compromises.

"I came this close to sleeping with him. At that time, I think we used to call him Tom. Spots was his last name. Or short for it. Technically, I suppose you could say we did engage in sex, although it was quite brief."

She recounted an incident at a dance party that turned into an orgy. She and Spots had been in the same bed, but with different partners.

"He came on to me a few nights ago," I said. "I found him rather obnoxious."

"You always preferred cats you thought you could tame."

"I don't know if I've tamed my cat as much as I'd hoped."

"Problems?"

"Vivi Cairo is recording at Wonderland Sounds. Billy's helping write, produce, playing bass. He comes home one night in four."

"The key to understanding men is to realize that they are basically beasts. From agriculture to democracy, civilization is the creation of women. Men play in our fields."

"I don't know, Deirdre. I'm kind of hung up on old-fashioned ideas like caring for the children conceived during those romps in the hay."

"You sound like my mother."

I laughed. "That's what I am—somebody's mother."

We chatted for a few minutes about my kids. She'd never met Smokie, but she'd been in LA during my pregnancy with Keith. She knew what I'd been through with Billy. I'd forgotten how relaxing it could be to talk to an old friend whose past had been tawdrier than mine and who didn't make judgments. As the conversation drew to a close, we came back to the issue of Spots. She'd heard rumors about the source of his income, that he had connections with big-time dealers, but she knew nothing specific.

"What's this all about?"

"Well," I said quietly. "There's a little problem of murder."

"Not Spots?"

"No. He admits to having been the lover of a woman who was an activist in Greymont. Her name was Cassandra Dunne. Last week he and the band stayed in Greymont before driving up to Vermont. The night he stayed over, she died. The police are calling it murder."

Her voice was somewhat strangled when she finally spoke. Spots, she confided, had a habit of disappearing for a month or two at a time, then reappearing flush with money. The assumption had been that he dealt drugs.

"I suppose you should know. He had a violent side. Nothing to do with sex. He was one of those people who occupied that nether world, part techie, part tough guy. Criminals. The men with scars, black leather, chains, motorcycles. He moved in and out of that crowd. And, Zoë, if there's a chance he's involved in something illegal, steer clear. He might be dangerous."

"That name," I asked, "Cassandra Dunne. Ring any bells?"

"What did she look like?"

"I'll fax you a photo," I said, after describing the lopsided face and different color eyes.

"A high school yearbook picture would probably jog my memory more than anything recent."

"I haven't been able to trace her back to a hometown."

"Really?"

"No. The trail stops just before she moved to Greymont. Spots mentioned having an affair with her at Silver Wind Farm. She shows up two or three years later in Greymont with a mission to preserve every piece of land offered for development. That's what she seems to have devoted herself to for the past dozen years. Her bio on an old sheet for elections to the Select Board mentions growing up in Wisconsin, but there's no record of anyone of that name at the high school or in town."

"Dunne is fairly common."

"There were no female Dunnes in the high school records for the right years."

"Any mention of college?"

"None."

"Hmm. Sounds like she might have been one of the ones who slipped off the grid."

"That's what Spots said. Off the grid."

Later I reached a friend at a New York news magazine who had access to archives and databases. He offered to run a search for me. At the end of the week, he called with the following information: He could find no record of Cassandra. But he unearthed ample information on Spots, whose real name was Tom Sporkartch. Spots for short.

I asked my friend to run the name through his databases. A couple of days later, I received a three-page fax with a birthplace on Long Island, Amityville, a Social Security number, and a list of jobs. It ended when he was fired from a major label. Rumor had it he'd come in stoned one too many times . . . and screwed up a job that had cost the company mega-bucks.

Sporkartch then disappeared and reemerged as Tom Spots, apparently with the same Social Security number and a legal change of name. A member of the Silver Wind commune, he bought property in Sparrowville, Vermont, and founded Wonderland Sounds. He was a co-owner of land formerly incorporated as Silver Wind Farm, reincorporated as WonderWind Enterprises. Court records turned up only the name change and the filing for incorporation. There was no record of any arrest.

A more thorough search for Cassandra Dunne turned up the series of court papers filed in Massachusetts, the same cases I already had records of—suits over land use in Greymont. He found no driver's license. No bank account. No birth records.

I called the town elections office. Yes, Cassandra was a registered voter. The Social Security number on file, after a search by my New York friend, turned out to have been fabricated.

Well, I thought, Spots, you didn't make it completely off the grid. But your friend Cassandra certainly had.

On Thursday morning, the rain still pouring down, I checked in with Whit.

"One more thing," I said, after going through the upcoming Town Meeting stories. Whit looked at me from behind his antique mahogany desk, poised to return to his computer after our pre-deadline conference.

"I've dug up some interesting facts on Cassandra Dunne."

The benign expression on Whit's narrow face shifted subtly. The space between his eyes creased. The pointed chin pushed forward perhaps a quarter inch. The near smile flattened. He said nothing.

I drew in a breath, realizing that it was time to pitch.

"Brannigan's investigation is proceeding. I checked with him this morning, and there's no arrest pending. I think he's reached a dead end. I've done some digging through back channels"— I waited, but Whit didn't seem inclined to interrupt. My words echoed weakly in the air—"old friends in the music business. Two facts emerge. One is that the owner of the studio where Vivi was recording, Spots, knew Cassandra. They'd been lovers before she moved here. He has a shady past, with rumors, nothing confirmed, of drug dealing. He was here the night she died. By the way, he was out most of the night—where I don't know. I have nothing at the moment that we can go to print with, but I think it bears further investigation."

Whit's body was absolutely motionless. After a few seconds, he tapped the eraser of his number two editor's pencil on his blemish-free blotter—a fine robin's egg blue—which perfectly matched the ocean on the antique globe on a stand near the glassed-in bookcases. Behind him, through the bay window, leaves scattered and swirled in eddies of wind.

"And the other?" he said.

"I've tried to trace Cassandra various ways. She knew Spots during the time she spent at his commune in Vermont over fifteen years ago, before she came to Greymont."

He pursed his lips. "And?"

"And . . . I can't find a trace of her before that."

"Have you questioned Brannigan about this?"

"No."

"Well, that's where you've got to go first."

"Don't you think it's odd that there's no trace of her in the town high school she lists on her bio?"

Whit picked up the phone, pressed a few buttons, and after a moment asked to speak to Detective Brannigan. After another moment, he turned the phone over to me.

I got off after a few minutes. "He says they have no information on her previous to her arrival in Greymont. They ran a fingerprint check with the FBI. Nothing turned up."

"So she hadn't broken any laws."

"No. She hadn't been arrested. And there's John."

"An accident."

"That's what it looked like."

Whit's pencil drummed the blotter. He put down the pencil and pressed his thumb against his lower lip. He stood up, walked to the bay window, and gazed out beyond the Common and the brick Town Hall to the distant towers of exclusive Greymont College, his alma mater.

"There are rumors, Whit, that Spots made the money to build his studio illegally."

"Did they check out?"

"There are no arrest records, if that's what you're asking."

Whit returned to his desk, standing. "I'm going to put Mark on the story with you. Don't even think about objecting. Have a meeting with Brannigan or one of his people and fill them in before you go off on a wild goose chase."

"He's not going to give me inside information."

"He will confirm if he knows you already have it. You don't want to interfere on a lead he's already following. Keep a healthy distance. Don't go charging in like a bull in a china shop asking questions of anyone who might have had a hand in the killing. Understand?"

"Yes."

"Document everything. Work the paper trail and stay away from lowlifes. That's a job for the police."

"Yes."

Dancing with Mr. D

I was gathering my papers, trying to escape before he had a chance to impose more limits. Just as I was about to leave, something extraordinary happened.

Whit's lip twitched slightly. And then he smiled. It was such a surprise I stopped in my tracks. "Is something wrong?" I asked.

"No. No, not at all." He turned and gazed out at the Common with the leaves dancing in the quickening wind. "They're predicting a hard freeze tonight."

"Really?" I cast a thought to the bulbs I'd bought for a school fund-raiser that I still hadn't planted.

"I love that hint of frost in the air. My favorite season," he said. For Whit this was veritably voluble—three sentences about the weather. Probably the most intimate dialogue I'd ever heard from him in the year and a half on the paper.

"Do you like autumn, Zoë?"

"Halloween's kind of tough," I said, curious about his sudden foray into personal territory. "The kids, costumes, all that candy. They get kind of wild."

"With Billy recording, you must have your hands full. Why don't you take Halloween off."

"Gee. Thanks. Maybe I will."

He smiled at me awkwardly, seemingly unsure how to follow such a generous and uncharacteristic gesture for a flinty New Englander.

I let him off the hook. "We're going to throw a huge party when the recording is done. I hope you'll come."

"Sure," Whit said, "Love to."

"And bring a friend," I added with an insinuating smile. I'd thrown this in because I was curious to see his reaction. He didn't color as I'd expected, or stammer. But the room seemed to darken. He withdrew back into his workaholic shell.

"Well," he said somberly. "Time to get back to work."

As I was halfway out the door, Whit called. "Remember, from now on you're working with Mark on the murder story—especially about this character Spots."

"Yes, sir," I said, eager to get away.

"Take Mark on all—you hear that—all interviews."

"Yes."

"For corroboration. Understand?"

"Yes, sir."

He frowned, meeting my gaze. "Don't be foolhardy."

"No, sir."

I kicked myself for having raised Whit's concerns about danger. I didn't want to put myself in jeopardy, but neither did I want Mark cramping my style.

Several hours later, finished with my stint until Town Meeting tonight, I grabbed my Madonna bag, threw in my notes, and prepared to go home to regroup. I wanted to make some calls to find more on Spots, and I was determined not to make them within earshot of Mark, even if Whit had assigned him to partner me on the story.

I was about to leave when I heard the familiar "Hey Szabo, *qué pasó?*"

I'd just put on my jacket, quilted cotton Chinese with a pink peony painted on the back, something I wore when I needed to cheer myself up. Bright colors presented a brave face toward the rain and the dark thoughts I'd been fighting since John's death.

"Hey," Mark said. "What are you doing this afternoon?"

"I'm busy."

"Weather report says it might clear later. Maybe I can come kick the ball around with Keith."

"Thanks, but you've done more than enough already.

And even if the rain stops, it's going to be a sea of mud out there."

"Hey, a promise is a promise. Besides, Whit gave me a new assignment." He raised both eyebrows tauntingly. "Partner."

"Relax. The story's on hold till after Town Meeting." That would get rid of him for at least two more weeks. Plenty of time to finish my investigation.

"Don't give me that candy-corn smile, Szabo. I'm hip to your tricks."

I assessed his rough features, ruddy with health. His blue jersey with white raglan sleeves hung untucked over his snug khakis. "Yeah," I responded. "And I'm hip to yours."

"How about a quick lesson on getting a credit report?" His eyebrows went even higher. "Who do you want to check?"

Oh, for a look at Spots's or Craig's financial records. I repressed the urge to rise to the bait.

Chapter 19

Friday, the rain tapered off to a drizzle, then to overcast skies. Tim Boudreau lived in a small two-family dwelling situated on a pond in North Greymont, not far from a system of trails you could follow all the way into Maine. It was mid-morning. Ever since hearing Kate's gossip, I'd wanted to find out more about Tim. As I was scouting out the territory, a man emerged from the apartment next to Tim's. He had an energetic black Lab on a leash.

I stopped to pet the dog and struck up a conversation. Middle-aged and stooped, the man told me he was on disability. "Otherwise, I'd be working." He lit a cigarette, pulling in his sallow cheeks.

"I'm a reporter," I said. "I'm working on the Cassandra Dunne murder. Did you know her?"

His bug eyes widened. "Yeah. You want to know about her, talk to my neighbor. They were pals."

"Tim Boudreau. You often saw them together?"

"She used to come by here a lot." He lowered his voice. "Say, you think he was mixed up in it somehow?"

"I'm checking out backgrounds. Had she visited recently?"

He frowned. The dog jumped at the leash. "No. They had a fight. Last spring, I think it was. She stopped coming by."

"A fight?"

"Yeah. He's a quiet guy. Doesn't bother anyone. But her. Christ. Shouting something awful."

"Do you have any idea what it was about?"

"He came by later and apologized about the noise. Says they disagreed about something they were planning. He's one of these guys always pushing the environment. But he's nice about it. He built something around the culvert over there so the beavers couldn't dam it up. A swish, but . . . live and let live, you know?" He puffed on the cigarette. The black dog panted, drooling.

"Do you remember the night of the murder?"

"Sure. Last Wednesday."

"Did you notice any activity?"

"No. No activity. Boudreau was out."

"He was away that night?"

"Yeah. Last few weeks, he's been going out almost every night. He leaves around ten or so. Comes back around four, five in the morning, then he rides his bike to school. He teaches at the high school. Chester here wakes me up. I wish I could train this dumb dog not to bark when the bike drives up. He hears the door over there. Thinks it's robbers."

"Let me confirm. You're saying that Tim Boudreau came home at four-thirty on Thursday morning after being out all night? How can you be sure?"

"Easy, the police asked me the same question a couple of days ago." He grinned and then made a rasping sound that was part laugh, part cough.

That night after Town Meeting, I checked in on Smokie, who slept fitfully, always throwing the blankets aside. I pulled them up, tucked her in, and kissed her soft cheek. In Keith's room, I found him asleep with the light on, wearing his lexovisaurus costume, hugging two dinosaur figures made out of hard plastic. Poor kid. The dinosaurs were his best friends. I was grateful to Kate for having made the costume.

"Hey, sweetie," I whispered after I'd turned off the lamp.

"Mmm?"

"Want to change into pajamas?"

He was half asleep. I helped him out of the costume and into his nightclothes.

"Mom?"

"Yeah?"

"Is Dad coming home tonight?"

"I don't think so, honey."

"I want him to see me play."

I kissed him, brushing back his hair. "I'll give him a call. But don't get your hopes up, hon."

"If Dad says no, can you call Mark?"

"Oh, boy. Let me think about it."

"I love you."

"I love you too."

Later, I typed up my story, then read over my notes on Cassandra's death, and tallied up everything I'd learned.

She had been a lonely person, shrill, a zealot about the environment who alienated even her allies. All, that is, except Ann Chatsford. She was a good carpenter, handy with tools, at fixing things. She'd had an affair with Spots when she was young. In her twenties. If I'd read Spots correctly, she'd left him for someone else. Maybe someone she'd followed to Greymont.

In Greymont she'd worked closely with Tim Boudreau and Ann. She'd fought many battles with the biggest developer in the area, Craig Detweiller. Craig was a womanizer. Tim hinted that Cassandra was hung up on

Dancing with Mr. D

Craig. But they'd been bitter enemies. She'd caused him untold setbacks. She'd crossed swords with a number of others, namely people who'd tried to sell property to subdividers, for example, the Braithwaites.

People who had no alibi included Spots and Tim. I wondered about Ann. No, Ann was unable to climb a tree. I wondered if there were someone else. Some rival. Maybe the murder had nothing to do with the environmental battles she was waging. I kept getting the feeling it was personal. I wondered whether I should reread those clips and find other people whose land deals she'd ruined.

Then I thought about John's death. If it was purely a coincidence, an accident, then all the above still held. But say, for the sake of argument, it was murder. That meant someone at the studio had a hand in both deaths. Or someone from Greymont suspected John of having witnessed the murder. Someone sly enough to follow me to Sparrowville and then hide outside, lurking, lying in wait until John wandered off by himself. That meant there was a predator, capable of striking again if he—or she—suspected someone was close on his trail.

I thought about Mark with his smarmy grins. Whit was right, no matter how annoying Mark was. I had to be careful. I considered phoning him about soccer tomorrow. Keith really wanted him there. I checked my watch. Way too late. I'd call in the morning.

The wind gusted suddenly and I heard a crack at the window. Startled, I jumped. I looked out into the night, but saw nothing. To be on the safe side, I drew the curtains and double locked the doors.

Feeling lonely and frightened, I dialed Billy. So it was after midnight, I thought. He'd be up. They were probably still recording.

"Hey, babe," he said as if nothing were out of the ordinary.

"Coming home soon, or should I send out a search party?"

"We're making progress," he answered. "We finished the bass tracks tonight."

"Keith would love you to see him play soccer tomorrow."

"When?"

"In the morning—at nine. If the fields are dry enough."

He sighed. The weight of the world sat on his shoulders.

"You could drive down tonight."

"Hey, I'd love to, but I'm beat."

"I'm getting tired of unraveling my weaving every night while you're up there in the land of the lotus eaters playing with Circe."

He laughed lightly. "You're the only one I want to eat lotus with. You know that, babe."

"Sure."

"You're reading this all wrong."

"Prove it."

"We're coming Sunday."

"Is that the royal we?"

A silence.

"Billy," I pleaded, "it would be so nice to make it just the two of us. Can't you take an afternoon off from that woman?"

"She said you helped plan it. That's why we're coming down. She's got a big show scheduled."

"What?"

"Vivi's found a political theater troupe. She said she'd called you. Guess it slipped her mind."

"About what?"

Dancing with Mr. D

"She claims you cooked up this scheme."

"Huh?"

"The rally for Cassandra."

My mouth went dry. I'd figured it was just a momentary mania that would pass like a dream. I swallowed. "Me? It was all her idea—well, mostly."

"She was on the phone for an hour last night with a woman from *People*. And there's a film crew."

"A what?"

"They did a documentary on the Amazon a few years back. They're based here in Vermont. They seem to think this is a gas—you know, the Chico Mendes of Western Massachusetts."

"Don't laugh. It's not funny. When is this happening?"

"On Sunday. I told you."

"Great, she could have at least clued me in."

"Viv, Zoë's on the phone. Wants to know about your newt protest."

"Zoë!" Vivi's mellow soprano sang into the phone. Whatever doubts she'd suffered seemed to have been overcome. "Billy told you? *People*? And a mother lode of other magazines. We're doing it Sunday afternoon in that gorgeous square across from your paper. I wanted to stage it at the base of the tree where she fell, but the police prohibited it. My publicist has been working overtime. The press releases were faxed today. Didn't you get one?"

"No." I suspected she'd made sure I didn't hear of it until there was no way to stop it. Jeez. What would Whit say? There my reporter's objectivity went—right out the window. I felt myself sinking into hot water.

"Tell those Greymonters to hold on to their hats, because Vivi's coming back to town. And we are going to *boogie*."

"Is Spots coming?" I asked.

"No, he's going to take advantage of the quiet to put together a rough mix. We are marching on this album. Something pulled us all into focus. I'm starting keyboards tomorrow." She paused. I thought she might mention John, but she didn't. "Billy's such a sweetheart," she added breathily, "he's rewriting some of my charts."

"So, how about tomorrow?" I persisted, once Billy was on.

After a heavy silence, he said, "I don't think so."

"Why not?"

"Recording, babe—"

"But you finished with the bass. It's Vivi tomorrow."

"Listen," he murmured quietly enough so I could tell he didn't want her to hear, "she needs me."

"Keith doesn't?"

Silence, then a rush of air as he exhaled. "Tell Keith I'm sorry about missing the game. We'll talk Sunday after the rally."

"You're not participating, are you?"

"If there's publicity, I want my share."

"Sounds like some diva is rubbing off on you."

"What's that supposed to mean?"

"Nothing. Sorry."

"Hey, listen. We'll go somewhere, just the two of us, when all this is over."

"Yeah," I said quietly. "I'd like that. God, Billy, I miss you so much."

We disconnected. The channel between us was suddenly gone. I held the receiver, listening for words still caught inside—an unarticulated message he'd meant to impart. I pressed the button and switched off the power.

On Sunday, the weather cooperated with Vivi. The sky was bright blue with a few thin threads of clouds. The leaves lay scattered on the green Common. The colors had faded. What only a few days before had been bright red and gold had turned dusty brown.

The publicist had called the local radio stations touting the free concert to launch a new campaign for Vivi's foundation and to announce her forthcoming album, *Eve's Ambition*. They'd notified the national media, a surprising number of which had shown up. There were *USA Today*, *People*, fan and music magazines, even a couple of women's glossies.

The film crew hovered about with cameras. The political theater troupe roamed on stilts and in whiteface doing a dumb show. One was dressed as Cassandra, a cross between a witch and Joan of Arc. Another was dressed as a backhoe. Another as a tree. Another as a spotted blue newt. There were even a couple of evil developers chasing each other around merrily, providing ample entertainment for the children.

At two in the afternoon, the band took the stage.

"Ladies and gentlemen," Billy announced, playing MC, "I am pleased to introduce a lady who needs no introduction—" Applause. The crowd grew restless. Finally, Billy shouted her name: "VIVI CAIRO!"

Vivi climbed onto the small wooden stage, mike in hand, dressed in a flashy green costume. It was made out of shiny material, with a hint of a tail, a tall spray of bluish gauze framing her face, sprinkled with glittery blue. I supposed it was intended to represent the newt, but it looked more like an outfit from a futuristic movie than any creature I'd ever seen. Duck was a developer in a top hat. Cerita was Mother Earth. Morgan, in an Uncle Sam costume, had been made an honorary member of the band. He played harmonica.

"If you get lost," Duck had said when Morgan objected that he couldn't keep up, "Just toot loud. Everybody will think you're right and we're wrong."

The music ranged from familiar hits from Vivi's vast repertoire to new tunes she and Billy had written for the upcoming album. After about half an hour, Vivi began a breathy speech into the mike while the band quietly vamped behind her.

"Is everybody having a good time?"

Applause. Shouts.

"I can't hear you!" Holding her hand to her ear—joking, the shouts had been uproarious. "Can you tell me, a little louder?"

More shouts. Whistles. Catcalls.

"Ladies and gentlemen," she said, "boys and girls. I want to dedicate this next number to a very special lady. Unfortunately she can't be with us today. You know, ladies and gentlemen. We can only enjoy the beautiful sky. The bounty of this vast, green, beautiful earth. The rich colors of your beautiful New England autumn—if we are willing to do what it takes to protect it!"

More cheers. Music going up. Vivi vamping, then coming to rest, things growing quiet.

"I want to dedicate—do you know what that means, ladies and gentlemen, that word 'dedicate'? I looked it up in the dictionary last night . . ."

I wandered about as she spoke, leaving the kids watching the concert with Dania. Mark, who had shown up at the soccer fields on Saturday to Keith's delight, was on duty reporting. So I was free to scout out the townsfolk.

Kate, sour again after I'd mentioned the event, had deliberately stayed away, as had her whole family, with the exception of Ron's wife, Sandy, who stood on a rise alone with her two children, looking on from a distance.

Dancing with Mr. D

Cletha Fair and Ann Chatsford stood with the environmental crowd. I saw Tim Boudreau, but, like Sandy, he seemed out of place. He'd lost friends since switching sides on the Plaza.

At the edges I spied Whit, with the town's leading lights. Mavis French. Stuart Livingston, Greymont's town manager. Several selectmen and women. Even Craig and his wife, Jenny.

"Hi," I said, approaching this group.

Whit nodded. Craig offered a pleasant hello.

"Hi," I said to Jenny.

She smiled brightly, her teeth small, her gums thick. Her hair was in a bouncy pageboy. She wore what appeared to be rabbit fur, all white and fluffy. Not the best choice for an environmental rally.

"Like your jacket," I said.

"Thanks."

"What do you think of the turnout, Craig?"

"Vivi Cairo's a particular favorite of mine," he said genially. "Most people are here to see the show and have a good time."

After a while, Vivi, taking a break in the music, called, "Now, I want to introduce someone very, very special. She's ninety-two years YOUNG!!!"

A few people applauded. I noticed Cletha whooping with her group of activists. The kids whose hair was shaved, or dyed outrageous colors, or worn in dreadlocks. The earnest women in bulky sweaters and baggy jeans. The mellow men like Boudreau, with shaggy hair, faded pants with frayed knees, and running shoes with holes in the toes.

They clustered around Ann Chatsford, applauding loudly as she briskly walked to the stage. Billy helped her up. Her back slightly stooped, her thinning curls white as the clouds and just as wispy, she mounted with difficulty. She walked toward Vivi center stage as if she belonged there.

"Hello, dear," she said loudly into the mike.

"Ladies and gentlemen—ANN CHATSFORD!" Cheers spread through the crowd. People were taken with the old woman.

Vivi laughed breathlessly into the mike. "When we spoke earlier, she asked me when was the last time I hugged a tree." Vivi paused. There were titters of laughter. "I admitted, I never had. So when we met this morning, she took me to the place I think some people are calling the Plaza site. And she and I"— breathy pause— "took a few minutes of quiet. We put our arms around the magnificent maple, its foliage absolutely breathtakingly ablaze—" Now this was an exaggeration. The leaves had been battered by the week's wind and rain. But people called out and applauded.

"We stretched our arms. The two of us together, and we still couldn't reach all the way around it. What do you say, folks. Is this a tree that should fall to the developer's ax?"

Shouts of "No!" and "Save the tree!" and "Save the newt."

"Habitat." Vivi added. "That's what it comes down to at the end of the day." Breathy pause. "Habitat.

"Why don't you tell them what you told me this morning?" Vivi coaxed.

Ann cleared her throat. "You have such a beautiful voice. Nobody wants to hear my old croak."

Cries of encouragement. "Speak! Speak!"

"Trees need what humans need," she began. "Fresh air. Clean water. Nourishment. Sunlight."

Vivi smiled dubiously. "Even love?"

Ann chuckled. "Yes. Even love. They procreate, send off their seed. New trees grow at the base of the old."

The crowd applauded as Vivi cooed, "Isn't that sweet?"

"So," Ann continued, "the best way to protect ourselves is to protect the trees. It's lovely to see all of you out here today. Contact your representatives in Town Meeting. Ask them to vote for our proposal to make the Plaza site into a park, in memory of Cassandra . . . and as a tribute to the trees."

The crowd broke out in cheers of support. It was a moving moment.

I glanced toward Craig, standing near Mavis. He smiled coolly. They might as well have been applauding him, his attitude seemed to convey.

Jenny turned to me. "I can't believe they're doing this. She was such a nasty person."

"Did she do anything nasty to you?"

"Lots."

"Such as?"

She leaned toward me, confiding. "When we got married"—her eyes indicated Craig—"she came to me and said all kinds of awful things about him."

"To your house?"

"Yeah. I had to call Craig before she would leave."

"Really. What did she say?"

"Crazy, witchy things."

Mavis murmured something to Craig. The two of them laughed.

"Such as?"

Jenny looked reluctantly toward her husband.

"A lot of people have told me she was nasty, but I've heard no concrete examples."

"She wouldn't come out and make a direct accusation," Jenny whispered. "But she said Craig was a criminal, that he was a womanizer, that he—" She flushed, suddenly remembering she was speaking to a reporter. "I can't remember all of it."

"What kind of crimes did she say he committed?"

She shrugged vaguely. "Crazy things."

Meanwhile, on stage, Vivi and Ann were winding up. Vivi was singing "Froggy Night." She taught Ann the chorus and everyone sang.

The rally concluded with Vivi urging everyone to STOP THE PLAZA PROJECT.

I watched Craig through the whole rally. He seemed mildly amused, above the fray. Mavis looked disdainful, irked, but Craig jollied her out of it. "Loosen up, Mavis," he kidded her. "This is democracy at work."

"Honey, where I come from, a bunch of white folks screaming is called a lynch mob."

He smiled. "Rest easy. I'm the target here. Right, Zoë?"

"I'm just an impartial observer."

Craig turned to Whit. "You train them well."

Whit said nothing, but the glance he aimed at Craig wasn't his most amiable.

While the cameras, the film crew, the political theater troupe, the TV folks, and the magazine sycophants crowded around Vivi, Billy stood near the stage, speaking with a woman from *People*. Beside them was Dania, with Smokie and Keith, who jumped all over his dad like a puppy.

I split to corner Tim Boudreau, who was on his way to the parking lot.

"Hey, Tim," I said, catching up with him.

"Hi." His green eyes were friendly enough, but he seemed a bit on edge.

"Just give me a word or two on the rally."

"No comment."

"No comment? From one of the town's leading environmental activists?"

"I don't like to be pigeonholed."

"Are you still backing the Plaza project?"

He paused. Then, very quietly, he said, "Yes."

"The heartfelt pleas of nonagenarian Ann Chatsford didn't affect you?"

He seemed to lose patience, then he snapped himself back under control. "I admire Ann. I happen to disagree with her on this one issue."

I had my pen and pad handy. I jotted that down. "Is somebody pressuring you?" I asked.

"No. I'm evolving."

I never trust people who start talking about their spiritual evolution. My skepticism must have showed in my face, because he went on.

"Evolving my views. Fighting over a few acres in the middle of downtown is a total waste of energy. If people want to do something, they should be up in arms about the loss of wilderness. This is a diversion. And if you want my opinion, Cassandra thought so too. Look at her history. Look at it. She usually didn't fight downtown development."

"Oh, but she did. I have the records."

"She made a show of it, but she always backed down. She chose her battles. Never before did she go to the mat over a downtown space. I just don't get it."

He was shaking when he finished.

I was about to ask more when we were interrupted by a shrill scream.

Tim and I ran in the direction of the shouting. A crowd had gathered around Vivi's van. At first, I didn't want to push my way through, because of what had been there waiting for me twice in the past few weeks. Please, I prayed, don't let anyone—

Despite my misgivings, I elbowed my way into the tight knot of townsfolk, some familiar, some strangers, who pressed to see what had elicited the screams.

And then I saw.

EVE'S AMBITION. The mural that decorated the side of the van had been vandalized. The portrait of Vivi, with her animals in her hands, had been touched up by a mischievous joker.

A streak of blood cut across the woman's throat. Violent gashes of red paint had been splattered across the rest of the mural in a malevolent fury. At first I thought they were just random slashes, and then I realized they spelled out a message:

NEXT TIME YOU DIE

Chapter 20

Mark wrote the story on Vivi's event and the threat on her van, since I was too personally involved. Whit slapped on a headline categorizing it as a publicity stunt. He placed it low on the arts page under the fold. So much for star power.

Brannigan had come by to look at the van. The police said they were investigating the matter, but privately Brannigan told me—off the record—that he thought Vivi's public relations staff might have cooked it up. Vivi seemed so frightened that I didn't believe it was a stunt. However, I couldn't be sure.

As soon as the event was over, Billy and the band drove back to Vermont. Badly shaken, Vivi insisted on getting out of Greymont as quickly as possible. When I suggested to Billy that Vivi go with Duck and Cerita in the van, so he could spend the night, Vivi heroically agreed.

But as she drew near the van, she fell apart. "God," she said at the last minute, clutching her neck and gaping at the vandalized portrait. "I can't."

Her Abyssinian eyes exuded vulnerability. "Maybe we can fit everybody into the Carrera and Billy you can drive the van in the morning." But of course, with the instruments, that was impossible. Knowing it was useless to argue, I silently gritted my teeth.

The kids and I had to content ourselves with a fifteen-minute chat over coffee at a local snack shop while Duck and a roadie packed up the van. Smokie stroked Billy's cheek and put her fingers into his ears. Keith described his lexovisaurus costume and the new drill Mark had taught him after yesterday's game. Only half listening, Billy and I exchanged somber glances across the table.

Before leaving, while Vivi watched from the passenger seat of the silver Carrera, Billy held me close. The kids hugged his knees. I folded myself into his arms and entreated the gods for his safe return.

On Monday, Mark pestered me to put our heads together about the murder story. I finally gave in. We spent an hour going over what I'd discussed with Detective Brannigan: the possible time of death, the bulldozing, the people I'd called who'd heard noise during the night. To keep him busy, I suggested he research Delstar's finances. I kept my suspicions about Craig's personal connection and my growing concern about Spots to myself. No need to confuse Mark with these minor details.

I took work home and made calls in the afternoon. I managed to find an old friend of Spots who was willing to talk. Yes, Spots had had many lovers. About drug dealing, aside from a few innuendoes, the friend was more circumspect. No, he couldn't recall a Cassandra Dunne. I faxed him the photo from the paper. That failed to ring any bells. The first thing I had to do was find an old picture of Cassandra, which meant another visit with Ann Chatsford. Then I remembered I could easily talk to her that night.

The Town Meeting beat had turned out to be fun. Since people liked to read their own quotes in the paper, I had to take down the occasional rhetorical flourish. But the cool thing was observing the behind-the-scenes plotting in the back aisles.

Tonight I watched Craig Detweiller work the room. He wandered about the edges of the large W-shaped middle school auditorium, its back section of seats awkwardly split by a lighting booth. I finally cornered him, asking how he intended to stop the motion.

"Zoë, you know I'm a believer in that old adage, 'Where there's a will there's a way.'" He cast sparkling eyes on me, touching my shoulder.

"How about a preview. What are you offering those nice old ladies in lieu of their park?"

"There's no reason why we can't all agree."

"Oh?"

"A fountain surrounded by flowers in an inner atrium with a skylight. Just a little remodeling. That's all we need."

"An atrium in a mall to commemorate a radical ecologist?" The guy's shamelessness astounded me. He got away with it too.

"I have my architect working on it right now. Come on, loosen up." His cold eyes courted warmth as they met mine, reading me loud and clear. The guy wasn't stupid. He knew what he was doing. "Ann thought it was a lovely idea. Ask her."

I duly noted his design idea in my notebook.

Finally, it was time to debate the motion brought forward by Ann and Cletha to stop construction. The town had donated some of the land for the project, so they could do that, if enough people wanted.

Craig rose to speak. Whatever their views, people liked Craig. He was smooth. He laced his comments with humor and was never defensive.

Craig didn't urge or cajole. He was more subtle. He told a little joke that illustrated what could happen if one put off action too long. He looked boyish and friendly. He reminded people of the eyesore of having a construction site open over several years. He mentioned how much money it would take to turn the area into a park.

"One can admire one's adversaries," he said. "Cassandra Dunne was the most worthy of foes—intelligent, articulate, impassioned. It is only fitting we build a memorial in her honor." What could be more appropriate than a rustic atrium fountain in a skylit garden at the center of the new Plaza Mall? He described it in great detail. When he was finished, the auditorium was hushed. Gosh, I almost wept.

In response, my old friend Cletha Fair stood. She spoke pleasantly, but a bit more forcefully than Craig, relating her memories of Greymont all the way back to her youth.

"I don't want to be seen as a Luddite, but neither do I want national chains to gain a foothold in downtown," she argued. "What will we lose? Friendships with local merchants. The natural beauty of the village area, the trees, the mix of homes, businesses, and parks. I've spent this week perusing early photographs of Greymont. It's surprising how much that was here a century ago has remained.

"Why? Because my grandparents and great-grandparents—and many of yours—honored tradition. Their first instinct was to preserve beauty, to preserve nature, to preserve town landmarks. I would like to pass on their legacy to my great-grandchildren and yours.

"As for an atrium, an indoor atrium. What kind of memorial would that be for the Cassandra Dunne I remember?" She aimed a laser glance toward Craig. "An undeveloped green space would be far more appropriate."

She sat down to a warm round of applause. But I counted. The applause came primarily from a section seated around her, the radical fringe. I estimated that Craig would win hands down.

Just as the vote was about to be called, Ann Chatsford moved to amend the original motion. She wore a blue pants suit with a frilly blouse. Unlike many female Greymonters who eschewed makeup, Ann wore a smear of red lipstick and rouge. As the oldest member of Town Meeting, she got away with things no one else could. So people listened while, voice quavering with age, she offered an amendment that would delay a final vote until spring.

"After all," she said, "Mr. Detweiller has put forth some fine proposals. I think we ought to have time to consider them carefully. Perhaps he might alter his design to allow for an outdoor garden, which would be more in keeping with Cassandra's spirit."

Craig in a rare show of pique objected, though pleasantly, saying this would delay the process unnecessarily. Mavis French rose to support him, as did several other shopkeepers. But, after some procedural jousting, Craig lost to the little old lady in blue. It was as if Cassandra had reached up from the cold grave with ghostly hands and cheated him of his victory, just when it was finally within his grasp.

For an instant, and only an instant, he actually showed signs of ill humor. Then he returned to his smiling, easygoing self. He heartily congratulated Ann on her motion, chatted her up, and presented the idea that they both really wanted the same thing.

Later I drew Ann aside. After congratulating her on her victory, I tried to maneuver the conversation to the subject of Cassandra's finances.

"Could you tell me how she came to live with you?"

Ann related that it had been right after the Gemini Hill Farm fight. "She was looking for a place," Ann told me. "We worked out an arrangement. She'd help me keep my house up. I'd rent to her at a price she could afford."

"How much was that?" I'd learned early in my journalistic career to go for an exact figure.

"Well, this was fifteen years ago. I charged her $125 a month, including electric."

"Whew. That's cheap."

"She fixed anything that broke. Plumbing. Toilets. She even built new steps for the porch. She did the mowing and kept up the vegetable garden. I'm right in town, and she didn't want a car. She always walked or took the bus. Always paid on time, first of the month."

"Did you ever raise her rent?"

"No. She was such a convenient tenant and the mortgage is all paid off. It was nice to have something coming in, helped with the property tax."

Guessing the value of Ann's place, I knew the rent couldn't come near to paying the taxes. "Did she have a job?"

"She had inherited a little money, so she didn't need to work. But she wasn't lazy. And she was very frugal. A small stipend, she called it. From a distant uncle."

"And she gave you a check on the first of every month?" I was angling to find out which bank she used.

"No."

"You just said—"

"She paid me in cash." Ann leaned forward and imparted this as if it were a delicious secret.

"Always in cash?"

"Yes. Always."

"Where did she get her money?"

Ann looked me in the eye. "I don't know."

"I wonder if the police found cash in her place."

"I don't think so."

"Why not?"

"They didn't look very hard. Just between you and me"—she checked to make sure no one was listening—"I don't think she kept it here."

"Then, where? Did she have a bank account? A safety deposit box?"

"Oh, she was secretive," Ann told me, her eyes shining. "I don't trust the police." She shook her head. "They didn't like her. I agree with what that pretty singer—Vivi—said at the concert. Did you see what they did to her car? Next they'll come after me."

I felt my smile fade.

"Is Vivi a friend of yours?" Ann asked.

"My husband and she are recording an album."

"Hmm." Ann scrutinized me. "Well, you keep an eye on him."

"Oh, I will. Who were you saying didn't like Cassandra?"

"The police chief. Bob Sodermeier. Told me I should get rid of her as a tenant. And Craig, Stuart, even Whit. Nobody liked her. They won't even investigate that threat painted on Vivi's car." She scrutinized me more carefully, looking deep into my eyes. "You find her killer."

I demurred. "I'm just a reporter."

"No, you'll flush out the rat."

"I'll try."

Ann nodded approval. "The only way around Craig," she confided, "is to flatter him. Make him think you're going along. Otherwise he'll make mincemeat of you. Cassandra was the only one willing to fight him openly. And even she chose her battles."

Town Meeting had emptied. I offered to drive Ann home, mentioning that I could use some early photos of Cassandra to aid in my quest for the murderer.

"Usually I walk," she objected. "Oh, all right."

On the way, she told me more about Cassandra's secret source of income.

"She'd get low on money. Then she'd disappear for a few days. Sometimes as long as a week. When she returned she'd have cash. I wasn't supposed to notice, but it's hard to live so close to a person without knowing her business."

"Do you know where she went?"

"She had a place in the mountains. She outfitted herself for hiking when she went on her excursions. She'd take a bus to Springfield. When she first moved in, I had my car. I offered many times to give her a lift, but she always refused. She didn't want me to know where she went."

"Did you ask?"

"Once or twice."

"What did she say?"

"She told me she went various places. The White Mountains. The Adirondacks."

"And you think she was lying?"

"Oh, I know she was."

"How?"

"I followed her," she whispered gleefully.

"You did?"

"I was so curious, I couldn't help myself. You have to admit it was strange. She had no job. Never wrote a check. Once she told me she didn't trust banks. I asked where she cashed checks. She said she never got checks. I asked, 'Where do you get your money?' She said she 'sort of clipped coupons.' Well, Henry left me a few of those bonds with coupons, and I know darn well you need to cash them at a bank."

"So you followed her?"

"Yes.

"Where did she go?"

"She bused down to Springfield, then took the train."

"Where?"

"Vermont. What was it? Darn. Oh yes, a place named after a bird."

"Sparrowville?"

Ann studied me shrewdly. "How did you know?"

Chapter 21

Ann Chatsford told me she'd followed Cassandra several times. On each occasion Cassandra took the train to Sparrowville. Although I'd promised Whit I'd stick with Mark when working on the Cassandra Dunne story, I reasoned that this trip didn't really count. If Sparrowville turned out to be a dead end, the two of us would have wasted a day. And if I did find something, I always had my cell phone.

Early the next morning, after giving last-minute instructions to Morgan, who had agreed to ferry the kids to school, I slipped out of the house. I left before six, thereby being certain to elude Mark, who would most certainly cruise by around seven as he had the previous day. I certainly didn't want him around when I checked the public records on Wonderland Sounds to see what kind of financial and legal arrangements propped up Spots.

I wore a black and yellow parka, snug purple corduroys, and a matching purple poorboy sweater with one thick black stripe across the chest, bordered by two narrow pink ones. It was hunting season, so I wanted something bright. I took a backpack of Smokie's, just big enough to fit a two-liter bottle of spring water, fresh reporter's pads, pens, my micro-recorder, minicassettes,

Dancing with Mr. D

batteries, flashlight, a tiny pearl-handled jackknife—a gift from my mother when I'd expressed an interest in whittling at twelve, and, of course, my cell phone. My Honda started without difficulty. All was well with the world.

With the mercury in the mid-forties, the chill of fall filled the air. I climbed the mountains of the Interstate ascending into Vermont and slapped *Rubber Soul*, one of my favorite traveling albums, on the cassette deck. My shoulders bounced to the beat as the Civic sped up the Interstate cheered by the buoyantly tuneful "Drive My Car," "Norwegian Wood," and "Run for Your Life." One great song after another.

The rising sun painted the horizon pale yellow and gold. As Paul and John preached of sunshine and love, the morning rays bathed the evergreen mountains in brilliant color. The vistas sang of farmlands, faded old barns, rusty weather vanes, village hamlets with white church spires, and wooden houses with gingerbread trim.

An hour and a half later, I arrived in Sparrowville. I pulled into a gas station and showed the attendant a photo of Cassandra. She looked familiar, he said. The mechanic slid out from under a truck long enough to suggest I stop at Bella's Cafe. Bella knew everyone.

Down the road I found the restaurant. The pine interior was packed with customers. Most wore workclothes. But a few were dressed as flamboyantly as I, obviously tourists, even though the height of the foliage season had passed.

I sat down at the counter and scanned the menu. Pancakes. Waffles. Eggs and bacon. I thought about how my corduroys clung to my thighs—still a tad tight.

A middle-aged waitress with a face like a cherub approached.

"Is Bella here?"

"I'm Bella."

I ordered a poached egg.

"Sorry. Scrambled or fried?"

"Scrambled. Thanks."

She took the menu.

"I wonder if you could help me. Do you recognize the woman in this photo? At the gas station they said you knew everyone."

She squinted at it. "Mmm. Why?"

"I'm an old friend. She has a place around here somewhere. I'm trying to find it."

"We have a phone book over there."

"She doesn't have a phone. It's a rustic place up in the mountains. No electricity."

"I think I know who you mean. She has a place up on the other side of the mountain. You have to hike in." She frowned. "You know who could help you—Spencer Prouty."

After eating a bite or two of the eggs, I followed her directions out of town. I drove straight past the turnoff to Wonderland Sounds. Instead I went down a small road that led up between the shoulders of two high mountains, over a pass, and into a rural area surrounded by rugged green peaks.

After a wrong turn, I retraced my path and finally came to a dilapidated house with four vehicles parked in front, two of which were junkers on blocks. Behind the farmhouse was a large falling-apart barn. The place smelled of earth and manure. I squished through the mud, past a chicken coop, to the front door. Luckily, today I'd worn my Reeboks. After a few moments, I was greeted by a man with a broad, pockmarked face and squinty blue eyes. He wore a red cardigan sweater, overalls, and blue slippers.

"Mr. Prouty?"

"Yup."

I introduced myself. "Bella at the cafe said you might be able to help me."

"Kick off those shoes. They're covered with mud. Come on in. Got a fire in the kitchen."

I followed him into a small kitchen. The windows and table were decorated with green print curtains and cloth. The cabinets looked homemade and old, all painted pale green. The walls were papered with pink roses climbing up green trellises. A wood stove stood on an elevated stone hearth and radiated heat. We were high in the mountains, somewhere in the middle of the state. Despite the bright sunshine, the day was cold.

"I have some cake, if you'd like. Hot cocoa?"

"No thanks."

"Sure now? I'm having cake. My daughter, she comes by and leaves it for me."

He insisted on serving me cocoa and cake.

"Mr. Prouty, I wonder if you could help me. I'm looking for a woman named Cassandra Dunne. She has a place up here somewhere."

I showed him my photos. He put on glasses and examined them awhile. "Yup," he said. "There's a woman got some land up the mountain. This looks like her. She comes through here a few times a year. Hikes in, lots of gear, stays a week or so, hikes out."

"It's really important." I said. "Could you give me directions?"

He paused, casting a shrewd eye on my clothes. "You're not with that big resort outfit are you?"

I stared at him blankly. "What outfit?"

He snorted. "The one that wants to buy everybody out."

"No. I'm not."

"Yup," he said, growing more relaxed. "They've been pestering me to sell my land. I thought you might be going up there to pester her too. They bought up just about everybody around here. They're going to build a resort. Condos. Ski trails. Lifts. Going to be another Stratton Mountain."

"I hadn't heard about it."

"I thought you might be one of them. They've been trying to convince me to sell. Course my land isn't so important. They can build around me. But that Dunne woman. She's got a prime piece and she's a real holdout. Almost eighty acres. Lots of good springs and water. Course, my daughter, she can't understand. 'Why not take the money, Dad?' she keeps saying."

I listened a little longer, impatient to get directions to the land. Finally, he finished the story of his trials with his daughter. He found an old topographical trail map of the area and marked it for me. He showed me how to find a logging road, the only way into the territory.

"Course they're building another one. Back around here. But your best bet is to go in from the west side. I'll show you. You're going to need to park here." He marked an X on the map. "It's about a two-mile hike from that point. You'll see a big boulder and an old stone wall. If you look carefully, you'll find a trail right here. That's my land over here. I used to log up there, believe it or not, with a horse and a sled.

"You walk up this way, you'll see some old gravestones. The trail isn't well marked. You might have trouble following it. Got a compass?"

I shook my head.

"I have one somewhere." He rummaged in a kitchen drawer and found one. "I'd go out and help you find it, but I've got a bad leg and my daughter—"

"You've done more than enough already. Thank you ever so much." I flashed my pearly whites.

"Hmph," he said, looking at me skeptically. "You going to be warm enough in that?"

"Yeah. I think so."

"Take water with you."

"I've got lots in the car."

"You should know the Mount Silver people don't like trespassers. Be careful not to wander off her land."

"Mount Silver?"

"That's what they call it. Everyone's always called it Beamon's Mountain, but that's not fancy enough for them. Word is they're going to start building in the spring. They've got the go-ahead from the state. That Dunne woman had a lawyer working on it, but folks around here, many of them want the jobs. Course, as long as she holds on to the land—"

He went to a desk near his telephone, rooted around in the top drawer, and drew out a silver business card with an elegant logo in blue and black. Mount Silver Resort and Mountain Properties. Printed on the card was a name, which I didn't recognize, an address in Montpelier, and an 800 number.

Going back to the map, he marked a line around the general area of her property, not that I'd have any idea if I did wander off it. "You'll find a little cabin up here. If she's there, she'll probably be in the cabin or nearby. I saw her at the beginning of the month, but I don't know if she's come back."

I thanked him again, folded the map, dropped it into my daypack with the compass, and drove away.

After following the meandering trails, I eventually found the logging road. A wooden bar stretched across it. I got out of the Honda, moved the bar, drove through, stopped, replaced the bar, and drove on.

Twenty minutes later I'd found the boulder Mr. Prouty had described. I was near the top of a high mountain with amazing views down the forested flanks into the valley and across to other rugged hills and mountaintops. The logging road switched back and forth, steeply climbing. Mostly I was in deep evergreen forest, but occasionally the road would emerge to a cleared area and I could see out over a panorama of mountains in rolling peaks, hillsides of gray and spruce, valleys full of mist. The blue of the sky had grown pale, and a bank of gauzy clouds clung to the horizon to the west.

Cassandra's land was posted with NO HUNTING signs. The Mount Silver land was marked by a huge sign saying ENTERING MOUNT SILVER RESORT AND MOUNTAIN PROPERTIES—CONSTRUCTION ONLY—FOR SALES AND RENTAL INFORMATION . . . It repeated the name, address, and phone number on the silver card Prouty had given me.

I parked the Honda behind a dense stand of firs, hoping it was hidden from sight. I grabbed my daypack, took out the map and compass, locked the car, and started to hike.

Carefully following Mr. Prouty's directions, I arrived at a narrow trail through a thicket of firs. I followed it, coming to a row of trees with more NO HUNTING signs posted every few feet. After crossing the narrow wooden bridge Prouty had mentioned, I was confronted by an outcropping of huge granite boulders. The trail seemed to stop.

I scrambled up the boulders to get a view. Across the

valley wisps of fog rose among the dark greens and smoky grays of the mountains. And then my eye caught a glimpse of the wood-shingled roof about twenty yards to my left. I slid off the boulders and forged through the brush until I found a small foot trail. Within minutes, I found myself before an exquisitely built wooden cabin, not more than twenty feet square. Every log appeared to be hand-cut, every shingle hand-hewn. Moss filled the chinks. A covered porch extended the length of the small edifice. The pillars were constructed of saplings, stripped of bark and polished. They cradled the corners of the porch roof between notches where the stubs of branches reached like fingers stretched in Ys. The door was padlocked, the windows shuttered tight from inside.

I tried each window just to make sure. I shimmied up one of the pillars and climbed onto the roof. Another thirty or forty feet down the slope, I noticed a small outhouse. I scrambled along to the small stone chimney, hoping somehow to find a hole large enough to crawl in. The chimney was covered. I pried a piece of slate off the top and looked down into sheer blackness. It was too small a space for me to slither down.

I dropped back to the ground, walked down to the outhouse. The door was latched from the outside to keep animals out, I supposed. I unhooked the lock and opened the door. It smelled faintly of lye and eucalyptus.

A branch of dried aromatic leaves hung in a high corner. A roll of toilet paper rested on a knob made of driftwood. The seat was covered with a finished oak board with a polished driftwood handle. Everything appeared to be carefully and lovingly crafted. I took out my flashlight, picked up the seat cover, and looked down the hole. Just what you would normally expect to see. No trunk full of money. I felt mildly disappointed.

As I was examining the walls of the outhouse for signs of hidden objects or secret panels, I heard a noise.

I froze for a second and listened. Twigs snapped as something moved through the brush. My heart turned to ice. I could make out footsteps and voices approaching.

I inched open the outhouse door a crack and peeked. All I could see were tree trunks, scraggly underbrush turning brown with the onset of frost, evergreen boughs, and withered leaves. A hint of sky. I could see no one, but the trail to the cabin was hidden from my view.

I closed the door. I locked it with a hook and eye.

The voices drew closer. I shrank into a corner near the door, and listened. All of a sudden, they were loud enough to make out actual words. Men. Two of them.

I was dying to see who was out there. But I didn't dare crack the door to peer out.

The steps approached closer. I heard leaves rustling under the heavy steps. Twigs and brambles snapped.

"Check there?" a deep voice said, so close I would have just jumped if my muscles hadn't been paralyzed with fear.

Something hard bumped the thin wood slats on the other side of the wall where I pressed my body. I hoped they wouldn't try to enter.

"Yeah. Look inside." This voice was higher pitched and had a hint of an accent.

I glanced at the flimsy metal hook and whispered a silent prayer. If they couldn't open the door, they'd know someone was inside. Not much of a yank would break the lock.

With trembling fingers, I reached up and unhooked the lock. I squashed my body into the narrow space between the door frame and the front corner of the sturdily built outhouse. I made myself as flat as a pancake. I drew onto my tiptoes so my feet wouldn't stick out. Like a little kid playing hide-and-seek, I shut my eyes and waited to be caught.

Fear stilled my pounding heart. Fear glued me to the spot. If the men didn't lean inside, there was a chance they wouldn't notice me.

The door burst open.

I sensed the size and heat of a body just outside. A man's heavy steps sounded on the earth right in front of the door, within inches of me. His hand bumped the wall.

I held my breath and waited for him to lean in and discover me. I was too paralyzed to scream or to breathe or to think.

"Nothing in here."

"What?" the other voice was saying. "Come on. We've got a visitor coming up the road."

The outhouse door pushed closed.

"Lock it," the voice instructed.

I heard the latch shut.

Chapter 22

Several minutes passed before I dared try the door. I couldn't hear footsteps or voices any longer. Despite the icy cold, sweat poured down my body. My forehead and neck were dripping. I took my water bottle from my backpack and drank.

Then, listening to make sure no one was outside, I tried to decide what to do, examining the walls of the narrow room in which I sat. The faint odor of dung invaded my nostrils. I glanced up at the eucalyptus hanging from a nail in a corner. Natural light filtered through a translucent plastic ceiling, which was angled up over the front wall, creating a high narrow vent covered by a screen to let in fresh air. I climbed onto the outhouse platform, propped my feet on the ledge, and managed to hoist myself high enough to peer out.

I had a good view of the path leading up to the porch of the cabin. A large man in a dark sweater strutted out onto the porch. Over his shoulder was slung something black. It looked like a military weapon. I closed my eyes and opened them to make sure I wasn't hallucinating.

The man turned, giving me a clear sight of the weapon, a deadly-looking thing with a jagged stock and a short, thick barrel. The few bites of food I'd eaten that morning did a cartwheel in my stomach.

Dancing with Mr. D

Then I remembered I had my cell phone! I slipped back down ever so quietly. I opened my pack, took out the phone, turned on the power, and tapped 911. I held it to my ear and waited. Static.

With frustration and annoyance, I pressed send again. Nothing happened. I examined the phone to make sure I'd typed in the correct numbers. My eyes were almost blind with fear and confusion. The red "no service" message blinked at me mockingly.

I closed the phone, returned it to my bag, and agonized over what to do next. How long would I have to wait? How long would the men stay outside? I wondered if I could somehow sneak out, use the compass and the map to find my way through the brush, staying off the trail, and find my car.

I decided it was too much of a risk. The gun strapped to the man's back looked as if it would be lethal to anything in range of his view.

I found my pearl-handled jackknife and opened it. In a couple of tries I flipped up the outside hook and unlatched it. After retracing my thought process one more time, I realized I had to get out of there. Sooner or later one of the men might come to use the outhouse, and I'd be caught like a sitting duck—up shit's creek with no place to go but one. I didn't want to think about it.

When the men disappeared from view, I stole out the door and relatched it. I crawled into the bushes where no one could see me. I heard a commotion behind the cabin.

Dropping into the thicket of underbrush, I pressed my body onto the ground, cursing my penchant for purple and yellow, trying to hide in the leaves, praying the men at the cabin were nearsighted. My heart pounded so loudly I thought footsteps were rushing toward me.

I forced myself to focus and poked my head through

the boughs to see what was happening. I crept toward the cabin, slithering through underbrush as stealthily as I could. Now I heard talking. A loud clap—like flesh on flesh. Another. A man's deep grunt. The thud of something heavy hitting something hard.

Inching my way up the hillside, I hid behind an outcropping of rocks and peered around the corner. I saw a group of three men.

One was the big man with hulking shoulders in the dark sweater. The other was bald, wider, and shorter. He wore a black leather jacket and gray slacks.

They held a third man, whom I instantly recognized.

His body was tall and athletic, his hair short and sandy, his features rough. He wore faded blue jeans, hightops, and a baseball jacket with the insignia of the State University.

The man with the assault rifle punched him in the stomach and he slumped forward. The other man held him.

I felt a surge of annoyance and frustration, mixed with terror and dismay. The man in the middle was Mark.

For a moment all I could feel was anger. Anger that he'd followed me. Anger that he'd managed to get himself mixed up with this, that he'd let himself get caught by these men. The anger beat through me. It warmed the icy blood in my veins.

I closed my eyes and forced my paralyzed brain cells to think. The anger dampened my fear. It clarified my mind. I watched as the man with the gun slugged Mark a couple more times. He muttered something about private property, asking if he knew where he was. Mark grunted sickeningly as they punched him.

They shoved him toward the cabin. The windows were still shuttered, but the door was wide open. They disappeared into the cabin.

Dancing with Mr. D

* * *

About fifteen minutes later, I was hidden in the lower branches of a spruce near the boulders, about eight feet above the ground. Below me in a crack in the rocks, I'd left my micro-recorder turned on as loud as it would go. I'd inserted an old tape of an interview from the summer. Stuart Livingston talking about the town budget.

In my hands, I gripped a heavy rock, which I'd dug out from a rocky area behind the outcropping of boulders. I'd fit it into my backpack, tied the strap onto the lowest branch, then climbed up, and hoisted the pack and tied it to the branch above me. I slipped down, set the recorder, and scooted up again. Now I sat on my perch, my parka turned inside out—the black fleece lining providing meager camouflage—and waited, breathing slowly, and watched.

Soon, the tall bulky man in the sweater appeared. He cocked his head toward the sound. He held the automatic weapon in one hand, tucked against his ribs. As he approached, I held my breath, hoping he wouldn't look up. He came close, probing around the rocks. I could have reached down and touched him. I clung to the branch with my legs, the rock poised, waiting for just the right moment, trying to summon the courage to act.

I must have slipped and made a noise. His face tilted up into the branches. His eyes met mine for an instant. I didn't stop to breathe or think. Fear and anger fused in a rush of overwhelming voltage. The boulder burst from my hands. It hit his skull with a muffled thud. He went down. The weapon fell from his hand.

I slung my pack over my shoulder and dropped out of the tree. Gingerly picking up the gun, having no clue how to carry it, terrified I would accidentally shoot myself, I sprinted toward the porch and crawled underneath. A long black snake slithered away. A gasp froze in my throat. I lay prone, about three inches of headroom above me, cheek to cheek with the dirt.

Footsteps sounded on the floorboards above.

The bald man called out. "Carlos?" He muttered an expletive. He strode to the birches. An all-terrain vehicle was parked in the shadows. He spoke into a walkie-talkie.

In his other hand, he loosely held a pistol. What in the hell was I going to do? Mark moaned in the cabin above me. I reached into the backpack and pulled out the cell phone, muttering silently the most sincere prayer of my lifetime, praying for a miracle. I opened it up and pressed the power switch but the "no service" light kept blinking.

I found my flashlight and knife. Sweat rolled down the back of my neck. I tried to ignore the trembling of my shoulders and arms.

"Carlos!" the man shouted, walking farther away. I said another prayer, then slithered out from under the porch and crept into the cabin.

The only light came in a shaft through the open door, illuminating a handmade chair and table, a pot-bellied stove, and a narrow bed. Mark lay on the floor, hands and feet tied with thick yellow rope. His face was bruised and he bled at the mouth.

"Szabo," he whispered.

I scooted over to him on my knees. With the dainty jackknife, I sawed the rope that bound his feet. I had just cut through a tough knot at his wrists when footsteps sounded on the porch. I dove under the bed.

"Shh!"

Only then did I realize that I'd left the military weapon on the floor near Mark's feet. I was afraid to reach out for it, although I could see it right at the edge of the bed. From my vantage point, only the man's shoes were visi-

Dancing with Mr. D

ble. Italian leather, I guessed, too good to be hiking around in the woods.

"Hey," he muttered. One of the expensive black shoes nudged Mark's chest. I saw the bald head as the man bent over Mark. With lightning speed Mark's fists lashed out. The next moment, the two of them were thrashing on the floor, rolling, kicking, punching.

A pistol fell. I crawled from the bed, knocked the larger weapon underneath, and grabbed the pistol.

Just as I did, the bald man slugged Mark in the jaw. Mark staggered back, falling against me. The man hit him again. Grunting, Mark kicked the guy in the stomach. As the guy doubled over, Mark kicked him again in the head.

I tried to get out of their range.

The guy dove at Mark. They rolled across the floor. I saw the gleam of metal. I gasped. The bald man, his face beet red, clutched a knife.

"Watch out!"

Mark held the man's wrist, keeping the knife at bay, but it seemed to take every ounce of strength he had left.

I lifted the pistol and pointed it uncertainly.

"If you shoot me, Szabo—" Mark grunted.

I was dimly aware of sweat trickling down my neck. I held the gun but my fingers were rigid with fear. I was terrified I'd kill Mark if I tried to shoot. I didn't even know if the gun would go off. The only time I'd ever pulled a trigger in my life was at a carnival shooting gallery—and I'd missed every time.

The two of them scrambled at each other, kicking and punching. The man clawed at Mark's eyes. Mark's grip on the hand with the knife seemed to weaken.

I brought up the gun, trying to aim it at the man's head. Mark managed to kick and threw him off. Mark jumped to his feet, clutching the chair. He held it in front of him, feet first, like a lion tamer.

The man dove over the chair and knocked Mark to the ground. For a long moment the two of them clung to each other in a sweaty ball. The knife pressed on Mark's throat. His muscles strained, but a faint line of blood appeared under his ear where the blade pressed.

"Point the gun and shoot!" Mark shouted.

"I can't!"

"Put two hands on it, Szabo, and shoot!"

The guy saw me. Jesus. He broke free of Mark and came after me. He grabbed for the pistol. I jumped out the cabin door onto the porch. He grasped my foot. I fell.

Mark pulled the guy by the back of his leather jacket.

The guy jabbed at Mark, the knife barely missing.

"Do something, Szabo!" Mark shouted. "Do something!"

Mark panted, winded. Blood poured from a cut on his eye, the slit under his ear, the gash at the leg of his jeans. His face was swollen and red. He was doubled over in pain.

"Shoot the fucking gun!"

I lifted the pistol again and pointed it. The man lunged, knocking Mark down, but Mark quickly rolled over and straddled him.

"No. Don't shoot, Szabo. Don't shoot. You'll kill me."

The guy threw Mark off. Mark lay on the ground. He didn't move. My God! I thought. Is he unconscious? Is he dead?

The man raised the knife high. I had a clear shot. I held the gun in both hands. As the guy lurched forward, his knife aimed at Mark's throat, I pulled the trigger. His knees crumpled beneath him.

I heard an enormous report.

Then it was quiet.

Mark stood up, holding on to the porch rail for support. He wobbled back and forth. Blood trickled down his eye. His face was battered. He bent over. Coughing. Retching. There was blood all over the porch. The man's leg, like a fountain, spurted red.

"Oh God," I said. "I shot him."

I don't know how fast we got down that mountain trail, but it seemed that we flew. I stumbled and fell. Mark was way ahead of me, but then he came back, grasping my arm, pulling me faster than my legs could run.

Suddenly we were at the gate where I'd left the Honda.

"Hey!" Mark shouted. We were both winded. He bent over, trying to breathe. I looked around. The little blue Civic was still there, behind the stand of firs. I unlocked the car and jumped in, tossing my pack.

"Get in!" I screamed.

"My car!"

"What?"

He ran up the road, then down again. "My car. Someone took my damn car."

"Get in!"

He jumped into the passenger seat. I turned the key and heard a resounding click.

Click. Click. Click.

I started cursing.

"Push." Mark muttered.

I heard the sound of an engine in the distance.

"Do you think someone's coming?"

"Just fucking push, Szabo!" Mark shouted.

"You don't have to get testy," I said.

I was out, the two of us pushing the car onto the road. Luckily there was a long downhill stretch, even if the road was poorly maintained gravel.

As the car began to roll, I jumped in. It took three tries, but I finally popped the clutch, the spark ignited, and the engine turned over. Mark hurled himself in and slammed the door.

"Step on it," he said.

The Honda lurched forward.

I went through the gears and pressed the pedal flat on the floor. The Honda sprinted down the mountain, over the rutted dirt road, around hairpin turns, down a twenty percent grade. I kept her in fourth gear most of the way, downshifting only on the switchbacks, the gravel pinging, the tires squealing, the rocks rappelling down the cliffs like torpedoes.

"Don't look now," Mark said. "But there's someone behind us."

Chapter 23

I glanced in the rearview mirror and wished I hadn't. Behind us loomed a big black Lincoln. I drove as if our lives depended on it, swerving as I took the curves. The Lincoln tried to catch us, but the car was large and cumbersome. On the straight ways it closed the distance. But as soon as a curve came, my old Honda hugged the road like a skier on the giant slalom; the Lincoln began to fishtail and had to slow down.

"You did it, Szabo!" Mark shouted, as we hurtled around a hairpin turn at warp speed. "They stopped. They're getting out!"

Two men holding guns stood beside the Lincoln. I heard a popping sound. I slammed my foot on the pedal, but it was already against the floor. I sped away from the spray of gunfire, taking curve after curve down the mountain road. I didn't breathe until we reached hardtop.

Mark removed the baseball jacket from over his eyes. "Where'd you learn to drive?"

"New York," I said. "From an actor who was an ex-cabbie."

"Are we dead yet?"

I glanced at him. His face looked like a train wreck. "God, you look bad. How do you feel?"

"I'll live." He winced and put the jacket back over his face.

In another quarter hour we were on the Interstate. I stopped at a McDonald's and left Mark in the car with the motor running, worried that we wouldn't be able to get it started if I turned off the engine. I ordered a jumbo soda, lots of ice, hold the soda. The kid behind the counter gave it to me free. I stole a pile of paper towels from the rest room and returned to the car.

While Mark went inside to wash up, I fashioned an ice pack. He returned with three Quarter Pounders, two jumbo fries, and two sodas. Groaning, he eased himself slowly into the passenger seat.

I took a sip of the Diet Coke he proffered.

"How did you find the cabin?"

He attempted a smile, but his lip was too swollen. "You couldn't spot a tail on a dog. Ever hear of a rearview mirror?"

"You followed me!"

"Homing device." He touched my earlobe. "I planted one right here."

"I know something better you can do with those paws."

"What?"

I handed him the ice pack. "Hold this against your lip."

He leaned back in his seat and groaned again. "I hurt."

"Sorry."

"It's worth it, Szabo. Just to hear you apologize."

"No," I said quietly, contemplating the clotted blood on his neck. "It isn't."

I pulled onto the Interstate and pressed the pedal to the floor. My Honda is one of those cars that takes fifteen minutes to go from zero to sixty, seventy, eighty. Once I'm there I don't like to slow down. Takes too long to get back up to speed.

"We're a couple thousand miles from Daytona," Mark said, "You don't need to set records. I'd like to get home in no worse shape than I am right now."

"I'll take good care of you. Don't worry." I glanced into the rearview mirror. Nobody back there, as far as I could tell.

"Have a burger," Mark said after a while.

"That's okay."

"Not eating?"

"No. Not today."

I took another sip of soda.

"Want music?" I asked.

"What have you got?"

I pointed to the box of tapes on the floor in the backseat. He grabbed it and started rummaging.

"Anything but Vivi Cairo."

"How about this?" he said, his mouth full of French fries. The strains of "Yellow Submarine" filled the tiny car.

"Why?" I said.

"Keith says it's your favorite."

I laughed. "It's the kids' favorite. I can't stand it."

"Okay. Then what do you want?"

"What do you listen to?"

"Whatever's on the radio."

"I would have pegged you for Beastie Boys. Maybe Metallica."

He found another tape. Liz Phair.

I glanced at him sideways. His jersey was torn and filthy from dirt and blood. His face looked like a punching bag that had gone one too many rounds. He unwrapped a burger and took a bite. In minutes it was gone. He unwrapped another.

Mark ate. I drove. Liz sang.

* * *

The sun was just setting when we arrived in Sheffington. I drove Mark straight to the hospital. After a wait, they gave him a tetanus shot, sewed three stitches in his slashed thigh, taped up his left hand, which had a broken bone, and sent him home with a prescription for painkillers.

While he was being attended to, I found a pay phone and called Dania, telling her I'd be home sometime after dinner. Then I called Detective Brannigan.

"Mark and I ran into a little trouble today," I said.

"I'm busy."

"Detective, you'll be annoyed if I wait with this one." I told him about the cabin. When I reached the part about men with guns, he said, "Where are you?"

"The emergency room at Sheffington General."

End of conversation. He slammed down the phone.

The next order of business was to contact Whit. I dialed the number. Sharon answered.

"He's working at home tonight."

I called the home number and left a message on the machine. Then I called the cell phone.

Whit picked up. "Yes?"

"Zoë, here. Mark and I had some trouble today."

"If this is a dispute about a byline—"

"No. It's important. But I don't think we should talk about it on the phone."

"Can it wait until tomorrow?"

I hesitated. "I guess so."

"I'm not in Greymont," he said tentatively.

"Oh."

"If you really can't discuss it by phone—"

"No. Better not."

"Meet me in my office first thing tomorrow."

"Sure."

I found Mark in the hospital lobby. Brannigan was there with another detective. As we explained what had happened, Brannigan's scowl deepened. He brought us back to the Western District office and made calls to the Vermont State Troopers' headquarters. There was no report of anyone injured or shot in the Mount Silver Resort area. Yes, they would send someone to look. No, there was no report of a red Miata with Massachusetts plates. They took down the information about the missing vehicle.

I wondered if the gunmen had anything to do with Cassandra's death or if they were security guards with a mission to protect the cabin from intruders at all costs. Drugs. That was the only explanation that worked, I kept thinking. Why else would they have had weapons like that?

One of the police officers showed me a book. I'd picked out what the military weapon looked like—the one the man had carried slung over his shoulder.

The officer whistled. "Are you sure?"

"I'm no expert," I said, uncertainly, "But it's the closest to what I saw."

"Detective," the officer said to Brannigan. "She says they had one of these."

Detective Brannigan glanced at the picture I'd identified. "You sure you didn't just see this in a movie?"

"I just talked to Joe in forensics," the officer said. "Matches the bullets they took out of the fender of her Honda."

Brannigan's face folded into a fierce scowl. The light in his eyes faded as they held mine. "You know what this is?"

"No."

"Take a good look."

I did.

"This is an Olympic K23. Even though the barrel is only six and a half inches long, it's a machine gun. It's used by the Venezuelan Army and bootlegged to Colombian drug gangs. They like it because it looks macho, it's light, and it's loud. The damage it causes is devastating. One of these can mow down a field full of charging linebackers in ten seconds flat."

Brannigan glowered at me. "These are not people you want to play footsie with."

I nodded, my throat catching.

Mark stood near me. The office was the district attorney's suite in the Carnavon Hotel in Sheffington, temporary headquarters of the Western District homicide squad. The large room was jammed with bulky metal desks covered with papers and coffee cups.

Large windows overlooked downtown Sheffington. Brownstone office buildings and shops lined the broad Main Street shopping area. Against a sea of black, currents of automobile lights streamed back and forth on the street four floors below us.

Brannigan said, "I'm going to get to the bottom of this. Make me a promise."

"What?"

"Stay home. You too, Mark."

"I will," I promised.

Mark added his assurance, and then we left.

It was like one of those horrible nightmares where monsters keep appearing in places where you'd expect everything to be perfectly normal. You go to school; your teacher is Godzilla. You go home; it has turned into a war zone. You go to your neighborhood grocery; it has been replaced by a spaceship swarming with fourteen-foot aliens that look like giant cockroaches.

The Honda, having tricked me in a pinch, now decided to behave. The engine turned over without a hint of complaint. I dropped Mark off at his apartment in a ramshackle house near the State University.

I finally arrived home around nine, exhausted. After Dania left, I kissed Keith good night. Smokie was fast asleep. I thought about eating, but my stomach was tied in knots. I double locked all the doors and windows, went upstairs, and crawled into the queen-sized bed without taking off my clothes.

I decided to rest for a few minutes and figure out exactly what to tell Billy when I called. In spite of everything, I knew how much he was riding on this album. A few more days wouldn't make much difference, I told myself. Maybe it was crazy, but that's the way I'd been raised. No matter what—family problems, illnesses, acts of God—the show must go on. When my mother was dying, my father, who'd been on Broadway at the time, spent every day in the hospital and every night on stage. Even the night she'd died. He'd done the show, then gone to the hospital. She'd waited. He was with her at the end.

Maybe it wasn't normal for me to face danger and not tell Billy, but that's the way I was born and bred. The bad news can wait until the final curtain has fallen, the last echoes of applause have faded, and the theater is dark. Then the problems of the real world can be attended to.

At three in the morning, I sat straight up in bed. I'd slept soundly, but now I was hopelessly awake. My poor-boy sweater was ripped. There was a gash in the side where the Colombian had grabbed me when he went after me with the knife. My corduroys were torn from brambles and briars. Every muscle in my body ached.

I took a shower. Examining myself, I found bruises on my knees and thighs, and a big one on my side where the gash in the sweater had been. My shoulders and legs were terribly sore. There was a cut on my face where some branches had scratched.

Suddenly the terror welled up so fast that I stopped myself from remembering what had happened. What frightened me the most was the look of alarm stamped on Brannigan's face. And the memory of how close Mark had come to having his throat sliced open. Shuddering, I forced the image from my mind.

I emerged from the hot steam of the shower, feeling better but not good. I studied my hair. It was time for another go with the peroxide. If I was going to shoot it out with dope dealers, I might as well look like a punk. And then I went beyond the surface and looked into my own eyes, irises a mixture of green and blue, the makeup smeared round my lashes. Who was in there? In some ways, I didn't know her very well.

Sadness overwhelmed my soul, drilling me like a hard rain. I suddenly saw a vision of the man's grimace as the shot I'd fired hit his leg. Mark staggering. The knife gleaming. I pushed the memories from my mind. I wasn't going to think about it. Just wasn't. Again, I remembered Brannigan's scowl.

By now it was four. I'd agreed to meet Whit at the *Eagle* at six, but I'd forgotten all about the kids. I looked out the window to see if Morgan's light was on yet. No.

I went downstairs, made myself a cup of chamomile tea, and called Whit at the office. No answer. Believe it or not, Whit often goes to the office that early. I wandered into the living room and glanced over my notes on Cassandra's case, which I kept in a plastic file box on a shelf. To fend off the darkness that kept pushing into my consciousness, I set to coloring the maps I'd started the night of John's death. With a yellow Crayola pencil of Keith's, I filled in every parcel that Cassandra fought over during the last fifteen years, starting with the Gemini preserve. I wrote in the names of the original owners. That took over an hour. She had been a very busy lady.

As five-thirty rolled around, I'd begun a second map showing how the parcels had eventually been disposed. The Gemini property, for example, had been bought from Carver Pruitt by Saragossa. After a protracted battle, it had been bought by Delstar, Craig's company, and then donated to the Green Trust.

In Massachusetts there is no unincorporated land. Each town comprises the central village area plus all lands up to the boundaries of the neighboring towns. So Greymont contained a town center, as it is called in New England. That's where the *Eagle* was and the shops and restaurants along Stanhope and Main.

Greymont College owned a good deal of land in the south end of the town center, reaching from South Stanhope toward South Greymont, which was more rural, with horse and dairy farms. Orchards, riding stables, and flower, vegetable, and fruit stands were interspersed with the homes of the wealthy.

Whit owned a magnificent old Georgian house in that section. I'd never been invited to his home, but I'd driven past it many times. Situated at the intersection of two main roads, it was easily visible from the road and had many acres of rolling hills and fields, a pond, and a small orchard.

My friend Cletha Fair, on the other hand, lived in North Greymont, which was also rural. Her farm had been in her husband's family for generations. Formerly a dairy farm, it consisted of a barn, now used for storage, fields hayed by a neighbor, and a 1790 farmhouse with a large vegetable garden for her own use.

Craig Detweiller's $4.2-million home was located near the southernmost boundary of town. I wondered what that much money could buy. I found his lot on the map. Hmm. That was interesting. Craig's mansion was built on land that Cassandra had battled against developing. I studied the sales records and old newspaper clips. The original owner had attempted to subdivide the property for suburban development. Cassandra had fought and won. A year after the owner's planning board petition had been denied, Craig had bought the property at a fire sale price.

Chapter 24

I realized it was getting late. Looking out the kitchen window, I saw Morgan's light and called him. He quickly agreed to get the kids off to school again. I thanked him profusely.

"Nonsense," he said. "I'm happy to help out."

I left him with a pot of fresh decaf, cinnamon rolls reheating in the oven, and instructions to take them out in fifteen minutes. At five of six, I arrived at the *Eagle* offices. The sky was dark. The door was locked. I let myself in, locked the door behind me, and went up to Whit's office. It was shut tight. I knocked. No answer. Surprising that he wasn't in yet.

In the kitchen, I brewed a pot of coffee, wondering what was keeping Whit. Then I went to my desk, found my Discman, and put on the *Eurythmics Greatest Hits*. Returning to the kitchen, I switched out the lights and sat in the big comfortable chair, sipping coffee in the dark, headphones on, gazing out the windows. The lamps dimly illuminated portions of the deserted parking lot.

Annie Lennox sang about hearts broken like china cups.

It seemed like a month since Billy and I had had a real conversation. Life would get back to normal, I told myself, as soon as the album was done. If they broke through with a hit, the sacrifice would be worth it. Financially things had been strained for a quite a long time. With the money from his song on Vivi's last album, we'd finally been able to pay off a chunk of the debt still owed from the crisis. The idea that we might soon be free of that weight lifted my spirits.

Then the gunmen, the car chase, came flooding into my mind. I didn't know which was worse, worrying about Billy or reliving the events of the last twenty-four hours. But now that I'd inadvertently summoned it, the nightmare forced its way into my consciousness and refused to let go. What was it those men hadn't wanted us to find?

I thought of Craig's house built on property Cassandra had contested. I considered Spots. Where did he fit into the equation? He lived near Mount Silver Resort, near where Cassandra had her cabin hideaway. Did she keep money there? Had she been blackmailing Craig? Or had he found something out about her past? Had she and Spots had something to do with drug dealing together? If Craig had found out, maybe he'd forced her to let go of her battles when she contested development deals in which he was involved. He said he always researched his enemies. What had John and Spots seen the night she died? Was Spots in danger? Or was he a killer?

The blackness had begun to fade into a predawn blue when a car drove up and pulled into a parking space near the back of the *Eagle*. A Volvo. The headlights shut off.

Whit, at last. It was nearly six-thirty. He'd never been

this late. I was about to go greet him when a man emerged from the passenger side. Tall. Lanky. Graceful. The driver got out. A lamp behind the Chinese restaurant next door shed a yellow light on him. He wore a top coat—camel hair. Although I couldn't make out his face, I was sure it was Whit.

He went to the back of the Volvo, which looked faintly blue in the early light. He opened the trunk. The other man, whose back was to me, wore a parka. He pulled out a bicycle. Whit dug out a wheel and handed it to him. The man in the parka fastened the wheel to the front of the bike. He took a pack of some sort and attached it to the rack. He propped the bike against the car and approached Whit.

He touched Whit's cheek—tenderly. They held each other for a moment. I glimpsed his face as he turned toward the light. It was Tim Boudreau. He mounted the bike and rode off. Whit closed the trunk. He stood looking after Tim as the bicycle veered round the corner, through the lot, past the Community Center, and out onto Revere Street toward the high school.

Annie Lennox was singing about angels playing with her heart.

Five minutes later, I turned off the Discman. I left the player and my CD on my desk and went upstairs. Whit's door was open. The light was on.

I tapped on the door.

"Yes?"

He was hanging up his camel hair coat. Whit's narrow face seemed freshly shaven. He had color for a change, as if he'd been outside walking.

"Zoë, I didn't hear you come in."

"Do you want coffee?" I asked. "I have some brewing downstairs."

"That would be nice. Shall we talk in the kitchen?"

"No. Here's fine. I'll be right back."

I ran down and poured two mugs. Whit took his black. I added milk and two packets of sugar substitute to mine. No one else was here. Whit served as the early-morning rewrite man on his paper. Also the publisher, editor, and business manager. I'd even caught him sweeping the steps and polishing the brass doorknobs.

I returned with coffee. He thanked me. "Ah, that's good," he said, uncharacteristically making small talk. "I just drove back from Boston."

"So early."

"I had a ticket to the symphony last night. I decided to make a little vacation of it. Have you ever been to the Pear Tree?"

"No."

"You must try it. They have delicious quail."

"Maybe we will, if this album—"

"How is it going, by the way?"

"Everybody says it will be finished in another week or two."

Whit's face darkened. "That Spots character. Is that what you wanted to talk about?"

"Actually, Mark got into a fight."

"A fight?"

"He's okay. Just kind of beat up."

"Where was this?"

I swallowed. Whit folded his hands together. His eyes met mine. I sat there for a few seconds, my eyes fixed with his. Eye contact, I thought. Bicycles.

"We drove to Vermont. We found property of Cassandra's. Some men there beat Mark up, and, well, we got away. Brannigan knows the whole story."

Whit hesitated for a moment. "Friends of this fellow Spots?"

"I don't know, but—maybe."

"Zoë," he said, growing serious. "I think we're going to have to back off and let the police do their job."

I nodded.

"I've been looking into the Green Trust," I said after a pause. "And Craig. You know I've found . . . a pattern."

He frowned. "Didn't we agree that the Green Trust was a dead issue?"

"Yes, but—"

"Is something wrong?"

I remembered Cassandra saying, *Your boss doesn't like me. I know too much about his personal life.*

"Something's wrong, Zoë. I can sense it."

"It's Billy—just personal."

His face shut down. Even the word "personal" made him withdraw.

"You must be concerned for his safety," Whit said after a minute. "With his protracted visit up there . . . with Spots."

"Yes, I am. That's why it's hard for me to ignore this story."

"But Brannigan is fully informed?"

"Yes." A dart of fear pierced my heart and wove its way through my arteries.

"That strange drowning. Quite a coincidence, coming directly after Cassandra's death."

"Yes."

Whit met my gaze. "If you want to investigate Spots's

drug dealing, go ahead. As long as you stay away from the man himself. You have a friend, you said, who has computer access to public records?"

I nodded.

"Why don't you call him today. See if he can find out more. I have some old friends on the *Globe* who might have ways of getting information on Vermont records. What's on your agenda today?"

"Just Town Meeting wrapping up. Whit, let me give you a hypothetical."

"Sure." His smile looked like a jack-o'-lantern trying not to be scary.

"Do you think Cassandra might have been killed because of a secret she was harboring about someone in town?"

His awkward smile vanished. "Possibly. That's why, I'll admit, the chance of this man Spots having a motive—"

Motive, I thought. And opportunity. Spots had been out walking with John at night. No one at Morgan's had seen them after one in the morning. Brannigan had never revealed the exact time of death, but it was clearly sometime between one and five. My guess was two, from my conversations with the neighbors. I wondered where Tim Boudreau had been on the night of Cassandra's death. I'd already found out he wasn't at home. Tim was agile enough to climb that tree. Was Whit shielding Tim?

I became aware of movement, noise, the sounds of people arriving for work, the newsroom beginning to hum. Light streamed in from the east-facing windows that overlooked a small park and fountain. The sun shone on Whit's face. I shook off my doubts.

* * *

After taking the Honda to the shop to get the starter replaced and the holes in the rear fender plugged, I spent the rest of the day on the phone.

Brannigan told me that the Vermont police had contacted Mount Silver Resort security. They reported no problems. A trooper had visited and had found nothing out of the ordinary. Brannigan intended to drive up to Cassandra's cabin himself. He was filing the necessary paperwork to do a search. However, he told me, he'd discovered something faintly troubling.

"Who told you the land belonged to her?" he asked.

"Didn't it?"

"It's in someone else's name."

"Whose?"

He hesitated. "Off the record—a woman named Kathryn Dunnaston. Sound familiar?"

"No." I thought for a moment. "The farmer. Mr. Prouty. He called her Dunne. He recognized her from a photo."

"I'm not liking this," he said. "You're not going anywhere today, are you?"

"No."

"Good."

When I got off the phone, I looked up the number of the high school in Rheinlander, Wisconsin. I asked if they'd had a student registered there named Kathryn Dunnaston. It would take a while, they said, to search their old records. Two hours later, I got the answer. Bingo.

I called my friend at the newsmagazine and asked him to run a search on that name. He rang back an hour later.

"She was supposed to be a witness in a drug trafficking

case on Long Island. Never showed up at the trial."

"When was that?"

"Summer of '78."

"Who was the defendant?"

"A local mobster." He mentioned the name, but I didn't recognize it.

After hanging up the phone, I began to think the thing through. Kathryn Dunnaston is involved with Spots. He's the kind of guy who had a lot of women. Maybe she took it more seriously than he did. They spend time together at Silver Wind Farm. Maybe she's hiding out there. The commune disintegrates through lack of money. Kathryn is slated to testify in a drug trial in Long Island, but disappears instead.

She reemerges as Cassandra Dunne, owning a prime piece of pristine land in the mountains. She moves to Greymont and becomes an activist opposing all development. Many of the deals she contests end up as donations to the Green Trust.

Spots, formerly Tom Sporkartch, has a mildly tarnished reputation as a result of possibly dealing in drugs—no proven connection. After an affair with Cassandra, he becomes the owner of a state-of-the-art studio, Wonderland Sounds, on the land of the former commune. All the other members have dispersed.

I thought, I should go look up these real estate transactions in Vermont. I remembered my promise to Brannigan not to leave town. I certainly didn't want to show my face anywhere near the Mount Silver Resort.

But if I went to Montpelier . . . No one would be looking for me there. It was several hours from Sparrowville. A different part of the state. Besides, the state attorney general's office would have other records—corporate and business filings.

I called Ann Chatsford and asked if Cassandra had ever mentioned the Mount Silver Resort in Vermont.

"No," she said, "but Cassandra hated ski resorts."

"Really?"

"Oh, she railed against them incessantly. They ruined the environment."

"What did she have against them?"

"Snowmaking."

"What's wrong with that?"

"Uses water and energy. And building condos on steep slopes causes erosion, silts pristine mountain streams, kills all aquatic life. That's just the tip of the iceberg. She went on and on so much about ski resorts that I finally asked why. We have none here."

"What did she answer?"

"A global conspiracy. When she started in on those I turned off my hearing aid."

Enough of this, I thought. Tomorrow I'd go to Montpelier, look up property and corporate records, then maybe I'd check on Billy.

Just for the heck of it, I fished out the Mount Silver Resort card with its fancy writing on the silver paper. I picked up the phone, blocked Caller ID, and punched in the 800 number. A woman with a crisp British accent answered. The voice sounded familiar.

"I'm doing a story for *Travel America*," I said, raising my voice a few tones in pitch. I spoke as I imagined some dizzy travel writer might—someone, say, angling for free accommodations in return for a plug. "I'd like some information on Mount Silver Resort."

"Could I have you name and address? We'd be happy to send you something."

I told her I was Courtney Lennox, after two of my favorite divas. I gave her a phony address in New York City.

"Is there someone who could answer a few questions for me right now?"

"Perhaps I might help you," the woman answered.

I asked about the general plan for the resort. It was just as Prouty had said. Lifts, scads of trails of all levels and types, cross-country, downhill, state-of-the-art snowmaking, outdoor and indoor skating rinks, a condo village and shops, several restaurants, ski bar, four hotels with heated pools, saunas, a full gym, a chalet village near the mountaintop, activities for children including a mini amusement park, and miles of scenic hiking trails.

I asked about permits and construction schedules. The permitting process had been going on for over a year. They expected final approval in the spring and hoped construction would be under way by summer.

"We've already begun working on road access. That has caused some delay, but a primary obstacle has just been removed. By spring our paperwork should be in place."

"Could I speak to someone in management—a president or vice-president?"

"I'm vice-president of the company."

"Sorry. You answered your own phone. What did you say your name was?"

"The name is Kai. Alida Kai."

"Well, thank you," I said, trying to suppress the quiver

in my voice. I didn't want Craig Detweiller's assistant to discern my discomfort. "Thank you very much."

I hung up and thought about it. I kept adding up two and two and getting twelve.

Chapter 25

The next morning, after dropping the kids at school, I drove to Sheffington. I left the Honda, with its brand-new starter, in a lot, did my best to make sure I wasn't being followed, and rented a Ford Escort. That way, it would be harder to be spotted by any unsavory characters.

I drove the three hours to Montpelier. There I researched property ownership papers at the Hall of Records. Then I spent a few hours at the state attorney general's office going over corporate and tax filings. When I was finished, I had culled the following information:

Silver Wind Farm was incorporated as a nonprofit in the mid-seventies. Later its assets were divided between SilverStar, a corporation registered in Andorra, and WonderWind Enterprises, registered in Vermont.

WonderWind Enterprises owned Wonderland Sounds, which listed Tom Sporkartch, otherwise known as Spots, as president. I didn't recognize any other names on the corporate filings.

Mount Silver Resort and Mountain Properties was owned by SilverMist, a corporation registered in the Cayman Islands. Of all officers listed, I recognized only Alida Kai, vice-president of Mount Silver. SilverMist, being offshore, the clerk informed me, didn't have to file papers listing officers or board of directors.

At the Registry of Deeds, I typed in Mount Silver Resort and Mountain Properties. The Beamon's Mountain property had been bought from a company called WolfStar, also offshore, which had bought pieces of the land starting in 1974, and a company called SilverSeed, which had made small purchases during the early 1980s. WolfStar showed a sale of property on Beamon's Mountain in 1978 to a Kathryn Dunnaston for $1.

SilverSeed rang a bell. I checked my notes. Aha. That was the company which had paid the Braithwaites for a right-of-way that they'd never used.

But when I ran Craig Detweiller's name at the Registry of Deeds, nothing turned up.

I checked my map of Montpelier and found the Mount Silver card given to me by Mr. Prouty. I drove to the address listed on the card. It turned out to be a lawyer's office in a fancy building near the state capitol. I wanted to go in and ask for information, but the memory of the gunmen stopped me. By that time it was five o'clock and everything was closed.

Starving, I grabbed a quick dinner of soup and salad at a vegetarian place, and began the long drive home. As the overcast twilight darkened to night behind the gray-green mountains, I battled with the temptation to go to Wonderland Sounds.

Even though Detective Brannigan had warned me to stay home, throughout the day I'd watched my back. Nobody had followed me. I was dying to ask Spots about Kathryn Dunnaston, about her failure to appear at the trial in Long Island, and about her land. I was curious to see what he'd say if I mentioned the names of Craig Detweiller and Mount Silver.

So, against my better judgment, I found myself taking

the exit for Sparrowville, leaving the Interstate in search of Wonderland. I entered the network of dirt roads leading to the old commune. A drizzle began to fall. The paintings on trees and on the sign marking the turnoff seemed drab in the rain.

My rented Escort bounced angrily in response to the potholes on the poorly maintained dirt road. I pulled up alongside the EVE'S AMBITION van. Someone had cleaned off the ugly threats that had been painted on it and retouched the mural.

I walked across the wet grass to the brick path leading through the trees to the barn studio. Music issued forth and lights blazed invitingly. The sky was dark. It was a little after eight o'clock.

No one answered when I knocked, but the door was ajar. I let myself in. The recording light was on over the door of studio A. I followed the long hallway covered with kilim runners to the control room.

Inside, Spots sat on a director's chair. He wore a green long-sleeved shirt and baggy white pants held up by dark blue suspenders printed with half moons and stars. Padded earphones pressed against his hair, which was pulled into a bushy gray ponytail. He listened intently, making small adjustments on knobs on the big board.

Through the expanse of soundproof glass I saw Vivi, standing alone in the studio. She too wore earphones. Over the speakers I could hear a rough mix of tracks laid down earlier: piano, drums, bass, and guitar.

Vivi's eyes were closed. She wore a simple blouse over a shimmering gold skirt of some synthetic material. She sang without moving, her voice soaring and then growing intimate, exploring all the funky cracks and crannies in the music.

Dancing with Mr. D

As the music intensified, the rhythm grew more tricky, the spiky melody more intricate. Spots's frown relaxed into an expression of admiration. The piano and drums engaged in a kind of hand-to-hand combat, then joined together, and jogged to a stop. Spots turned some knobs and the system went silent.

"What do you think?" Vivi said. "My voice cracked on the bridge." She hummed a bit of the tune.

"I like that crack," Spots said. "I get this grainy, old-school feel. Marlene Dietrich in the rain."

Vivi lifted her shoulders and began a gravelly "Falling in Love Again."

Spots unobtrusively pushed up the level, recording without Vivi's knowledge. Her Marlene imitation was uncannily accurate: the aloof half smile, the heavy lids, the soft German accent. She sang about three-quarters of the way through, then erupted into giggles. Spots maneuvered levers on the board.

He said into the mike, "We're in Weimar. I see the fog, the misty lights. The figure in the trench coat in the shadows."

Vivi pushed her hair up with both hands, did a bump and a grind, and yelped. "Yeow!"

Spots chuckled. "Too bad we don't have a video cam."

Vivi saw me and waved. Spots turned and nodded hello.

A moment later, Vivi bounced into the control room. She gave me a showbiz hug and kiss. "You're looking marvelous today, dear."

"So are you," I responded. "Love the skirt. Where's Billy?"

"He's at the house," said Spots peevishly.

Vivi turned to Spots. "How was the take?"

"Judge for yourself." He leaned over the board and pressed a couple of buttons. While it was playing, he dug up a phone and made a call. "Hey, Bill," he said. "Your wife's here. We've got a beautiful vocal on 'Eve's Ambition.'" He handed me the phone.

"Hi, babe," Billy said. I detected strain, despite the upbeat tone.

"Hi. You okay?"

"Yeah. Great. How about you?"

"Had a rough couple of days, but—"

"Kids okay?"

"Yes."

"I called the other day, but you weren't there."

"I didn't get your message."

"Duck and I are finishing an arrangement. Give me two minutes. I'll be right over. You can stick around and listen while we record."

"Sure, Billy," I said, reassured by the invitation.

With Vivi and Spots, I listened to the rest of the cut.

Vivi's face was a study in contrasts. Her glossy enjoyment seemed sincere at first, but a white line of discomfort inched up from her knotted fingers. Her gold-frosted nails, short for the keyboards, pinched at her gold lamé skirt.

"Where did you get that guitar?" Vivi asked.

"Ghost tracks." Spots's lip curled in a sardonic grin. "The day John died, Viv. That's when he recorded this."

"It gives me the creeps."

"Me too," he said. "But it's great stuff."

Vivi raised an eyebrow suggestively. "I like it," she said to him. "Don't know about that Marlene crap."

"Trust me." Spots's two front teeth were stained. "What do you think, Zo?"

I'd been distracted, watching Spots as he spoke about

John's death, wondering how to begin to question him, but I grinned. "Sounds great."

"See, Viv," Spots said. "The voice of the media."

"I'm going to take a break. Come on, Zoë. Let's find that laggard husband of yours."

"I'll be right there." I wanted to talk to Spots alone. His eyes flitted past mine toward the door that Vivi had just closed.

"I've been thinking," I said.

His mouth was very pink, lips very full. "What about?"

"Cassandra." I breathed slowly to calm my pulse. "You had an affair. She found out too much about your dealing . . ."

I watched his pink mouth curl into a strange smile. He'd been fiddling with some dials on his huge console, but his hands stopped when I uttered the word "dealing."

"She found out too much about your dealing," I continued, watching his face for signs that I was hitting on the truth. "You had a falling out. She threatened to testify against friends of yours . . . and then she disappeared. You found her two weeks ago in Greymont, and you—"

"That's an interesting tale you weave, but you've got the story wrong."

"Set me straight."

He thought about it. Finally he snorted dismissively.

"What can you tell me about a woman named Kathryn Dunnaston?" I pressed.

His lips pursed and drew into a mocking grin. "I can see you've done some homework."

"I have."

He turned, gazing absently through the soundproof glass to the half-lit studio. After a while, he cocked his head. "Old Kat, we called her in those days."

"She slipped off the grid and became Cassandra."

His eyes were guarded. He said nothing.

"Why?" I thought aloud. "Why did someone come stalking John, when you saw nothing?"

"John," he said. "That was an accident."

"If you believe that, why won't you tell me what you saw? He told me you went to see Cassandra when she was up in the tree. I haven't mentioned this to the police yet, but you're not giving me any reason not to. I did tell my editor. He urged me to ask you to tell us what you know. If you make a statement off the record, the evidence you have could come out without anyone knowing where it came from." Okay, I was embellishing. But it seemed to work.

His complexion grew paler. He closed his eyes and thought for a moment. When he spoke it was in a whisper. "This goes no further than this room. Get it? Anonymity?"

I nodded, worried that it was only me and him, wishing I had another set of ears to corroborate anything he might say, hoping I could verify whatever he told me through a second source.

His eyes narrowed. "I don't want to be involved in any way."

"You have my word." God, I hoped I wouldn't be tested. Certainly didn't want to go to jail guarding the identity of a source who was an eyewitness to a murder.

He let go a breath. "Yeah, we went to see her. We exchanged words. Ya know? Kidding back and forth. Joking around about the Kat stuck in a tree. I hadn't seen her in about a dozen years. I wanted her to give it up, come down, get stoned with us, but, shit, I couldn't talk her out of it. Old times." He shook his head; his fingers pinched his misshapen nose.

"John and I blasted out our brains, sniffing a little of

this, a little of that. Felt like two days later, John wakes me up says we'd better get out of there fast. I have no idea where, or when, or why. We just hightailed it."

"He saw her fall?"

Spots grimmaced and gazed into his distant galaxy. "So he said."

"Why didn't you go to the police?"

"Hell, you kidding? I didn't want to get hauled in on a possession charge. Besides, police start nosing around in some old history they might find something. Listen, Zo, I don't want anyone messing in my past. Not you. Not anyone. I'm reminding you, Zo, this is Billy's ticket back. You don't want to mess that up."

"No. I don't."

He wiped the palm of his hands against his thighs. They left a streak of perspiration on the white cloth of his pants. He squinted.

I remembered Tim Boudreau saying, *I think, maybe, she was hung up on Craig.*

I took a wild guess, "What about Craig?"

His eyes darted up. "You have been doing homework—overtime."

"He was here, wasn't he?" Saying it with a confidence I didn't have. From his expression, I could tell I'd hit the truth. "A member of the commune?"

"Nothing as formal as memberships. People just came through. Only, old Craig, he came to stay."

"And Kathryn—"

"Craig and Kathryn. The love affair from hell."

Spots opened his mouth and made a face like he was laughing, only no sound came out.

"Tell me about it."

Spots handed me a pair of earphones. "Want to hear a demo?"

He opened a cabinet and found a tape—it looked like something you'd slip into your VCR. He inserted it into a slot in the console and flipped a couple switches. It could have been recorded yesterday afternoon. There were three voices. A soft tenor—a young Craig. A woman, unmistakably Cassandra, a voice that swooped up and down, with an edge of hysteria running through it. The third was the slow, hip drawl of Spots.

"We'll bury it so deep," Craig's voice said on the tape, *"there won't be any way to trace it to us."*

"They're after me. They going to kill me!" Cassandra's voice sounded high-pitched and wild. *"There were six of them waiting. They're coming after me! I know these guys."*

"Kat, lie low for a few months. At least until these creeps stop hunting you. You don't have to worry about money."

"What about us? You and me."

"I have a plan for the money, but we have to cooperate."

"Craig," said Spots on the tape, *"that's what intrigues me. How's that work—with the money?"*

"Offshore accounts . . . I'll take care of it."

"How do you do that—I mean with the money? It concerns all of us. We want to know."

"Told you I'll handle it." But after a moment, the young Craig ran through a rough sketch of setting up accounts and corporations. As he spoke, he grew more loquacious. Bragging about how smart he was, how clever the scheme.

"No one can ever trace the money," he added. *"I've got a plan to funnel it into land, small businesses. It comes back into the country clean. Legitimate payments for services."*

Spots snickered. *"What if I told you I had this on tape?"*

"If it were Kat's old friends," Craig said, *"a move like that could kill you."*

The laughter grew louder.

"This is Tom Sporkartch. I made this tape on July 17th, 1978, at Wonderland Sounds. Participating players: Kathryn Dunnaston of Rheinlander, Wisconsin; Craig Detweiller of Greymont, Massachusetts. This is an insurance policy. If you are listening to this tape, one of us is dead."

I spent a few minutes absorbing what I'd heard. I took off the earphones.

Spots leaned toward me, a cynical gleam in his eye.

"A short story," he said. "Long ago and far away, a wild child named Kathryn comes to Silver Wind Farm by way of Chicago. She and I, we got it on. Not bad as things go, ya know? Then Craig, a college boy, stops in one snowy night. Kat, well, she's never seen anything so nice and sweet.

"Seems she's been trying to escape some friends. But these friends arouse Craig's curiosity. You see, they have big-time connections. Craig has big-time dreams. Me, I've got friends who like to buy.

"Five years later, I've got a studio that's the envy of every independent in the business. Craig, he's set for life. And Cassandra—Kat at the time—she buys herself a mountain. Craig helps her do the paperwork. A place she says she's going to keep forever wild. Some people get religion, Kat has found the wilderness. Trees. Birds. Fish. Never did like people very much. Everything she earns, all her share, she pours into groups trying to save the earth.

"I heard you talking about her the night she died. A

wave of nostalgia hit. For old time's sake, I took John to see this friend of mine, see what happened to her.

"I thought it was pretty darned funny, she was sitting up there in that tree, protesting some deal of Craig's. Like a mongoose. She sinks her teeth, she's not going to let go of the cobra. Fifteen, twenty years. I kidded her about it."

I scanned his face, etched with character. Laugh lines bordered his mouth. His eyes were sunken, and though they were laced with glints of humor, I could see a hint of deep sadness in them.

"And so she ran away," I said, thinking about the tape, trying to make sense of it.

"Off the grid, so the Colombians couldn't catch her. And three weeks later we've got some drug task force dudes from New York banging at the door asking for a Kathryn Dunnaston. Seems there's going to be a trial. Old friend of hers. They think if she talks, he won't walk. Hey, maybe that bad deal was a setup. What do you think, Zo? I heard from Billy that you're a fair detective."

"The money," I said. "She came back here for money."

"She hid that last stash. Somewhere on her mountain."

I was thinking, I'm going to have to work like hell to get confirmation, but what a story. MOUNT SILVER RESORT ALLEGEDLY FUNDED BY DRUG MONEY I could see the headlines. I almost laughed thinking of the look on Craig Detweiller's face when he read it.

Spots narrowed his eyes on me. He scratched under his moon-and-stars suspenders. "Yesterday, a cop shows up. Says they found a footprint down near the lake the night John died that didn't match any of ours. Too big. Asks if I have any friends who wear size fourteen.

"I'm beginning to wonder whether Craig hasn't grown greedy. Maybe he's hired an assassin. He got the lion's share. Cassandra was happy with her mountain. Me, I've got the studio. And John, I keep thinking, man, did he see something he shouldn't have? And if so, hey, I was with him. You know? I'm beginning to worry about my health.

"What I want from you, Zo—aside from keeping this little story to yourself—is to go tell my old friend Craig what you've heard. Remind him that the tape and some papers to back it up are squirreled away in a safety deposit box. Anything happens to me, the world will know. After all, he's the guy with a reputation to protect."

Chapter 26

The rain was pouring down heavily when I stepped outside. I ran across the path toward the farmhouse and burst in the door, eager to see Billy, excited about the information I'd just dug out of Spots.

When Billy was working, he lost track of time, just as I did when I was driving down a lead on a hot story or conducting an interview with a hard-to-reach celebrity. If he said he was working on an arrangement with Duck, I figured it had turned out to be trickier than he'd expected. But it was getting late, and I had a lot of new material to sort through. I was eager to get home and find out what Mark had discovered in his computer search of Delstar's finances.

Which is why I entered the farmhouse without waiting for someone to come to the door. I stopped in the front hall long enough to hang my drenched jacket on a hook by the stairs. I glanced through the French doors to the left leading into the living room. It was empty. I checked the kitchen. No one there either. I opened the door to the study.

Duck sat on the dark leather sofa. He was bent over a broad coffee table, on which were arrayed several pages of music paper. He was copying notes in quick, sure strokes from a master chart. Cerita stood at an upright piano, playing a tune with two fingers, singing a harmony, as if testing it.

"Billy here?" I asked.

"Upstairs," Duck said.

"He'll be right down," Cerita said. "Wait. I'll get him."

But I was already gone. I clambered up the stairs, eager to check in with Billy and then get back to Greymont with my scoop. Wow, I kept thinking, this is really explosive. Even Whit couldn't keep the lid on this new information.

There were several doors off a central hall. One was open—a bathroom. I took a wild guess and knocked on the first door I came to, then opened it without waiting for an answer. Billy was there, and Vivi.

She was standing by the bed. As I entered, Vivi turned to look at me, her mouth open in an "O" of surprise. Several feet from her, Billy stood near the window, beside an old bureau with a glass top. He was bent over, holding something close to his face.

My eyes immediately went to the spot that he seemed to be inspecting with utmost care. He finished the line of coke before he looked up. It was only half a second. I guess he thought it was someone else. I don't know. Maybe he'd forgotten I was there. Maybe he'd forgotten he'd told me he'd be right over as soon as he finished that chart with Duck.

His head turned sideways. Vivi's mouth seemed permanently stuck in the "O" of surprise. I froze. We all did.

Billy, caught red-handed, put down the little straw.

"Hi, babe," he said nonchalantly. As if nothing had happened. His pupils were little points, despite the low light. There was an undertone of defensiveness in his attitude, his look.

I went to the bureau, put my pinkie into the bit of residue left on the glass, and tasted the bitter substance.

About five seconds rolled by. I was dimly aware of the clatter of heavy rain on the roof. The memory of his pallid body after the OD, the tubes running in and out of him, in the hospital bed in Kyoto, flashed before my eyes. Then Smokie's small fingers caressing his face.

I stared at him, comparing the way he looked now to the way he'd looked then.

"How could you do this?"

He grinned sheepishly.

"Hey, Zoë," Vivi interceded, "we're working on overdrive. We need a pick-me-up once in a while. It's my fault. I talked him into it. We were working on a song and it wasn't coming together, and I thought—just one hit. It helped. It really did."

"Vivi," I said, "could you excuse us?"

"Don't screw it up." Her eyes narrowed unpleasantly. Her pupils were huge. She uttered a mild curse.

The little green cloud that had been collecting particles of dew for the last few weeks froze in my chest, becoming a hard block of ice. I felt myself shaking.

"Vivi. Get the hell out."

She swept to the bureau, picked up her implements of abuse, shot me a deadly glance, and left, slamming the door.

It was a good minute before Billy or I spoke. I kept listening to the sound of the rain on the roof above, the spatter as it hit the windows.

"Did the stuff come from Spots?"

"Zoë. Leave it alone."

"From Spots?"

"No. Vivi has her own supply."

I took him in: the slender body, the chiseled features,

the pretty dark eyes, all the poetry and molten lava. A stubble of day-old beard marred his jaw. His hair was tousled. He wore a denim shirt, sleeves rolled up. It was unbuttoned, hanging loose over a white undershirt and jeans. His feet were bare. His toes were slender and delicate.

Irritation flashed through his eyes and then subsided. A telltale redness showed at the edge of his right nostril.

My eyes scanned his face, which had grown noticeably paler in the past few weeks. If I'd lost a few pounds on my self-imposed starvation diet, he'd lost more weight. His cheeks were hollow. A pale bluish vein ran up the side of his face like a streak through polished marble. It thrummed slightly.

I listened to the rain.

"Dania watching the kids?" he said, as if we were just chatting over nothing. "Everything copacetic with them?"

I grasped at this fragment of normality as if, maybe, if I let myself believe it, nothing would have changed.

"The soccer seems to be doing some good."

His hands were cold, his fingers quivered. "You care so much."

"I do."

"Sorry I can't be as good as you want me to be."

It was very quiet. I listened to the rain grow heavier and then diminish.

I thought about the five hundred excuses, explanations, denials, and promises I'd accepted in the year leading into the crisis.

"It's really over this time, Billy."

I heard myself say it. I hadn't meant to, it just came out.

"I could use love. Not another guilt trip."

His stare was angry, scornful. Not really Billy.

I was swept by confusion. Part of me was unconnected to the emotion jolting through my veins. I wanted to pretend it hadn't happened, that we weren't really here.

I wanted to take him in my arms, to beg forgiveness, to have him beg me for forgiveness. I wanted to rewind the tape and play it over, doing everything right this time. I wanted some power greater than the two of us to give us one more chance.

"I've got to record," he said. "I don't have time for a scene."

"All those promises . . . two years ago."

I knew better than to start in on this, but I couldn't help myself. Sometimes feelings overrule logic.

"Leave it alone," he said angrily. Cocaine in him, making him defensive, suspicious, surly, and aloof.

"Billy."

"I'm going to the studio. I'm going to lay down the bass track. We're running a rough mix of the entire album over the weekend. I'll be home Tuesday. We'll talk about it then."

I knew from experience that you can't save someone who doesn't want to be saved, that you have to walk away when every muscle in your body is screaming not to.

I walked away.

The wind changed direction. The water sprinkled from the shivering evergreens. The sounds of the trees rustled above the deep drumming of the rain, the splattering in the puddles, the tapping on the shingle roofs.

Chapter 27

Maybe I would have been better off if I'd screamed and yelled. Sometimes when things are beyond repair, I lose my ability to express what I'm feeling, or I don't allow myself to feel at all. I drove back down to Sheffington, turned in the rental car, picked up my Honda, and drove home.

It was nearly eleven when I got in. I worked out the schedule with Dania for the rest of the week. A little numb, maybe, a little distracted, not making my usual small talk. But, observing myself interact with her, I felt I held things together fairly well.

"Mark called," she told me.

"Okay."

"Is everything all right?"

"Fine," I said, forcing myself to smile. I wanted her to leave as quickly as possible. I wanted to be alone with my emotions.

We said good night, and in a sleepwalk, I went upstairs to check on the kids. Touching Smokie's soft forehead as she slept, I remembered the image that had come to mind when I'd faced Billy—of her putting her fingers on his cheek. I forced it all out of my mind. Couldn't bear to confront it now. Later, I thought. Later I'd be brave. Right now, I just wanted to escape.

The first thing I did was pull the plugs on the phones. I didn't want to talk to him. If he tried to reach me, I wanted him to worry. I wanted him to know what that felt like. I went to the kitchen, opened the refrigerator, found the bottle of Chardonnay, and poured myself a glass. Then, having second thoughts, I poured the wine back into the bottle and made myself chamomile tea.

All I wanted was to sleep, to forget everything: Billy's addiction, Vivi's arrogance, Cassandra's death and John's, the tape Spots had played me, Craig Detweiller, Whit and his secret, Mavis French, Tim Boudreau, Ron Braithwaite, the men who'd shot at Mark and me, the bullet holes in the left fender of my Civic.

But as I sat at the kitchen table and sipped the tea, which frankly did nothing to counter my agitation, I thought about Billy. About the defensiveness mixed with scorn.

Don't have time for a scene. Be home Tuesday. We'll talk then.

The ice in my chest burned—the way an icicle scorches your tongue if you lick it on an extremely cold day. I was way below zero by now . . . and descending. Anger, fiercer than anything I'd felt in my life, gnawed at my stomach. If he'd been there, I would have given in to my rage, but you can't fight with a ghost. The muscles in my back and abdomen stiffened, squeezing the emotion into a ball, hugging it deep in my chest.

Desperate to distract myself, I found the property transfer records, the old clips of Cassandra's many crusades, and I continued coloring the maps. I forced myself to concentrate, to banish my troubles from my mind. It was like working a jigsaw puzzle, focusing on one bit at a time, with the belief that eventually a picture would begin to form. When I completed the second map—the one that showed how each of the contested lots was disposed, I compared it to the first. The pattern jumped out as clear as day.

I went back through the clips, through my notes on the corporate filings I'd taken that morning, double-checking just to be sure.

I suddenly became aware of the sound of a car in the drive. I made sure the doors were locked. I lowered the light in the kitchen, where I'd been working. I heard footsteps. Rain had been drumming all night. Now the wind tossed droplets against the windows. There was a wild clattering. The rain came down harder. The gutters overflowed with a splash.

There was a knock at the mudroom door.

My pulse quickened. I froze.

The knocking grew louder. "Szabo?" I heard Mark call.

I sighed with relief.

"I'm spooked," I said as I opened the door. "I thought you were somebody coming to get me."

His height always surprised me. He stood six-feet-two. "Hi, Szabo," Mark said, grinning in his superior way. He wore jeans, a jersey, and a wet navy fleece vest. His hightops were soaked.

"Where'd the car come from?"

"Kate lent me hers."

"How nice of Kate."

"She wasn't doing anything tonight. Listen, I found something I thought you might be interested in."

"Come on in, I've got a load of new information too."

I felt calmer, in control. Hey, I told myself, you're doing fine.

Mark looked at me funny. "Where's Billy?"

"In La-La Land with the band."

We'd reached the kitchen. I turned up the light. "Want a glass of wine or beer?"

"I'll have a beer. What have you got?"

I listed the exotic brews Billy collected, thinking I should have insisted he quit alcohol too, not just the illegal stuff.

Mark wrinkled his nose. "I'll take that." He pointed to the Amstel light.

I handed it to him and poured myself another cup of tea. He twisted the cap of his beer, tossed it in the garbage pail, and walked to the table, pawing through my papers.

"What's this?" He took off his fleece vest. The jersey he wore was clean and tucked in. He sat down and looked over my colored maps. I found a floppy rabbit of Smokie's on the floor. I picked it up and hugged it. My stomach began to cramp.

"I figured it out," I said, ignoring the hurt inside.

Mark read through the material several times. He looked at the maps. He glanced at me, raised his eyebrows, and whistled. "This is what you were doing today?"

"No. I, uh, I checked some records in Montpelier."

He glanced at me with a mixture of annoyance and alarm. The swelling on his eye had diminished somewhat; the cut on his lip looked less fierce.

"You're asking to get yourself killed," he said quietly.

"Sorry. I couldn't help it."

I showed him the list of properties and corporations that had turned up. But I didn't explain.

"I also talked to Spots," I added. "He played me a tape."

"You went to Sparrowville?" His rough face no longer held any trace of snide conceit. He was angry. His eyes met mine. "Do you have a death wish?"

Dancing with Mr. D

"I had to see Billy."

I picked up my mug and took a sip. I put it down. I felt my hands trembling, but I ignored them.

"What's going on with you?"

"Look at all we found out," I said, "it's there in black and white and colored pencil. It's obvious. Doesn't it look like they were working together? She fights a sale to developers. He appears to oppose her, but then, when the deal falls through, he's there to pick up the pieces—at a very good price—every time."

"Wait a second," he said, burrowing into the maps, looking confused. "What are you talking about?"

"Craig. Craig and Cassandra. Look. See this property? Saragossa attempted to develop it. Saragossa is registered offshore. My guess is that Craig owns it, though I don't have proof. Cassandra fights the development. Two years later they donate the entire tract to the Green Trust." I showed him the Gemini conservation area on the map.

"So? She beat him."

I shook my head. "But at the same time, this piece here—on the highway. This area, not owned by Craig, is offered for sale. A strip mall is proposed. But the area is zoned for farming, not business. She fights like crazy when they petition to change the zoning. Two years later, the farmer—an old guy looking to retire—gives up after she scares away several developers. Then Craig buys the land for a third of what the farmer originally asked."

Mark scrutinized the map. "Okay, so Craig buys the land."

"You know what that piece is now?"

Mark looked at me. Then he suddenly grinned. "Strip mall with the motel."

"Craig held the land for two years, then he pushed through a zoning change. Cassandra didn't make a peep.

He built the mall, then sold it, clearing a $2-million profit."

"Wait a second. This is a different company. WolfStar."

"Yeah. Here's a list of corporations, most of them registered in places with very lax business and banking laws. Anytime one of these companies is involved, Cassandra folds her opposition to downtown development. In the case of a rural site, the land is donated to the Green Trust. It happens over and over again. Notice that Craig gets the lion's share. The value of the parcels he develops far exceeds what he paid for the pieces he donates to the trust."

"Okay," he said, after we carefully traced three of the properties. "Craig clearly profits. What does she get?"

"I think she wanted the land preserved. She had a crazy way of doing it, but I think she was sincere. And she was hung up on Craig."

Mark shook his head. "An odd couple."

I told him what I'd learned from Spots about Craig and Cassandra, about the drug deal gone bad, about Kathryn Dunnaston and the mountain.

I fell silent. The icicle in my chest burned deeper. I held the rabbit, stroking the ears.

Mark gazed at me with a penetrating stare. "Something's wrong."

"It's just Billy," I said quickly, hugging the floppy rabbit, then I pressed on with Craig's land deals. "But then, there's the Braithwaites. From what I hear, Craig made them an offer, typically low, but they refused to sell. One of his companies, SilverSeed, paid them $20,000 when Drew was dying. Maybe Craig felt a pang of conscience."

Mark pulled some papers out of the inside pocket.

"Here." He tossed them to me. There were some records of checks paid by Delstar to Ron's company, RB

Dancing with Mr. D

General Contracting. One a month for the last year, all for $5,000. The last check was paid in August.

"Where'd you get this?"

He grinned. "I'm not telling."

"We can't use it."

"But we know it. Look here," Mark said. He handed me a credit report on Craig. The guy had real estate all over the country. He sat on the boards of several corporations, none of which I'd heard of. He held major positions in banks and other stocks. His $4.2-million home had no mortgage. He owned it outright. The guy had to have some source of money other than Delstar, whose operations seemed pretty small. His assets were just too extensive.

"You know what I'm thinking," I said.

"What?" Mark leaned close to me. His gaze fixed on mine. His bruised eye looked sad, his thick lip swollen.

"I'm assuming Craig controls Mount Silver."

"Okay."

"I'm assuming Cassandra's property was more than a minor inconvenience. Let's say it threw a major monkey wrench in his plans."

"Okay."

"I'm assuming Craig doesn't like to give away money. I'm assuming he wants something in return."

"Okay."

We fell into silence. The papers outlining Craig's deals and Cassandra's past were spread out before us, telling their sad story of an unhappy woman who'd thrown herself at a man who hadn't wanted her. Allowed herself to be used by him, her values betrayed. Like a kid trying to buy friends by giving them all his toys.

I heard the tick of the antique clock. Each second was accompanied by the dry click of the hand moving.

Mark squirmed in the chair, which seemed small for him. His fleece vest lay on another chair beside him. He'd shaved before coming over, I noticed, seeing the smoothness of his broad cheek. I became aware of his physical presence. His long legs nearly touching mine. His feet, which he kept shifting to avoid hitting mine as I leaned forward poring over documents and maps. His muscular upper arms and shoulders and large sturdy hands.

He stared at me. "Tell me what's going on. You're not yourself tonight."

I closed my eyes and pulled Smokie's rabbit close to my chest. "It's Billy. He's . . . he's on coke again."

"Again?"

"You didn't know? Billy almost died a few years ago. From an overdose. That's why we're here." I bit back tears. I felt the tightness in my chest. "Once he starts, I don't know where it's going to end. I just found out tonight."

Mark studied me, not smiling, no snide grin. "Sorry," he said quietly.

"I'm going to get some water," I said. "Do you want anything?"

He glanced toward me. I could smell the faint scent of mint and Amstel Light on his breath.

His face was serious, eyes soft. The bruise had faded to a greenish blue.

He looked at my hands and the rabbit, which rested on the table. My green glitter nail polish was chipped; the stars I'd painted on for Smokie were dented at the points. Time for another manicure, I thought.

"Cute," he said.

"What—the nails?"

He touched the tip of my index finger with the tip of his.

I told myself I didn't like it.

"I love the way you decorate yourself. The earrings. The nails. The hair."

"Every Halloween I just go as me."

"Billy doesn't appreciate what a lucky guy he is. If I were him—"

"You're not."

"I wouldn't leave you alone like this. I wouldn't hurt you."

I met his gaze. So serious it hurt. I averted my eyes. The second hand moved another tick. The clock struck two. *Bong. Bong.* Then it stopped.

I laughed lightly. "Time to go."

"I'd rather stay."

"Please. Don't make this difficult."

His stare was intent. A standoff. After a moment, I touched his shoulder. His kiss was wet, sloppy, and urgent, with lots of tongue. The kind I never used to like. The coldness tore at my chest. I drew closer, trying to escape the chill.

After a few minutes, I became aware of a high-pitched sound. It came from far away. I pulled back. Ending the sloppy kiss was even harder than allowing myself to indulge in it. Mark's hands grasped my shoulders. I pressed my fingers against his lips.

"Mommy?"

It was Keith upstairs.

"Yes?" I called.

"Mommy, I'm scared."

"Did you have a bad dream?"

"Yes."

"I'll be right up."

* * *

In Keith's room, I went to my small son and held him in my arms. He buried his forehead into my neck, face hot from crying.

"What's wrong, sweetie?"

"When's Daddy coming home?"

"Soon."

"Why does he go away?"

"He's working."

"Other dads work, but they come home at night."

"He's a musician. They're different."

"Is he coming home?"

I didn't know what to say. I wanted to believe he would, even though the memory of my words this evening echoed in my mind. *It's really over this time, Billy.*

"Of course," I heard myself saying. "They'll be finished in a few days. And everything will be the way it was."

"You're sure?"

"Mmm hmm."

I held him in my arms. After a while, I heard the thud of the front door opening and closing. I heard footsteps, the crack of a car door shutting. I heard the car drive off. I heard the rain falling.

Chapter 28

I slept only fitfully. Finally, at four I gave up, showered, dressed, and had coffee. The fierce sting of last night's icicle inside my chest had been replaced by a hollow ache that I felt I could handle. I was determined to see my investigation through to the end. Billy didn't have time for a scene. Well, I thought bitterly, neither did I.

That settled, I trained my attention on work with a kind of robotic precision. Today, I had to talk to Whit despite my reluctance. I was ready at last to interview Craig and get the denials that I was sure would come. I wanted to ask him to explain certain evidence, such as the pattern of land deals he'd engaged in with Cassandra and Spots's assertions about his drug dealing and money laundering.

Nervous about confronting Craig, I decided that I needed to bring Mark in on the conference, both for safety and for corroboration, despite my misgivings. Remembering the men with the guns at Mount Silver, I feared what might happen, not during the meeting with Craig, but right afterward.

I'd dressed for battle in a snug skirt that shimmered with silver and a short-sleeved chenille sweater in a color called Ice, with a metallic thread in the weave. It was as if I hoped the glint of metal could provide armor against the enemy.

I read over my notes and organized my documents until the clock rolled around to seven. I found my Madonna bag and stuffed the documents inside. Then I woke and dressed the kids, gave them breakfast, dropped them at school, and drove to the office.

Outside, last night's rain had left the sky a freshly laundered blue. The air felt so clean that it was almost painful to breathe. The mercury had dropped to forty. Winter licked her lips, gathering the force to swoop down and consume us.

I wore suede pumps with tall heels and a row of tiny rhinestones down the toe, which I considered subtle enough for work but still fun. Glitter is my variation on whistling in the dark. Sometimes it's the only thing that pulls me through, making a show of bravado when inside I'm ready to go down for the count.

I paused long enough to hang up my coat and greet Sharon, who was just coming in. I avoided the newsroom because I didn't want to run into Mark. Not after last night. I needed at least one more cup of coffee before I could face him. At eight-thirty, I wasn't sure Whit would be able to give me the time I needed to lay out the story. Nevertheless, I rapped on his door, which as usual was partly open.

Whit was at his desk. The bay windows behind him displayed the Common, the bare trees, the buildings of the college in the distance. He glanced up from the computer. "If it's new for deadline, come in. If not, come back at ten oh five."

"Will do," I said.

That meant I had to go into the newsroom. I considered going to see Craig Detweiller right now on my own, but a shiver of fear dove through me, even in my relative numbness. First I needed to tell Whit.

I entered the newsroom. It felt strange not to have a deadline story. Mark was bent over his computer, working on a story of last night's basketball game. He glanced up as I approached my desk. Kate ran in to ask him a question about photos and saved me.

I booted up the computer and began tapping out the story of Craig Detweiller's real estate empire being built on drug money, of his tortured and long predatory relationship with Kathryn Dunnaston. Then I wrote a story of a young woman from Wisconsin, who in the early seventies left home. She got mixed up with the wrong sort of people in Chicago, tried to escape to what seemed to be a happy, peaceful commune in Vermont that turned into a nightmare. She escaped again, this time leaving behind her name and former life. She delved into environmental activism with a vengeance. I wondered how it had been with her: obsessed with Craig, angry with him for spurning her, for using her as an avenue to money, then leaving her at the first sign of danger. Had she worked with him? Or had he only taken advantage of her tactics of fighting development?

At the end, I believed, she'd decided to break with him completely. He wanted to take everything. He wanted to develop her mountain. He wanted to build a mall, where she saw a patch of wilderness even in the middle of the town. And she made her last stand. How convenient for him to have her die, I thought. And how inconvenient it would have been for him to have her go on living, threatening to expose his past. Perhaps he wanted to make a break himself, go clean with his new wife. With the ski property and condos, he could probably make tens of millions. Especially with Cassandra's property.

Spots, I realized, was the only other person—besides me—who knew the whole story.

I wrote it down. Of course I'd have to go back and painstakingly document it all. I had the motive. How did he go about killing her? If I were Craig, what would I do?

By that time, it was ten o'clock. Deadline passed, and the climate in the newsroom changed. People went to get coffee. A low buzz of murmurs arose. Phones began to ring.

"Szabo," Mark said at my ear.

I felt like I was back in high school. His presence was that discomforting. Grow up, I told myself. I forced myself to meet his gaze. The robot took over.

"I've got a meeting," I said, smiling hastily. "I'll catch you later."

"If you're going to talk to Whit," he said with a swagger and a "gotcha" grin, "I'll join you."

"This is just a preliminary meet." I blinked innocently. On second thought, it would be better if I handled this alone.

"The trouble with you, Szabo, is you don't know how to share."

He grabbed his notes. I grabbed mine.

"Come on," he said, a hand on my elbow, as we headed to the stairway. One kiss and he thought he owned me.

I shrugged the hand away. "I've been managing stairs on my own since I was two."

"Can't blame a guy for trying to be polite." He flashed me a jaunty grin.

I almost said something, but decided now was not the time or place.

"We have the whole story ready to lay out," I said when we entered Whit's office.

"Fair enough." Whit glanced at my stuffed bag and the sheaf of notes Mark held. "Why don't we sit at the table."

To the rear of the room was a library table with six

Dancing with Mr. D

leather chairs. I spread out the property maps, labeled and in order. I handed Whit the summaries I'd written of my interview with Spots and the information I'd culled from public records. Mark set down his outline of Craig's intricate web of financial dealings. I included the list of companies that I felt might, if traced to their source, have the same controlling owner.

I added a map of the Beamon's Mountain area, with Mount Silver's and Cassandra's properties outlined, showing the road Mount Silver wished to build through her land. I'd found it filed with the permitting agency in Vermont.

Whit strode stiffly to the table, donned his tortoiseshell reading glasses, and perused our presentation. He'd dressed in brown today. His nubby tweed jacket whispered of quality. It seemed more a part of the world of the past than of the present.

Mark shot me a glance, another of the "jaunty" variety. In my mental to-do list I entered: *Quash innuendo-drenched looks from co-reporter.* And then I kept my gaze firmly fixed on Whit.

After about ten minutes of speed reading, Whit looked up with a frown that deviated from his normal expression. If I had to qualify his look, I'd call it troubled.

He rested his hands on the table, cupping his fists, and gazed toward the portrait of his great-great-grandfather. The stern, stout man had Whit's rectangular face, but his jowls and rosy color contrasted with Whit's narrow sallowness.

"The tape," I began, deciding I had to jump in and sell this. It was going to be a hard sell, because I could see Whit wasn't buying—and I thought I knew why. "The tape could be a fake, but the rest is solid. Mark and I have overlapping pieces on the corporate holdings and financial deals. We need to do more searching for corroboration, but the structure is clear.

"I want to find the files on the trial. I think those records will give us the names of the people who were supplying the drugs to Cassandra. Now, admittedly, it's going to be hard to tie in Craig because all we have is Spots's story and the tape. But he says he has things like checks he didn't cash that are signed—"

"By Craig?"

I stopped. "Knowing Craig, I would assume not. Spots says he has physical evidence in a safety deposit box though. By the way, this isn't going to go any further than this room, is it?"

Whit's look was harsh. "What are you trying to say, Zoë?"

My heart started thumping, dully at first.

Whit glanced at Mark, who stood at the table like an eager puppy. "Sit down, Mark. Zoë, you too."

Mark sat across from him. I took a seat kitty-corner.

Whit studied Mark for a moment. Then he turned, taking off the glasses and wiping them with a lens paper he drew from his jacket pocket. He put his hands on the edge of the table in front of him and pushed his seat back.

"I know the two of you have put a lot of work into this," he said. "I appreciate your effort. And I don't like the look of that bruise. Zoë, I know you have your heart set on solving another crime. Personally, I don't see the connection between the ski resort here, the Green Trust there, this crazy story about drugs. You have an item from a newspaper from fifteen years ago. But I see no other evidence—"

"Except that she changed her name. See the high school photo? That's Cassandra."

"People change their names for all kinds of reasons.

Dancing with Mr. D

She had problems. Delusions of grandeur. I've talked to Detective Brannigan. He says it was murder. I have to take his word. But my feeling is that it could easily have been an accident—or—even suicide. I thought she was unbalanced. Even you did when you met her."

"Whit. You said it yourself. Brannigan says it was murder."

He frowned again. His skin was so pallid it was nearly green.

Mark jumped in. "Those guys who shot at us."

"Shot at you!" Whit cast a startled look toward me.

Mark turned to me. "You didn't tell him?"

"Uh—" I stammered.

"That does it," Whit stated matter-of-factly. "No more. Take this—whatever you've found. Give it to Brannigan."

"Wait a second, Whit," I broke in. "We've worked hard on this story. We have solid facts here. Take a minute to look at the property scams Cassandra and Craig were running. I think we're ready to go to print on that, if nothing else. I can interview a few people who lost fortunes—albeit small ones—but real nest eggs they were counting on, mostly for their old age, by being forced to sell to Craig for almost nothing. He donates half to the Green Trust and develops the cream for himself. He's made millions. We owe it to people in Greymont to let them know what he's done."

"You have no proof."

"Look at the maps. The purchase and sale prices. The *Eagle's* own accounts of Cassandra's opposition, which melts once Craig has control of the property. He makes a donation to the Green Trust—of land—about three months before he makes a sale of other prime lands he's scooped up after her opposition killed all deals."

"Zoë," Whit said abruptly. "Enough."

"I can't believe you're saying this!"

Whit stood, his face growing as dark as a Lou Reed lyric.

"The tape—"

"Enough."

Mark pressed my knee with his. I shot him an angry glance and stood.

"Whit, I don't believe you want to suppress this story. Not in your heart of hearts."

"I won't touch it, Zoë."

"Why not?"

"Because . . . I'm too closely involved."

"How?"

Whit glanced toward Mark. He turned back to me.

"Craig is an old friend."

"Because he's your friend, you'd let him get away—"

Mark tugged at my arm, frowning, giving me a signal, saying, Let's go, this is getting us nowhere. I ignored him.

"I don't understand," I said, staring at Whit.

"There's no proof here," Whit said. "Now I have other work."

I reluctantly packed up my papers. Mark went ahead of me. I waited for a moment, signaled him to go on without me. I stopped and closed the door.

"Whit," I said. "I just can't let this go."

He looked surprised to see me still standing there, challenging him.

"Give me a week. I'll find solid sources that will expose these deals for what they were."

"No."

"Three days."

"The story is dead."

"So you're going to let him win."

"You're taking this too personally."

His remark intensified my urgency. "Maybe that makes two of us. What if I gave you incontrovertible proof that he murdered her?"

His fingers, pale, with the veins firm and blue, closed over the back of the leather chair by his side.

"You'd let him get away with it?"

Whit's gaze fixed on the globe in its antique stand. He didn't speak, but he seemed to hesitate.

"So there is a limit to your loyalty."

"We're not anywhere near that limit now. I think we've pursued this long enough."

"I've looked up to you." Not flattery, just abject pleading. "Don't let me down."

"The subject is closed."

"Are you protecting someone?"

"Some debts, Zoë, supersede all other matters."

"What do you owe Craig?"

"I suggest you leave before either of us says something we will both regret."

"Like, 'You're fired'?"

Whit blanched. "Possibly."

"Or maybe like, 'Is Craig Detweiller blackmailing you?'"

It was so silent that I could have sworn Mother Nature stopped the flow of the atmosphere around the planet.

Finally Whit looked at me. "Discretion," he said quietly, "may be a waning virtue, but it is one I value."

"Is that a synonym for cover-up?"

His pale lips twitched. "I suggest you check your thesaurus."

The atmosphere slowly started moving. I heard the shudder of the glass as the wind rattled at the pane.

Chapter 29

"Any word about your car?" I asked Mark as he adjusted the passenger seat in my Civic. He pushed all the way back, but his legs were still cramped.

"*Nada*," he said.

I risked a glance at his face. Still in pretty bad shape.

"Mark, about last night—"

His swollen lip jutted forward. His droopy bruised eye caught my glance.

I stared at the steering wheel, car keys in my hand. "Billy and I may have problems, but I love him."

He touched my finger. I cocked my head, meeting his gaze. His shrug was casual, his grin forced. "I get the picture," he said after a few seconds. "You don't have to spell it out."

I put the key in the ignition. The engine turned over immediately. Well, I thought, that was easier than I'd expected.

"Got the starter fixed."

"Yeah. You don't mind if I take the lead on this interview?"

"Do it any way you like, Szabo."

"Thanks."

"*De nada.*"

We rode in silence.

Dancing with Mr. D

* * *

Permetti's was one of the out-of-the-way places that people in Greymont might go to meet if they were having an affair. It was darkly lit, more like a Florida bar than a New England eatery, with booths that were private. Few people went there during lunch hour, so it was a good bet you wouldn't be seen.

The owner, a short, balding man, an Italian by way of Argentina, led us to a booth when we told him we were waiting for Mr. Detweiller. I'd set up the lunch meeting shortly after leaving Whit's office. For once I was happy to have Mark along on an interview. The memory of the gunmen at Cassandra's cabin had convinced me to bring him. I felt protected with him by my side.

We had breadsticks, olives, and fizzy mineral water while we waited.

Craig arrived when we'd almost given up on him. Dapper as always, although discreetly so, he found us easily. He slid into the booth next to me.

"Hi, Zoë," he said amiably.

"This is Mark Polanski," I said. "My associate."

Craig laughed. "Yes, I know Mark. How are you doing? I still remember the perfect game you pitched in your senior year. It doesn't get much better than that."

Mark modestly bowed his head as if he were ashamed to be reminded of his glory days.

Craig glanced around, alert, friendly. He caught the waitress's eye effortlessly. She came as if drawn by a magnet. He complimented her, mentioned the last time he'd been in, thanked her for being so lovely to his companions. "Does Reggio have anything back there that's not on the menu? Anything special?"

"The calamari is perfect. Flown in fresh this morning."

Craig turned to us and asked if we wanted some.

We both declined. Craig ordered it with an appetizer of melon and prosciutto. I passed, not wanting food to interfere with my interviewing. Mark, disappointed that he couldn't have a meatball sandwich, ordered spaghetti alla Bologna, which Craig recommended.

"What can I do for you," Craig said, smiling at Mark, including him almost as an afterthought. Mark had agreed to let me do the talking. He was going to listen carefully, so we could compare notes after the interview. We both wanted to catch Craig in a lie.

"We thought you could fill in background. And confirm some facts we've uncovered. You've been in town a long time."

"All my life."

Mark said, "Except for that short period when you went away to college."

Craig regarded him for a split second, then smiled at me.

"When did you first become acquainted with Cassandra Dunne?"

"Let me see . . ." He took a few moments to ponder. It was very difficult for him to dredge up the memory. "It must have been during the Gemini Hill Farm fight."

"You never met her before?"

"It could have been a few months, even a year before. I believe she arrived here in . . . uh, your article said '78."

Memorized the article, I thought.

"Do you have any idea where she moved from?"

Again he took time to think. "Can't say that I do. Tim Boudreau might. They were good friends."

Mark said, "Yeah. We're going to talk to Tim."

"Good," Craig said. "You do that."

"I'll tell you why I'm asking," I said. "I can't find any trace of her before she moved to Greymont."

Dancing with Mr. D

"Really?"

"She seems to have been conjured up out of thin air."

He smiled.

The appetizers came. We paused while the waitress passed the food around.

Craig dug into his melon.

"I was just wondering," I said, as if throwing it off, "if she might have had something to hide before she came here. Something she didn't want anyone to know about."

"I suppose it's possible."

"Don't you always check people's backgrounds before you do business?"

His icy eyes met mine. "Always." He took a sip of imported water. "For example, I've looked into yours."

He took a spoonful of melon, chewed it thoughtfully, swallowed, and took another.

"And Whit's?" asked Mark.

Craig hardly acknowledged the remark. "No need to check on an old friend."

I continued. "What do you know about Wonderland Sounds?"

"Is that where your husband is recording with Vivi Cairo? The woman who has openly accused me of conspiring to kill Cassandra Dunne?" He smiled thinly. "So that I can single-handedly cause the seas to boil?"

"Do you know anything about the way the studio was built?"

"Not much more than you do, I'm sure."

"Do you know Tom Sporkartch? He also goes by the name of Spots."

Craig smiled calmly. "It sounds familiar, but I can't quite place it."

"How about Kathryn Dunnaston?"

Craig seemed completely at ease. "Never heard of her."

"And your company, Delstar. Does it have any connection with an organization named Mount Silver Resort and Mountain Properties?"

He paused. "My assistant, Alida Kai, is involved with a company by that name. But, of course, you know that since you called her the other day." He laughed mildly. "I don't know why you attempted to disguise your voice and use a pseudonym. Perhaps you enjoy playing games. Usually I don't have time, but I'm willing to make an exception, since your boss is a friend."

I swallowed. "Have you heard of a company called SilverSeed?"

He gazed at me, scrutinizing. "I'm not sure."

"It paid $20,000 to the Braithwaites shortly before their son died. For a right-of-way they never used."

"Oh, yes," he said calmly. "I heard about that. Have you looked up their board of directors?"

I glanced at Mark.

Mark said, "The company is registered in Andorra."

Craig nodded.

"But," Mark added, "it seems SilverSeed has done quite a lot of business over the past few years with Delstar. Funny you never heard of it."

Craig smiled congenially. "A bright young man like you could go far."

Again we paused while the food was served. Craig's calamari. Mark's spaghetti.

When the waitress left, I decided to cut to the chase. I handed him the list of companies that kept turning up whenever we investigated the land deals in Greymont or Wonderland Sounds.

"Do you serve on the board or as an officer of any of these corporations?"

He read the list to humor me. Like it was a childish prank that he was going along with because he was such an amiable guy.

"I don't know." His voice grew intimate, his smile cozy. "Mind if I keep this list, so I can check?"

"No. I guess not."

"Thanks." He tucked the paper in the inner pocket of his jacket, then began to eat his lunch. Mark glanced at me. For once he refrained from indulging his appetite.

"Go ahead," he said, noticing that Mark hadn't touched his food. "It's delicious. The best."

"I'd love to hear the story of how you entered the real estate business," I said. "You grew up in modest circumstances."

Craig ate slowly, with good manners. He wiped his mouth with the cloth napkin. He turned his eyes on me. He took a sip of his water. He took all the time he needed.

He patted his stomach, which seemed fairly flat for a man of his age. "Thirty pounds. I lost it in the last year. Since I got married. You see, Zoë. A man will give up his vices for the right woman."

I blinked.

Craig nodded almost inconspicuously to the waitress. He asked for an espresso with a twist of lemon peel. "Either of you care to join me?"

Mark and I shook our heads.

"Put mine on my tab. I think they're going to pay separately." He looked at Mark, then at me. "Don't want to do anything that looks improper, do we?"

"No," I said.

When the waitress went, I said, "You didn't answer my last question."

"I didn't? Oh. Modest circumstances? Yes. Anything else I can help you with?"

"You made a lot of money in the past fifteen, twenty years."

He glanced benignly at Mark. "You've checked my credit?"

Mark didn't answer, but it was clear he had.

"My research," I persisted, "shows you had ties to known drug dealers."

Craig smiled as if we were just chatting about the weather. He waved to the waitress and asked her to add a shot of Amaretto to his espresso.

I thought, Okay, he knows how much I know. Instead of beating a measured retreat, I pushed forward, despite the fact that under the table Mark was stepping on my foot so hard that it hurt.

"My research also shows that certain evidence will come to light if anyone at Wonderland Sounds is harmed."

"I used to love smoking," Craig said, "a great cigar after a good, rich meal. Now I'm married to the woman of my dreams and I have to give up all the pleasures of my earlier life. But once in a while," he added after a few moments, "I indulge myself."

He drew a cigar from his inside pocket.

"Would you like one?" he asked Mark.

"No thanks," Mark said.

"Nasty habit," Craig answered.

I watched as Craig snipped off the tip with a silver clipper, struck a match, and then puffed luxuriously, almost gulping in the smoke. With a soft blow, he extinguished the flame and tossed the match in an ashtray the waitress had provided. No smoking was permitted in Greymont's restaurants. Nobody complained.

I realized then that the very last thing I should have done was set up this meeting.

On the way back to the office, I said, "He was just sitting there, while I opened my big mouth and told him every last bit I had on him. He knows now. He knows."

Mark winced as I took a curve going about ten miles faster than I should have. My old Honda hugged the road.

"Sometimes you've got to put the ball over the plate. You're taking a chance, but it's up to your opponent to swing. Sometimes he misses."

"Mark, I'm afraid."

"You've got one thing in your favor."

"What?"

"He knows there are two of us. He's got to assume we've told Whit. If he killed her, that means we're closing in on him and he's got to take all of us out."

"That's supposed to set my mind at ease?"

"How's he going to get out of this trap, Zoë? Spots is in Vermont with the goods in a safety deposit box. Whit is sitting on the story. What's he going to do? Send the four of us on a cruise and sink the ship? He's too smart not to want to get away clean."

Chapter 30

"I hear you're off the Cassandra Dunne story," Kate said Friday after deadline.

"Officially as of this morning," I said.

She flashed a smile. "Now if I could only get my mom to let go of the past. She seemed to be getting back on her feet, but the last few weeks have been—as you say—nightmare time."

"My life hasn't been exactly a piece of cake in recent weeks either. In fact, I could really use a friend. What say we get together and commiserate?"

"Sure, name your day."

"Tonight? My place."

"You're on. I'll bring some Chinese food. Movie?"

"Keep it upbeat. So it doesn't get too teary when we unload afterward. Any gossip?"

"I might have a few tidbits."

Throughout the day, in between work on the new story Whit had assigned—the mentoring program at the high school—I tried to get in touch with Billy. The only response at the studio was the answering machine. *We're recording platinum*, it sang in harmony, *Leave it or lose it*. On my third try, I swallowed my pride and left a message asking him to call me. He didn't.

I spent a few hours doing interviews at the school.

Kate went with me and took photos. Afterward I made a trip to the library. In an exercise in futility I searched the microfilms of the New York papers. I scanned through the weeks in the summer of 1978 around the time when Spots said he'd recorded his incriminating demo, looking for some reference to the shootout or the trial at which Kathryn Dunnaston had been requested to testify.

Finally, in a tiny item in the Metro section of the *New York Times*, I found a mention of two men found dead in a Greenpoint warehouse, attributed to a mob killing. No mention of drugs. No mention of an escaped witness. I phoned the precinct in which the killings had occurred. I spent a half hour talking to an old timer with a long memory and a fondness for reminiscing. One of the guys nabbed had turned informant. He named Kathryn Dunnaston as someone who could confirm his story. The narcotics squad had wanted to nail the seller. They issued a subpoena for Dunnaston but it had never been served. The dealer they'd been trying to bring to trial had been indicted and convicted in a conspiracy to distribute case five years later.

"So eventually these guys get caught," I said.

The police detective sighed. "Don't kid yourself, honey. Plenty are running around loose. I could tell you stories."

Kate arrived at seven. Keith insisted on wearing his lexovisaurus costume while he ate. Smokie banged on the keyboard, preparing for Monday by making up a Halloween "song" with every sound effect imaginable: screams, ghoulish laughter, echoey organ, and, of course, her favorite, dentist's drill.

After I put the kids to bed, we decided not to watch the movie she'd brought. Instead, I told her about Billy.

Anger mixed with confusion roiled through me as I talked, though I tried to cover with an outward show of bravado.

"The thing that worries me," I said when I'd finished describing what had happened, "is that they say you don't just start slowly and work up to what you were using before. They say you start where you left off. Where he left off, Kate, he was spending several thousand a week on his habit. Where he left off, he barely escaped a fatal aneurysm. He was in a coma for two days."

So much for the bravado. Well, at least I had someone I could confide in.

"Have you listened to his side?" Kate asked.

"He said he didn't have time for a scene. That he'd talk to me Tuesday. I've spent most of today hanging on the phone trying to get through but no one picks up at Wonderland Sounds."

"So you haven't spoken to him since?"

I shook my head.

"You have to give him a chance to explain."

"Oh, he could talk the birds out of the trees. I don't want to go through that again."

"He adores you," she said, her voice throaty. "Anyone can see it whenever he looks at you. And he's so sweet with the kids."

I swallowed. The sounds of an automobile driving by for some reason silenced us both. I watched the lights move through the room. I tried to bury my emotions. Pressing them deep. Trying not to think about the sweet things Billy had done since we'd passed through the crisis. Little things, like the way he held Smokie's hand and looked deep into her eyes when he talked to her, taking her seriously.

Like the way he helped Keith put together an intricate Lego kit, not doing it for him, patiently letting him make mistakes and figure them out for himself, and taking real delight in the finished product, no matter how lopsided.

Like getting up at four A.M. with me when I couldn't sleep and listening while I rambled on excitedly about a story I was working on, asking perceptive questions, bantering back and forth, trading ideas.

"Ron and his wife have had some hard times. But they've been working on it. You can't just give up, Zoë."

"What am I supposed to do? See a marriage counselor?"

"Maybe."

"Oh, please."

"What if he made a commitment to get counseling. And join some group, like Narcotics Anonymous?"

He'd tried the group stuff, but after we'd moved to Greymont he just wanted to put all that behind him. "Billy wants to live the way he did when he was in his early twenties at the height of his fame."

"Maybe part of him wants that, but part of him wants more."

"Enough about me," I said. "Tell me. To what—or whom—do we attribute the new spring in your step?"

"It's too early to tell. But . . . I've made a decision." She smiled. "I haven't done anything yet. But I thought maybe I'd make the first move. You know—with Mark. What do you think?"

I thought about it. "What's your plan?"

"Well, you know how he likes sports?"

"Mmm."

I remembered Mark's fingertip touching mine. I pressed the spot. The taste of mint and beer. Yesterday in my car. The casual shrug, not so casual grin. How stupid could I be? A dumb jock with an ego the size of the Astrodome.

"One of my uncles has season tickets to the Celtics," Kate was saying. "I can probably talk him into giving me two tickets to one of the games. I've been feeling so miserable lately. I'm ready to put the past behind me. Do you think Mark would say yes, or would he be insulted, my taking the initiative?"

I pressed her shoulder, feeling friendship for her, wanting her happiness. "Go ahead. Be brave."

Her eyes clouded. "What happened with the murder story? Have the police made any headway?"

"You don't want to hear about Cassandra."

"I should learn to let go." Kate put her feet up on the coffee table and rested her head against the back of the sofa. "Test me."

I laughed. "You want to hear my theories?"

"Why not?"

"Well," I equivocated. "There's not much to tell. I'm worried this guy in Vermont might get hurt before I can convince him to tell what he knows to the police." I was thinking maybe I should try to call Spots again. I would, as soon as she left.

"Do you have any idea who killed her?"

I scanned her forthright face. She was so Ralph Lauren, I could almost see her in the saddle taking a jump. She wore a preppy navy blue sweater and pressed jeans. Her long braid was tied with a matching velvet ribbon.

"Whit has been giving me lectures about corroboration, facts versus conjecture."

We fell into thought for a few minutes. I kept thinking about Billy, the way he'd looked at me, the eyes lit unnaturally by the drug, the guilt making him defensive and accusing. I rubbed the glittery polish on my index finger, touched the dented star.

"Cassandra really hurt you, didn't she?" I asked.

"Yes. She caused my family so much suffering. I'm glad she died. She deserved it."

"That's a hard attitude, Kate. Unforgiving." Maybe I was talking to myself.

"You didn't have to sit and watch the life seep out of my brother inch by inch, day by day. Ron was always difficult. Belligerent. He used to beat me up when we were kids . . . but Drew was the sweetest—" Kate pressed her hand against her mouth. "He made a, um, special place for me. A hideaway, when I was seven. So Ron wouldn't bother me with his stupid trucks. Even then he loved trucks, my jerk of a big brother. But Drew was sensitive. He had so much potential. He shouldn't have died."

I touched her shoulder. It always came back to this. I handed her a tissue and she wiped her eyes.

"It's hard to get over someone's death," I said. "My mother. I still remember how weak she was. I wish I'd been nicer to her. I was such a rebel. Some moments you wish you could relive."

She nodded. "It's been hard on the whole family."

"You and your mom seem to be taking it harder than your brother or your father."

"No. It's just that we show it differently. Ron always had trouble with his temper, but recently it's . . ." She looked at me and made a small confession. "Sandy's come to my place a couple of times. Afraid he might hurt her or their kids."

"I'm sorry."

"Funny. When it happens to other people, you think . . . I don't know . . . you empathize, but you wonder how could they let it go that far. When it happens to you, it really feels shameful. I don't want to tell anyone. Mom is completely unable to function, so she's useless. Sandy . . . she's embarrassed. I did convince her to go to counseling. And it's helping. I wouldn't be telling you this if you weren't having problems with Billy. Talking it out with a professional can help. Needless to say, this is confidential."

I studied Kate. Her strong jaw and earnest brown eyes. It was at that moment that the details I'd been overlooking snapped into place. I hoped I was wrong, but I couldn't avoid them anymore. "Kate," I said tentatively. "You said you were with your mom and dad the night Cassandra fell."

Her eyes reflected wariness and distrust. "Yes."

"And Ron was there."

"Yes."

"What time was that?"

It was quiet enough to hear that ticking clock.

"He came just before midnight."

"When did he leave?"

"He didn't. He stayed the entire night."

"Forgive me for asking, but how do you know?"

She glared at me without speaking for several seconds. But then she answered. "We were all awake. The entire night."

"That's unusual, don't you think?"

"No."

"Why not?"

"Because it was the anniversary of Drew's death. And that's the way we . . . remember him."

"Kate," I said delicately, "that guy in Vermont. The one who drowned. He might have witnessed the murder."

Anger flared in her dark brown eyes. "What's that got to do with me?"

"As a reporter I have to come up with what-if scenarios. A lot of times I'm totally off base. But if you know something—let's say you fell asleep that night for a couple of hours, you should go to Brannigan and get it off your chest. He's a nice guy. He'll understand."

"I've already talked to Detective Brannigan."

"And?"

Her jaw stiffened, her eyes brightened. "You are so—ruthless. Taking advantage of my friendship to pry."

"Ruthless? Kate, go to Brannigan and tell him the truth before it's too late."

Our eyes met. Her face hardened. We stared at each other. The antique clock on the mantelpiece ticked dryly. I counted the seconds. She flushed.

"You're just like all the other outsiders," she spat suddenly.

"Sorry," I said, reaching to touch her shoulder.

She wrested away. The anger made her face ugly. "Trying to grab all you can get and lord it over us with your snob appeal, your politically correct bullshit, your green that and green this, making it impossible for people who grew up here to survive! We can't build a goddamn fence without a permit! We can't pay the goddamn property taxes because you want schools and conservation land!"

She pulled away from my calming gesture.

"Kate. I'm honestly sorry."

"Damn you!" she shouted.

"Kate, this isn't about being outside or inside. You're risking being an accessory to murder. I'm trying to help you."

"Help? That's a laugh."

"What are you going to do?"

"Nothing."

"Nothing? Kate, I'm pleading with you. Go to Brannigan. Go tonight. Go before it's too late. He's killed twice already. Don't let it happen again."

"You're wrong. Ron was with us all night. He didn't kill anyone."

I didn't know whether to believe her or not. I just wasn't sure.

She grabbed her jacket and rushed out the door. I heard her pickup roar, the gravel spitting as she fled. I thought, She's a friend. If there were a reason for her to call Brannigan, if she were providing an alibi she knew to be untrue, she would change her mind. I had faith in her.

Too much had happened. John had drowned. I wasn't sure it was related, but what if it were? I remembered the night he died. I'd driven up to Wonderland Sounds, the bright headlights behind me. Mark saying, *You couldn't spot a tail on a dog.* And the threat painted on Vivi's van? NEXT TIME YOU DIE. Who was the intended victim? Or was it just a cry of undirected rage?

I heard the clock ticking again. I wondered if I should call Brannigan. No, I'd give Kate the benefit of the doubt. I'd see her at the soccer game tomorrow. If she didn't agree to talk to Brannigan, I would go myself. If Ron hadn't committed the murder, then—no matter what, I'd lost a friend, one I'd come to treasure. If she went to Brannigan herself, there was a chance the damage might someday be repaired.

Chapter 31

On Saturday morning the clouds were low, the air was cool, and the sky threatened rain. The sturdy oaks still held their foliage, though the onslaught of frost had turned the burgundy to brown. Smokie was at home with Dania, who would take her to a birthday party later in the morning. Keith's team was scheduled to play Ellis's. Hugging my quilted jacket, trying to warm myself, I scanned the panorama for Kate. She was nowhere to be seen. Ron hadn't shown up either. Maybe Kate had called Brannigan. Maybe they had both gone to the police.

My confusion and fears had dug in during the night. As my glance swept the fields, I caught sight of Mavis French. Craig and Jenny Detweiller kept her company. The sight of Craig, rubbing his hands, huffing with the cold, sent a chill through me. Mark had another interview with the basketball coach this morning. He'd offered to stop by and catch the first half hour, but I'd begged off, despite the fact that I knew Keith would have loved to see him. Now I wished I hadn't been so hasty.

The wind scurried across the grass. The game between the Turquoise and the Green team started. My heart sank as I caught sight of Ron Braithwaite jogging from the parking lot. Despite the weather, he wore a dark green T-shirt, sleeves torn off to display his biceps. He shouted instructions, waving away the assistant coach. Was it my imagination or did Sandy, whom I spotted at the sidelines with her stroller, seem to tense when he appeared? Stopping for a moment, he shielded his eyes and scanned the crowd. I slid behind a group of mothers at the sidelines, hoping to avoid his eye.

"What team is your child on?" the woman beside me asked. I pointed to Keith.

"My daughter's the one with the pigtails." She indicated the super-athletic little girl I'd noticed before, the one on Keith's team who ran with the lead pack of boys. We chatted as I shivered. The wind whipped through me.

During the next half hour, I was so preoccupied I could barely follow the action of the game. The coaches shouted instructions, running down the field with the kids, yelling all the way. The children went in and out of play.

"Mom!" I heard Keith calling at some point. "Watch. I'm going in!"

Though I'd always considered him to be awkward, today Keith seemed to be able to stretch his long legs and keep up with the small knot of boys and the super-athletic girl. According to my neighbor, the score was zero-zero. "This is a great game," she kept effusing.

"The kids seem happy," I responded. To me it was just blotches of turquoise and green bobbing back and forth across the centerline.

"Good play!" she screamed.

Keith's coach shouted, "Attaway. Watch your left!"

Ronnie Jr., by some miracle, was running the ball down the field, a pack of kids behind him. Keith and the athletic little girl ran down to guard the goal. Ronnie kicked. Keith intercepted and began dribbling in the opposite direction. He passed to the super-athletic little girl. Between the two of them they ran the ball down the entire length of the field.

I was watching the ball at Keith's feet. Suddenly it wasn't there anymore. I looked up just in time to see the goalie fall. The ball bounced into the net. I was so surprised that at first I thought it must have been a mistake. I became aware of cheering, of Keith grinning toward me, of the super-athletic girl's mother next to me shouting cheers. Several of the kids crowded around Keith, punching his shoulder, saying, "Nice play."

Mavis, a few feet away, called to me. "Open your mouth, girl! Your son just scored a goal."

I raised my arms and cheered at the top of my lungs. When the game was over I ran to Keith and threw my arms around him. "Wow! That was awesome. Great job!"

Keith tried to hide his joy with a light shrug. I gazed at him, teary with motherly pride. His eyes were shining. "Too bad Dad's not here, huh, Mom?"

I tousled his hair. "He would be so impressed."

"Can I go for ice cream?"

"Last game of the season," his coach told me. "Sponsor treats."

"Gee, I have to work this afternoon." I checked my watch. Nearly noon. Time to call Kate and Brannigan. I glanced around, spotting Ron across the field in a huddle with Craig Detweiller. What was that about?

Keith pulled at my jacket, "Can I Mom? Can I?"

I was dimly aware of Ellis with a group of kids nearby. Mavis stood near Keith. Elegant as usual in a cream turtleneck, suede coat, and perfectly pressed wool slacks, she met my gaze.

"I'll bring him home," Mavis offered. "Ellis is going. It's about time those two started to learn to speak to each other with respect."

I stared at her uncertainly. "You *knew*?"

She raised an eyebrow. "Mr. Keene called last week. You might have said something. Instead of barging into my store and making outrageous accusations."

"Accusations?" I bristled. Then I shook my head with a conciliatory smile. "I'm sorry. I should have called about Keith."

"Hmm," she said after a moment's thought, "as I've told Ellis, sorry is a good place to start." She glanced toward our sons. Ellis and Keith had joined a circle of boys who were kicking the soccer ball back and forth.

As I followed her line of vision, my eye took in a scene far beyond the children. On the rise near the parking lot, Ron Braithwaite was gesturing wildly. Craig reached toward him. Ron's arms moved threateningly. Sandy watched in alarm, hands covering her mouth.

"Excuse me. I've got to run." I hastily scribbled my address, explaining when the baby-sitter would be there. Mavis assured me she'd keep Keith until Dania returned from the birthday party with Smokie. By the time I'd kissed Keith good-bye, Ron had disappeared.

I ran to Sandy. "Where's Ron?" I shouted.

She flushed as if I'd caught her doing something wrong. "He had to go out on a job."

"A job?" I said sharply. At first I thought it was my tone of voice that upset her, but another glance told me it was more. Her hands fluttered nervously. "I'm so ashamed."

"What are you talking about?"

She gazed at me numbly. Her face reddened. "We hated her so much. You have to understand."

"Tell me! Where is he?"

Sandy had tears in her eyes. Her face flushed, her mouth twisted. She shook uncontrollably. "Kate told me

Dancing with Mr. D

this morning that she was going to the police. He swore to me he was at his parents that night. He swore! And Kate—I'd believed her. They lied to me. She told me not to tell him what she was doing, but I—"

"You told Ron that Kate went to the police?" Of course she told him. I read it in her eyes.

Sandy's face contorted. "Craig tried to calm him down. But he took the car. He was screaming about the crazy hippie in Vermont. He's going to get them all. He's—"

"Vermont?"

"Craig said there was a witness—"

Not waiting to hear more, I ran to my Honda, jumped in, and started driving. If I could catch up with him, maybe I could figure out a way to get the police to stop his car. I took out my cell phone and called Detective Brannigan, but he was out. I left a message that I thought Ron Braithwaite was on his way to Wonderland Sounds, that I was following, to please send help.

I called Mark at the *Eagle*. Sharon answered. "He's on an interview." I rang his cell phone and reached his messaging service. I left word where I was going and why. I tried Brannigan again, leaving an even more desperate message. I called Wonderland Sounds. *"We're recording platinum,"* the machine sang. *"Leave it or lose it!"*

I drove as fast as I could, making the same calls over and over again, reaching no one. The body of my Honda shook as the speedometer crept past eighty-five. I hadn't spotted Ron's dark green Grand Cherokee. Although he had only a few minutes lead on me, his vehicle could travel much faster than my Civic. I scanned the side of the highway, praying that I would spot the Cherokee pulled over with police lights flashing behind it.

I climbed into the mountains just over the Vermont border. As the altitude rose, my Honda lost power. The

Grand Cherokee would reach Wonderland Sounds far ahead of me. Again I made my phone calls, again to no avail.

In desperation, I hit the 911 key. But the dispatcher couldn't understand what I was trying to tell her. An enraged man with a hair-trigger temper. An accidental drowning that was actually murder. A second witness, whose life was in danger.

"Are you with him now?" she said.

"No, but could you send a police car to make sure they're protected. I can't get through by phone."

"Where are you?"

I told her I was driving.

"I'm sorry, ma'am," she said. "Unless you actually have witnessed an incident, there's nothing I can do."

I shouted the address as the connection began to break up. "Call Kevin Brannigan—"

But I had lost them. From here on the cell phone was useless.

Twenty minutes later, I arrived at Wonderland Sounds. I sped down the dirt road and pulled into the row of cars and vans. Despite the icy fog that had begun to settle, my eyes quickly spotted the green Jeep Grand Cherokee. I parked and made a final attempt to use my phone, but the "no service" message blinked unrelentingly.

The reality of the situation began to settle over me. I'd done the drive in record time. The whole way I'd been telling myself that I was overreacting. That Ron wasn't going to Wonderland Sounds. That my imagination was playing wild tricks on me. That I would burst in on the band while they were recording and everyone would laugh when I explained why I'd come. What a tale I'd

Dancing with Mr. D

have to tell Brannigan. What a ribbing I'd get from Mark about the desperate messages I'd left.

Now I saw it was no joke. As the realization sank in, another darker one began to overwhelm me. What could I do? I was completely unarmed and I was certainly no match for Ron. I wondered if he had a gun.

The trunk of the Cherokee was open. With a sense of unreality, I examined the contents. Tools, blades, cutting implements of all kinds. Cans of oil and gasoline. I looked for a rifle or a shotgun. Certainly Ron carried one. I didn't see any. The best thing to do, I decided, would be to find out where he was, then run for help, or find a phone.

And that was when I heard the sound. At first the rumble was faint. Like a motorboat starting up. The sound whined high, then the pitch dropped lower, roaring crazily. I looked up at the telephone and electric lines that ran through the trees toward the house and barn studio. My eyes traced the wires until they reached the pole that began to sway. It crashed down through the branches.

My hands fell on the first familiar implement in Ron's open toolbox. A hammer—what I could do with it I had no idea, but I wanted something for protection.

As I stole through the woods toward the studio, the phantasmagoric faces painted on the tree trunks loomed out of the icy fog. I followed the buzzing noise. Remembering the tricks Spots played with sound, I told myself that I was hearing a synthesizer, not a chain saw. I stopped and crouched, peering through the fog. Ron's hulking figure became visible through the strands of mist at the studio door not ten feet away. Sweat glistened on his arms. He wielded an enormous chain saw, its red paint flaking, its blade snarling angrily. He worked quickly, expertly, cutting a circular panel out of the thick oak door. The saw fell idle. Ron kicked in the panel, the wood splintering noisily. He ducked inside.

My eye took in the downed pole, which had fallen on the path near the huge barn, painted in swirls of blue and pink and purple. I'd never seen it before in daylight and the intensity of the color struck me. The phone line had been severed.

My gaze fell to the claw-headed hammer. I clutched it like a talisman and slipped through the hole in the door into the studio.

Once inside, I flattened myself against the wall, my eyes adjusting to the darkness. Fog drifted in on a shaft of light from outdoors. The chain saw rattled through the control room door, about twenty feet down the hall. After slicing it like butter, Ron idled his saw and stepped inside. I heard the shouts, recognizing the voices—Duck's growl, Spots's higher-pitched cry, and Billy's startled baritone. Again I heard the motor rumble louder. Oh, God, I thought. We're all going to die.

I crept to the control room door and peered through the hole that Ron had sawed open. The sight that met my eyes was horrifying. Ron Braithwaite, his back turned toward me, all two hundred and fifty pounds of rock-hard muscle straining, was swinging the roaring chainsaw back and forth like an enormous baseball bat. In various stances facing him were Duck, Billy, and Spots shielding themselves with laughably inadequate implements. Duck held a high hat aloft like a shield. Spots grasped a heavy black music stand. Billy raised a shiny chrome mikestand the mike and cord still attached.

A curtain of blood clouded my eyes. For a split second I thought I'd gone blind, then my vision cleared. They were all so intensely focused on the spitting blade that no

Dancing with Mr. D

one had any idea I was there. The small room reeked of gasoline. Out of the corner of my eye, through the glass to the studio, I glimpsed Vivi and Cerita, mouths open in silent shrieks.

Billy brought his metal stand up. It hit Ron's arms. For a moment the two men held each other at bay, muscles straining. But Billy, though scrappy, was no match for Ron's massive strength. The saw blade moved toward Billy. I screamed, lifting the hammer in my hands and throwing it. The hammer hit the whirring blade and recoiled, bouncing back into Ron's face.

He staggered toward me, his expression grotesque. As I dove to the floor, Duck and Spots lifted their makeshift weapons—the high hat and the music stand—bashing him on the head. He turned around, like a bull stung by a mosquito, and threatened them again.

Just above me was the red flame front Gibson Les Paul with the Clapton signature. Ron stumbled, swinging the chain saw drunkenly. The blade veered toward Duck. Spots pushed it away and it shot sparks. Billy dove at Ron.

My body went numb as I stood up. Ron held the saw poised over Billy, like a reaper prepared to cut through hay. Vivi and Cerita stood at the glass like sculptures, mouths wide open, arms imploring. I grasped the Les Paul guitar by the neck. I saw Spots's mouth cry, "NOOOOO!"

I swung the guitar with every ounce of strength in my body. It crashed against Ron's wrist. I heard a loud *crack*. Duck smashed Ron's wrist right after I did. The saw jumped out of Ron's grasp. Suddenly set free, it bounced and growled and spit. Then, coming to rest on the carpeted floor, it stalled.

As Ron bent, reaching for it, Billy hit him over the head with the mike stand. Duck lunged at his back, arm around his throat. Spots attacked from the other side. Together, the three of them wrestled him to the ground.

"Phone," I screamed. "Call 911!"

"It's out! Out!" Spots shouted.

Of course it's out, I said to myself. I became aware of the adrenaline coursing through my veins, of the blood pounding in my ears, of my skin stretched over my muscles, of my bones and flesh. Terror and relief collided in a momentous rush. Just as my knees buckled, Billy's arms grasped me tightly. He held me close. I felt like one of Smokie's floppy rabbits, with no bones, just a bit of silk for skin, a few feathers for stuffing.

Spots dug cables from a drawer. He and Duck wrapped them around Ron's arms and legs. I glanced through the glass at Vivi and Cerita, who gazed back at me. The ringing in my ears sounded like the distant crash of surf on shore, the pebbles washing back as the water withdrew into itself again. The cartilage in my legs stiffened back to bone. My calf muscles tensed. I could stand on my own two feet again.

Dumbly, Spots reached out and took the Les Paul from me. It was cut in two, the strings frayed where the saw's teeth had sliced them. He took the damaged instrument in his arms, bowed his head, and wept.

"Hey, man," Duck said, putting a hand on his shoulder. "Be grateful it's not your goddamn arm."

Ron lay on his side. We stood around him, as if by keeping him within the circle of our bodies we could prevent the bad karma from leaking out. But the karma filled the air. After a few moments of stunned silence, we began to move again. To think what to do next. I looked around in a daze and wondered what had happened.

Spots held the polished instrument with its red flame

top sliced down the middle. "Clapton played this. His signature's right here."

"Man," Duck muttered, "I know a guy who'll make it look like new."

Vivi and Cerita burst in from the studio. Vivi wore her gold skirt, her white silk blouse. No makeup, but beautiful as ever. Cerita, behind her, in red, was pale and trembling.

Billy's arms still held me tight.

Vivi seemed none the worse for wear. You wouldn't have known that only a few days earlier I'd told her to go to hell. She threw her thin arms around me and kissed the air next to my cheek as if we were at a Hollywood party.

"Zoë, honey," she gushed. "You sure can swing that ax."

An hour later the police had come and gone, taking Ron Braithwaite with them. The paramedics had taken Duck to the hospital. His leg had a nasty cut, but he'd suffered no lasting damage. I'd driven to a neighbor's to make the call. While I was there I phoned Mark. He assured me he was at the border, on the way. "You might as well turn around and go back," I said. I told him what had happened. I told him we were all okay. "Call Kate," I said. "She needs someone right now."

As the sun was setting, Billy and I took a walk around the lake. I thought about the painted threat on Vivi's van. About the size fourteen footprint Spots had mentioned the police had found near the lake. About the photo of John in the newspaper, which Ron, of course, had seen. I thought about the fact that whoever killed Cassandra had to have climbed the tree. And that Ron lurching away from the scene of the murder must have stumbled into John. I imagined a moment where they exchanged a look and Ron realized John had witnessed his violent act. And Spots—maybe Ron had seen him too, reeling around in his drug-induced daze.

I'd discounted Ron in my obsession with Craig. But I should have known better. Craig Detweiller was a guy who kept his money laundered and his hands free of blood. I should have realized he wouldn't climb a tree to kill someone. As the men at the cabin demonstrated, he had others who could do his dirty work. Once Cassandra was dead, maybe he wanted to make sure she'd left no incriminating statements behind, no will that would keep her prime piece of Beamon's Mountain out of his grasp forever.

I remembered Whit saying that I was too personally involved in the story. When drugs are tearing apart your happy ending, you want to get the dealers. Craig and Spots, those were the people I'd focused on. Still, despite everything, I wanted to believe that Cassandra had been sincere in her efforts to save the environment. I wanted to believe that Craig had manipulated her. I knew about falling for bad boys. I'd done it one too many times. Perhaps Cassandra had thought she could force Craig to buy part of the world to keep it safe from the worst kind of exploitation. I could understand Cassandra's panic; I was no champion of mass extinction. How long had it taken her to learn that if you make a bargain with the devil, only the devil stands to win?

People could change, could find something to believe in, could straighten themselves out. I wanted to believe that Cassandra had tried. Maybe Craig, knowing her secrets, held the strings and made her dance. She couldn't object when he developed a property, because he knew too much about her past, and he was ruthless enough to use it. But one day, facing a battle over the mountain property, she decided not to give in, to be brave, to carry the battle to Greymont's town center, a place too visible for him to act. They'd been playing out a deadly chess match for years; this had been the end game. She'd held him momentarily in check by climbing the tree. But someone else had made a move, an unexpected player.

Billy and I wandered along the paths to the lakeshore. The fog settled on the placid water. All around were mountains, pointing toward the sky. The air was cool and moist. A single star gleamed in the far distance. Peace. Everywhere but in my heart.

"That guy is as strong as an ox," I said as we walked. "It's a miracle we weren't all hacked to pieces."

Billy strolled by my side. "Zoë to the rescue," he muttered. "It's getting to be a regular habit."

"You have your habit. I have mine. It's an equal partnership."

He touched my hand. I shrugged him off.

"Don't be like that," he said.

"I'll be whatever way I want."

We stopped to sit on a rock. Billy found a flat stone and flung it sidearm toward the water. It must have skipped a dozen times before it disappeared into the mist.

"There's one rescue I can't accomplish."

I felt him tighten. Defenses up. Brandishing his blame. I told myself that his poor choices were not my fault. The anger and hurt rose inside me.

"I was wrong," he said at last. Even though he'd swallowed his pride, his eyes wouldn't meet mine.

"What are you going to do about it?"

"I don't know."

"When you figure it out, give me a jingle."

He kept his eyes averted toward the place where the skimming stone had slipped beneath the surface. *It's really over this time.* I remembered hearing myself say the words. I remembered the reassuring feel of his arms grasping me when I felt my bones turn soft.

"God, Billy. I wish this weren't happening to us."

He took in a breath, but didn't speak. What could he have said that would have made a difference? I didn't know, but I kept wishing he would try.

We watched the sun dip below the fog. The pink sky went lavender. Then it darkened.

"Did I tell you?"

"What?"

"Keith—he made a goal today!"

"No kidding?"

"Yeah. It was like a dream come true."

He took my hand. He kissed the inside of my palm. We sat together long after the sky went completely black.

Chapter 32

Brannigan, whose purview was murder not land deals, thought the information Mark and I had turned up might be of use in a civil suit, but there would be no police investigation. As far as the drug dealing went, I received a one-word response:

"Conjecture," he'd snarled. The leads were cold and most were out of his jurisdiction. "Ms. Szabo," he said, looking me straight in the eye. "Bring me a body, and I'll work night and day to nail the bastard who did it. As far as I'm concerned, the case is closed. The perpetrator is behind bars."

Brannigan's logic was blunt but irrefutable. Ron Braithwaite had pled guilty to murder and aggravated assault. He'd killed Cassandra at three in the morning. He claimed to have been trying to talk her into coming down. She'd started throwing stones. He'd lost his temper and scrambled up the tree, threatening her. She'd lost her balance and fallen. The police evidence contradicted him.

I spoke to the medical examiner, who told me he'd noticed bruising in the neck muscles inconsistent with the fall from the tree.

"My best guess," he told me, "is that she suffered a fatal blow, most likely a karate chop, to the back of the neck before the fall. Darned hard to detect. An artery at the base of her skull burst. We looked closer and determined that resulted from the blow, not the fall. It must have taken the murderer some time to untie her and push her out of her seat. When she hit the ground, she was probably dead."

The skull fracture had occurred on impact with the ground. There'd been a rock right under her head. Initially, that had misled him.

The boot print at the lakeside in Vermont forced his confession on John's drowning. On his way from the Plaza area to his car, he'd bumped smack into John. They'd exchanged a few words. John asked if he'd heard screaming. Ron panicked and fled.

The next day Ron saw the picture of the band in the paper. When he'd heard from Kate that I was going to visit the studio, he followed me. He'd lain in wait outside the house. When John emerged, he'd followed him to the shore, pulled him under water, and held him until he drowned. The scary thing was that he had been nearby, lurking in the dark, the whole time we had been trying to revive John.

After Vivi's rally, Brannigan had started to question his alibi. Ron had begun to lose control. At first he'd wanted to scare us. But when he heard from Craig at the soccer game that someone else in Vermont had seen him at the scene of the crime, he'd gone berserk. I tried to get an interview, but Ron refused.

True to his word, Whit gave me Halloween off. The holiday fell on the Monday following Ron's capture. Billy had come back home with me, but for the next few days neither one of us broached the difficult subject of our future. As we walked behind the kids trick-or-treating through the neighborhood, we barely spoke. I watched Keith parading happily in his lexovisaurus costume, and reflected on Kate. I'd called her several times but she refused to talk to me. Her entire family was in a state of shock. Erwin insisted that they'd provided a false alibi for Ron only because they'd believed steadfastly in his innocence. With the history of the enmity between the family and Cassandra, they knew he'd be a prime suspect.

The morning after Halloween, after dropping the kids off at school, Billy finally raised the subject that had been on both our minds. He returned from chauffeur duty with a dozen roses.

"You know, Billy," I said, putting them in water, "I love the flowers, but—"

He pulled out a chair for me with a gentlemanly gesture. "Please," he insisted.

I frowned, ready to lecture.

His dark eyes met mine, plying their charm. "What if I told you I called a clinic?"

"We've been through this. Remember?"

"You won't believe it, but since you caught me, I've been clean."

"You're right. I don't believe it."

He squinted toward the gray light coming through the windows. It was overcast and drizzling. "I'd give anything . . ." His voice trailed off.

"Yeah. So would I."

"Well, I'm going into this rehab program."

"When?"

"Shit. As soon as possible. I, uh, I hooked up with NA."

"Narcotics Anonymous?"

"I went to noon meetings the last couple of days."

"Good luck with the program."

"I'm going to win you back." He flashed the seductive grin, eyes full of poetry and molten lava.

"Are you? This time I'm not sure you can." I fought back the tears. I didn't want to show my weakness.

The rest was what you'd imagine. We talked about the children, about not knowing what would come next. He spent two weeks in the rehab program and then came back to Greymont. He rented a room from Morgan to be near the kids. He's been on his best behavior, making dinner when I can't get home till late, running errands, kicking the soccer ball around with Keith when the weather's mild enough. He's going to counseling and attending NA meetings religiously. He's been courting me. He wants to move back in, but I've told him I'm not ready for that yet. Maybe I never will be. I just don't know.

On a happier note, I made amends with Whit one day in December. Mark, angry about the loss of his Miata, which had been found crashed and burned in a ravine, came up with a key piece of evidence. He'd discovered a shared account that seemed to prove Craig and Cassandra's collusion. Delstar had made deposits and she, as Kathryn Dunnaston, had drawn money from it on occasion. I'd done a great deal of footwork. I'd elicited quotes and corroboration from various landowners. Together we put together a story we considered airtight.

Whit had changed in the month since our confrontation. He'd assigned Barbara Warwick to oversee the daily operations of the paper for a few weeks. He'd spent time at home, coming in only to put together the front page and the editorial pages.

Dancing with Mr. D

"Yes," he said when Mark and I knocked. Behind him the windows on the Common showed the first snowflakes of winter, drifting in the soft wind. The branches of the trees were black lace against the gray glow of mid-morning.

"Excuse us," I said as we entered.

Whit had aged. He seemed weaker than he had only a month earlier. Perhaps it wasn't him. Perhaps I was the one who'd changed. I'd grown up.

"We have a story that we'd appreciate your considering. We've worked late, on our own time. We feel we have enough to go to print."

"Leave it on my desk. I'll get back to you."

"Do you want notes, sources? Most were willing to have their names used, but there are a few—"

He shook his head. "I'll get back to you after I read it."

On the way out, I took an appraising glance around the room. It hadn't changed. But it seemed smaller, less impressive. The furniture that I'd reverently viewed as priceless antiques now just looked old and faintly shabby.

"What do you think?" I asked Mark.

His large shoulders contracted under his jersey. "He and Craig have been friends for a hell of a long time. I don't think he's going to bite."

"If he doesn't, I might take it elsewhere. I've got an editor friend who's just landed a plum job at the *Globe*. Think we've got a shot at the magazine section? Craig's newsworthy. That ski resort, I hear, is going up this spring."

One sole relative of Kathryn Dunnaston, a cousin, had inherited the property, and Craig made an offer he couldn't refuse. No will had ever been found. I still think that the gunmen searched the cabin. Though I can't prove it, I'd lay odds they found a will and destroyed it. Craig bought his last piece of the mountain. Cassandra's sanctuary would be gone in a few brief months. Another rent in the tapestry of life. How many more would it take until the fragile fabric collapsed?

I woke the following morning with a sick feeling. Whit had never placed the call to Mark or me. I was sure he didn't have the guts to tell us to our faces that he wouldn't run it. I told myself I forgave him. I told myself I understood.

I moped the whole morning. Then at noon, someone brought me that day's edition.

Hot off the presses—figuratively speaking, anyhow—front page, above the fold. It was a monster. The headline alone must have taken a gallon of ink. DEVELOPER DENIES TIES TO GREEN ACTIVIST. Records Show Payments Linked to Closings. Trust May Have Benefited.

If I hadn't been wearing heels to rival Tina's, I would have taken the stairs two at a time. Whit was standing at the window when I burst in. The room suddenly looked as big as the world.

"You did it!" I said, exploding with admiration, with . . . astonishment. I threw my arms around him and kissed him.

Whit's shoulders shrank uncomfortably, but he allowed the gesture.

"You published!" I exclaimed. God forgive me, it was even better than Keith scoring that goal. "You're right up there on the top of my list of personal heroes."

About ten seconds ticked by. "Not a bad job of research," Whit said gruffly. "Some of the language, though, was a bit—"

"I resisted 'drenched.'"

"Yes, but—" He bent over the front page which lay open on his desk, "gauzy Madonna of the over-ninety set'? and 'primping like a hipster gone Hollywood'?"

"Wait! I didn't write that."

"Yes, you did." He paused, and the faintest hint of a smile flitted across his lips. "Quotes from the clips you showed me when you applied for the job."

However, in the following weeks, Whit paid his pound of flesh. Someone on the school committee claimed that a parent had complained about a remark Tim had made to his son. It didn't go much beyond that, but a few calls to the superintendent's office requested an investigation. Rumors flew. A flurry of letters to the editor—some anonymous, but many boldly signed by leading citizens—complained, in crude language, about the paper's slant, or about the editor himself. Several advertisers dropped away. Craig himself never openly retaliated. But I wonder, sometimes, if he's just biding his time, waiting until we're off our guard, coiling until the time is right to strike.

Also on the dark side, Keith is still struggling to get along with his classmates. Ellis isn't openly hostile, but they aren't best friends. And neither are Mavis and I, although we had a pleasant conversation during the book drive at school in December. Mark's offered to teach Keith baseball come spring, but I demurred. The kids don't understand why their dad is living next door, not at home. Billy and I are sorting out where our relationship is going to go from here. Keith and Smokie have been lobbying for him to move back in. Despite my resolve, I admit there are days when I find myself wavering.

And then, there's Kate. For me that's the most painful

part of the story. Give her credit, she did go to Brannigan and admit that she had lied. How much Kate suspected and when, I had no idea. She decided her mother's health was more important than the truth. I don't know. I probably would have done the same.

I tried to tell her that, but she wouldn't speak to me. She's moved to a town about thirty miles west, a quiet farm town in the hills. I rarely hear about her. Mark and she never did get together. Well, I didn't expect they would.

Who's left? Oh. Yes. There's Vivi Cairo.

Four months after Ron's arrest, on a cold night in late February, the launch party for *Eve's Ambition* was held at the Glass Onion in Sheffington. For the event I'd bought a brand new dress. It was a slim sheath with spaghetti straps, teals, creams, and lavender in shimmering sequins. I'd dyed a pair of spike heels to match and sprinkled them with glitter. A blue-green Dorothy, back home in the Emerald City.

I'd even added a dash of blue-green to the ends of my bleached platinum hair. I missed that streak of pink, and darned if at the last minute I didn't decide to add a dash of fluorescent fuchsia to the mix. I looked a bit weird. My head drew stares even among the pierced.

Billy was his beautiful, vain self, in a burgundy velvet shirt, black leather slacks. Vivi wore red Chinese pants, a pink satin halter, and a loose silver chiffon jacket.

The lights changed hues on every song. Cerita sang backup vocals in a clear descant. She was a gypsy, in bright orange and acid yellow, dripping rhinestones. Duck, his leg completely healed, wore Armani and played his drums with class. Spots filled in on his newly restored Les Paul. His playing was tasteful, not flashy. In a tie-dye T-shirt, baggy jeans, and red bandana, he looked his part—a horny, doped-up, techno-hippie, future senior citizen of sleaze. But, hey, what a great producer. We all had high hopes for the album.

The music crashed. It roared. It simpered. It flirted. And Vivi—well, Vivi was Vivi. A flapper. A slut. A virgin. A temptress. She danced. She wriggled. She shouted. She crooned. She sang of lost love, of charisma, of dying and rebirth. She sang about frogs chanting their joy after sudden rain and, so help me, she put it over. She was cynical, manic, reflective, and coy. Everywoman and a lost child, a brassy provocateur, a harlot, a thief, a seer with a mission.

If I'd been worried that the album would send Billy catapulting back into the lofty ether of fame, I needn't have bothered. Vivi held the spotlight. She wouldn't have it any other way.

I listened awhile, at a table with a group from the paper: Whit, Barbara Warwick, and her husband, Fred, who'd made a solid recovery. Morgan was there. Tim Boudreau had brought Ann Chatsford, Vivi's guest of honor. At some point in the evening, Craig came by to pay his respects. He cast his reptilian eye on all as if bestowing a benediction.

"Ann," he said. "Looking lovely as usual."

"Thank you, Craig. How are you?"

"Wonderful. Jenny's been appointed to a post on the Arts Council. We're hoping to renovate the old movie theater. I have an architect working on the plans." He smiled pleasantly and shook a finger at her. "Dear, I hope you won't fight me on this. You're a formidable opponent."

"Yes, I am," she said, pursing her lips. They were

bright with a bold purple lipstick she'd borrowed from me. Dark Temptations was the name. "But Craig, I like the theater idea."

"Glad to hear it."

The Plaza Mall was still under contention. They were set to go tooth and nail come May when Town Meeting started up again. It was kind of like boxers touching gloves before they retreated to their opposing corners to await the bell.

Craig started paying homage to Whit. His mealy-mouthed compliments on the paper's ability to weather stormy seas left me breathless. The guy was totally without shame. I excused myself and joined Mark at the bar.

"Hey, Szabo, *qué pasó?*"

"Kind of stuffy back there." I nodded toward the table.

"Buy you a beer."

"I don't drink anymore."

"Soda?"

"How about a Virgin Strawberry Daiquiri?"

"You like that sweet stuff? It's a girly drink."

"I'm a girly girl."

The slushy drink arrived, topped with a strawberry, an orange slice, and a pink umbrella. I took a little sip through transparent purple straws.

I watched Billy running a bass riff, the instrument low on his hip, the groove tightening. Vivi's eyes riveted on his. He moved toward her. She moved toward him. She held the microphone high and they sang together, a close, and somewhat harsh harmony. The rhythm was like an undertow, pulsing with concealed danger, energy straining to be unleashed.

We watched Vivi strutting and singing, flirting with Billy, their eyes locked, bending toward each other as she sang and he thumbed up the bass.

"They're in the same groove, wouldn't you say?"

"How's he doing?" Mark asked.

"Sticking to the plan. No booze. No drugs. Counseling. Daily attendance at NA."

Mark's rough lower lip jutted forward. He fingered the strap at my shoulder blade. "Nice dress."

I studied his features. No poetry. No molten lava.

"There's Brannigan," I said. "Gotta go."

Mark pressed my arm. Craig Detweiller had just approached Brannigan's table. I decided what I had to say could wait. We watched the two of them talk while the music pounded.

For a moment the room grew quiet. The music took over. Spots played his beloved Gibson, which looked as good as new. His fingers ran up the scale, flowing into a bittersweet riff, bending the blue notes, milking it. Even Craig watched.

Spots looked up and saw Craig. For an instant, their eyes seemed to meet in a hostile stare. If I'd wondered what Spots's feelings toward Cassandra had been, I had my answer. From the enmity between them, I guessed that despite his facade, his feelings might have run deeper than the brief bout of lust he claimed.

The keyboards pounded; the bass began to drive. Billy seemed to be looking straight at me. But it was dark and the spotlight was in his eyes. The colors were smoke and lavender. He was singing. The drums were rapping out something syncopated. Vivi, at the keyboards, was letting it rip, the high notes were doing the dirty with the low notes, and Spots's lead guitar tiptoed between them like a sandpiper wading through the surf.

In the midst of all the pounding, I heard Billy's bass going through a modal progression. A hint of Irish roots. The echo of an O'Carolan tune, as pure and innocent as

Malibu beach at dawn. As plaintive as the sting of autumn air when the frost is settling and the last yellowed leaves are falling from the nearly naked branches. A melody so elusive and forlorn, it could almost break your heart.

Discover the
Deadly Side of Baltimore
with the Tess Monaghan Mysteries
by Agatha and Edgar Award-Winning
Author
LAURA LIPPMAN

BALTIMORE BLUES
0-380-78875-6/$6.50 US/$8.99 Can

Until her newspaper crashed and burned, Tess Monaghan was a damn good reporter who knew her hometown intimately. Now she's willing to take any freelance job—including a bit of unorthodox snooping for her rowing buddy, Darryl "Rock" Paxton.

CHARM CITY
0-380-78876-4/$6.50 US/$8.99 Can

BUTCHER'S HILL
0-380-79846-8/$5.99 US/$7.99 Can

IN BIG TROUBLE
0-380-79847-6/$6.50 US/$8.50 Can

And in Hardcover

THE SUGAR HOUSE
0-380-97817-2/$24.00 US/$36.50 Can

Available wherever books are sold or please call 1-800-331-3761 to order.

Nationally Bestselling Author
of the Peter Decker and Rina Lazarus Novels

Faye Kellerman

"Faye Kellerman is a master of mystery."
Cleveland Plain Dealer

SACRED AND PROFANE
73267-X/$6.99 US/$9.99 Can

JUSTICE
72498-7/$6.99 US/$8.99 Can

SANCTUARY
72497-9/$6.99 US/$9.99 Can

PRAYERS FOR THE DEAD
72624-6/$6.99 US/$8.99 Can

SERPENT'S TOOTH
72625-4/$6.99 US/$9.99 Can

MOON MUSIC
72626-2/$7.50 US/$9.99 Can

THE RITUAL BATH
73266-1/$6.99 US/$8.99 Can

AND IN HARDCOVER
STALKER

Available wherever books are sold or please call 1-800-331-3761 to order.

DEATH AND DINING IN SOUTH DAKOTA
The Tory Bauer Mysteries by

KATHLEEN TAYLOR

COLD FRONT
Murder is best over ice. . .
0-380-81204-5/$5.99 US/$7.99 Can

MOURNING SHIFT
Murder over easy. . .
0-380-79943-X/$5.99 US/$7.99 Can

FUNERAL FOOD
The Special today is murder—
served blood rare
0-380-79380-6/$5.99 US/$7.99 Can

THE HOTEL SOUTH DAKOTA
You can check out anytime
you like. . .permanently
0-380-78356-8/$5.99 US/$7.99

Available wherever books are sold or please call 1-800-331-3761 to order.

Edgar Award-winning author

EDNA BUCHANAN

"Buchanan again proves that she is the mistress of Miami crime... deftly delivers on suspense and emotion."
—PUBLISHERS WEEKLY

CONTENTS UNDER PRESSURE
72260-7/$6.99 US/$8.99 Can

MIAMI, IT'S MURDER
72261-5/$6.99 US/$8.99 Can

PULSE
72833-8/$6.99 US/$8.99 Can

―――――― And in hardcover ――――――

GARDEN OF EVIL
A BRITT MONTERO NOVEL
97654-4/$24.00 US/$35.00 Can

Available wherever books are sold or please call 1-800-331-3761 to order.

EB 0200

The Joanna Brady Mysteries by National Bestselling Author

An assassin's bullet shattered Joanna Brady's world, leaving her policeman husband to die in the Arizona desert. But the young widow fought back the only way she knew how: by bringing the killers to justice . . . and winning herself a job as Cochise County Sheriff.

DESERT HEAT
76545-4/$6.99 US/$9.99 Can

TOMBSTONE COURAGE
76546-2/$6.99 US/$9.99 Can

SHOOT/DON'T SHOOT
76548-9/$6.50 US/$8.50 Can

DEAD TO RIGHTS
72432-4/$6.99 US/$8.99 Can

SKELETON CANYON
72433-2/$6.99 US/$8.99 Can

RATTLESNAKE CROSSING
79247-8/$6.99 US/$8.99 Can

OUTLAW MOUNTAIN
79248-6/$6.99 US/$9.99 Can

Available wherever books are sold or please call 1-800-331-3761 to order.

Explore Uncharted Terrains of Mystery with *Anna Pigeon, Parks Ranger* by

NEVADA BARR

LIBERTY FALLING   0-380-72827-3/$6.99 US/$9.99 Can

While visiting New York City to be with her sister, Anna invesigates when a teenager falls—or is pushed—to her death from the Statue of Liberty.

TRACK OF THE CAT
0-380-72164-3/$6.99 US/$9.99 Can

A SUPERIOR DEATH
0-380-72362-X/$6.99 US/$9.99 Can

ILL WIND   0-380-72363-8/$6.99 US/$9.99 Can

FIRESTORM   0-380-72528-7/$6.99 US/$9.99 Can

ENDANGERED SPECIES
0-380-72583-5/$6.99 US/$8.99 Can

BLIND DESCENT   0-380-72826-5/$6.99 US/$8.99 Can

Available wherever books are sold or please call 1-800-331-3761 to order.

BAR 0900